Sugar Scars

Travis Norwood

Cover Design by Greg Simanson

This is a work of fiction. Names, characters, places, brands, media, and incidents are either the product of the author's imagination or are used fictitiously. Any resemblance to similarly named places or to persons living or deceased is unintentional

ISBN: 979-8-3986-2970-5

For Layah,

You will survive this, and you will find your family.

When the end of the world came, I had one thought on my mind, and it isn't what you think. I stepped out of my house, glad to be outside and alive, after a week of being cooped up and expecting to die. I drove straight to Walmart, desperately hoping they still had what I needed. The parking lot was virtually empty, and I pulled right up to the front, parking in a handicapped spot, still feeling a reflexive twinge of guilt.

I hurried to the entrance and nearly collided with the glass doors that didn't automatically open like the past hundred times I had been there. With my face an inch from the door, I realized that no one was there to unlock the store. Almost everyone in the country had done as the government said and sealed themselves in their houses, hoping to avoid the virus.

No one would ever come to unlock those doors.

The government spokesmen claimed that as many as a third of the people would survive if they stayed indoors and waited for the virus to go dormant, but I had tracked the stories on the Internet and knew that wasn't true. They just said that to keep people calm and contained. The virus started in China, killing all but 1 in 9,600 and kept nearly that exact ratio as it marched across the globe. If you've read other journals like this, I'm sure you've seen everybody else round that number to 10,000, but I don't round. I'm good with numbers and don't need them to be even.

The government said they had released a counter-virus, but now that was obviously another lie. I can't blame them. It kept people mostly under control. Some countries had erupted in chaos as the virus approached. It was airborne and nothing seemed to stop it.

I stood there wondering what to do. I thought about just smashing the doors with a rock or even my car, but that didn't feel right. This wasn't an apocalyptic wasteland. I was still just a simple teenage girl. This was still my beautiful hometown of Tallahassee.

Well, except for the fact that almost everyone else was dead, which I guess is a pretty big exception.

The building was huge. These couldn't be the only entrances, so I drove around back to the loading docks. The big garage doors were all pulled down, and even if they hadn't been locked, I couldn't possibly raise them. But I saw a simple, ordinary door with a handle on it.

I pulled the handle, hoping for luck, but it didn't budge. I wasn't about to complain about bad luck. I was one of the few immune, having survived against enormous odds.

It didn't seem so bad to break the door in the back, but the only thing that could knock a door down was my car, and I wasn't about to damage her. I loved that car, a yellow Ford Mustang convertible that I had named Bella, after my mom, Isabella. I had briefly thought about naming her after my dad, Henry, but the car was definitely a girl.

I had bought Bella with some of the small amount of money I had gotten from a trust fund my parents left me. I had dreamed about having my own car for years, but the trust fund didn't kick in until I turned eighteen. The trust specifically stipulated that I could get a car, so I thought of her as a birthday present from my parents.

I drove to the neighborhood behind Walmart, looking for a car I could use. Vehicles of all kinds lined the streets and filled most every driveway. I wasn't used to this new, empty world, and it still felt wrong to be thinking of taking someone else's property.

I wasn't about to go into the houses to get keys. I didn't want to see what was in there. I wondered when it would start to smell. Most people had sealed their houses, so maybe that would contain it for a while.

After a few minutes of searching, I found a pickup truck with the keys still in it. I imagined the owner had been in a hurry to get inside. There was a very small chance (0.0104 percent, my mind automatically calculated) the owner was still alive, so I forced myself to walk to the door and knock. I wasn't a thief. I knew how much my car meant to me, and I wouldn't do that to someone else.

I started counting to thirty, hoping no one would answer. Please understand that I wasn't hoping the people inside were dead. It was simply habit. Every time I'd ever knocked on a door or called someone on the phone, I'd always hoped that no one answered. I'm not a people person. I like to be alone.

Well, that problem had been solved.

I don't mean to sound so callous, but I had no one who I really cared about to mourn. I had been on my own for a little more than a year after the foster system was promptly done with me on my eighteenth birthday. My most recent foster parents had occasionally checked in on me. They were good people and wanted to make sure I was okay, but I had lived with them for only about six months.

In some ways, I was the perfect person to be left alive like this. The idea of a world with barely any other people didn't scare me. In fact, it sounded sort of nice. I didn't want everybody dead. But I could handle it now that it had happened.

But in another way, a very important way, I was the exact wrong person to survive. On TV and the Internet, everyone had speculated on how people would survive in the depopulated world. They worried about having enough food.

Virtually everywhere in the United States had stores on every street, each teeming with food. There was more food than we could possibly eat in our lifetimes. I was sure of it because I did the math. The canned and dry goods would last years. When those ran out, there were vast fields of crops left and slow, meaty farm animals that would now reproduce unrestricted. The bigger problem would be avoiding being overrun by cows, chickens and pigs.

On the Internet sites I checked, people filled pages with their endless worries of how they would survive the first winter. They made plans to stockpile firewood. Why wouldn't they simply get in their cars and drive to Florida for the winter? Our winters, if they can even be called that, are easily survivable.

Everything people could need would be available in endless supply. Survivors had their pick of cars, and there was enough gas left in the gas station tanks to keep us all driving for more than a century. I've run the numbers on that too. I had a glamorous job at a convenience store, and I knew just how many gallons the huge underground gas tanks held.

We were left in a world of no responsibilities and virtually unlimited resources. Everything a normal person could want sat waiting on unwatched store shelves. But I'm not a normal person.

Food. Water. Air.

That's all an ordinary body requires. From these it produces everything else it needs. Not mine. On that first day, when I stepped out of my house realizing I was one of the few immune, my thoughts were for one thing.

Insulin.

I don't have the easy kind of diabetes that can be handled with proper diet and exercise. My body is self-destructive. Specifically, my immune system, in its glorious overzealousness to defend from outsiders, gets confused and attacks the insulin-producing cells. I imagine the white blood cells feel quite proud of themselves as they slaughter the innocent pancreatic cells that want nothing more than to do their job and be left alone.

Over the years I've learned to live with my condition quite well. I had to if I wanted to survive. The various foster parents I've lived with were all good people, but started out knowing almost nothing about how to help monitor and keep my blood sugar at the right level. I methodically checked it every few hours. I learned just how I would react to each food. What sent my blood sugar rising and how quickly it fell. God forbid if I ever ate more than one slice of pizza. I never went anywhere without at least one syringe in my purse. Insulin was literally my life's blood.

Okay, if there are still grammar Nazis in the future reading this, I realize it wasn't literally my life's blood, but it might as well have been. I couldn't live long without it. I can't tell you how many lectures from doctors and social workers I've had about this.

I reached the thirty count, and no one answered my knock, so I turned to take the truck. I would have to figure out how to knock the Walmart back door in without hurting myself or causing too much damage.

Something made a low sound, and I screamed and nearly tripped. A man's muffled voice called from behind the door, "Is it safe out there?"

For the rest of my life, however short it might be, I would regret what I said next.

"Yes.

I turned back to the house. I hadn't paid attention at first, but now I saw that this house was completely sealed, far more than the others around it. Duct tape, caulk and even what looked like tar covered every conceivable opening or crack so air couldn't get in.

The knob turned, and then the man thumped against the other side of the door, breaking it free of the tape that sealed it. The door sprang open, and a large man stumbled into the sunlight, blinking.

He took a huge gulp of air and said, "Finally."

Something felt wrong. The mathematical part of my brain was trying to tell me something about the odds of finding another immune survivor so quickly, but I was surprised and didn't think things through.

"Is everybody else dead?" he asked.

I nodded.

"Suckers," he said. "The first thing we're gonna do is remove the shutoff timer from the power lines going into the neighborhood."

I had forgotten, but the government had sent people around installing automatic power shutoff timers. I thought it was pretty smart. It would have only taken a few people dying with the stove still on to burn down most of the city.

I was going to watch how he did it, so I could do the same with the timer for my neighborhood. He hopped in his truck, and I followed him in Bella to the neighborhood entrance. It turned out that it was just a clearly labeled off switch, which I could have easily figured out myself.

"I'll be glad to have the air conditioning back. I had it off because I had all the vents sealed."

It was late April, which can get warm in Florida, especially inside a sealed house.

"So what's next?" he said. He scratched at the stubble on his chin, which looked like it had been growing for the week or so he had been in his house. "I'll have to shut off each house by flipping the circuit breakers, but that will take a few days."

"I need to get into the Walmart, but it's locked."

"That's smart," he said. "Stock up on food supplies before the other survivors start hoarding."

Hoarding wasn't a concern. He didn't understand how few people would be left. I wasn't worried about food. I needed insulin. I barely had enough in my fridge at home to last through the week of waiting. My convenience store job only provided enough money to have one or two vials at a time.

That morning I had carefully checked my blood sugar, done an injection, and waited about half an hour to eat a simple breakfast. My entire life was a constant computation to keep my flawed body alive.

"We could smash our way in," he said, "but there's no need for it. One of the managers lives … lived just over there." He pointed to a house across the street. "I'll go get the keys." He wiped sweat from his brow. It wasn't hot yet this early in the morning, but it must have been stifling cooped up in his perfectly sealed house.

The Walmart manager's house had only superficial taping. The door was locked, and the man had to break a window to get in. I'm glad he was the one going in there and not me.

He came out a few minutes later with a large ring full of keys. "That was nasty," he said. He looked pale, which was understandable, given what he had just seen. "Apparently the virus speeds decomposition."

Everything about the virus was fast. There was plenty of speculation about what had caused something so deadly, but that was irrelevant now. All that mattered was that we were immune.

Wait.

"You had your house perfectly sealed?" I asked.

"Yeah. I had oxygen tanks. But they were almost gone. I just had to wait for the virus to go dormant, like they said. Once I saw you walking around, I knew it was okay. You and I are some of the smart ones."

I wasn't smart. My genetics, which I had always considered so defective, had saved me. "I didn't seal my house," I said. I had learned enough to know it was pointless.

"Then how did you … ?"

"I'm immune," I said. We both stared at each other for a horrible moment. "I'm sorry." I was a fool. I expected him to scream at me.

But he just said, "It's okay."

It wasn't okay. I had killed him.

"I would have run out of oxygen in a day or two," he said. "It doesn't go dormant, does it?"

I shook my head. I didn't know what to say, so I did the thing strangers always do in normal circumstances, when a virus isn't killing one of them. I asked his name.

"Robert," he said, "but everybody calls me Bob. What's yours?"

I told him. I hated my name. I didn't want anyone in this new world to know it, but he wasn't a part of this new world.

He wanted to spend his last moments in his home. We didn't know how long he had, so we drove back to his house. Coming out to flip the power shutoff switch, he had driven fast, excited to have cheated death. Now he drove slowly, easing back into the driveway, parking the truck carefully.

It turned out he didn't have long.

-3-

I sat with Bob for two hours. That's an incredibly fast time for a virus to kill someone, but an immensely slow time to watch someone die. I took a small comfort that it didn't seem painful. More than seven billion people had just gone through this. He lost almost all feeling within a few minutes.

He kept looking down to see if I was still holding his hand. I listened to him talk about his life, until he started slurring his words and then lost speech completely. Within five minutes of that he was gone.

I thought about burying him. It seemed like the right thing to do, but I didn't have the strength to move his large body or to dig a big enough hole. I kept trying to convince myself that I had only cost him a couple of days before he would have been forced to leave his house anyway. He had told me his birthday. He had lived 16,496 days. I had shortened his life by just 0.012 percent. But those numbers didn't help me feel any better.

I closed the door behind me and took the manager's key ring from the passenger seat in Bob's truck. Everyone else in this neighborhood, the city and the world had gone through what Bob just did. Some earlier, if their houses weren't sealed well. Some later. Like them, I had stayed home and waited, hoping and praying someone would find a cure in time.

Well, I didn't actually pray for a cure. That's just something you say. I figured if there were a God powerful enough to stop this, then he was powerful enough to prevent it. If he did exist, then he probably caused it. I can understand how he might not be bothered with the troubles of one insignificant girl in Tallahassee, but the end of the world had to get his attention. I was pretty sure he was aware of it, and my whining about it wouldn't make much difference.

Whether by divine intervention or genetic luck of the draw, I had survived, and if I was going to keep surviving, I had to get insulin. I drove Bella back to Walmart and after ten tries found the key that unlocked the back door. I made my way through the back offices and out into the empty store.

Stepping into the grocery section, I realized just how much food there was. I did a quick calculation in my head. If I remembered right, and I always remember numbers right, Tallahassee had a population of 195,000. Dividing that by 9,600 would leave 20 people. I'm sure the real number wouldn't be that exactly, but it was probably within five either way.

There had to be at least twenty groceries stores, probably more. I took my phone out and googled "grocery stores in Tallahassee" and the first link listed more than a hundred. Not all were as big as a Super Walmart, but that was still a lot of food. Five full stores per person.

With that in mind, I took a shopping cart and headed straight to the pharmacy. I went behind the counter, feeling like it was wrong to be there. There was a fridge in the back, and I opened it and found the insulin. They had seven long-acting, eleven intermediate-acting and eight short-acting vials. I had stabilized on short-acting, but I took them all. Then I felt guilty and put one vial of each back. There were probably nearly as many pharmacies in the city as grocery stores, but I didn't want to leave a fellow diabetic desperate if they came here in an emergency.

For a brief moment I wondered, in horror, if the gene for immunity was tied to the gene for diabetes. I imagined a future of fighting everyone else for insulin.

But the numbers didn't work out. The ratio of diabetics to non-diabetics was much more than 1 in 9,600. I thought about whether my parents, my real parents who shared my DNA, would have lived through it also, but that was irrelevant now. Another kind of death had found them long ago.

With the insulin in my cart, I felt better. I could go to other pharmacies in the city and get a supply to last a lifetime. While I was in this section, I took a few other basics I would need: blood sugar meters of every kind, test strips, shampoo, toothpaste, toothbrushes and "ladies' things," as my last foster mom called them.

I had barely made any money working at the 7-Eleven, and I thought about going through the store and getting all the things I had wanted but couldn't afford. I was wearing a cheap, worn-out bra. When I had gotten dressed that morning, I had briefly thought that I could get by without one digging into my shoulders, but I wasn't quite ready to abandon all the trappings of civilization, yet.

On the way to the women's section, I got a top-of-the-line toaster and a fancy coffeemaker. I would grab a few more things, some groceries and then find more insulin.

Now I had to think like I never had before. I'd always lived my life thinking about the near future, the short term. Regulating my blood sugar for the next few hours. Keeping my current foster parents happy until they got tired of the girl who was all the work of a child with a medical condition, but none of the joy of having a daughter.

I stayed in my room almost all the time. They just didn't seem to understand that I liked being alone. I wasn't crazy or psychologically scarred from my childhood. I'm just not that into other people.

There were a lot less other people now. The world's population had been reduced by 99.9895833 percent. Now I had to start thinking about the long term. The *really* long term. Before I had trusted in the vast network of people who worked the machinery of our economy that kept the insulin flowing. Now that was all gone. I had to get enough to last a lifetime. No one would ever manufacture it again.

Well, maybe not ever, but certainly not in my lifetime. It would take many generations to rebuild the population enough to have people who worked on ancillary concerns to society like keeping the diabetics alive. I thought about trying to calculate how many generations it would take, but I couldn't take that kind of time then. I'd always enjoyed figuring out mathematical problems, but that one would have to wait.

If this pharmacy had insulin, then there would be others that did too. I could stockpile it all. The day had started out badly, but now everything was going as planned.

Until I heard the crash of glass shattering at the front of the store.

4

I ducked behind one of the aisles and listened to what was happening. I heard someone struggle to pull a cart from the long line of interconnected carts at the entrance. Then they pushed it forward with a squeak and a rhythmic thud every few feet.

An old woman's voice said, "Every time. Even now. Every time I get the bad cart with a busted wheel."

She pushed the cart aside, and I listened to her mutter to herself as she picked through three different ones until she found one that rolled smoothly. An old woman fussing with a shopping cart at Walmart didn't sound too dangerous, so I stepped out from behind the aisle. Her car had smashed the front doors in. She had pulled it back, but it was still covered in glass.

The woman startled and said, "Oh, sweetie, you scared me there for a minute."

"I scared you?"

"Sorry about the front doors," she said. "I thought it was the only way to get in. Apparently not."

I held up the key ring. She looked at it and smiled.

"Well, seeing you answers the big question," she said. "Someone else did survive. I was wondering why God would leave an old woman as the last person on Earth."

"If the survival rate worked out the same in the US as the rest of the world, about one in ninety-six hundred survived."

"Oh, my." She stepped out from behind her cart. "Well this sounds strange to say under the circumstances, but it's nice to meet you. My name is Edith."

An old woman's name. Which is, of course, perfectly appropriate for an old woman. Not so much for a nineteen-year-old girl. I didn't share her name. Mine was far worse. I don't know what my parents were thinking when they named me.

She waited through an awkward pause. "And what's your name, honey?"

"Um. I don't know."

"What? Did the virus take your memory? I hadn't heard of that."

"No. I mean I don't know what my new name will be yet. I don't like the name I had." And I figured now was a good time to change it. I didn't have to worry about records or forms or official processes. My name would be whatever I told people it was.

And, no, I'm not going to tell you either. That old name will die with me. I suppose all names end up sounding like old people's names, eventually. Mine did from the day I was born. My parents probably named me after a grandmother or something, but I was too young to ask them before they died.

"Are you okay, um, dear?" Edith said. "You look so young."

"I'm an adult," I said, but felt the opposite with her looking at me like I was a child. "I've been on my own for a year now. I'm okay."

"Would you like to shop with me? I hadn't looked forward to shopping in an empty store."

I had actually thought that shopping in an empty store for once was wonderful, but I said, "Sure," to be nice. I got my cart and pulled up next to her. She glanced at the vials and other things but didn't say anything, which I appreciated. We rolled up and down the aisles filling our carts, mostly with perishables that wouldn't be good when we came back for the next shopping trip.

"I'm keeping a diary of these end times," Edith said as we rolled past the boxes of Mexican meals. "I'm so glad to know now there will be future generations and that someone will read it."

"How do you know there will be future generations?" I asked.

"Because of you, dear," she said. "You're young. You'll find some young man who survived, and then nature will take over from there."

Finding a man was the last thing on my mind.

"It will be like the old days," Edith said, "when people needed lots of children. You'll have baby after baby and put them to work when they're still youngsters."

Edith kept talking, and she didn't seem to need me to say anything, which was fine with me. I wondered how she was able to act normally, given the circumstances.

"I guess you're like me," I said.

"How do you mean?"

"You didn't have anybody close to you who you lost."

"Oh, no, honey. I lost three children, eight grandchildren and more friends than I can count."

"Then how … "

"How am I okay?" she asked. "I lost my husband three years ago. We had been married forty-nine years. He died a month before our fiftieth anniversary. I was devastated. I felt so alone. I barely left the house for a year. I just wanted to die and be with him."

We turned down the paper products aisle, and I picked up a huge stack of Styrofoam plates. I was never going to do dishes again, and I didn't have to have any guilt about hurting the environment since I was just making use of what already existed, and no one would ever make any more of the nondegradable products.

"But this time was different," Edith said. "The loss is so complete that it doesn't feel like a loss at all. I guess it feels like I'm the one who's lost. Like I stepped into another world."

The refrigerated section held more meat than the two of us could keep in our freezers at home, so we moved it all to the aisles of frozen foods. We or some other survivor could use it later. I started to shove my heavy cart to the exit when Edith headed to the checkout line.

She saw the look on my face and said, "I want to bag the groceries up, so I might as well ring it up and see how much I'm getting for free. Can you operate the register and the bark code thing?"

I didn't correct her. She was a little hard of hearing and said a few words wrong.

"My cart's four hundred fifty-seven dollars and thirty-eight cents," I said. I counted only the groceries. I didn't include the cost of the medicine, which would make it *much* more. "We got almost the same things. Yours is probably within thirty dollars either way."

"How on earth do you know that?" she asked.

"I'm good with numbers. I don't even care what the prices are, but I can't help adding up things. It's how I got my job at the 7-Eleven."

"Don't they have cash registers to do that for people?"

"The cash register was broken, and the clerk and the manager couldn't get it to work. I was in a growing line of irritated people while the employees stood there clueless about what to do. So I stepped behind the counter and just started adding up everyone's purchases and telling customers their change. The supervisor looked at me like it was magic and offered me a job."

"I'd think a girl as smart as you could get a better job than at a convenience store."

For that I would have had to have graduated high school. I left the day I turned eighteen and got access to the trust fund. It was a small trust fund with a small monthly stipend, so I still needed a job. But I was able to live on my own in a tiny rented house. I was finally, deliciously alone and on my own.

Everyone had told me I was a fool. That I needed an education. A lot of good that would have done me now.

We bagged her groceries and exchanged phone numbers. I'd answer if she called. She was a nice lady and would probably be lonely for human contact.

I threw the pile of groceries into my trunk and the backseat, putting up the top on the Mustang so nothing would blow away. I went to the CVS across the street and cleaned them out of all but one of each type of insulin.

Dosage and usage varies based on a lot of factors, but each vial should last about a month. In just a few hours of work, I had enough to last years. The amount of insulin in all the pharmacies in the city should last for years beyond that. That was assuming there were no other insulin-dependent diabetics in the city, which was probably a good assumption with only twenty or so people left.

I stopped at my 7-Eleven on the way home and filled the tank with gas. I passed other gas stations on the way, because I knew how to authorize the pumps at mine. Thankfully I'd never have to work that job again. I'd spent many tiring hours in the past year dealing with all the people who flowed endlessly in and out, getting gas and overpriced, sugar-filled food.

I stopped at the entrance to my neighborhood and flipped the switch on the automatic power timer. I would flip the circuit breakers on a few houses every day, until every one but mine was safely off.

I arrived home tired but satisfied. I had the insulin that I needed to live. Food, water and shelter would be easy. Each was in virtually infinite supply.

I felt secure.

And, like with so many other things, I was very wrong.

5

Over the next few weeks, I gathered up all the insulin I could find. And it was a lot, even more than I had anticipated. I kept the fridge in my house filled with food, and there wasn't enough room for the food and all the insulin. I was beginning to run out of fresh food, but a lot of the cans and jars needed to be refrigerated after I opened them, since they were sized for families, and I usually didn't finish them in one meal.

I was going to need another fridge.

I didn't know how I would get it home, but as far as end-of-the-world problems it didn't sound too bad. I didn't know where else to go, so I drove to Home Depot. Mainly because the bright orange building stuck out in my mind, and it seemed like the kind of place where people might have bought fridges. I thought about using or taking a fridge from one of the neighbor's houses, but that would require dealing with something I had managed to avoid so far.

Dead bodies.

I was hoping nature would handle that problem for me. A quick Internet search showed it could be quite a while for some of the bodies to decay, depending on how tightly sealed up the houses were, but it also seemed like the virus might increase the rate of decomposition.

Strangely the Home Depot parking lot was empty. I figured this was the kind of place people would have gone to buy stuff to seal up their houses. With the speed of the virus, I thought some of the people would have been caught here. Government workers had distributed some home-sealing supplies, so maybe that accounted for it. Everybody had basically stayed home or, in pointless desperation, gone to the hospital. I hoped I would never have to go there. It must be a nightmare of death and decay.

The doors opened automatically as I approached the entrance, which surprised me. I stepped inside to the smell of paint and sawdust. The air conditioning was running unchecked and unrestrained, and it was quite cold inside. I had been here once before when I'd considered building a deck on the back of my house, but the helpful employees threw so many choices at me that I left intimidated, and abandoned the project.

I expected the store to be ransacked, but it was neat and organized. I wandered the aisles for a few minutes looking for anything that might be useful, but most of it seemed far above my skill level. I supposed I would have been the kind of person who paid someone else to do repairs or home-improvement projects, but that option was gone now. I guessed I'd figure out how to repair each thing as it broke.

Or just move into a new house every few years. I could have a mansion if I wanted, but I loved my little house. I had named her Rosy, for the beautiful bushes that grew in front, which bloomed even though I did nothing to attend to them. Rosy had everything I needed, and it was the first place that felt like home, after my parents died. There's nothing like opening the door to a place where no one has any expectations or demands.

After a few minutes of not finding anything interesting, I wandered to the back where they kept the appliances. The washers, dryers and stoves looked amazing and could apparently do anything you could imagine. I'd have to bring one of each home later, but those were just nice-to-haves. I needed another refrigerator to keep the insulin safely cold and protected.

I went with the simple theory that the best would be the most expensive and walked over to a shining, stainless steel beauty with a whopping price tag of $5,129.10. I couldn't have imagined ever spending that much on a fridge before.

But now money was meaningless.

I opened my purse, pulled out my wallet and took out a crisp new twenty-dollar bill. It had come fresh from the bank when I cashed my last paycheck. Standing there I could hardly convince myself that it had no value anymore. Tentatively, I held it up with both hands, my fingers pinched together at the top. I took a deep breath and then ripped it in half.

I felt equal amounts of freedom and remorse, but I kept tearing it into smaller and smaller pieces, finally letting it fall to the floor in a tiny green blizzard. I looked at the massive fridge and wondered how I would get her home. The name Bertha popped into my mind, and I decided it was a good, solid name. She would be large, firm and reliable.

I supposed that I would need a truck. They must have some around here. I'd never driven a truck before, but that was a secondary problem. First I had to move Bertha without crushing myself beneath her. A simple dolly wouldn't do.

They must have had something around here for moving things like this.

"Hi, there, sugar. Can I help you with anything?" a man's voice with a thick Southern accent said from behind me, and I nearly screamed. I turned around to see a young man in his early twenties wearing a bright orange Home Depot jacket.

I didn't know what to say, so I said the dumbest thing possible. "Do you, um, work here?"

"Well, not anymore," he said. "But I live close, and I come by to help anybody who pulls up. It's a good way to meet people. Especially pretty young ladies."

If anybody else had said something like that, it would have sounded creepy, but he had such a simple, easy confidence about him that it seemed sincere and almost charming. I've never considered myself particularly pretty, but I suppose that all things are relative, and with the limited options available, I may have looked gorgeous to him. Unlike many men, he kept his eyes firmly locked on mine and didn't even steal a quick glance up and down.

Then I remembered that I hadn't worn a bra that day. It had started seeming so pointless. The overzealous AC was freezing my skin, raising goose bumps on my arms. To my horror, I glanced down and saw I "had my high beams on" as Edith had said the week before when we met for coffee at Starbucks. It turned out we couldn't actually make coffee, because the automatic timer had shut the power off in that area. But I still loved the smell that permeated the store, and there were a few treats to eat.

I tried to casually pull the thin shirt away from my chest. To his credit, he kept his eyes on mine.

"My name's Kyle," he said and held out his hand. He wore an old ball cap that, like everything else left in this world, had seen its better days.

"Hi," I said and briefly shook his hand. He waited for me to introduce myself, but I still hadn't decided on a name. Edith was the only other person I'd seen, and she just called me honey, sweetie, darling or any of a hundred other affectionate terms. I changed the subject away from introductions.

"This seems like a strange place to try to meet people nowadays," I said. "Wouldn't a grocery store be better?"

"I figured there are so many grocery stores," Kyle said, "and places to get food that the small number of people left may not run into each other. It turns out my hunch was right. Everybody needs something from a store like this eventually, and this big orange building seems to stand out in their mind."

"How many people have you met?"

"Ten so far, including you," Kyle said and smiled. "I can help you get anything but caulk and duct tape. We're completely out. Everybody used it to try to seal up their houses. Are you looking at that refrigerator? It's the top of the line."

"Yeah. But I don't know how I'm going to get it out of here. I've never tried to move anything that large." I honestly wasn't trying to get him to help. I was simply sharing my problem with him. I knew almost nothing about men.

"Oh, I can get it for you. That price includes delivery and installation."

I had to make a quick decision. His help would be wonderful, but then this stranger would know where I lived. But thinking about it for just a moment, I realized that if he had any bad intentions, he could have already done anything he wanted. He was a foot taller and had large, powerful arms. I would have no chance against him. And all the barriers of society that kept bad people in check were completely gone.

So I guessed he had already proven his trustworthiness, and being handsome and charming didn't hurt either. "Thanks," I said.

Kyle handled everything. He got a forklift and carried Bertha out to a large flatbed truck. He even wrapped her in plastic wrap to protect from dings and scrapes. He followed me home, stopping to carefully push a few cars out of the road. I had just driven around the cars, trying not to think about what was in them. Most of the bodies were slumped over, so I couldn't see them.

"I try to do that everywhere I go," he said when he stepped out of the truck. "It helps to make the driving smoother for whoever's left."

He used a mini-forklift on the back of the truck to get Bertha down and to the front of the house, then a simple dolly to heft her over the step up onto my tiny front porch. He had me push to get her over the step, but I think it was just to make me feel like I was helping.

She wouldn't fit through the front door, and I didn't know what we would do, until Kyle took the doors off, from both the fridge and the house, and managed to barely squeeze her through. He wheeled her into the kitchen and said, "I can haul off the old one."

"I'm keeping both."

"Yeah, I guess that makes sense. Keep as much food as you can, especially frozen stuff that will last. You never know what will happen. Do you want me to just put it here in the dining room? It will be a little cramped in this place, but I can fit it in if I push the table up against the wall. You probably won't be hosting any big dinner parties anytime soon."

I nodded and, before I could move to help, he slid the table over like it didn't weigh anything.

"Do you have an extension cord? There isn't another plug available over here."

I didn't have one, so Kyle went back to the store for a cord. While he was gone, I tried to push the food fridge, Phred, over to make more room, but he wouldn't budge. When Kyle came back, I had him put Phred on the cord and plug Bertha directly into the wall. She would have the insulin and needed to have the most reliable connection.

When he finished putting the doors back on and getting everything hooked up, Kyle looked around my house. "I can get you other new appliances and hook them up. We have awesome stoves, dishwashers, washers and dryers. You might as well take advantage of this … situation."

Kyle had stayed happy and charming the entire time, but a brief look of sadness flashed across his face. The smile returned, and he stood there waiting for me to say something.

"I think I'm fine for now," I said. "But I may call you if something breaks."

"Sure. Give me your number, and I'll text mine back to you."

I did and he turned to go. "Would you like to stay for some dinner?" I asked. It seemed like the right thing to do after he had worked so hard. He turned around without hesitation.

I decided to grill some steaks out back on the tiny square of concrete that I called my patio. I got the charcoals started while we chatted. Like me, Kyle had lived in Tallahassee all his life. We had even gone to the same junior high, but he was five years older, so we hadn't been there at the same time.

Kyle didn't mention who he lost to the virus, and I didn't ask. I don't like people to pry into my personal life, so I don't do it to them. He didn't push on any subject that I hesitated about. I told him about growing up in the foster system after my parents died. At that point everybody always asked how they died, but he didn't. He seemed to intuitively sense what I wanted to share or not.

He actually respected my privacy.

That's a trait I'd never experienced before. The boys who had been interested in me always wanted to know everything. I think they thought it would make us closer. But it just pushed me away. Two people, friends or romantic interests, don't have to share it all. There's something nice about not knowing everything about another person.

About thirty minutes before the steaks would be ready, I excused myself to step inside and get a syringe, a meter and a vial of insulin from the fridge. I stepped into the bathroom to do the familiar process. I wasn't embarrassed by my diabetes or the shots, but it's a lot for a new person to absorb.

I put a test strip in the meter and then pricked my finger and watched a drop of blood form. It was the only situation where I could stand the sight of blood. You're supposed to wipe your finger with an alcohol swab first, but that gets forgotten after about the thousandth time. I touched the blood drop to the test strip, and within a few seconds, the meter showed a reading. I lifted my shirt and carefully gave an injection into my abdomen.

We took two dining room chairs and ate the steaks on paper plates out on the patio.

"You're a fine cook, Sugar," Kyle said after finishing.

He was saying it to be nice. The steaks were okay, but I really didn't know much about cooking. What I knew about was how to carefully control my diet to keep my blood sugar under control. It took a constant balancing act of what I ate, when I ate and how much insulin I took. Adding the skill of actually preparing a good meal with multiple dishes was still a little too much to tackle.

I thought that Kyle might try to stay longer, but he stood and said, "Well, I've got an early morning at Home Depot tomorrow. The boss hates it when I'm late."

He had helped me with something I might not have been able to do by myself. We had a pleasant time, and then he left without overstaying his welcome.

He'd been a perfect gentleman, and we'd had a perfect day.

6

With the new capacity Bertha gave me, I gathered insulin from everywhere in the city but the hospitals. I wasn't going to those places of death. But I didn't need to. I had her filled to the brim and had more than a lifetime's supply.

Kyle called a few times to see if I needed anything, and we ended up talking for over an hour each time. I hadn't realized before that, but I really did enjoy spending some time with people. When I lived with my foster parents, I would go to school all day and then come home exhausted, and spend all night in my room.

On my own, I worked at least eight hours a day at the 7-Eleven with customers coming in, talking to me and asking for things the entire time. When my shift was over, I wanted nothing more than to hide away in Rosy and recharge my batteries.

Now, in a life of almost complete isolation, I found myself sometimes craving company. Before, I had thought my desire for other people was zero. It was small, but it was definitely a non-zero value.

When I met Edith at Starbucks (this time Edith brought coffee), she wanted to hear everything about Kyle. I told her what I knew. He hadn't shared anything with me that I thought he wouldn't want someone else to hear.

"What a nice young man," Edith said.

"He was very helpful."

"I'd like to meet him. You're the only other person I've seen," she said. "And he's a handyman. Maybe he could fix the missing shinkles on my roof."

I didn't point out her mistake. I always hated when people corrected others when they clearly understood what was meant. Most of the time they did it to make themselves look smart, not to actually help.

I called Kyle that evening, and he sounded delighted that I had called him.

I told him that Edith would like to meet him.

"Let's get everybody together," he said. "I've met a few people through the store."

I normally would have shied away from a large group gathering, but I decided to try it out. Kyle made all the arrangements and set it up for Friday at noon at the Applebee's near the Home Depot, a landmark everyone knew.

He picked me up that morning in his gargantuan red pickup truck. I had wanted to go on my own, in Bella, so I could leave whenever I wanted to, but Kyle had really wanted me to go with him. He said he'd take me home whenever I wanted him to.

I wore an outfit that I actually gave some thought to, a yellow sundress, and I made sure to wear a bra. Kyle got us there early because he had to set everything up, but that worked for me. I dealt with crowds better if I got to meet people one at a time. Kyle had dressed nicely, in slacks and a button-down shirt with a collar, but he still wore his beat-up ball cap.

I hadn't seen him without it. He occasionally took it off, briefly, and then would put it right back on. I had no idea why, since he always wore it in the exact same position. For the few seconds his head was revealed, I could see a small spot where the hair was beginning to thin.

Everyone was supposed to bring a different dish. Kyle assigned me mashed potatoes, and I cheated and just made them from a box of Hungry Jack instead of real potatoes, which I assumed would take a lot of work. I hoped they tasted good. I rarely eat potatoes. They're not worth the sugar.

We arranged the tables to seat twelve people, and I stood fidgeting as they arrived one by one. Edith was first, and she gave me a big wink when she saw Kyle. He gave her a warm hug and said that he felt like he already knew her from talking with me. A man in his forties came next with three bags of Lays potato chips in his hands. He had a beard, but it looked like it originated more from a lack of shaving than a real choice about his appearance.

A couple, perhaps in their early thirties, came in next and from the way they acted it looked like they had been married for quite a while. They both had on matching wedding rings. That struck me as strange. The odds of a husband and wife both surviving were 1 in 92,160,000. That's 9,600 times 9,600. I got to thinking mathematically and didn't stop to think socially when I asked, "Do you know how rare a phenomenon you are?"

"I'm sorry?" the husband said.

"The odds of both spouses in a marriage surviving are less than one in ninety-two million. You're probably the only surviving married couple in the United States." I lit up with excitement over this freak mathematical chance being in our city, but the husband's and wife's downcast faces let me know I had said something awkward.

"We were married before, but not to each other," the wife said. "We met each other right after the virus. Bill proposed, and we were married a week ago."

"We figured why wait?" Bill said. "Who knows what the future holds? And I certainly won't find a better woman."

I wanted to ask about how they made their marriage official. Did they find a preacher or a justice of the peace? Or did they just declare it? But I had made enough social awkwardness. Kyle deftly steered the conversation to easier subjects and then greeted the other people as they arrived.

I began paying attention to what everyone had brought. Kyle had assigned the main dish to one of the women, who had owned a restaurant. He had no idea what she would bring. She was the next to last to arrive, and everyone else was excited to learn what she had fixed.

Eating an unknown meal is terrifying for a diabetic.

I had to guess at the insulin dosage before I left the house. And you can't just go with a large dose to be safe. Too much insulin is more dangerous than too little. The restaurant owner arrived to much fanfare with heaping pans of lasagna. She brought a feast of carbohydrates that would readily turn to sugar in my blood.

I resolved to eat polite, tiny little bites, enough to hopefully even out with the insulin, and go home hungry. We all stood around the restaurant waiting for the last guest to arrive, and when he did, he yelled, to my horror, "Hey, I know you!"

I immediately recognized him as a boy from my high school. We barely knew each other, but I remembered his name, Gill Barnes, and I prayed he didn't remember mine. I had thought I could leave it completely behind.

"This is incredible. What are the odds?" Gill said.

One in sixteen. Not really all that remarkable. There were 605 students when I dropped out.

Gill walked over, and Kyle immediately stepped away from the people he had been talking with to stand close beside me.

"I'm so glad you made it," Gill said. I didn't know if he meant to the dinner or surviving the virus.

"So how are you doing?" he asked.

He hadn't used my name yet, and he looked awkward, like he felt he should know it but couldn't remember.

"We're doing great," Kyle said and put his arm around me. The clear gesture of claiming me might have felt too forward in other circumstances, but now I felt protected. Gill was looking me up and down, sizing me up like a piece of meat. I regretted wearing the dress, which showed a little bit of cleavage that seemed to have caught his eyes.

Kyle called everyone, twelve people in all, to the table. Gill picked a seat, and Kyle selected a pair of seats for us at the opposite end. We all sat down and picked up our utensils to dig in, when a small, almost bald man named Ralph at the end of the table said, "Let's say grace and give thanks to God."

Everyone stopped and put their forks down. Ralph bowed his head and began a long prayer thanking God for his provision and protection in bringing us together and keeping us alive through the virus. The married couple, Bill and Laura, prayed fervently with their eyes closed, hands folded and their heads bowed. Gill sat looking around. He winked at me from across the table.

Kyle had his head bowed politely, but kept his eyes open, staring at his plate. Most of the other people did the same. When the prayer finally finished, everyone began passing the food around.

We talked and ate, getting to know each other. I took cautious nibbles at each item, trying hard to control myself. The food was so good that I wanted to tear into it. Many of these people were experienced cooks, especially Deena, the restaurant owner who had made the lasagna. It was an unfortunate reminder of how bland my food at home was.

"What did you say your name was, dear?" Ralph, the man who had prayed, said looking at me from across the table.

Edith spoke up. "She hasn't quite decided yet. Things are so different now. If I wasn't so old, I might change my name also. I've always dreamed about being called Consuela. It sounds so exotic."

I almost laughed out loud, but I could tell she was serious. I looked to Gill to see if he would remember my name and tell everyone, but he took my glance as flirtation and smiled slyly back.

"Sugar," Kyle said, "you can take as long as you want to decide."

"Okay," Ralph said. "Um, well, Sugar, will you please pass the peas?"

It took me a moment, and then I realized he meant me, and I passed the peas down the table. The conversation continued on as the food disappeared, and I got repeated admonitions to eat more.

Edith said, "You won't keep that girlish figure by starving yourself. Men like a little something to hold on to."

I blushed and pushed the food around my plate. But I wasn't really embarrassed. I could tell it was just friendly teasing. It wasn't like the bitter, vindictive society of high school that I had left as soon as I could. This was a small community of leftover people. No one here wanted to hurt anyone else. The world had seen enough loss.

Deena went out to her car and surprised everyone when she came back in with a huge chocolate cake, thick with icing. I had to will myself not to eat more than one bite. I looked around the table and saw men and women, black, white and Hispanic, people of every age. Young, like Gill, Kyle and me. Old, like Edith and most every decade in between. The immunity gene had been even in its distribution.

But something was missing. It wasn't even. Gill and I were the youngest there, at nineteen.

"Where are the children?" I asked out loud without intending to.

The table went silent.

"I haven't seen any," Sofia, a middle-aged Mexican woman, said.

Others around the table shook their heads. "The immunity is genetic," I said. "There's no reason children wouldn't have it. There should be about twenty survivors in Tallahassee. So there should be four or five children from infant to eighteen."

"Well, an infant … ," Gill started to say.

He didn't complete the thought, but we all knew what it was. An infant wouldn't have survived these past weeks on its own. While we were all thinking of our own survival, a young child had likely died, left on its own.

"I've seen a boy, maybe eight years old, running around," Ralph said. "I've tried to approach him, but he runs away. He looks well fed though. I saw him in a grocery store once."

"And he's probably having the time of his life," Gill said, trying to lighten the mood. People got back to chitchatting and enjoying the company, but I couldn't stop thinking about a child being out there alone.

After we said our good-byes, we exchanged numbers and made plans to meet each Friday. Kyle started to drive me home. "No," I said.

He turned and looked at me. "You want to look for the children."

I nodded yes, glad that he understood. Despite being careful, I had eaten too much of the rich food, and I felt my blood sugar rising. It always started with a slight sting in my eyes and a tingling right behind my nose.

Kyle had to find out some time. I took a meter out of my purse, put a test strip in, pricked my finger and pressed the blood drop to the strip. It read 220, about 80 over the high end of normal. I took a fast-acting insulin syringe out of my purse. I couldn't easily or modestly get to my abdomen in this dress, so I pulled it up a little and injected into my thigh.

Kyle said nothing and simply waited until I finished. This was what I really liked about him. I didn't have to talk or explain if I didn't want to. He just accepted me for who I was and what I was willing to say at the time.

We drove around with the windows down, looking and listening for any signs of children. The same mathematical part of my brain that realized that the children must be there somewhere also realized we had little hope of finding them. Four or five children in a city that used to hold tens of thousands of them. I absorbed the grim fact that any child under about three, who couldn't open doors, wouldn't likely have survived the past month since the virus.

"What do we do if we find one?" Kyle asked.

I hadn't thought of that. I never thought long term. Until the quest for insulin, everything in my life had been short term. I certainly couldn't care for a child, but someone in the group could.

The married couple, Bill and Laura.

They would be perfect. They had each had children before and were probably desperate for a child to love. I couldn't handle everything children would need, but I could do my part and find them.

7

Kyle and I went out every day, driving through the city in a systematic pattern looking for any children. We packed food and insulin into a picnic basket and stopped only to eat lunch and then dinner when the sun went down. Most days we took Bella, because we could put the top down and see clearly in every direction.

If we ran into a road that was impassable because of cars left in the road, we'd come back the next day in his truck to push them out of the way. I suppose it would have been more efficient to go in separate vehicles and even to split up, but I liked spending time with Kyle. He was as dedicated to the search as I was. But here's the real truth of it:

I felt safe with him.

I didn't think there was anyone dangerous in Tallahassee. We'd met most of the survivors at the get-together already, and they were fine people just trying to survive themselves. We met four more adults during the search. We told two middle-aged women about the community, and they started coming to the Friday lunches and chatting with everyone on an Internet site one of the survivors set up. Facebook and some of the other big sites had starting acting flaky, so we didn't use them.

We met one older man who simply wanted to be left alone, and he appeared to be able to take care of himself, so we did. We saw another man wandering the streets one evening when we stayed out past dark, thinking the children might come out in the cool of the night. Kyle made me stay in the car with the engine running while he stepped out and approached the man.

I feel bad now to say that we judged the man by the way he looked. He wore ragged clothes and walked without purpose. He was a large black man with a thick head of curly hair and an unkempt beard. As strong as Kyle was, this man could have broken him without a second thought. I had told Kyle to leave him alone, but Kyle wanted to let everyone know we had a community, of sorts, and that they could be a part of it.

The man, Thomas, turned out to be a gentle giant. He was just broken and sad and grieving all the loss he had endured. We talked with him for hours into the night. Knowing someone else was still alive seemed to brighten his eyes.

After three full weeks of searching, we gave up and simply put signs up telling the children, or anyone, where to go to find the other people. Thomas came to each Friday meeting. We now had fifteen people attending. No one seemed as grief stricken as he was, but everyone dealt with loss in different ways.

Thomas had lost a wife, seven children and both parents. I had never asked Kyle if he had lost anyone. Over the weeks I had told him almost my complete life story, but, strangely enough, I knew little of his. I loved that he respected my privacy and never asked or pressed on anything that I didn't want to talk about.

I wanted to show him that same respect, but I also longed to know more about him. I had never felt this way about anyone. I'm not talking about physical desire, although that was there too, or any of the storybook romance feelings. I'd had crushes and infatuations like any young girl.

But I'd never before had the genuine desire to know someone. To care about what another person felt or thought or had experienced in their life. So I took a step I'd never taken before and began to ask about him.

"Did you lose anyone close to you?" I said one morning as he worked on building a deck on the back of my house. I had mentioned my story about the one time I had gone to Home Depot and been too intimidated by the process to try building a deck, and he leaped on the project immediately. I felt guilty, but he seemed to love it. I knew he was trying to impress me and win my affections, but even more so, he seemed to just love working for a purpose.

He stood with his shirt off, but his ball cap on, in the hot Florida sun, covered in sweat and sawdust. "Come over to my house tonight. I'll make dinner."

I couldn't tell if it was an answer to my question or not. Would the house reveal something, or would he tell me more while I was there? But it was the answer he gave, and I respected that. I pried no more. He knew I wanted to know. He would tell me more if he wanted to.

Kyle went home at five o'clock to shower and make dinner. He told me to come over at seven. I hate the way this next part sounds, so please don't judge me. I don't know what kind of society will have formed years from now, if the world is able to recover, or what kind of morals you'll have when you're reading this, but I had to be thinking long term in everything.

On my way over I stopped at the Walmart pharmacy and found birth control pills. I wouldn't let anything happen that night or maybe for a little while, but I had to be realistic and plan ahead. Our relationship was going in the obvious direction, and I had no desire to stop that.

But I couldn't possibly handle pregnancy with the medical complications from diabetes and the simple, unimaginable responsibility of caring for a whole tiny person. I never really intended to ever have kids, even before the virus. Let my defective genes die with me. Now more so than ever. The population would be rebuilt from a relatively small gene pool. Why infect it with my impurity?

I did some Google searches (which were getting increasingly slow to return results) on my phone and found the pills I thought were right for me. I took a supply that would last for years. Unsurprisingly, the pharmacy had more birth control than insulin.

I arrived at Kyle's house promptly at seven. I had never been there before, but it was easy to find since it was directly across from the Home Depot like he had said when we first met. I would have normally still used MapQuest or Google Maps, just to be sure, but they were both down that night.

Kyle had a nice house, well cleaned, especially for a bachelor. He must have lived neatly, because he couldn't have possibly driven home, showered, fixed the meal and cleaned the house up in two short hours. He still wore the ball cap, but it looked like his hair was combed neatly underneath it. We ate a simple meal of french fries and hamburgers. He made mine without the bun, which helped keep my blood sugar in check.

Our conversation was simple. He said nothing about his family, but I got the feeling the house would tell the story. After dinner, while he cleaned up, I looked around at the many pictures that covered the walls and lined the surfaces of his end tables and entertainment center. A woman and man who were clearly his mother and father featured prominently in many of the photos.

There was no one family photo with him and all his siblings, but I was able to piece together that he used to have two sisters, both older I thought, and a much younger brother. He'd had numerous friends, which didn't surprise me at all. He'd had guy friends that he worked with, played softball with and frequently went to the beach with. Women were always around him in the photos, but no one who he held in an affectionate or romantic way.

Kyle saw me looking and opened a drawer on one of the end tables. Inside there was a photo album labeled "Our Engagement Album" in a woman's elegant handwriting. I looked through the pictures from his proposal to the bridal photos. I knew nothing about engagements or how things timed out in the elaborate pre-wedding process, but I didn't have to, since everything was clearly labeled with dates in the same elegant handwriting.

The last entries were one week before the virus panic took hold in the US and everyone fled to seal themselves into their homes.

8

Kyle spent the next week working every day at my house on the deck. It wasn't that large, and I knew he could build it faster. He had worked in construction before Home Depot and knew how to build or repair almost anything, but he dragged it out. And I didn't mind.

I offered to help a dozen times, but he wanted to do it entirely on his own. So I watched him work in the hot sun and brought him iced lemonade regularly. It was June, which is hot in Florida, and within a short amount of time each day, he was drenched in sweat and would take his shirt off. Kyle had a well-muscled chest, but not a gym-sculpted look. He had built his muscles with real work. Something about a man exercising just to make himself pretty to women wasn't attractive to me at all.

We ate with the community that Friday, this time at Deena's restaurant, and she fixed everything. He finished my deck that afternoon, and we went back to Home Depot in his truck to get some furniture.

We got a table with chairs and two luxurious lounge chairs. We set them up and had a celebration dinner at the deck table, with real plates and utensils, instead of the disposable paper and plastic we normally used and threw away. Afterward we lay in the lounge chairs and watched the sun slowly set in the sky.

"Do you need a shot?" he asked.

"No," I said. "I think I got the pre-dinner dose just right."

"Does it still hurt?"

"Sure. But you get used to it," I said. "I was deathly afraid of needles when I first found out I was diabetic. But you can learn to get over anything. It's amazing what you can do when you have no choice."

"Where do you inject them usually?"

He wasn't normally so inquisitive, but I didn't mind. "On my abdomen. My stomach."

"Does it … does it leave scars? After so many injections?"

"Tiny bumps sometimes, if you don't get the needle in just the right depth or reuse the same spot. But I've gotten pretty good at it. I have a system to keep from injecting the same place before it has time to heal."

He looked over at me. I was wearing shorts and a T-shirt, and I pulled my shirt up to show my stomach. "I work best when I think in numbers."

He nodded. He had learned that after spending so many hours with me. I pointed to twelve tiny tattoos on my belly.

"I've always pictured the face of a clock on my belly. When I turned eighteen and was on my own, I had these tiny upside-down numbers tattooed." Each number was less than a fourth of an inch in size.

"Noon is a little below my belly button, and six is just under my, um, breastbone." I pointed to the two spots. "I start the first injection at noon and then move to one o'clock, two o'clock et cetera … If I take three or four injections a day, it will be three or four days before I repeat a site, giving it time to rest. I always remember numbers, so I always remember where I did the last injection."

"And no bumps?" he said.

"Not so far. See?"

"No," he said. "Not in this light."

The sun had almost gone down completely. He sat up and reached his hand over and placed it flat on my belly. He rubbed his hand around slowly.

"No bumps," he said. "What time on the clock was the last injection?"

"Three," I said.

He put his finger at three o'clock. "And if I understand the system right, then the next one would be at four. Here." He moved his finger to four. "And then five. And then six." He traced the clock points, stopping on six, just below my breasts. After a moment, he continued on counting each hour down to twelve, below my belly button.

With each touch on an hour, my insides trembled. He moved slowly, making sure I wanted this.

We made love on the lounge chair out in the open under the dimming light of the sun and the rising light of the moon. We had no concerns that anyone would see us. We were utterly, deliciously alone.

-9-

We lay naked in the lounge chair under the moonlight for quite a while. The night was warm, and I thought we might just fall asleep out there, holding each other. After some time, I felt nauseated and dizzy. I had begun to sweat even though the night air wasn't that hot.

I recognized the feeling of low blood sugar. The excitement had gotten my heart pumping, and the insulin must have absorbed faster than usual. Kyle had fallen asleep, with his right hand cupped on my left breast. I slipped out from under him and stood up. I had to steady myself against the wall for a minute, and then I walked into the house.

I slowly got a meter from the cabinet, and it showed 50, definitely low, getting dangerous. I was glad I hadn't fallen asleep. That could have been very bad. I was going to have to teach Kyle the signs to look for of high and low blood sugar and what to do if I was unconscious or unable to treat myself. I opened the food fridge and stood there unsteadily with the door open, enjoying the cool air flowing over my body.

"You look beautiful in the glow of the fridge light," Kyle said, smiling.

I turned and he stood there, also still completely naked. I looked down and saw that, amazingly, he was turned on again. He was going to have to understand that at the moment I couldn't be more turned off. I knew I was irritable in this condition, so I tried to keep my voice under control.

"My blood sugar is low. I need to get something to eat. Why don't you go get our clothes?"

There was nothing all that arousing to me about looking at a naked man, but I knew men were visual. Covering up should help cool him off.

Kyle smiled, understanding, and started to say something when suddenly the light in the food fridge went off. We stood in darkness. I closed and opened the door again, thinking that the fridge must have a shutoff timer on the bulb, but the light stayed off. I stood there, baffled, and then I looked

36

around.

The clocks on the microwave and the stove that normally glowed a soft green were off also. The ever-present soft hum of the air conditioning was now silent.

I don't know why I had expected the power to keep flowing forever. Like the manufacture and supply of my insulin, it all depended on a vast and complex system watched over and maintained by thousands of people. The government had apparently done all it could to keep the power going for a little while after the virus. I slammed the food fridge door to hold in what cold was left.

The world started to spin, and I sank down onto the floor. I felt like I was falling off a cliff. Kyle opened the door on Bertha, the insulin fridge. I screamed at him to keep it shut. He couldn't see, and I heard him knock a precious vial to the floor. It shattered.

"Flashlight!" I said. "In the drawer. Behind you."

He fumbled around, found the flashlight, turned it on and shined it into the fridge. He handed me a vial and a syringe. My heart was pounding and my vision blurred. I took a minute to focus and read the vial.

"I need fast-acting," I said.

Kyle put it back and started fumbling through the other insulins. He had no idea what to get.

"Novolog!" I shouted.

He finally found one and handed it to me. I took it and tried to insert the needle through the top, but my hands were shaking, and I couldn't do it. Kyle took it from me and asked how much to draw up.

That simple question saved my life.

My brain started dealing with the numbers. My blood sugar was 50 at the last check and probably lower now. I pictured the hundreds of insulin dosage charts I had looked at in my life. You found your blood sugar in a range on the left column and slid over on the same row to see how many units to take. I did that in my mind, but the row had asterisks in it.

What did that mean? I couldn't make sense of it. I pictured the row below it on the chart. It said "0 units." If a higher blood sugar needed no units, then what did the asterisks mean?

It came to me as Kyle sat there on the floor, naked, with the needle penetrating the vial, asking over and over again how much to draw up.

"I don't need insulin. My blood sugar is low. I need food."

Kyle dropped the vial, stood and opened the food fridge.

"Orange juice," I said. He poured a glass quickly, his shaking hands spilling a good bit onto the floor. I drank it down. We waited there for a few minutes until I began to feel better. In the glow of the flashlight, I could tell Kyle was scared, and he definitely wasn't turned on anymore.

"I'm okay now," I said. The meter showed my blood sugar at 75, and I munched on a graham cracker while Kyle got our clothes from the deck.

"Let's go to bed," he said as we dressed in the kitchen. "We can go get a generator in the morning. Frankly, I'm amazed the power lasted this long." The automatic shutoff switches probably made a huge difference. The city didn't use a hundredth or maybe even a thousandth of the power it did before. He held on to me as I stepped into my panties and shorts so I wouldn't fall, but I didn't really need it. I was fine now.

"No," I said. I couldn't sleep through the night with Bertha sitting powerless. I knew it was ridiculous. Insulin can sit for a while without refrigeration, and she would hold in the cold for a bit, if we didn't open the door.

Kyle didn't argue. We drove to Home Depot and got the largest generator they had. I called the generator Scotty, like the engineer on *Star Trek*, because it would keep everything else running. Kyle had no trouble setting it up. He had done it before. But we needed gas to run it. We drove to my 7-Eleven. Of course, the power was out there too, so the pumps wouldn't work.

Kyle started working on opening the underground tanks, but that proved to be difficult. It turned out that gas station owners didn't want you stealing their gas. I had the idea of getting another generator to power the store and the pumps, and with a few more hours of work we had that hooked up.

We were left with a chicken-and-egg problem of how to get the first gas, but that was easy since many of the homes in the area had gallon gas cans in the shed with the lawnmowers and other power equipment that would never be used again. We got dozens of empty gas cans from the store and filled them up in the back of Kyle's truck. We turned on the generator for the station only long enough to pump the gas and then shut it off again.

At my house, we turned off the power-hungry air conditioner and unplugged everything but the fridges, since Kyle said anything plugged in could still draw a small current even if it was turned off. We crawled into bed at 4 am, exhausted.

I could rest secure now, knowing the insulin would be preserved.

Kyle pressed up against me, and I could feel that he was turned on again. With my exhaustion, I wasn't in the mood at all, and realized how little I understood men. But he didn't try anything and soon fell asleep.

I knew now that I loved him and he loved me. But that wasn't what I thought about as I lay there with him holding me. I could have died a few hours before if he hadn't been there to help me when my blood sugar was low. He had done the wrong thing by trying to give me insulin, but that was a simple matter of teaching him.

I don't know if I could have hooked up Scotty, the generator, by myself, but he had done it easily, like so many other things he had the skills to do. We were now facing a world of limited power where many things would have to be done manually, and the strong arms that held me now would be so very useful in all those tasks. I loved him, but more importantly, that night I realized this:

I needed him.

Within a few days, we had a complete system of turning on the station's generator long enough to pump the gas we needed to power Scotty for a couple of days. The air conditioner became a thing of the past. I didn't miss it as much as I thought I would. I could now wear cooler, less modest clothing around Kyle. It often turned him on, but that was an easy, and admittedly fun, problem to handle.

I did miss running water, which stopped working when the power stopped supplying the city's pumps. We brought water up from a nearby creek and used bottled water, still in vast supply, for drinking. Kyle talked about building an outhouse, which I dreaded, but I found out the toilet still flushed if we kept the tank full. He said he knew this, but didn't want to do all the water hauling needed for it.

One look from me, and that issue was settled. If I could meet his seemingly insatiable desires, then he could darn well haul some water so I could keep that wonderful aspect of civilization. Kyle helped the others set up generators at their houses, and with a little work figured out how to get into the underground tanks at gas stations near their houses. They had hand pumps to draw the gas out, because it wasn't safe to have anything electrical running near the open tank that might spark an explosion.

In the old world, Kyle had worked construction, and when the economy took another downturn, he got the job at Home Depot earning ten dollars an hour. Men in suits came in to buy tools he couldn't afford and they wouldn't really use. He was on the bottom rung of the economic ladder.

But in this new world, he was the most valuable man in our city. Bill, a lawyer who used to earn $350,000 a year (I know because he mentioned it frequently) was next to useless and constantly needed Kyle's help and advice.

After a week or so, Kyle started living at my house. One of the reasons was simple practicality. Maintaining one house was simpler than two. The other reason, to my amazement, was that I wanted him there.

Having him around constantly, day and night, didn't bother me like I thought it would. He liked to talk and be together far more than I did, but now being alone took almost no effort at all. When I felt a little cramped, even with Kyle's gentle company, I simply had to think of an errand to run, and I stepped into a vast emptiness.

The world had reversed.

Home was the place of people and interaction. Out in the city was the place of aloneness where I could recharge my batteries. And Kyle drained those batteries less than any other person I had ever met. He was often gone during the day running errands or helping the other people in the city. At night we ate dinner and talked, something I had never enjoyed with anyone.

During what I thought of as the honeymoon period, we made love nearly every day with an almost aching passion. There was no reason to hold back. No thoughts of "Is he really *the one?*" The math of it made the thought meaningless. In this city he was literally the one, the only man within fifteen years of my age. Gill Barnes, the boy who had gone to my high school, hadn't been seen in a while. We assumed he was out questing for a female to mate with.

The lack of choice didn't make our love any less. In fact it made it much more. If you're reading this and living in some future world, like the old world, where there are plenty of people to choose from, you may find romance in the choosing of one from the many. But there is a dark side of choice.

All choice leaves doubt.

I gave myself to Kyle completely. Unreservedly. Unlimitedly. With no doubt whatsoever that we would be together for a lifetime.

Sometimes at night, Kyle would whisper, "Just the two of us, Sugar. That's all we need. We're young, and nothing will take us until we're old and gray. There won't be a car accident, because there are hardly any other cars on the road. We won't get sick, because we're immune to the virus and other diseases could hardly spread through the sparse, separated population. I'll never lose anyone I care about again."

From talk like this, I knew he didn't want kids, which fit my plans perfectly. Edith had asked, "When are you going to start your family?" for the first few months. One time she came over and brought a gift basket, filled with coffees and cookies. I thought she was just being friendly or wanted an excuse to visit. After she left, I went through the basket. I looked beneath the treats and was mortified to find massage oils and even a tube of KY Jelly.

Eventually she got the message. Two people can be a family. That's all it takes.

I supposed we had a marriage of sorts, although we never did anything to formalize it like Bill and Laura had. They still valued the trappings of the old world and had Ralph perform a ceremony. Ralph wasn't anything official before the virus, just very religious, always carrying a Bible. They had met him in the first weeks and had him officiate. This was enough in Ralph's mind to make him the new city pastor, a job he relished, and we all tolerated.

We didn't use the words, but Kyle was my husband and I was his wife. We fell into mostly traditional roles. Kyle protected and provided. I fixed the meals. I wasn't good at it, but it made sense, since I had to be so careful of what I ate.

One evening, as the fall air grew a little cool, which isn't much in Tallahassee, Kyle said, "I'm going hunting tomorrow morning. Would you like to come with me?"

I had no problem with eating animals and was glad he would provide some fresh meat to cook, but the idea of killing a living creature myself was one of the most repulsive things I could think of. Kyle had talked about his love of hunting before. A lot of it seemed to be in just being outdoors, but a part of the experience definitely centered on the killing. I hoped to live my entire existence without ever directly taking another life.

I was a little worried for Kyle to go out into the woods, but he said he had been there many times before. I was deathly afraid of snakes, and years ago I had researched how to identify poisonous ones. I made Kyle listen to me lecture about the dangers, but I knew he was just placating me. He didn't seem to be afraid of anything.

Kyle took Bill and Thomas and returned proudly with a dead deer in the back of his truck. In the old world he would have taken the carcass to a processing plant, but strangely, bafflingly, he seemed to look forward to cutting it up himself.

He brought a freezer back from Home Depot just to store the meat from this and the other kills he anticipated. I started to object, because it would use the gasoline in Scotty quicker, but he was so proud to have provided food that I kept silent.

Even after years of taking my own blood, I couldn't stand the sight of it in any other circumstances and stayed away during the grizzly process, which he said would take a few hours. But Kyle had never done this himself and underestimated how long it would take.

I returned home and stepped out back to a sickening scene of gore. My beautiful deck was covered in blood and the insides of the deer. Its eyes stared at me from a lifeless, severed head, and I vomited, falling to my hands and knees in the congealed blood.

I stood up and instinctively ran to the shower, throwing my clothes off. I stood under the showerhead and twisted the faucet to full blast, but of course, no water came out. I ran out of the house, naked and covered in blood, and down the street to the creek that ran just outside of our neighborhood.

I lay down in the cold water, barely six inches deep, and began washing the blood off. Kyle arrived in a minute and helped me clean up. He stood me up, wrapped a towel around my shivering body and carried me home.

Kyle continued to hunt. We and others in the city needed the fresh meat. He just processed the carcasses somewhere else, far away from me. I had no trouble eating the meat, but I was firmly resolved that I was done with killing and blood.

I thought that the only blood I would ever see again would be the tiny drop that welled up on my finger when I took my blood sugar.

-11-

The winter, if it can be called that in Tallahassee, passed quietly. Kyle and I briefly considered moving to a larger house, but I loved Rosy and she had everything we needed, even if she was a little cramped with two refrigerators and a freezer.

I named the freezer Nimrod, one of the few names I remembered from Bible stories. One set of foster parents had made me go to Sunday school, and the phrase Nimrod was "a mighty hunter before God" stuck in my brain. Nimrod held more meat than we could eat in a year, but Kyle kept hunting anyway. Sometimes he harvested (the hunting word for killing) deer in a painstaking wait in the forest, and sometimes he simply drove out of the city and killed a pig on one of the farms.

Edith, still quite strong at nearly seventy-five, butchered the pigs. She had grown up on a farm, and her first husband had been a butcher. So we all had all the pork, bacon, sausage and ham we could eat. This will sound incredibly naïve, but before I hadn't actually known that all those meats came from the same animal. My knowledge of the world was random. I hated school and had done the bare minimum to get by until I dropped out.

I learned nearly everything of interest from YouTube videos. I could explain how the event horizon of a black hole worked, but I didn't know what it meant for a man to be circumcised. This, by the way, Kyle was happy to explain and show me one evening.

I suppose I would have learned these many tiny things ordinary people knew if I had spent time with the families I had been in. This general knowledge of the world must be transmitted in thousands of conversations over dinner tables or sitting in the living room watching TV.

My various foster parents handled most things for me, like most parents would do, but because they didn't expect to have me for long, they didn't spend time teaching me how to do things or how the world worked.

That first year on my own was a rude awakening. I didn't know about insurance or how to write a check, which my stupid, backwards, stuck-in-the-twentieth-century landlord required for the monthly rent. The trust fund got me started and allowed me to buy my beautiful Bella. After that it provided just five hundred dollars a month, but that made all the difference. Mom and Dad couldn't be there to teach me, but they had provided enough to let me be on my own, which is all I ever wanted.

Kyle and I taught each other constantly. I knew obscure facts and interesting oddities, and he understood the simple things needed for day-to-day life in the strange new world we had entered. He kept Scotty going, which kept Bertha running, which kept the insulin safely stored, which kept me alive.

One morning, a few days into spring, almost a year since the virus, I stood in the kitchen in my pajamas beginning to prepare a simple breakfast of oatmeal and asked Kyle to get the insulin out of Bertha. I had trained him in what to do in case of high or low blood sugar and for regular doses to always get the vial I was currently using.

"Let me do it this time," he said.

"Do what?" I asked, but I knew what he meant.

"Let me give the injection. I need to practice."

I had never let anyone except a doctor give me an injection, and I hated to let the doctors do it. I didn't like the idea at all and decided to try to distract him. Fortunately, men are easy to distract.

"We could try that, or we could try something a little more fun." I unbuttoned the buttons on my pajama top.

He looked interested for a moment, but then said, "No. I'm serious. I want to try it."

He must have really been serious. I took a deep breath and said, "Fine."

He got the current vial out of Bertha and a syringe. "How many units?"

"Ten should be fine. Roll it a few times in your hands to mix it."

He drew out the insulin and approached me with the sharp needle. "What time is it?"

"Eight o'clock."

"No," he said, pointing to my stomach. "What time on your belly?"

"Oh. Five."

He pushed my pajama top apart and found the five o'clock position, a few inches above my belly button and little to the right.

"It needs to go into the fat layer underneath the skin," I said. "Pinch the skin first."

He pinched a fold of skin, much too hard, and it hurt.

"Put the needle at a forty-five degree angle, and then push it all the way into the skin."

He held the needle against the skin.

"Do it quickly. You're freaking me out." I had done this myself thousands of times, but Kyle was making me nervous. It didn't make sense, but I don't have to make sense. He pushed the needle in all the way and then injected the insulin in one smooth motion.

He pulled the needle out and said, "That wasn't so bad."

For him.

But he had done well and learned the right technique. I buttoned my top closed. There wasn't going to be any fun. I didn't want to associate those two things in his mind.

Kyle squinted and looked at the vial. "How much longer should this last?" he asked.

"About two more weeks," I said.

"Okay. That should be fine then."

"Why?" I asked.

"Do you see this tiny print that starts with 'EXP'?" he said.

I looked back at him blankly.

"It expires in a month."

It seems so obvious now, but I can honestly say the thought of expiration never crossed my mind. I knew food could expire and go bad, but I didn't realize that applied to medicine. I'd never come close to that before. The insulin moved from the store to my fridge to my body in a never-ending cycle. I simply hadn't needed to think about how long it would last if left to sit on the shelf, because it never sat for long.

I was diagnosed at eight. I'm sure the doctors explained about expiration to my foster parents at the time, but if I even heard it, it didn't register in my child's mind. The foster parents bought all the insulin and were reimbursed by the state of Florida. Perhaps some of them stocked up and threw away expired insulin, but I never knew about it. When I was on my own, I could only afford to have a couple of vials in the fridge. I used one after the other in order, buying just one more when I emptied a vial.

I opened Bertha and began going through the vials. Each had an expiration date anywhere from a month away to just under two years. I felt shaky, but not from high or low blood sugar.

"Really they just put those on there to make you think you have to buy more," Kyle said.

I'm sure that was partially true. The manufacturers would be motivated to put on a very conservative expiration date, both to ensure customers continued to buy it instead of hoarding and to avoid liability. But if there was an expiration date, there had to be a point when the medicine actually expired. It wouldn't lose all effectiveness the day after the expiration date, but some day, weeks or months later, using it would be like injecting useless water, and my blood sugar would continue to rise unabated.

I put it in terms Kyle would identify with. "Have you ever had milk a day or two after expiration?"

"Sure," he said, "and it tasted fine."

"Have you ever tried it a week or two after expiration?"

He apparently remembered just that, and a look of disgust crossed his face. "You can freeze it. Thaw it out when you need it."

"No," I said. "Freezing destroys it."

I stood there in stupid disbelief, looking at the vials on the fridge shelves.

"So what exactly happens after you run out of insulin?" Kyle asked.

"I die."

-12-

"What do you mean?" Kyle asked. He staggered back and dropped down onto a dining room chair.

"It won't be immediate, but I have to have insulin to live."

This felt like the time just before the virus. It took about a week to reach us once it had hit the US. Like billions of other people, I progressed through the stages of grief. I had watched a YouTube video about them. It turns out knowing the stages doesn't keep you from going through them.

At first I was in denial. I couldn't comprehend my own imminent death. I thought I would be one of the lucky immune. Of course this actually turned out to be the case, but it was completely irrational at the time given the odds.

Then I got angry. I thought I was angry with God, but I couldn't work up enough belief in him to be angry. I just hated the world that had created this monstrous thing. Then I started making promises to this God I didn't believe in. I said if he would let me live, I would help rebuild the world. I would form a community of good and destroy evil and all sorts of other promises. Even then, I knew that was ridiculous.

I was deeply sad for a day or two, and then I accepted it and waited to die. I guess it was a lot easier on me than most since I wasn't watching any loved ones die. The one time Kyle ever talked about his experience, he just said he wished he hadn't survived. It had been too painful for him.

"I don't know if I'll last just days or weeks or months," I said, "but it's inevitable. If I eat enough to live, my blood sugar will rise too high and my body will destroy itself."

I didn't mean to be so matter of fact, but he deserved the truth. We still had at least two years, more if the insulin kept well beyond the expiration. I had to seize these years and enjoy them. I wasn't going to mope and whine through it. This was all I had left.

I'd force myself to move straight through the stages to acceptance.

We could make this work, together. At the end, I'd even help him find someone else. I'd be a good wife until the last.

"We'll make it through this, Kyle," I said, taking his hand.

"*We* won't make it through this," Kyle said. "I will." He got and up and went to the bedroom.

Who the hell was he to be getting upset? I was the one who was going to die. I was so mad at him I wanted to scream. And that's what I did. I went outside and yelled until I lost my voice. Then I got in Bella, still in my pajamas, and just drove. I'm not sure how long I drove or where I ended up, but when I looked at the fuel gauge it was on empty.

I turned the car around. I needed to head home. That much I knew. I felt stupid and then a little scared. My phone couldn't call anymore with the power gone from the network, but the phone itself worked. I kept it charged, because I still used it to tell the time and date, take pictures and play games. I opened the map app on the phone to see where I was, but it didn't work.

The screen showed a flashing blue dot to indicate my position, but it couldn't load the maps, which made sense when I thought about it. The maps were downloaded from servers on the Internet, which was dead, but the GPS that figured out my position in latitude and longitude listened for signals from satellites that must still be working fine.

With Bella stopped in the middle of the road, I took my hands off the wheel. They were shaking and wet with sweat. I needed food. Kyle had given me the insulin injection, but I hadn't eaten. Now the insulin was processing the sugar in my blood and dropping it lower and lower.

I didn't know how far Bella could go once the dial hit empty. I had never let her get that low. I drove slowly, gripping the wheel tightly, hoping and praying for a gas station that would have the fuel that both Bella and I needed. I passed a sign that showed I was on I-10. I realized I was driving on the wrong side of the road, but it didn't matter since I had it to myself.

I swerved, nearly running off the road and had to slow even more to keep driving straight. It became a matter of who would run out first, me or Bella. I asked her to try to keep going until the next gas station. I saw it as I passed a bend in the road, but she didn't have it in her.

Bella sputtered to the exit ramp and then refused to go any farther. The sign said the gas station was a tenth of a mile away, but it might as well have been a hundred. Like a car, the body is a machine, and when the fuel is gone, it can't move anymore. I stumbled to the top of the hill and could see the green BP sign beckoning to its shelves filled with convenient packages of quick sugar.

I fell on the side of the road, and the last thing I remembered was the taste of grass in my mouth.

***

The taste of grass turned to Coke. I coughed as it poured into my throat

49

and even some in my nose. Someone was holding me up and keeping my mouth open while pouring the Coke in. I swallowed and began sucking at the warm can, drinking in the life-giving sugar.

When I finished, draining every drop, I closed my eyes and let my body recover, feeling the life flow back into my limbs. After a few minutes I looked up and saw Kyle's face. My head rested in his lap.

I sat up and he said, "I wouldn't have found you if it weren't for that stupid bright yellow car right at the exit."

He held me for a little longer, and I ate half a Pop-Tart from the pile of sugary treats he had dumped beside me. When my blood sugar reached normal, I walked around some to clear my head and then injected again before a meal of two beef jerky sticks and a can of tuna fish.

Kyle didn't want me to drive, but I assured him I was fine. He got the port to the underground gas tanks open. I watched so I would know how to do it. He pumped some gas into a can with a hand pump. We filled Bella up and drove home slowly, Kyle staying close behind in his truck.

We made love that night, and I went to sleep with thoughts of what to do running through my head. I needed to learn how long after the expiration date the insulin was actually still effective. I'd have to experiment with the vials that would soon expire, carefully watching how I felt after using the insulin from an old vial.

I woke in the morning with a plan to sort all the vials by date, but I was stopped by a note taped to the fridge.

I stared at the note.

I'm sorry, Sugar. I can't take losing anyone else. Good-bye.

I looked out the window and saw that Kyle's truck wasn't in the driveway. I remembered that some of the drawers in the bedroom had been slightly open when I got up, so I went back in the bedroom and saw that he had taken all his clothes. The bathroom was cleared of his toothbrush, razor and deodorant.

He usually woke up before me, and this time he must have quickly gathered his things while I slept soundly, stupidly secure in our love. What had last night been? We had made love and fallen asleep in each other's arms. Was he just getting one last thrill before going on his way?

He had left his shaving mirror by the bathtub. How many times had we lain in the tub together? It was so much work to fill a bathtub with hot water that we usually bathed together. I picked up the mirror and threw it against the wall, where it shattered in a hundred pieces that all fell into the tub. One of those sharp pieces could cut a thin red line on my wrist.

It would be easier than the death I had ahead of me. All I had wanted before was to be left alone, and now that's all I had. Two years of emptiness and then an agonizing death. I had nothing to look forward to.

But I still wanted to live.

It made no sense, but my desire to live was even fiercer now. Last night I had accepted my fate. Now I raged against it.

I went to Bertha and set to sorting the vials, putting those soon to expire in the front. The first was just two weeks away. I would save that one, leaving it perfectly sealed, to experiment with first. I took my morning injection from a vial I had already been using, then worked on getting rid of everything of Kyle's that he hadn't taken with him.

I wasn't going to go after him. I wouldn't beg him to come back to me.

If he couldn't handle what the future held for me, then I didn't want him. I'm not saying I didn't still love him. The love was real, and that doesn't just disappear in a moment. I don't know if it ever does.

I put his stuff in a cardboard box and drove it down to the dump. Of course with no trash pickup, we had to handle it ourselves. We could have just thrown it somewhere out of our sight, but I insisted we take it to the dump. I had known we would have to live here all our lives, and it would eventually pile up. I didn't want our city turning into a desolate wasteland.

I had asked Kyle to get a riding lawnmower, and he kept the yards around us mowed. We couldn't maintain the whole city, but we could at least keep the parts we had to see every day looking like civilization.

Would I keep that up now that he was gone? Now I would have to do all the chores he had helped with. Endlessly hauling gas from the station and water from the creek. Shopping, cooking, fixing things on the house. It would keep me busy, and that's what I needed.

I dumped his things into the landfill, but kept the cardboard box, since it was always useful to have. Kyle had left the many practical things needed in our life. Dozens of gas cans and water jugs. I guess he would go back to his house and set up his life there. Maybe he would leave the city and look for another woman about his age. One that would live a long time.

But he'd find that another woman wouldn't be like me. Kyle hadn't wanted kids and neither had I. He was afraid of losing them. Our more primitive life would be hard on fragile children. Much more would die like in the old days.

But any other woman would want to have kids. I know the desire they have. It's natural. And was probably in overdrive now. The biological imperative is to continue the species, and our species was having a bit of trouble.

Maybe he just didn't want children with me? He didn't want to let my flawed genes replicate themselves. Had he ever intended to stay with me for long?

A man as valuable as he was in the new world could have any woman he wanted. He could have as many as he wanted. I bet there were women who would be fine with being in his harem as long as he kept them safe and kept their homes powered and repaired.

I shut thoughts of Kyle out of my mind and started on the business of staying alive. I didn't attend the weekly community meetings anymore. Edith came to check on me after I missed two. She knew about Kyle. He still came and had told people we had "broken up."

Broken up?

That's what silly kids in high school did. Bouncing from one relationship to another. Crying for an evening over their loss and then flirting the next morning with the next cutie who came along. We hadn't broken up. We were a family. We didn't have the paperwork, but we were husband and wife, and he had divorced me.

When the first expiration date passed, I finished the vial I was on and then two days later used the expired vial. Even though I knew it wouldn't instantly degrade, I was scared. I injected it slowly. Not the quick, well-practiced motion that was deeply ingrained in my muscle memory. I felt like I was taking poison.

I waited thirty minutes and then made a simple lunch of a venison hamburger, a combination of protein and carbohydrates that would turn to sugar. I ate it, and the taste of the deer meat made me think of Kyle.

I sat at the table with a fast-acting vial and a syringe ready to go. My body processed the food, and I stayed at the table for an hour just staring at the vial, ready to use it at the slightest sign.

And I was fine.

I put the syringe and vial in my pocket and went on about my day. The insulin lasted just like it always did, and I had a good afternoon of shopping at the mall. I got a car GPS to put in Bella. My theory was right. My phone downloaded maps as needed, so it wouldn't work, but the car-mounted GPS didn't connect to the Internet. It had the maps built in, so it worked perfectly, connecting to the satellites that would hopefully keep working for many years.

I drove around unfamiliar parts of Tallahassee, trying to get lost and failing, delighted this piece of the old world still worked. It did tell me that I needed to purchase a map update, because the roads may have changed. The poor machine didn't know the roads would never change again.

I stopped at a gas station and used the technique Kyle had showed me to get the tanks open. I retrieved the gas with a hand pump. That was one thing that I had never done by myself that I could now check off the list.

I used the expired vial for a month, until it was empty, without incident. Then I used an unexpired vial next, just to see if I had gotten used to the weaker expired insulin, but there was no perceivable difference. The months passed in a simple routine. The pleasant spring turned once again to the all-engulfing heat of a Florida summer.

I cleaned out and maintained a pool in a house a few down from mine just so I could cool off occasionally. Modern houses were designed to keep everything tightly sealed in so the air conditioners could work efficiently, which meant they got hotter without AC. But I learned to open doors and windows the right way to allow airflow, and Scotty could handle the extra load of a few fans.

The only person I saw was Edith, and she had the good sense to realize I didn't want to talk about Kyle. She kept me informed about the others in our city. She said Bill and Laura were trying to have a baby. I always thought that was a funny thing to announce to people. Basically you're telling everyone you're having a lot of sex.

I supposed we would find out how difficult it was to have a baby without a doctor, but billions of women before us had successfully had babies before doctors and hospitals and all their fancy gadgets. Laura had even said that the women of the community were invited to the birth. Part of me was intrigued to see how it worked. Was it really like in the movies? But I couldn't handle all the blood, so I politely turned down the invitation to that party.

Ralph had claimed a small church as his own and held a service there every Sunday morning. Edith, Bill, Laura, Thomas and Deena attended. Deena invited me, but there was no way that was ever going to happen. Ralph was a little annoying in person with his constant Bible-thumping. And I mean literal thumping of a Bible. He carried it at all times and used it to punctuate all his points. I couldn't have stood to be around him in a church where he had a prerogative to act that way.

I got the impression he hadn't been that way before the virus. He had been an insurance salesman. Now he had transformed into the community preacher, and he was of the fire-and-brimstone variety. I suspected that was how all current preachers were. If you believed in God, then you had to believe he had just brought judgment down upon the Earth. There was no other way to reconcile it.

I think making God all-powerful was one of the biggest mistakes the writers of the Bible ever made. If he were good and very powerful, but not all-powerful, he would make for a very compelling character. A force for right struggling against evil. But there is no struggle when he can do anything. There is just this constant question: Why isn't he wiping out the evil immediately?

I did take one lesson from the church. I used my Sundays for rest. My life now was constant chores, many of them quite physical. Like in the Bible, I did extra work the day before my Sabbath to prepare everything so I wouldn't have to do much on Sunday.

One particular Sunday in July, I swam in the pool. I didn't swim laps or anything. The point was to relax and cool down. I was tempted to swim naked, rather than change into a swimsuit, since no one was even vaguely close by, but that still seemed a little weird for my tastes. I hadn't even felt comfortable parading around naked in front of Kyle, and he had seen me naked plenty of times.

I got out for the third time in the past forty minutes to pee. I didn't like going into other people's houses, mainly because of the dead bodies, so I just went in the yard. I thought I was peeing so much because I was drinking so much, and I was drinking so much because it was so oppressively hot.

I got another glass of unsweet tea from the cooler and noticed a thermometer hanging on the outside wall of the house. It read only eighty-one degrees. Eighty-one degrees is nothing to a lifetime Floridian.

I drank down the entire glass and wanted another one, and I still felt like I needed to pee again. I didn't want to accept it, but I knew what was happening. I walked over to my purse and took out a meter. I pricked my finger and waited for the result.

It read 362, a vastly high blood sugar level. Mine hadn't read that high in many years, not since I'd learned how to carefully keep it in check. I knew I had injected before lunch and eaten a reasonable meal.

I looked at the insulin vial I had used. I had opened it for the first time on my last injection. It had expired a little more than four months ago. The sugar in my blood was rising unhampered by the old insulin in my veins. I walked home and quickly injected an unexpired, fast-acting insulin and waited for it to take effect. With no one else here, if I ever slipped into a coma, that would be it. I had heard many stories of family members finding a diabetic who had lived alone, dead when they finally came to check on them.

So that was it.

The last expiration date was in about a year and a half. If I were lucky, it would last four to twelve months after that. I had enjoyed the peaceful solitude of the past months and had even fooled myself into thinking the insulin might last long past expiration. That I might have many years left if I kept it all carefully refrigerated.

One day the insulin would all be ineffective. I would die as my body destroyed itself. Edith would come for a visit one day and find me dead lying on the floor and shake her head.

I looked at the calendar I had hung on the wall. The stores didn't have current ones, of course, so I had carefully made one by hand. I flipped through the pages, looking to see when the expected date of my death would be.

No.

There had to be a way.

-14-

I wouldn't give up.

I could do a lot in two years. Who knew what was possible? I might still end up dead, but I would go out fighting until the last breath. I didn't know the history of how insulin was discovered and manufactured, but someone had done it the first time. I know they didn't have insulin shots hundreds of years ago. Diabetes used to be a certain death sentence. Someone had figured out how to make it.

I didn't need to produce vast quantities for shipping to millions of diabetics across the nation. I just needed to make enough to keep one tiny woman alive.

I needed to research how insulin was made. Without thinking, I got out my phone, opened the browser and googled "How is insulin made?" only to get an error message. And then I cursed myself for wasting the precious months while the power was still on everywhere and the Internet still worked.

For more than a year I had hauled water from a creek and sat soaked in sweat without air conditioning, but I never felt more primitive than when I stepped into the library. I had never been in one before. I had passed this local library many times and always wondered why it still existed. Why would anyone ever go there if they had the unlimited information of the Internet at their fingertips?

This library wasn't very large, but it still held ten or twenty thousand books. It was divided into sections, and some I could obviously ignore, like fiction and children's books, but otherwise I had no idea how to search for the books I wanted. Signs pointed to computers that could be used to search, but those computers, like everything, sat powerless.

So I got a cart and went up and down the rows, reading the titles of books and grabbing anything that seemed useful. After several hours, I had a small stack of books that didn't seem promising. I flipped through a general anatomy book and found a diagram that showed where the pancreas was located, which was educational, but useless. The other books had passages about the function of the pancreas and how it made insulin, but they didn't have anything about how insulin was manufactured.

The information I had spent all day gathering would have taken seconds on the Internet. I needed to know how the first scientists, in the most primitive conditions, learned to make insulin that humans could use.

I went home that day discouraged, but my resolve wasn't shaken. For a moment I wished I had someone to talk to, a feeling I had never felt before. The time with Kyle had changed me, and it wasn't for the better. I needed to be able to do this myself. No one else would be as motivated. It wasn't their life on the line.

The next morning I decided to try a better library, if there was such a thing. A university seemed like the right place to start, so I drove to the Florida State campus and hoped they still had a library building. Maybe librarians had somehow convinced the university presidents that their positions and the libraries themselves were still valuable.

Amazingly they must have, because FSU had more than one library, and each was massive. After reading just a few signs on campus, I saw with delight that they had an entire medical library, named after somebody who must have been famous or given a lot of money, Charlotte Maguire. I liked that it was named after a woman. She could be my patron saint.

I had been delighted to find out they had an entire medical library, but that isn't what I felt when I walked in. Intimidation. That's what I felt. I had never seen so many books. How did anyone ever deal with this amount of information without a computer? I knew libraries had existed for centuries, maybe even thousands of years. There must have been a system for organizing the books so you could find the one you were looking for.

Of course that system had been abandoned and replaced with technology. I saw dozens of computers from the spot where I stood, stupefied, near the entrance. But they had to have the books organized in a logical fashion, keeping the related ones near each other just to save time. I started roaming around studying the section titles.

After some time I found a section on historical medical books. I pulled book after book from the shelves, flipping through, looking for anything about insulin or diabetes or the pancreas. Most everything was over my head. These were books for doctors or brilliant medical students. They all assumed prior knowledge that I didn't have.

Then I found a beautiful book. It wasn't beautiful to look at. It had a plain and nondescript cover. But it was written beautifully. Simple and clear. It was called "The History of Modern Medicine" and it was unpretentious and understandable. The chapter titles weren't helpful, just numbers, but then I made an amazing discovery. The end of the book had an index, like computer databases have, with key words and concepts in the book along with the page number they could be found on.

Insulin was there in the list, and the index told me to turn to page 394. I flipped the pages and found a clear description of how insulin had first been discovered and how they manufactured it. Modern insulin was made by genetically modifying microorganisms to give them human genes to produce insulin. I had no chance of doing that.

But before that, it was extracted from animals. Frederick Banting and others had done it in the 1920s. If they could do it in an age before computers and television, then I had hope. Like a Wikipedia page, the book had footnotes that referenced other books. After hours of more painstaking research, I found some of those books. Those books themselves had footnotes referencing other books.

It was like the World Wide Web in paper form. Usable, just a thousand times slower. And I don't say a thousand times slower in exaggeration. A click on the Internet might take one second. A thousand seconds is sixteen minutes and forty seconds. I was lucky if I could find a referenced book in that amount of time, and then I had to find the information in the book. So it was actually about five thousand times slower.

After a few days of work, I found a book that outlined the exact process manufacturers used to extract insulin from animals. I read that Banting had used dogs. I wondered how I would possibly capture enough, until I read that they used pigs and cows when they began to manufacture it in bulk. I knew from Kyle that there were pig farms nearby. There must be millions of pigs left in the US. All roaming around, eating, reproducing and waiting to be taken.

The process would be time consuming and difficult. I didn't really understand many of the steps, and I needed some unfamiliar equipment like centrifuges and various chemicals, but people before me had done this in primitive situations with limited resources. A man had done it with pancreases from water buffalos during World War II in war-torn Shanghai to keep his diabetic wife alive.

The top of the page detailing the process said a kilogram of pancreas could provide two thousand units of insulin. I didn't know how much a pig's pancreas weighed, but from the pictures it looked like a couple of hundred grams. Well, in my mind I thought it was about a half pound, and then I had to painfully find a reference book to get the conversion from pounds to grams.

It probably wouldn't work out exactly like it said in the book, but this meant the numbers were feasible. I usually needed about thirty units of insulin a day. If pig pancreases could yield even a thousand units, then that would last me a month. Once I mastered the process, it didn't seem unrealistic to think I could do ten a month.

I'd live on insulin and bacon.

I looked over the detailed list of steps. Preparing for each one would take serious effort on my part, either finding the equipment or chemicals or practicing the process. But it all started with one step. One horrible, terrifying, bloody, messy step.

I was going to have to get a pancreas out of a pig.

I don't know which step terrified me more: extracting the pancreas from a pig or finding out where the pig farms were, since Kyle was the only one who knew how to find the farms.

I cannot overstate how much I missed the Internet.

I was born after the Internet was well established, and I completely took for granted that any information could be found within seconds. The labor of gathering knowledge exhausted me like nothing else, because, as I had calculated, it was thousands of times more work than I was used to. Now I had to painstakingly read books, or in this case, even more painstakingly talk to people to find the information I needed.

When the power flowed I could have googled "pig farms near Tallahassee" and had the answer instantly, with driving directions to the nearest one. Now I had to ask people, and the person who knew best was the person I wanted to see least. I tried using the car GPS first. It had ways to find hotels, restaurants and amusement parks, but strangely not pig farms.

I arrived at the meeting early, so I could talk to the others and have a chance of getting the information I needed before Kyle arrived. The meeting was always in Deena's restaurant, but Edith usually arrived first. She was glad to see me and hugged me tightly. She had the courtesy and social sense to not ask why I hadn't been there in so long.

"Do you know where the closest farm with pigs on it is?" I asked.

"Hungry for bacon again?" Edith said. "I was going to bring you some, but I got the feeling you wanted to be left alone. I've got plenty at home in the freezer. I brought some this morning. I'll have it cooked up in a few minutes."

Edith had already started the restaurant generator, which powered the stove and a few appliances.

"No," I said. "I need to go out to one. Do you know where one is?"

"I'm sorry, Sugar. I've never been. Kyle always just brings a pig he killed, and I butcher it."

When she said his name, she looked at me to see how I reacted. I didn't flinch or at least I hoped I didn't. We chatted, which means Edith talked and I smiled or grunted at the right points, until the next arrival, Ralph.

He carried his ever-present Bible and dropped it onto the table with a heavy thud. Edith asked him without me having to say a word.

"Do you have any idea where a farm with pigs on it is around here?"

"No," Ralph said. "And I've been doing a lot of thinking about consuming unclean animals like pigs."

Oh no. I'd never get the information I needed if he started people arguing about religion.

"I've been thinking that we may need to return to Old Testament law. A new age has begun. God has wiped the world clean."

Neither Edith nor I took the bait, and Edith deftly asked me to help get some supplies out of the back. When I came back in, Deena, Thomas, Sofia, Bill and Laura had arrived. Laura had a beaming smile on her face. I could tell she wanted to say something, but she was apparently holding it for the entire group.

The others, except Kyle, arrived and sat around the table. While Deena and Edith cooked, Deena patted my hand and whispered, "I admire your courage." I didn't know what courage she was talking about. Facing Kyle or facing my own imminent death.

I asked and no one there knew where a farm was except the vague direction of somewhere north of the city. I thought about just leaving then before Kyle arrived and driving around until I found one, but that could take days. While two years seemed like a long time now, I knew I had a tremendous amount of work to do and would regret every day lost. The group chatted for a while waiting for the last member.

Kyle walked in and my heart leapt. I tried to act normal, but I'm sure the reaction showed on my face. The anger and betrayal surged up like it had happened yesterday. He sat down at the opposite end of the table. Laura, fortunately, dissolved the awkward moment with a shrieking announcement.

"I'm pregnant!"

The women oohed and aahhed. The men slapped Bill on the back and shook his hand. Laura even lifted her shirt to show the imperceptible bump of her stomach. That caught all the men's eyes. She was an attractive woman and pulled the shirt up so far as to show the bottom edges of her round breasts.

She didn't seem to care. She was delighted and beaming with pride. In moments like this I should keep my mouth shut. I don't mean to say some of the awkward things I do. But the mathematical side of my brain takes over, and I don't think about social appropriateness.

"I guess we'll find out if the virus immunity passes to children," I said, and the entire group fell silent.

Bill and Laura's faces drooped immediately. Laura sat down with a thunk. Everyone immediately began reassuring her. They said that clearly with two immune parents the baby would be immune. Some said that the virus was extinct with no humans who could host it remaining. Ralph said God would bless their children and protect them since their parents had honored his law and kept the marriage covenant, not fornicating like others. At this, he looked directly at me.

It was obviously a mistake for me to come. I stepped outside to get in Bella and leave. Kyle stepped out behind me and said the worst possible thing he could have.

"I thought you had died."

I turned around and wanted to punch him. "What?"

"Edith kept us updated about you, but even she hadn't seen you in the past couple of months."

"And you just stayed where you were? Thinking I was lying dead on the floor of my house or better yet, lying in a diabetic coma desperately in need of food?"

"Enough time had passed that I couldn't hope to show up at the last minute like last time. And I couldn't bear the thought of seeing you … gone."

"Well, we both agree about that."

"About what?"

"Neither one of us can bear the thought of me dying."

We stood in silence for a moment.

"I just can't—" Kyle started to say, but I cut him off. I didn't want to hear his excuses. He had made his choice.

"Where is the farm you go to for pigs?"

"What?" he asked.

"Just tell me where the farm is."

He thought a moment. "I can take you there. There's a couple. You pick. One's a big corporate farm. Huge. A lot of the animals died caged up in pens with no one to let them out. The other's a small family farm. The pigs just roam free now."

"The small one." That sounded best. I only needed one pig to start with. I just had to confirm I could successfully extract a pig's pancreas.

"Okay," he said. "I'll take you there now." He moved toward Bella.

"No." I knew what he was thinking. He missed me. He missed the sex. He'd renew the relationship for a while and then head out again before my time came. Strangely, if I had thought my fate was sealed, I might have let him come back. I would have put on my blinders and tried to enjoy my last days.

But I had a hope of living, however slim, and if I could live I didn't want him to be a part of my life. He had abandoned me when I needed him most. No one would ever do that to me again.

Kyle saw the look in my eyes and gave up. He scrawled an address onto a napkin, and I drove away.

I almost drove straight there. The GPS said it was only an hour away, but in a few minutes I came to my senses and realized I needed to gather supplies for the gruesome task. First I went to Walmart to get a change of clothes. But *get* was now the wrong word. While listening to the people in our group chat, I had noticed some small changes in language.

Deena had said, "I *got* some flour from my house." But she said, "I *bought* some sugar at the grocery store."

Of course, we didn't buy anything anymore, but there was a difference in getting something from your own personal items and getting something from the vast supplies in stores. The word *buy* had come to mean getting things from the stores.

So I bought some changes of clothes at Walmart. I would almost certainly dispose of these clothes when done, so I just got something that covered me, to hopefully keep the blood off my body. I shivered at that thought, but suppressed it. If I thought about it too long, I would chicken out.

Next I needed something to do the cutting. I went to the kitchen section. I found several sets of sharp knives, but I didn't need instruments for cutting processed meat. I needed surgical instruments. Scalpels and tools for cutting carefully into flesh, holding back skin or other parts and successfully extracting an organ. I wasn't going to find any of that here. I guessed there must be surgical supply stores or warehouses, but I had no idea where they were or how to find them. That wouldn't be in a library or in my GPS. In fact, there was only one place I could think of to find the right equipment.

The hospital.

There were two main places people went when the virus hit. Their homes, to seal themselves in as the government had ordered, or the hospital, in the vain hope of trying to fight their inevitable death. I had seen the news reports of hospitals overflowing. I had purposefully avoided driving anywhere near them. Everywhere else simply looked as if the people had disappeared. Their bodies were neatly contained in their houses or apartments, and I didn't have to think about them.

I drove to Tallahassee Memorial and saw the first full parking lot I had seen since the virus. In fact it was beyond full. Cars were everywhere—some crashed together, some crashed into the walls of the hospital. One was actually in the lobby, the glass of the front doors shattered everywhere. It must have been a mad rush at the end.

I was glad I had stayed home to die.

I pulled up and the smell hit me immediately. I took a shirt I had bought from Walmart and wrapped it around my face, covering my mouth and nose. Bodies were spread across the lobby, but they were mostly skeletal remains now. Two full summers had passed since the virus, and the Florida heat had done its part to speed the decay.

I wanted to run when I saw the dark red blood stains on the granite floor of the lobby, but I moved on through the doors where a clearly labeled sign pointed to the emergency room. I figured the emergency room would have supplies conveniently laid out so they could be accessed quickly. It was a good theory that might have been true before the virus. I opened the door to a chaos of bodies and bones spread everywhere.

All the supplies were scattered around, and I wasn't stepping through that field of death to get to them. This was a large hospital, and hopefully the supplies I needed would be stocked in a room that wouldn't be filled with remains. I thought for a moment. Where would surgical supplies be that people wouldn't have used at the end?

An operating room. No one would have done surgery at the end. You couldn't operate to stop the virus. Nothing could stop it. People irrationally scrambled for medicine, and doctors started giving it just to get the frantic crowds to leave the glutted hospitals.

I followed the signs directing to an OR on the second floor. It was dark in the interior of the hospital, and I used the flashlight on my phone. Skeletal bodies still lined the hallways, and I tried to pretend I was in a Halloween haunted house. I found the OR and opened the door. I shined the light around and saw a patient's mostly decayed body lying on the operating table.

The medical charts showed a scheduled C-section. I wish I hadn't looked at the paper because then I understood that two bodies lay on the table, one containing the other. The doctor's body was on the other side of the table. I hadn't noticed it in the dark when I came in.

I had to admire the doctor for working until the last. The physician must have been sick, but tried to get the baby out in an almost futile hope that it might be immune. Maybe the doctor knew performing the operation was completely irrational, but decided to keep going until the end.

I understood how he felt.

After opening a short cabinet, I found surgical masks and put one on immediately. I put the rest in a bag. I found three scalpels, each slightly different. I didn't know what the difference meant, but I took them all. I got clamps and things that sort of looked like scissors and other tools I didn't know how to use, but it couldn't hurt to have them. I scooped them all into the bag.

A box of surgical gloves I found in a drawer would hopefully save my skin from having to actually touch anything. I couldn't think of anything else I would need, so I left the gruesome place as quickly as possible.

I was never happier to be away from anywhere. Night was falling so I went home, dreading the day ahead of me.

-16-

I woke at five in the morning, unable to sleep anymore. I changed into the clothes I bought yesterday. Clothes I wouldn't care about losing. I put a change of clothes in Bella next to all the surgical supplies I had gathered. I injected and made a quick breakfast of ham and biscuits. I ate the biscuits, but felt uneasy about the ham and just left it on the plate.

I found a dozen things to do around the house. Scotty needed filling. A shingle on the roof had come off and needed to be replaced. I had already replaced three myself. The new shingles were exactly the same brand as the old ones. I spent a lot of time matching them, but the additions still stood out since they were new and unfaded by the sun.

By 10 am I was starting to convince myself that there were too many errands and chores to do, that the extraction would have to wait for another day. But I knew every day would be like this. There would always be something else I could find to do.

I entered the address Kyle had given me into the GPS. I had thought the GPS would be Bella's voice, so I hadn't named it, but the voice didn't sound like I'd pictured Bella's voice. I could remember my mother's voice, and that's how I pictured Bella sounding. The GPS voice was female, but much too stiff for the warmth of my mother's voice. I decided to name her Mandy.

Mandy announced that it was fifty-seven minutes to our destination, and I pulled out of the driveway. I enjoyed the drive in the countryside, with Mandy chiming in every few moments to let me know when to turn. But I didn't need the final directions. Pigs roamed everywhere.

For a minute I thought about pulling over and trying the extraction on one of the pigs alongside the road, but I decided to pull up to the farmhouse where there would hopefully be a flat surface to work on. The pigs didn't seem bothered by me and barely looked up as I parked and stepped out of the car.

The farmhouse was exactly as I had imagined it. Quaint and homey. I could picture a man in overalls with rough hands stepping out onto the porch in the early morning as his wife made breakfast and the kids rolled out of bed. An old barn stood off a ways from the house, and a pickup truck rusted out front, left there when the farmer had parked it for the last time.

A mother pig nursed a litter, if that's the right word, of piglets under an orange tree. Other pigs roamed around, some through the fields, others in and out of the barn. A small one walked up and nuzzled my legs, apparently remembering that humans brought food. I thought of Wilbur from *Charlotte's Web*, which my father, my real father, had read to me at least a half dozen times.

It was then that it really hit me. I would have to kill one of these trusting creatures.

I looked at the small bag I carried. It held a book on pig anatomy that I had got, no *bought*, from the library, a scalpel and a few medical tools. The scalpel was the only lethal instrument in the bag. I don't know what I was thinking I would do. Was I going to hold a pig down, cut its throat and watch it bleed out?

I wanted to get in Bella and drive home and forget this entire insane idea. If this even worked, it meant a lifetime of slaughter. Naively, I even had a cooler in the backseat for the meat I planned to cut off the pig after I removed the pancreas. There was no way I could eat it after looking into its eyes.

I stepped out of the warm sun and into the farmhouse feeling lightheaded and nauseated. I checked my blood sugar with a meter, but it was fine. I had to decide now. If I wanted to live, this had to happen. Probably hundreds of pigs had died to feed me in the past. That had never bothered me. Someone else had done the dirty work. But that age was gone.

I looked through a window at the mother pig. One of the baby pigs would be easiest to handle. I steeled myself and walked over. One of the smaller piglets was being pushed away by the others and couldn't get to a nipple to nurse. I carefully approached, and the mother pig didn't seem upset.

I picked up the small baby pig, cradled it in my arms and stepped away. It squealed a moment and then started rooting around at my breast vainly looking for milk. I looked at it, with it thinking I was its mother, and started trembling. I went back to the litter and pushed the other piglets apart and let the small one latch onto a nipple.

I needed an old, fat pig. One that had lived a long, full life and had a large pancreas. An old pig would have been from before and would have been intended for slaughter. It had been given a brief reprieve but would now meet its intended destiny.

But how would I kill it? I didn't think the farmers actually slaughtered animals on the farm, so there wouldn't be any equipment. I started to look around the farmhouse. The kitchen had several large knives, but that would be too brutal to stomach. I looked in every closet, rummaging through piles of clothes and opening boxes until I found what I was looking for. A small pistol in a shoebox. I didn't know the word for it, but this was the kind that had a spinning chamber in the middle that held the bullets. I thought they were all six-shooters, but this one had eight slots for the bullets.

It was small, the whole thing about six inches long, and I wondered if the husband had bought it for his wife to be able to use. The farmers were apparently conscientious and didn't have the ammunition with the gun. I had seen crayon drawings on the wall and other signs of the wear that children put on houses. I couldn't find the bullets anywhere until I finally pushed open the door to the master bedroom. The skeletal remains of a man, a woman, a boy and a girl lay together in a queen-size bed. I could only tell their genders from the clothes they wore. I found the bullets in a box under the bed.

I don't know what kind of protection this would have offered the family. With the bullets kept apart from the gun, an intruder would have had plenty of time to hurt them before it was loaded and ready.

I realized then that in all this time I had never thought of keeping a gun. In every post-apocalyptic movie I had ever seen, everyone carried guns and fought with dangerous strangers in the wasteland of society. But we had none of that. I suppose we had been lucky with the twenty or so people in and around Tallahassee.

There was nothing to fight over. Everything left was in virtually infinite supply. Well, there was one resource that was scarce, and I was one of those. There would certainly be some men left who would hurt a woman to get what they wanted.

I would keep the gun after this.

I shut the door to the master bedroom behind me and walked back down to the kitchen, holding the gun cautiously even though it wasn't loaded. I took a minute to figure out how to pop the spinning chamber out, and I loaded a bullet into each slot. When it was full, I hesitated a moment to push the chamber back in place, afraid the gun would go off, but it didn't, and the chamber clicked into place. From the movies I knew guns had safeties to keep them from firing accidentally, and I assumed these people would have kept the safety on. I looked all over the weapon, but I couldn't find anything that looked like a safety. I knew little about guns so it could have been there, obvious to anyone else. I guessed I would find out when I tried to fire it.

I put the gun in my bag and walked outside to find the sacrifice. The base of the tree was clear of oranges, so I assumed that meant the pigs liked them and had eaten them all. The lowest fruits were too high for the pigs but reachable for me on my tiptoes, so I pulled off five and walked into a grassy field where a large pig sat in a small mud puddle.

I held out an orange, and he ate it greedily from my hand. I stepped back about ten feet and held the next orange out. He hefted his bulk out of the mud, walked to me and sucked it from my hand. I felt like a child molester enticing a kid into a van with candy.

I lured him onto the porch at the back of the farmhouse where I didn't see any other pigs, because I couldn't stand for them to watch. I put the last three oranges on the porch, and he flopped down with a great creak of boards.

I turned and pulled the gun out of the bag, ridiculously making sure the pig couldn't see it. I should have tested the gun first, but I had never fired one and was afraid my resolve would flee with the shock of it. I turned back around and felt like I should say something to the pig. All that came out was, "Thanks and, um, sorry."

I pointed the gun at his head, hoping to get a clean shot that would kill him instantly, but my hand was shaking so much I would have missed or hit him in the body, leaving him to die in agony. I stepped closer as he slurped down the last orange and put the barrel an inch from his head. He finished the orange in a second and turned to look into my eyes.

I couldn't do it with him staring at me, so I waited until he turned his head. When he looked the other way, I forced myself to try to pull the trigger. I had no idea how much pressure it would take, and I hesitated. The gun and my resolve trembled.

The pig stood to go, and I couldn't imagine going through the stomach-lurching process of luring him again. I began to slowly squeeze the trigger. I expected it to be heavy to pull, but it was light, and it fired before I thought it would. The gun flew backward toward my face. The sound rang in my ears, and blood and brains splattered the porch and my clothes.

The pig's body crashed back down, and the blood poured from its head onto the porch. I put the gun down and kicked it away. I stepped away from the slowly expanding puddle, not having thought to bring a change of shoes.

Two other pigs came around, curious to see what was happening. I screamed at them, ashamed for them to witness what I had done, throwing a potted plant to scare them away. I had to finish now, or I had killed for no reason. I opened the anatomy book and turned to the page I had marked that showed a photo of a pig, cut open with everything clearly labeled.

Then I realized the pig in the book had been cut open from the stomach. This pig lay flat on his. I stepped in the pool of blood and gave the body a shove, but it didn't budge. It would have been far easier to get another pig and get it to roll onto its back before killing it, but I couldn't stand to do it again.

I found a rope in the barn, averting my eyes from the gaze of the other pigs as I walked past them. I drove Bella around back and tied the rope from the pig's two left legs to Bella's rear bumper. I slowly inched her forward, watching in the rearview mirror until the body flipped over on its back.

I stepped back onto the porch and took the scalpel from the bag. The instrument seemed so small compared to the pig's body. I thought of using the kitchen knife, but it might cut too far in and slice through organs that I needed to recognize to find the pancreas.

I put on the surgical gloves and mask and tried to imagine myself as a calm surgeon performing a routine surgery. I felt for the breastbone and cut a line straight down the belly. The sharpness of the scalpel surprised me. I didn't realize how easily it would cut through flesh. The first cut felt more like drawing a red line with a marker.

I had to make another cut to get through the skin and then again and again to get through layers of fat. The insides bulged against the seam I had made, until I sliced horizontal cuts at the top and bottom, and the two flaps spread apart, revealing the internal anatomy of the pig.

I lost the battle with my queasy stomach, and I had to step away to vomit onto the porch. I closed my eyes and let my spinning head settle down. When I felt better, I stepped back and looked at the inside of the pig.

And it looked nothing like the picture in the book.

The picture was bloodless and neat, and each organ had a distinct color. The inside of the pig was a red, gooey, fatty mess. I reached in to try to identify parts to orient with the book. The liver and intestines were clear, but I couldn't even find the spleen, which was far larger than the pancreas. I moved organs. I pulled and cut things out. At least three different things could have been the pancreas. I had no clue what I was doing. And then the truth, which was worse than killing and gutting the pig, became obvious.

I was going to need help.

17

I left my bloodied shoes on the porch and then changed into fresh clothes. I drove Bella back barefoot in defeat. I had failed at the first step, which should have been the simplest. I didn't even understand some of the other steps at all. I had no idea what it meant to "neutralize the filtrate with NaOH" or how to "adjust the acidity to a pH of 5.0."

I hated to admit that I wouldn't be able to do this all on my own, but it was painfully obvious. Who would know about the insides of a pig? Edith, my one true friend, butchered the pigs Kyle brought back. Maybe she could help.

I drove to Edith's house, which was only a few blocks from Deena's restaurant where the group met. Edith sat on the front porch and waved to me to come sit down beside her. I never was much for small talk so I just said, "Do you know how to find the pancreas in a pig?"

"The what?"

Not a good sign.

"The pancreas. It's an organ in the pig. Do you think you could find it?"

"I take all the guts and organs out at once. I don't sort them. I've heard of some people eating some of the organs, but I've never even heard of the pancretes."

I thought for a moment. "I need a doctor."

Edith looked worried. "Are you sick? Do you need some of your insulation?"

"No. Well, not yet. I'm going to need a doctor."

"Bill and Laura are going to need one too," she said. "The baby should be here in seven or eight months. They're not sure how far along she is."

That was true, but they had a chance without a doctor. I couldn't just take a guess at which organ was the pancreas. I had to be sure.

"How can we find a doctor nowadays?" I asked. "I can't just drive around to other cities looking for one. That could take too long."

Would it? I tried to estimate what percent of the population were doctors and how many would be left. But I had no good starting point.

"Do you have one of those listing books they used to print?" I asked. "People in old movies used them to look up phone numbers."

"A phone book?"

"Yeah. That's it."

Edith got up and looked through her house and came out with an old one. It was years out of date but would do fine for an estimate. I looked up doctors first, but it said, "See physicians." I turned to that page and counted through all the listings, including everyone but psychologists and other medical professionals, who wouldn't be any help in removing organs, reaching a total of 502.

Tallahassee used to have a population of around 195,000. That meant approximately 1 in 400 people in the population used to be doctors. The US used to have about 300 million people. Dividing that by 9,600 because of the virus deaths left about 31,250 people. Divide that by 400 and you got 78.

Seventy-eight doctors left in the entire United States. It was a rough estimate, but it was probably close. Less than two per state. How could I possibly find one?

"Ralph might be able to help," Edith said.

Ralph was the last person I needed. His skills as an insurance salesman were useless, and his prayers would be even less help. "Thanks, but I don't think so."

Edith laughed. "No. Not for his preaching. He has a radio. He talks to people on it."

I stood up immediately. "Where is his house?"

"I'll take you there," Edith said.

Edith got in the passenger seat, after I moved the bag. She looked in it and saw the strange contents including the gun, but didn't say anything. She directed me to Ralph's house. He answered after a few loud knocks.

Edith explained that we wanted to use his radio to look for a doctor.

"Come to church tomorrow, and I'll help you."

So his plan was extortion. I had go through his religious rituals to get anything from him. He saw the look on my face.

"No, Sugar. You don't have to come to church for me to help you. People don't listen to their radios all the time or even most of the time. It takes a while to find anyone. But quite a few of them listen to my Sunday service each week. I broadcast it." He looked proud. "I even have a couple of listeners in South America. One in Mexico and one in Venezuela."

I didn't tell him Mexico wasn't in South America.

"I'll let them know what you're looking for, and we'll see what they can turn up," Ralph said.

That was something. I went home, slowly filled the tub full of water from jugs and scrubbed myself clean for more than an hour. I crawled into bed and fell quickly to sleep, exhausted from the day's ordeal. I didn't have anything that I considered church clothes, so I woke early and drove to Sears in the mall and picked out a nice outfit, a blue dress with three large white buttons on the front.

I arrived a little before 11:00 am, the time God said in the Bible that all church services should start. Edith, Thomas and Deena, along with Bill and Laura, were already there. Everyone but Laura was glad to see me. She gave me a strange look, which I probably deserved after the stupid comment about whether her baby would be immune to the virus.

She still had no perceivable baby bump, but she held her hand on her belly and acted like it was the Messiah himself in there, come to save the world again. This time, however, not born of a virgin. Bill made it very clear to everyone that he had planted that seed.

"Are you sick at all?" Edith asked Laura while we waited for the service to begin.

"No," she said. "I've always felt great during pregnancy."

"Me too," Edith said. "When I was a young woman a lot of my friends were miserable in pregnancy, but I loved everything about gesticulating."

Ralph came onto the stage, or whatever it's called, at 11:05. He started up the radio broadcast and told everyone listening to stay tuned after the service for some special requests. Edith played the piano, and we sang some hymns. The only one I recognized was "Amazing Grace," but I have to admit I enjoyed singing it. It brought up a new flash of memory of my parents, and those were rare since they had died when I was six.

Ralph preached for fifty-three minutes on *one verse* from somewhere in a book called First John. I tried to find it in the Bible to get the context, but it wasn't anywhere in the first book called John that I came to. When he finally finished, he asked his radio congregation if anyone knew of a doctor. Apparently it was a two-way radio system, because the people talked back, one at a time. Ralph had said the word "ham" in regards to the radio, which must be some sort of acronym. The ten people listening didn't know of any doctors, but they agreed to ask others they knew around their towns and through other radio contacts around the nation and get back to us.

With that kind of network, I had a real chance. Ralph told them to call back later in the day when they had any information. Bill and Laura invited everyone over for lunch at their house. I thought she couldn't mean me, but she specifically came over and invited me personally. I asked what they were having, and she said it was a surprise.

Diabetics hate meal surprises, but I accepted anyway to be polite. I had to admit a real meal sounded good. I was happy to see it was pork roast (high protein, low carbs) cooking in a Crock-Pot since the early morning, but that wasn't the surprise.

Kyle was there, cleaned up and looking handsome. For the first time I'd seen (except at bedtime), he didn't have his ball cap on.

Laura said the roast needed another forty minutes, which would time out right if I did an injection right then. She fussed over getting everyone drinks and ushered everyone but Kyle and I outside, saying it was cooler than in the house, which was true. With the dress I was wearing, I would have to either lift it up high to inject in my thigh, or unbutton and pull the top down to inject in my stomach.

For a fraction of a second, standing there with just Kyle in the empty house, it felt like old times. And without thinking, I almost unbuttoned and pulled my top down, but that faded and he felt like a stranger again. Even worse than a stranger. If a stranger saw me in just a bra, I would be a little embarrassed and soon forget it.

The idea of Kyle seeing me made me angry and sick and sad all at once. I left and went into the bathroom. It only took a few seconds to inject, but I waited a full five minutes before coming out. When I walked back into the living room, Kyle was still there, stupidly holding his empty cup, looking at pictures on the wall.

"They said you're looking for a doctor," he said.

I nodded.

"Could he … fix you?"

"One: not all doctors are men. Two: diabetes can't be fixed. Nothing has changed. Without insulin, I'll die."

"Oh."

We stood for a moment in silence.

"I've been talking to Laura," Kyle said, "and I think I was more afraid—"

"You were more afraid of your pain than mine," I said.

"You didn't lose anybody close to you in the virus," Kyle said. "You don't understand."

"I don't understand losing someone that I love?" Could he step outside of himself for just a second to realize who he was talking to? I had lost my parents at six. I never dwelt on it nor used their deaths as an excuse for anything, but that didn't mean I didn't know the pain of loss. That pain became a part of me.

I believed Kyle was basically a good person. I didn't think he was purposely planning his actions to cause me the maximum possible pain, but that's exactly what he was doing. He abandoned me when I needed him most, then left me to heal on my own. With the healing almost complete, he returned and ripped the tender wound back open.

I thought killing the pig the day before was a horror, but I would do it a dozen times more rather than be there with Kyle. I wanted to flee again, but needed to eat now. The last time I had left upset with a fresh injection and no food, I had nearly killed myself.

I stepped outside, and Laura looked at me with questioning eyes. I didn't give her any sign of how things had gone and just joined the group to chat. Kyle came out in a minute. We both put on smiles and talked with the others. Laura finally served the roast and I dug in, skipping the potatoes, even though they looked and smelled delicious.

I wanted to leave, but Ralph had his radio there, listening to hear if anyone called back with information about a doctor. I could tell Laura was anxious too. I tried to understand what she was going through. The risk to her and the baby was real.

I was pretty sure my comment about the baby's immunity was off base. They knew it was a genetic immunity, so it should be passed to children since both parents had the gene. But many other risks remained. Plenty of women had babies without a doctor, but plenty of those women or babies died in childbirth.

The birth process clearly wasn't designed very well. So many things could go wrong when trying to push a baby out through such a tiny opening. God or nature had chosen to solve that problem with quantity rather than ingenuity. Just make the creatures of Earth crazy to reproduce, and if a certain percentage died in childbirth, then the numbers still worked out.

I wondered how long it would take to reach the old population levels, and once I think of a math problem I can't help but solve it. If we had about thirty thousand people in the US now and optimistically assumed that each generation doubled the population, then it would take thirteen or fourteen generations to reach 300 million. If a generation took just twenty years, that would be nearly three hundred years. So our children for generations would never know a world like the one we had grown up in.

I felt sorry for Laura, and I understood her fear. In a way, I guess I understood why she wanted Kyle and me to get back together. Her child would be the only child in the city. Kyle and I were the only other reproductively viable couple. She probably just wanted her child to have a friend.

For a moment I appreciated the appeal of being pregnant alongside Laura. Going through something with someone else makes it easier. But that wasn't the path for me. Even if I could find another man to love, I couldn't bring a child into the world when it was still very likely I wouldn't live more than a couple of years.

The radio squawked, and both Laura and I jumped.

The voice said, "This is Tim in San Antonio. We don't have a doctor in the survivors here. I'm not in radio contact with anyone else, but I talked to people here who have talked to others in the city. We figured that covers about two hundred seventy people."

I took the radio microphone from Ralph and pressed the talk button. "What was the population of San Antonio before?"

"One to one and a half million, I guess," Tim said.

"That should be a hundred four to one hundred fifty-six survivors," I said. "Did you have a higher survival rate?" The 1 in 9,600 ratio had been pretty consistent worldwide.

"Nah. It was probably a little over a hundred to start, but people have come in from all around, particularly Mexico. There's nothing to stop 'em crossing the border now. And, frankly, the more people, the better."

"Still, with only one in four hundred people being doctors, it's not surprising you don't have one."

"Sorry, honey," Tim said. "If you find one, let us know. A few people are sick here. And of course, the babies are starting to come."

The next call came from Gainesville, Florida. The caller had contacted people around the Panhandle and South Florida, but hadn't heard of any doctors. The others in our group made plans to get together with them since they were only two hours away.

We got other calls throughout the day, but no one told us about any doctors. The mathematics said that if we covered more than four hundred people, we should start finding doctors. But math doesn't account for everything. What if another community had a doctor but didn't want to share them? If we had a doctor here, would we send them away to help others?

One of the last calls came in the evening from New York City.

"This is Vince."

"Hi, Vince. Any luck?" Ralph said.

"No. We've been looking for a while, but I checked far and wide today. Nothing. No one's heard of anything."

He sounded sincere. And if he were trying to hide anything, he would have simply not called us.

"That doesn't make any sense," I said. "With the numbers we've covered today and especially with New York, we should have found a doctor by now."

"Yeah," Vince said. "One of our math types here figured it was about one in four hundred. Is that what you figured?"

"Exactly," I said. I knew I was right.

"But you math types don't figure for everything," Vince said. "The way I see it, the virus had two killing waves."

What was he talking about? I hadn't heard of anything like that. No one in Tallahassee had died after the virus first came through. It didn't affect the immune.

"The first wave is what you thought, killing nearly all but one in ten thousand," Vince said. "But the second wave is all the people killed from other things."

Everyone gathered closer even though the radio was turned up loud.

"As you've probably figured, there aren't as many children as there should be. They may have survived the virus, but little tikes couldn't make it on their own. Most under two or three probably died without anyone to take care of them."

We had realized this, but it was horrible to hear again.

"Other immune people were killed in the chaos of the last days," Vince said. "One in four hundred immune were doctors, but where were the doctors while others were hiding in their houses?"

Oh.

"Doctors are mostly good people who want to help others," Vince said. "Many went to try to help people at the hospitals or in their offices. The people looking for protection from the virus were going crazy. Some immune doctors were killed in the chaos."

Now I understood. I had seen the aftermath at the hospital. If a doctor survived the assault of the dying, they would find themselves surrounded by decaying bodies and disease.

"And then the suicides," Vince said. "Could you watch thousands die, including your loved ones, unable to help them, when you had dedicated your life to healing the sick?"

I had estimated about seventy-eight doctors were left in the US, but it might be far less. How could I possibly find one and then convince them to leave the community they cared for to help a girl who was almost certainly bound to die anyway?

We thanked Vince and said good-bye. Bill began reassuring Laura that it would be okay, and Edith said she had helped deliver cows and horses on the farm as a child. Kyle sat down in a lawn chair and asked if they had any beer. Deena whispered, "After Ralph leaves," and sat down in a chair beside him.

The last call came in from a small town called Conway, South Carolina.

A man named Eric with a thick Southern accent, but distinct from the Panhandle accent I knew, said, "I enjoy your service every Sunday, Pastor Ralph."

"Thank you, Brother Eric," Ralph said.

"Did you find anyone who has heard anything, even a rumor, of a doctor?"

"Well," Eric said, talking very slowly with long pauses that kept us waiting, "no."

So that was it. Our last contact hadn't turned up anything.

"Nothing," Eric said. "Not even a nurse."

Everyone deflated. Laura rubbed her belly. Edith mouthed, "Sorry," to me.

"Thanks for trying," Ralph said.

"No problem. I don't have anything else to do. I'm the only survivor around here. I've thought about heading down your way."

"You'd be welcome," Ralph said. "We have more than enough room and food."

"I thought I'd done it for a minute," Eric said, "when somebody on the radio mentioned an old man in Myrtle Beach. But he was just a veterinarian."

"That's perfect!" I shouted, and everyone looked at me like I was insane. Who better than a vet to know how to take a pancreas out of a pig? The old man had probably done that very thing in school. And his knowledge of other steps in the process of making insulin would be far greater than mine. If he hadn't done them before, he would probably at least know what they meant.

Laura started to say, "Well, I suppose … "

I interrupted. "Where in Myrtle Beach?"

"I don't know," Eric said. "It was really just a rumor. A few people had heard of a man who said he was a vet taking care of the local animals."

A rumor would have to do. I left the bewildered group immediately. I had preparations to make.

I was going on a trip.

18

Mandy, the car-mounted GPS, said it was seven hours and forty-three minutes from Tallahassee to Myrtle Beach, but I had to figure on a much longer trip. I didn't know what the roads would be like. The farthest I had gone out of Tallahassee was a little way down I-10 on the day I found out the insulin would expire and just drove Bella until she ran out of gas. The road had been relatively clear, but I had a lot farther to go this time.

My first priority was making sure Bertha stayed running. I had to plan on at least two days to get there and two days to get back. I had no idea how long it would take to find the vet. I had never been to Myrtle Beach.

Really I had hardly ever been anywhere. I had always dreamed of traveling to places around the world, South America or Europe especially. I guessed that would never happen now.

I'd gone to Disney World a few times with foster families and to the beaches near Tallahassee a hundred times, but never anywhere else. I liked beach towns because it was so easy to orient myself. Everything was relative to the ocean. I could use that in Myrtle Beach to help establish a search pattern, working east to west across the city.

I talked to Edith, and she promised to keep Bertha running. I was tempted to ask Kyle, since he could fix any generator issues or even hook up a new one, but his help wasn't worth the pain of seeing him. I asked Edith to check every day that Scotty was still going and power was flowing to Bertha. I emptied and turned off the food fridge and Nimrod the freezer so that Bertha was the only thing using power. Edith happily stored all the extra food in her freezers.

If Scotty or Bertha failed, I instructed Edith to quickly transport all the insulin to her fridge. My outer limit for the trip was somewhere around a month. That's about how long unrefrigerated insulin is supposed to be good for, but I hoped it wouldn't take nearly that long to find the old man.

I packed a few days' worth of clothes, but I could always easily find clothes almost anywhere. I knew how to open most gas station underground tanks, so fuel shouldn't be a problem, but I kept a few cans of gas in the trunk just to be safe.

I put the gun, with extra bullets, in easy reach in my purse in the passenger seat. I had decided to name it Clint. I think that came from a tough-guy actor who I'd seen with a gun in the movies. The people in Tallahassee had all been good, safe people, but who knew what kinds of people were out there with no law to stop them?

I packed four vials of insulin, even though I would probably only use part of one. Even if I lost all the insulin, I should still be able to get home in time. High blood sugar kills slowly. Low blood sugar is what can get you quickly. I kept packaged food of all kinds in the backseat, especially quick sugar-like cans of Coke.

The morning of the trip, I sat in Bella in the driveway, excited and scared. I had never gone on a long trip by myself, much less in a post-apocalyptic wasteland. This sounds completely stupid and childish, but I trusted Bella to keep me safe. She was my parents' only real gift to me, and in some way I believed they sent her to watch over me. She had protected me last time when I lost consciousness from low blood sugar, stalling at the exact place to let Kyle spot her, shining bright yellow in the sun, and then find me.

You might think Bella would have done better to have kept going a few hundred more yards and gotten me to a gas station to get the food. But Kyle had told me the store was completely locked, and he had to smash his way in to get the sugar I so desperately needed. No way could I have done that in the condition I was in, neither physically nor mentally.

We pulled out of the driveway, and within a few minutes we were cruising east on I-10. The speed limit sign read 70, but that was now meaningless. I thought for a moment I would hit the gas and see how fast Bella could go, but while there were no police to stop me, there were also no workers to maintain the roads or keep them clear.

To be safe, I decided to drive at forty to forty-five miles per hour, which meant the trip would take twelve to thirteen hours. It was probably unrealistic to expect no delays, and I didn't want to drive at night, so I accepted that I would have to stop somewhere for the night. I'd handle that a few hours before sundown.

The road was worse than last time and far worse than before the virus. Potholes dotted the asphalt, and tree limbs and other debris became more frequent the farther I got from a big city. It turned out that forty was the fastest I could safely go.

I hit Jacksonville around noon and stopped on the outskirts of the city to inject and have some lunch at a Winn Dixie, careful not to use my food supplies in the car unless I had to. The store still had plenty of food on the shelves, but someone had obviously been using it for a while. I opened a can of chili and tried to eat it cold. That was awful, so I found a small griddle and a car adapter to plug it into.

I got back in Bella and continued east on I-10, looking for where Mandy said I should merge onto I-95, going north. Mandy faithfully announced when I was two miles away and then one. When she said a quarter of a mile, I noticed something up ahead and slowed.

As I got closer, I saw a set of tables, with large umbrellas, in the middle of the road. Four people sat in chairs at the tables in the shade of the umbrellas. They appeared to be playing cards, but as I approached, they noticed me and stood up. I slowed to nearly a stop, not knowing what to do.

Was it an ambush?

I tried to think what they might want. There would be no point in stealing money. It had no value or meaning anymore. Food was still plentiful. They couldn't want a car. Thousands of cars, far better than my little Bella, sat idle waiting to be taken. I, a young woman, was one of the only rare resources left in the world.

If it were a group of only men, I would have turned Bella around and floored it, but I saw two men and two women. It looked to be two couples, an older pair and a younger pair. They saw me slow down and waved for me to come forward.

I took my purse, with Clint the gun in it, from the passenger seat and put it in my lap. I rolled forward and stopped about twenty feet from them. I had the top down on Bella and was now wishing I had it up to offer more protection.

"There's a toll to pay on this here road," the older man said. He reached behind his back.

I hesitated a moment in panic, not able to decide whether to hit the gas and crash through the tables or pull Clint out of my purse. In that moment the man pulled something out and held it in both hands, pointed at me. I had lost a critical second to react.

I tried to focus, but I didn't know what to do, and my heart pounded in my chest. Now I wished they wanted something so simple as money. In this world, the only thing I had to give was something I was terrified they would try to take. They all approached, two on the left and two on the right.

The man said, "But we pay the toll, not you."

It took a moment for that to register, and it made no sense. The older man handed me a small black book, and I took it, bewildered. The others handed me bottled waters, some canned food, a road map and a bag filled with other items.

"Just like we have paid the toll for you here so that you may go on, another has paid the price for your sins so that you may go to heaven."

Oh. They didn't want my body. They wanted my soul.

And they could have it. I was so relieved I would have said yes to anything they asked. The man kept talking in a preacher's tone, and when he paused and they looked at me expectantly, I said, "Um … yeah sure."

They all smiled and congratulated me. I think I was saved or redeemed or maybe reincarnated, but I'm not sure.

"How long have you been here, doing this?" I asked.

"About six months," the young woman said.

"How many have come through?"

"It's been pretty busy. This is a hub for many people coming from or to south Florida."

"How many would that be exactly?" I wanted real numbers.

The younger woman looked at the younger man before answering. "Would you say as many as five or ten a week? About as many coming as going."

He nodded.

"Have you heard of any veterinarians or doctors?"

The older man started to say, "There is only one great physician and—"

The younger woman rolled her eyes and smiled at me. "She wants a real answer," she said. "No. We haven't heard of any. I'm sorry."

I chatted with them awhile. The older man was a hundred percent on message, but the others talked like real people. They asked me religious questions, but they also just talked about normal things. The young woman was keeping a journal and showed it to me. I didn't share mine. This is for people to read long after I'm dead, which may not be long from now. They gave me some more supplies from their stash beside the road.

And they never asked me for anything in return.

I had always thought I understood the economy of religion before. Some people, just a few really, do it for the money. It employs preachers and a whole host of other workers. Some do it for the admiration. I think that's why Ralph does it, but I had to admit he did help me when I needed it.

Some people do it for the socialization. I was always miserable in church, because I'm miserable anywhere with large crowds, but I understood that most other people like to be involved in groups. But these people seemed to be doing this happily, sitting for hours and days without seeing anyone else. I couldn't figure out what they were getting out of it, except to conclude they actually believed what they said. It was refreshing to find people being good when it would be so easy for people not to be.

After an hour or so, I got back on the road. The missionaries, or preachers, or whatever they were, had given me an idea. They were trying to find people also, but they didn't go searching. They came to where people would naturally pass through. I could use that in Myrtle Beach in trying to find the vet.

I drove slowly up I-95, crossing plenty of rivers that fed into the nearby ocean. In the late afternoon I realized it was time to find a place to stay for the night. The cluttered road would be completely unsafe in the dark. I saw signs for Savannah, a place I had always wanted to visit, so I turned off onto I-16 with Mandy insisting that we get back on the intended route. I cancelled the destination and drove without her guidance.

I wandered around the city and then followed signs to the historic district and found a huge, beautiful park with a fountain that must have been spectacular when it flowed. I admired the old city, and then as evening came I picked out a historic inn. I picked one with no cars in the parking lot, to hopefully avoid any dead bodies.

I parked Bella outside and went in cautiously, but from the smell it was clear there were no remains here. The inn even had candles and matches, and within a few minutes I had myself set up in a quaint, lovely room that looked like it would be on the cover of a fancy magazine.

I slept soundly, almost lost in the soft bedding and overstuffed pillows. I woke in the morning with warm sunlight coming through the window. I went downstairs and found an unopened box of pancake mix in the cupboard, and I mixed it up in a bowl with bottled water. I stepped outside to cook the pancakes on the griddle that I had hooked up to run from the car adapter.

The parking lot was empty. Bella was gone.

19

I felt like a mother whose child had been taken. I had left Bella alone and unprotected, while I slept soundly. No smashed glass covered the asphalt. I hadn't locked her. I stepped back inside the house and saw my purse on the kitchen table where I had left it the night before. The keys had been attached, but they were gone now.

My purse didn't look like it had even been opened. Why would it? In this new world, the thief couldn't care less about money or credit cards or other things a woman might keep in her purse.

But why would he steal Bella? Thousands of cars had been left everywhere with the keys nearby. I couldn't fathom the mind of someone like that. There were just evil people in the world. People who would steal and hurt and kill just because they could.

I sat down on the kitchen floor and thought of the day I got her. I should have picked a car based on practical things like gas mileage and maintenance costs, but it was love at first sight. I could almost feel my mother pushing me toward the bright yellow car. Bella was the only thing I had that felt like it was from my parents.

And now she was gone.

I could still do what I had come to do. Like the thief, I could pick from hundreds of cars within just a few blocks. But it wouldn't be the same. Bella had made me feel safe on this journey. I had lost her, and the foolish sense of security with her. The missionaries in Jacksonville had made me feel like the new world was left with kind people.

I wanted to curl up in a ball and lie on the cold tile floor, but I needed food. And before I could have food, I needed insulin. I opened my purse to get a vial and syringe out, and I saw Clint, the gun, neatly tucked in with the other things in my purse. I took it out.

There is nothing in this world that can change your perspective like holding a gun in your hand.

What were the odds that the thief was just passing through town? Pretty low. With so few people in the world, two moving travelers wouldn't often encounter each other. I had picked a spot deep in the city, not on the outskirts like someone wandering through would do. The thief must have been a local and seen me. He wanted the car and stole it, but was probably driving it around town now. He would think he had nothing to fear from a small, young woman.

How would I find him? I could do a systematic search, but that would take a long time, and I might miss him, since he could be moving. I had to find other people. Like our community in Tallahassee, they would most likely know where each other lived. With fifteen or so people in a city this size, I could probably find one. Once I found one, they could lead me to others.

I injected, ate and got dressed in a hurry. I walked around looking in buildings with cars out front until I found a set of keys. It only took a few minutes of checking cars until I found one that matched the keys, a light blue Toyota Corolla. The ease of it made me even more furious at the thief.

The car was hesitant to start, but with a few turns of the key in the ignition, the engine started. I began to systematically move up and down the streets looking for anyone, but I realized I needed to always keep food ready. I had learned that lesson the day Bella saved me.

I drove until I found a grocery store, and when I walked in, a young woman, maybe in her late twenties, was pushing a cart through the store. I should have thought of this in the first place. People tended to go to certain places, like grocery stores or gas stations.

She seemed wary as I walked straight toward her. I'm sure I didn't look very happy. "I'm trying to find someone," I said.

"Hi. I'm Jane. Nice to meet you," she said, extending her hand.

I'm so bad at social situations. Of course, I should have introduced myself first. "Hi. I'm, um, Sugar. I guess," I said and shook her hand.

She looked at me strangely. I'm not sure whether it was from my unusual name or my uncertainty of it.

"Who are you looking for?"

"I don't really know. Someone stole my car."

"Then I know just who it is."

This search had gone quickly. Maybe the search for the vet would be as easy.

"His name is Rigby," Jane said. "He's a creep and a nuisance. He just loves to destroy things. One time he set fire to a building downtown just for the fun of burning it. Fortunately, Brian, my boyfr—" She stopped herself and looked me up and down. "Brian, my husband, was a firefighter. He managed to get it put out before all of downtown burnt to the ground."

"Do you know where I can find him?"

"He lives in the Publix. We never go there. He destroyed the sign, but you'll know you've found it when you see all the demolished cars in the parking lot."

Demolished cars? I had to get there quickly.

"When you find him, give that jerk a piece of your mind. I'm pretty sure he's watched Brian and me … enjoying ourselves in the backyard."

Jane gave me directions to the Publix. I hopped in the Toyota and drove straight there. Everything but the X in the sign had been torn off. The parking lot was filled with dozens of smashed and burned cars and trucks of every kind. One had been crashed into the wall, with most of the hood caved in and bricks scattered around. Some had crushed roofs and had clearly been driven over by a truck with massive tires, the only undamaged vehicle in the lot besides Bella.

I nearly cried in relief when I saw Bella, untouched, parked near the front. She had waited for me in this place of vehicular death. I started to weave the Toyota through the maze of dead automobiles, when a boy, who must have been Rigby, came out carrying a gas can. He appeared to be a couple of years older than me. He had a thin, scraggly beard and unwashed hair.

He hadn't noticed me, so I stopped the car and planned to sneak up on him while he filled Bella's gas tank. If he didn't try to leave, it might be easiest to stay hidden and then drive off when he went back inside. I held my purse, hunched over and worked my way closer, hoping he had simply left the keys in the car.

He took the cap off the gas can, and I wondered how he would pour it in the tank, since the can didn't have a spout and he didn't have a funnel. I stopped by a truck where I could stand up and watch through the broken glass.

Then he poured the gas all over Bella.

I screamed and he looked back at me. Then a sickening smile spread across his face. He pulled a lighter from his pocket, and with one well-practiced motion, he lit it and threw it onto Bella.

The fire caught, and within a second, she was consumed in flames. For a moment, I couldn't conceive of what I was seeing as Bella burned. Then I ripped open my purse, pulled the gun out and ran at him.

This scared him, and he started to turn and run. I pulled the trigger. The gunshot cracked through the air, and a chunk of brick flew off the wall. I can't tell you whether I purposely fired a warning shot or simply missed, but it stopped him. He turned around with his hands up, and Bella burning behind him.

I held the gun pointed at him, my arm trembling. "Why?" was the only thing that came out of my mouth.

"Please put that down," Rigby said. "It's just a car. There are thousands of them. I can find you another one just like it. Please, please put the gun down."

I liked the fear in his eyes, and I squeezed the handle of the gun tight. He had hurt me so much just for a stupid juvenile thrill.

"You're a thief," I said. He couldn't be allowed to get away with this. He had to be punished. What other evil things had he done? What else would he do if I let him go?

"I didn't know it was anybody's."

"Liar!" I yelled. "You took the keys off of my purse. You saw me pull up, and you waited until I fell asleep. You stole her, and then you killed her."

"No, I—"

"Shut up! You know it's the truth. Say it!"

"Okay. Okay. I stole it. I'm sorry. Please put the gun down."

"And you set fire to a building and nearly burned down half of Savannah."

"How did you … ?"

"And you watch people while they're making love."

"You talked to Jane. I only did that once. I wasn't trying to spy. They were doing it in their backyard where anyone could see. I came up to ask if Brian would let me use a fire truck. He has all the keys. I couldn't help it once I saw her naked. There's no Internet anymore. I hadn't seen a woman in so long."

"Pervert. What else have you done?"

"What?"

"What else have you done?"

"Am I on trial or something?"

Yes. He was. I hated him. I wanted to find a reason to pull the trigger and end his miserable life.

"What else have you done? Tell me!"

"Nothing. I just like to smash and burn stuff. I've never hurt anyone."

"Prove it."

"I can't … How can I prove it standing here? Just put the gun down, and we can talk."

I knew what kind of person he was. If he hadn't hurt someone yet, he would. He'd get bored with destroying cars. I could protect countless people if I just ended him here. There was no law anymore. People like him would do whatever they wanted. He had taken the only thing that mattered to me just because he could.

I put my finger on the trigger and raised the gun to look down the sight.

"Clint and I should just end you right now."

"Who the hell is Clint?"

"The gun."

"You named the gun?"

"Yes."

"Why?"

Why had I? Because I had named everything since I was a child. Stuffed animals and toys. It's something children do. And I was still a child, standing there pointing a gun at a man with my finger on the trigger, millimeters from sending the slug of metal ripping through his flesh.

I couldn't do it.

I couldn't kill someone for stealing a car. Maybe he was evil. Maybe he would do bad things later. But I didn't know.

I put the gun down at my side.

"I could have done anything last night," he said.

"What?"

"I saw you drive by and stop for the night," he said. "I watched you. You're beautiful. The only other woman near my age is Jane, and she's with that oaf. You fell asleep and lay there defenseless. I could have done anything. But I just took the car."

I never understood the power that desire held over men until I lived with Kyle. But I'm still not sure Rigby deserved any credit for not doing something evil when he was tempted. He started to say something, but I never heard it.

Bella exploded.

-20-

The world turned to light and heat.

When I could see again, I saw that Rigby stood there, the back of his shirt on fire. He didn't move, standing rigid in shock, so I pushed him to the ground to smother the flames. When I was sure the fire on his shirt was out, I dragged him away from the searing heat of Bella's corpse. He must have hit his head when I knocked him down, because he was now unconscious.

I turned him over and saw that he had burns on his back, but not the worst kind. I can never remember whether first- or third-degree burns are worse, but his skin was red and blistered, not charred. If that was it, I could have left him to heal, but his back and legs were riddled with sharp pieces of metal and glass. Some of them had been driven farther in when I pushed him down. I was relatively unscathed, because his body must have shielded me from the flames and debris.

I pulled him into the store by his shoulders to keep his face from dragging on the concrete. Like the outside, the inside of the store looked like a war zone. All the other grocery stores I had seen had been kept neat by the few survivors who shopped there. Rigby had demolished his acquired home. It looked like he had set up a shooting range. A variety of rifles and guns lay at the end of one aisle, and everything that could possibly be shot at lay at the other end: cans, bottles, toys and Barbie dolls in particular.

I went to the pharmacy section and got rubbing alcohol, sterile bandages, Band-Aids and tweezers. When I came back, Rigby had begun to stir.

"What the hell happened?" he said.

"Don't roll over," I said. "Your back is burned and full of glass and shrapnel."

"It hurts," he said.

I imagined it did. "Don't move. Your burns are like a super bad sunburn. That should heal, eventually. But I've got to get all this stuff out of you."

"Can you give me something for the pain? Please."

"There's a pharmacy in here. I'll go look for some painkillers. Do you know what they would be called?"

"Yeah," he said.

"And?"

"And I looked that all up when we still had the Internet. I took all the painkillers a while ago. I … I didn't handle it well when my mom and dad and everyone else died."

"Is there any alcohol?"

"I drank or shot it all," he said. "But I don't drink or do painkillers anymore. I got over that by breaking stuff."

"Then there isn't anything," I said.

He cranked his head around and grimaced. "What about that?" he asked, looking at the rubbing alcohol I had set down on the floor.

"I think that would kill you, not get you drunk," I said, but I wasn't actually sure. I knew I was in for more blood as I pulled each piece out. Hopefully it would be small amounts. I had to do it though. There was no way he could reach all of them, and he could die from the infection of the open wound.

The pain must have been tremendous, but he didn't cry or even whimper. I started with the little pieces dotting his back and lower legs. I didn't want to leave the pieces on the floor—even though the entire store was a safety nightmare—so I got a small bowl to drop them in. I got into a steady rhythm of pulling a piece of glass or metal out and hearing it plink in the bowl.

Rigby lay flat on his stomach, but craned his head around to look. To get all the little pieces I knelt by his right side, and then I switched to his left side. He painfully turned his head to the left.

"Just lie facedown. It'll be easier. I'll go find you a pillow," I said.

"No," he said. "I'm good."

"Did you shoot all the pillows?"

"No," he said. "Just keep going. You're doing a good job. Are you a nurse or something?"

"No," I said. I kept working, getting the small pieces, but I was worried about a large piece in his right leg and one in his lower left back. I had seen a YouTube video that said you shouldn't remove a large impaled object. It might have sliced an artery or vein, and it could be the only thing keeping the blood vessel from bleeding out.

I looked up and gave a false smile to try to reassure him that everything was okay, but he didn't even notice, even though his neck was stretched around to look directly at me. Then I realized he wasn't looking at my face. He was looking down my shirt as I leaned over, giving a clear view of everything he wanted to see.

I sat back on my heels and pulled the last few small pieces out. Then I opened a sterile cloth package and poured the rubbing alcohol over the cloth.

"Hey, give me a minute before—"

I rubbed the alcohol on the open wounds, and he screamed. I didn't feel guilty about inflicting the pain, since it was medically the best thing to do. I think.

When that was finished, and he stopped yelling, I told him about the two large pieces.

"I can sure feel them," he said.

"Is there anybody around who would know what to do? A doctor?" I asked and then I remembered my mission. I had completely forgotten it while focused on taking care of Rigby.

"Brian is the closest thing," he said.

Something close. My hopes rose. Maybe Brian was a vet or someone else trained in anatomy and surgery. "Who's Brian?"

"Jane's guy. He a fireman and a trained medic."

I remembered then that Jane had mentioned him. He wouldn't know anything about getting a pancreas out of a pig, but maybe he would know what to do with Rigby.

Rigby had trouble standing and walking with the shrapnel in his leg, and I couldn't support him without putting my arms around his back, which caused him agony. I went to the back, through the chaos of Rigby's store, and found a big dolly-type device that had a pallet on it. It must have been used for moving pallets of cereal boxes and such.

I pushed it back, and he scooted onto it. I rolled him out the front door and through the maze of demolished cars to the car I had driven there. He crawled in the backseat and gave me directions to Jane and Brian's house. When I pulled up and knocked on the door, no one answered. I went around the side to look in the backyard. They were both naked, fooling around on a large blow-up mattress by the pool. I can see how Rigby could have wandered upon this.

They didn't see me, and I went back to the car and blew the horn. A few minutes later they came out, Jane in a robe and Brian in shorts. He was large and well muscled and easily carried Rigby into the house and laid him on the kitchen table. Jane seemed put out by all of this, but Brian instantly went into his professional mode.

Brian whispered to me, "You were right to not pull out the big pieces, but all we can do now is pull them out and hope they didn't cut a vein or an artery. I'm trained to leave them in and get the victim to a hospital where they can handle it."

"What if he bleeds?" I asked.

"Then we try to stop it. Direct pressure. Bandages. I'll get them ready."

"He's on the kitchen table," Jane said.

"Yeah. That's easiest to work with," Brian said.

"That's where we eat," she said, "and he's filthy and bleeding and oozing and apparently about to bleed a whole lot more."

Brian ignored her and gathered his supplies. I went over and stood by Rigby's head.

"Could I die?" Rigby asked.

No one answered.

"Hey," he said. "How bad is it? Could I bleed out here on the table?"

Brian looked at the piece in Rigby's back and mouthed, "Distract him" to me.

"It should be fine," I said. "Brian has done this before." I tried to think of something to talk to him about. "Have you always lived in Savannah?"

"Yeah," Rigby said. "Where are you from?"

"Tallahassee," I answered without thinking, and immediately regretted it. Now he knew where I lived. I obviously didn't want to kill him anymore, but I didn't want this creep to be able to find me.

"I almost went there to FSU," he said, "but I had to stay home when Dad got sick. We thought the cancer would take him in a year or so, but he lived through it. Well, until the virus, of course."

Brian did the thing Catholics do when they make a plus sign over their chest, and then pulled the glass out of Rigby's back. He watched the bleeding, which was a bit, but it didn't seem to be gushing like an artery would. He bandaged it tightly and gave me a thumbs-up.

Brian studied the piece of metal in Rigby's right leg and made a "hmm" noise.

Rigby reached out his hand, and I stared at it wondering what he was doing. And then I realized he wanted me to hold his hand. This creep who had stolen Bella and burned her to ashes was hurt and scared.

I took his hand, and he squeezed tightly. Brian looked at the jagged piece of metal sticking out of Rigby's leg. It had flecks of once bright yellow paint on it. It was a piece of Bella.

Brian pulled the piece out in one smooth motion. Blood started pouring out onto the table, dripping down to the floor. Brian screamed, "Put pressure on the femoral artery!"

Jane leapt back, whether from the blood or the command I don't know.

"Where is it?" I said. Brian put his hand on a spot at the top inside of Rigby's leg. I put both hands there and pressed while Brian packed and wrapped the wound. Rigby started shaking and saying that he was cold. The blood soaked through the first bandage, and we added another and then another layer as the red spot pushed its way through the white fibers. Brian told Jane to get more bandages, and she just stood there until he screamed her name.

He wrapped another layer while I held the pressure, and this time the blood barely soaked through. We watched it a while more, and when Brian said I could, I released the pressure. Rigby was shivering hard, and we wrapped blankets around him. I held his hand, and Brian left the house to get something.

He came back in a few minutes with an IV pole and bags of fluid. He began setting it up, and I asked, "Could it have expired?"

"Maybe," Brian said, "but it's mostly water anyway. It'll replace lost fluids."

He started the IV. I took paper towels and began to clean up the blood. When I got it mostly cleaned up, I checked on Rigby. His eyes were closed, and he was rigid, lying on his chest on the table with his face turned. I didn't want to lay my hand on his tender back to check his breathing, so I put my ear to his mouth and heard the faint breaths.

Jane had stepped outside and was staring at the pool, smoking a cigarette. I joined her and said, "Brian did an amazing job."

Jane took the cigarette out, this time in her left hand, which I noticed now had an enormous diamond ring on it. She held it up there for quite a few seconds and then flicked the cigarette into the pool.

"I got the blood up," I said.

"I'm not going back in there," she said. "It soaked into the hardwood floors, and I saw some on the living room carpet. We'll just get a new house."

"This one isn't special to you?"

"Nah. We just picked it after we found each other. I was thinking of moving anyway. There's some bigger houses just down the street I've been looking at."

Why would anyone want a larger house? It was just more to take care of. The two of them couldn't need any more space. Then I realized why. Of course. "Babies," I said.

"What?" Jane said.

"I guess you want a bigger house for the children that will come along. Repopulating the Earth and all that."

Jane laughed. "Hell, no. I didn't much want kids before. I'm certainly not bringing any into this awful world."

What was so bad about it? Some people couldn't seem to get over the post-apocalyptic mindset.

"Brian really wants kids though," Jane said. "He asks me all the time, but I take the pill religiously."

"They'll expire," I said. "I learned that the hard way."

Her eyes grew wide. "Did you get pregnant?"

"No," I said. "Another kind of medication." I didn't want to explain it all to Jane.

She looked relieved. "Don't worry about the pills expiring. Brian says they'll stay good for decades."

"Really?"

"Oh, yeah. He's a medical professional. He knows that kind of stuff."

He had done a great job with Rigby so I guessed he knew what he was talking about. "I think he's going to make it," I said.

"Who?" Jane said.

"Rigby."

"Oh, yeah. Did you get your car back?"

I shook my head and walked back inside. Brian and Jane picked out a new house down the street, and Brian had their personal items moved in a couple of hours. I stayed with Rigby for three days until he could walk, eat and lie down on his back without much pain. I found some aloe cream at a pharmacy and rubbed it on his back. It seemed to help a lot.

He really wanted me to read his journal, so I retrieved it and read it cover to cover since it kept him from trying to talk to me. In the journal he referred to this time as post-apocalypse and saw the world as dark and ruined. He didn't seem to understand that he was the one ruining it.

When I started to pack up to leave, he simply said, "Sorry and thanks."

I nodded.

When the new car was packed with food, a few changes of clothes and a new GPS, and I started to pull out, he said, "Tallahassee?"

I said, "Yes," and backed out of the driveway. I drove by the Publix and looked at Bella's charred remains. I put a flower on her, but I didn't say any words. I got back on the road and started the drive to Myrtle Beach.

Alone.

-21-

The drive to Myrtle Beach, in the lifeless Toyota, took six hours. I saw a few people along the way but avoided them. One car, coming the other direction on the other side of I-95, slowed down and stopped when the driver saw me, but I kept going. He did a big, friendly wave, but I couldn't risk it. Who knew what his intentions were?

I stopped at a gas station just outside of town to fill up the Toyota. I spotted a red SUV that I liked better. Once I confirmed the keys were in it, I switched cars, abandoning the Toyota for the next traveler. The SUV was supposedly made for going off road, although I suspected the previous owner had never taken it anywhere but perfectly flat concrete.

I rummaged around the gas station and laughed when I saw a note behind the counter with instructions on how to set the pumps for the locals' price, substantially lower than the jacked-up price for tourists. At a stand of pamphlets for tourists, I browsed through brochures looking at all the attractions. One of them noted that the local population was only around thirty thousand. That meant I could expect there to be only three or four people, in a city sized for its tourist population, which might be in the hundreds of thousands.

With only a few hours of daylight left, I decided to wait to begin the search until the next day. I drove to the beach and waded into the water, enjoying the sunset. I wanted to swim, but I didn't have a swimsuit, and I hate the feeling of wet clothes. I'm sure thousands of swimsuits hung in nearby stores, but I didn't have time to find one before sundown.

I was tempted to just take my clothes off, but I didn't know who might be out there—their interest piqued by a young woman on the beach. I thought of Rigby, who felt like he deserved credit for keeping himself from raping me. I kept my purse near me at all times with Clint in it, loaded and ready.

The beach was lined with hotels, and I picked a tall one. I decided to stay in the penthouse on the top floor. That way in the morning I could look out and survey the land to see what there was to see. Also, I wanted to see what a penthouse in an expensive hotel looked like.

I had to spend a few minutes figuring out how to use the machine that coded the door keys, powering it with the adapter in the SUV, and then I began the long ascent. I overestimated my ability to climb twenty floors, and I had to stop three times to rest.

I walked up to the penthouse and slid the card, and the door clicked open. The room was grand, even in the dim glow of my flashlight. I had enough forethought to have brought candles, and I lit a few around the room. The romance of the room and the glowing lights made me think of Kyle.

One night I had come home after dark and thought the generator had gone out. But Kyle had turned the lights off and lit candles everywhere. He had a dinner prepared, but I hadn't injected yet and needed to wait at least thirty minutes after I did before eating. I quickly injected, and we waited while he kept dinner warm in the oven, but we couldn't control ourselves.

Within a few minutes, I had dropped my clothes to the floor, standing naked in front of him in the candlelight. He just looked at me for minutes, standing close, without touching. It drove me wild. When he finally touched me, I pulled him close, and we made love on the kitchen floor.

Those thoughts had no place in my mind anymore. I stepped out of my memory and back into the present. Romance is great, and sex is wonderful, but not if the person isn't willing to stay with you no matter what. I would have stayed by his side if he had gotten sick. I had thought that we were till-death-do-us-part. Apparently we were parting at just the chance of death.

I stepped out onto the balcony. The world below was black except for the faint light of the moon shining on the water. Years ago, before the virus, I would have looked out and seen lights for miles. There was one truly great thing about the electricity being out.

The night sky.

I had never known how many stars there were. In the old Tallahassee, you could see a few stars through the glow of the city, but nothing had prepared me for the magnificence of the sky when all the lights were completely shut off. And here, high above the world, looking out with the stars reflected in the black water, it was beautiful.

If I believed in the kind of thing, I would have called it a spiritual moment. I could certainly understand the ancient people looking up at a billion stars and feeling wonder at creation, God or nature or some combination of both.

Of course, it was the same God or nature that had spawned a virus that had killed billions of people. If I felt some spiritual twinge at the wonder of creation, it was only fair to feel horror at the avalanche of death that had covered the Earth. Maybe God had intended to completely wipe humans from the face of the Earth, and the virus was just phase one.

I looked out at the ocean and saw a pod of dolphins leaping in the moonlight. Perhaps it was time for another species to dominate. Well, good luck to them. I didn't know about the fate of the human race. All I could control was the fate of one small girl. A girl who felt even smaller looking out at the unending sea.

I slept that night in a luxurious bed and actually had a dream about sex, the first I had dreamt in a very long time. It was probably just the combination of the romantic room and the right time in my cycle. A billion years of evolution was all pointed directly at me to make me want to continue our struggling species. There is nothing more our genes want than to replicate themselves. But mine would stay with me, uncopied.

I woke early with the eastern sun in my eyes. I dressed, injected and had a small breakfast. Then I stepped across the hall to a less expensive room with a view of the city instead of the ocean. From the balcony, I could see for miles. Once I realized that I could actually figure out the distance to the horizon, I had to calculate it. With the Pythagorean theorem, a little algebra and knowing the radius of the Earth to be about four thousand miles, I calculated that I could see at least fifteen miles. Mrs. Hatcher, my high school math teacher, would have been proud.

Of course, that wouldn't really help me. I could barely see a person just a few blocks away at this height. And I had to find one old man in all this vast expanse. I thought of the missionaries in Jacksonville. They had stayed at one key crossroads, and people came to them. I had thought to use that here, but that would only work to find travelers. If this vet really lived here, he would probably stay at his house and only go to a few places like the grocery store. And being an old man, like the people on the radios had said, he would be even less inclined to wander.

So the idea of waiting for him to cross a key point was out. I could systematically cover the city, but I could easily miss him if he happened to stay inside the time I drove near. When I was trying to find Rigby, I found other people who led me to him, but this city, although about the same size as Savannah, had held a much smaller population.

This town would have just as many spots to find food, to support the massive tourist population, but a much smaller number of survivors, since tourists wouldn't have stayed when the virus hit. That meant my odds of finding him or someone else at a grocery store were significantly less.

It would take a big coincidence to be at the same place at the same time, but I could leave notes all over and tell people to meet me at a certain place and time. I drove to an Office Depot and got a laptop and a small printer. I charged the laptop and powered the printer by hooking them to the adapter in the SUV.

I made a one-page flyer that said:

Looking to meet other survivors.
Meet me at the Hard Rock Cafe any night at 7 pm.
1322 Celebrity Circle, Broadway at the Beach

I picked the Hard Rock Cafe because it was easily recognizable, and anybody who lived in Myrtle Beach should know where it was. I got hundreds of sheets of bright yellow paper and started printing as I drove around town. I taped or stapled the flyer at every place I could imagine that a survivor might go: grocery stores, gas stations and every other type of store that might have something useful.

After a long day, I stopped at 5:30 pm and drove to the Hard Rock, making sure I was there at least an hour before just to account for someone who might actually be observing daylight saving time. Everyone in Tallahassee had agreed to ignore that bad idea.

I didn't expect anyone the first night, and I just waited, looking through all the memorabilia in the restaurant. I stayed at a nearby hotel, this time on the first floor. The next day I repeated the process, covering more area, but no one showed up that night either. I settled myself in for a wait. I knew that when I was alone, I could sometimes go a week or so without getting out.

On the ninth day, after having put out more than a thousand flyers, I sat in the Hard Rock reading a book. My phone beeped to remind me it was seven o'clock, and at nearly that exact moment, I heard a knock on the front door. My heart leapt in my chest and I jumped up, leaving my book, my dinner and my purse sitting at the table.

The front door was glass, and an older man with a thick gray beard stood there smiling. He waved and I motioned for him to come in.

"Are you the one looking to meet people here?" he said.

That seemed pretty obvious, but I just smiled and said, "Yes. Thank you so much for coming."

"Well I thought you sounded lonely. It's always good to meet people. Especially these days." He looked around. "I guess we can just pick a table."

I took him over to the table I had been sitting at. I had a plate of dinner, but nothing for him. "Have you eaten yet? You could have some of this."

"No, thank you. I'll get my own," he said. "My name is Sam."

"Hi. I'm Sugar." I said it firmly this time.

"Oh, what a lovely name. That's what I call my daughter. It's a nickname, of course. She's Julie, but I always call her Sugar."

I thought he would be sad at the mention of lost loved ones, but it didn't seem to faze him. I couldn't wait any longer and just asked, "Are you a vet?"

He thought a moment and then smiled and winked at me. "Why, yes.

That's right."

Relief flooded through me. I had found him. He had probably been a vet for forty years and could take a pig's pancreas out with his eyes closed. He would understand the medical terms in the insulin-making steps that didn't make sense to me yet.

I decided that I needed to take it a little slower before asking for his help. I only had this one chance to befriend him and convince him to help me.

"What do you do?" he asked.

"I had a job at a convenience store. Now I just stay alive I guess."

"Oh, I think I've seen you. I thought you looked familiar. Did you work at the convenience store near my house?"

"No. I'm from Tallahassee. I've never been to Myrtle Beach before."

"Well I'm glad you came to visit." He looked around. "Where is that waiter?" he said with a smile.

I laughed. He seemed so easygoing. I thought it would be difficult to convince someone to help me, but this man had come to meet a stranger who left a flyer, and he would probably love to have the company and something to do. "Have you seen anyone else around here?" I asked.

"Just my wife today."

A wife would make it more difficult. She might not want to leave. Hopefully she was older like he was. With the slim pickings these days, I could see a younger woman marrying an older man. A younger woman might see me as competition.

"How long have you been married?"

Sam thought for a moment. "I'd say fifteen years, maybe sixteen years. I can never remember exactly."

They had been married before the virus. This was probably the only surviving married couple in the US. The odds were low, but it could happen. At least his wife was old also. I would try to get her to see me as a granddaughter. I wouldn't do anything to look like I was trying to take her husband. Maybe after a little while I would even start calling them grandparent names like Grandma and Grandpa or Nana and Papa.

I had never had grandparents. All mine had died before I was born. Grandparents seemed like such a nice idea. Adults who loved you like family, but didn't have to be parents, always worried about providing and disciplining.

I wanted to build the friendship. Get to know him. I could ask him to help in a few days after he and his wife became attached to me. They would be hungry for other people, especially a young girl, to take the place of children and grandchildren lost to the virus.

"Where did you meet your wife?" I asked. For a moment I wondered why she wasn't here, but it made sense. He didn't know what he would find here. It could have been a trick or a trap. He kept his wife safe, but was willing to take a risk to help a stranger. That's just the kind of person I needed.

"Oh we met a few years after I joined the military. I was flying F-4s then."

"You were a pilot too?" Wow. He must be a genius.

"I was in the Air Force. And I also flew in civilian life. I can fly anything with wings."

"What did your wife do?"

"She stays home with the kids."

"What did she do after the kids were gone?" I immediately regretted how I said that. I meant after the kids left home, but it sounded like I was asking what she did after the kids died.

He looked upset and said, "Where's the bathroom?"

I pointed to the rest rooms. "But, of course, they don't … "

Sam hopped up and walked straight to the men's room. He was in there for a few minutes and then came out.

"The lights don't work in there at all. I could hardly see except for the light through the little window. And the toilets don't flush. What kind of restaurant is this?" He looked around, confused. "Are you the waiter? I've been waiting for you to take my order."

"No."

"What's your name?"

"Sugar," I said, again.

His eyes lit up. "Sugar," he said and walked over and hugged me. "You came back. My little girl came back."

He held me tight, and I didn't know what to do. After a few moments he let go, and his eyes were red from tears.

"It's been so long. Let's forget this restaurant and go see Mom right now. She'll be so glad you came back."

"Um, … Sam?"

"Call me Dad. You're never too old for that."

"How long have you been married?" I asked, dreading the number he would say.

"I'd say forty-two years, maybe forty-three years. I can never remember exactly."

"Are you a veterinarian, Sam?"

"Call me Dad," he said firmly. "No. You still say it wrong, Sugar. I'm a veteran." He said the word slowly, emphasizing each syllable.

"Do you have trouble remembering things sometimes?"

He looked at me. "I guess you've talked to Mom already. The doctor said it's Old Timer's disease."

We talked for a while, Sam believing I was his daughter returned. Apparently they had fought at some point, and he currently thought he hadn't seen her for three years. I followed him home. He remembered exactly where it was. They had lived in the same house ever since he retired from the military, which was about thirty years ago from what I could tell.

When he got out of his car, I got out of the SUV to make sure he was okay. He looked around at his and all the other overgrown lawns in the neighborhood and said, "Oh. The virus. This is the time I hate to come back to the most."

For a few minutes, he knew exactly who he was and what was going on. "I'm sorry for my confusion earlier," he said.

"It's okay."

"I wish this disease would just run its course or leave me so rattled that I accidentally kill myself. I'm ready to go. There's nothing left here. But I've lived here so long, that no matter what time my minds slips back into I can still find food and water. I suppose that's all a body needs."

Not all bodies.

I hugged Sam good-bye, and we held each for longer than I've ever held another person, even Kyle. I wondered if the virus had just left those who would die soon anyway. Maybe we all had something wrong and would be gone in a few years.

I left him with his loneliness and his disease, and I took my loneliness and my disease with me.

-22-

I gave up on putting out any more flyers, and no one else came to the Hard Rock during the next three days. I checked in on Sam. Some days he remembered me, and some days he didn't. I told him my old name, so he wouldn't confuse me with his daughter. The effects of Sam's disease were strange. He would forget memories of his life, but he didn't forget things like how to drive.

"I could still fly a plane," he said. His entire career had been as a pilot. He had flown all over the world. "I remember everything about it. Maybe that's how I'll go someday. Find a plane and take it up and fly until it runs out of fuel."

I drove around most of Myrtle Beach and never saw another person. I decided to leave, defeated, and I stopped by one last time to see Sam. He was clear that day and said, "Did you ever find that veterinarian you were looking for?"

"No."

"Where's your pet?"

"What?" I asked.

"You're looking for a vet. You must have a sick dog or cat or something."

"No."

He gave me a strange look but didn't say anymore. I had never explained my situation because he would just forget it anyway.

"Where all did you look?" he asked.

"I put up flyers everywhere that survivors might go. I drove all around checking neighborhoods for signs of life. Nothing."

"If I were looking for a veterinarian, I would go to a veterinarian's office."

I started to say, "I don't need to take a pet … ," but then the obviousness of his statement hit me. I thanked him and went back to the SUV and searched for veterinarian's offices on the GPS. It listed five in the area.

I drove to the closest, and it obviously hadn't been used in more than a year. I looked at the next three closest on the map. I was sure I had driven by them before and not seen anything. The farthest one was on the edge of the city, and I had never been near it.

I drove straight there. As I pulled around the corner and got a first look at the building, a dozen or more dogs wandered around outside. More than twenty food bowls lined the front, and a car sat parked in the parking lot. I stopped, wary of the dogs, and rolled down my window.

Then I heard the most glorious sound.

A generator chugging away, giving power to the building. A sound I had grown so used to back home that I barely noticed it anymore. But now it stood out in the silence, almost singing of the life it represented.

I pulled up and parked as close to the doors as I could get. The dogs barely moved, undisturbed by my presence. I got out and got inside before one of them could decide to take an interest in me. The lights were on, but I didn't hear anything.

"Hello?" I said.

"Help," a man's voice cried out. "Now. Come back here and help."

I followed the voice to the back. A man wearing jeans and a T-shirt stood at a surgical table where a dog lay entangled in what look like barbed wire. It had dug deep into its flesh. The man and the table were splattered with blood.

He saw me and said, "Now. Come here and hold this." He held out a bandage and looked at me. I stood unmoving, and he said, "Now," again.

I walked over and took the bandage.

"I've gotten a lot of it off with just minor tearing, but here it's dug in deep. When I pull it out, it's going to bleed. A lot. Push the bandage on there while I get ready to sew. When I say to, pull the bandage away and hold the ripped flesh together as best you can with your hands. I'll stitch it together. I think I can save her."

I nodded, not saying a word. He clipped away other parts of the barbed wire, pulling it out with minor bleeding that he ignored for now. When he was down to the last piece, gouged deep into the dog's side, he told me to get ready. I wanted to leave the grisly, bloody scene, but I stayed holding the bandage.

He worked the barbed wire out, taking small chunks of flesh with it, sometimes cutting with a scalpel to make a cleaner wound. The sight was sickening. I could see layers into the poor dog's flesh, but the smell nearly made me vomit. The dog smelled of urine, feces and blood.

He yelled, "Now!" and took the final piece out, leaving a sizable rip through the flesh oozing blood and a yellow puss.

I held the bandage in place. It soaked through and onto my hands. He gathered his sewing equipment and handed me another bandage. I tried to throw the bloody mess of the first bandage into a trash can, but I missed and it landed with a sickening squish on the tile floor. I held the other bandage for what seemed like quite a while.

He said one word, "Antibiotic," and gave the dog a shot. When the next bandage didn't soak completely through, he told me to drop it. Then he took both of my hands and held them in place on either side of the wound, pushing it closed.

While I held my hands in the bloody fur, he stitched, pulling the flesh together. He moved quickly and surely. In a few minutes he said, "Well, she won't win any beauty contests, but I think she'll make it."

I stepped back. Once again I had blood on my hands. A bit had splattered onto my clothes.

"Do you know what the biggest risk is now?" he asked.

I shook my head.

"Infection."

I finally found my voice and said, "You gave her what looked like a huge dose of antibiotics."

"I did, but there's a problem with that. You'll never guess," he said.

"Expiration," I said.

He seemed disappointed for a moment. I guess I'd stolen his chance to explain it, but then he looked impressed. "Exactly. I've kept all the antibiotics refrigerated the entire time, but we're passing the expiration dates. It's not clear how long they'll be effective for. And then one day they'll all be gone."

"And then what?" I asked.

"I've thought about trying to make penicillin. The process starts pretty simply with growing common mold like you might find on old food. But of course it's trickier after that." He looked down at my bloody hands. "You can wash up in the sink. Do you have a change of clothes?"

"Yeah, in the car."

"I don't," he said. He was soaked with blood. He must have carried the dog in. "I used to have a bunch of extras here, but something like this happens a lot. I'll have to go shopping. I know a place that's really cheap."

He paused, looking at me, and I supposed that he wanted to me to laugh or smile at his joke. I turned and washed my hands, thoroughly.

"Thanks for your help," he said. "My name is John."

"Um, you're welcome. I'm Sugar."

"Seriously?"

"Yes."

"Well, I've got to get her cleaned up first, and then I'll go get some more clothes," he said. He unlocked the wheels on the table and rolled the dog into an area in the back. He pushed her near an area with a drain in the floor and a showerhead on a long flexible hose.

"This is the grooming and bathing area," he said. He turned on the water. He didn't rinse the dog off directly, but got a little in his hands and gently washed her fur to get the blood and dirt out.

"How long will she be out?" I asked.

"A few hours," he said. "That's something that I'll never have a hope of making."

"What?"

"Anesthesia."

"You have running water?" I asked.

"Yeah. I just modified the hot water tank to where I could fill it up. So I've got hot and cold running water."

He had a hot shower. That sounded amazing.

He gave me the exact same look and expectant pause as when he made the joke, and I tried to look sufficiently impressed. John finished cleaning the dog and then wheeled her over to another area, out of the way. He checked her heartbeat, blood pressure and temperature and seemed satisfied that her vitals were okay.

"I'm going to get some new clothes. Can you watch her while I'm gone, or were you going to head out now?"

Why did he think I was here? To pop in, get covered in dog blood and leave? "Sure. That's fine. What if she wakes up?"

"I'll only be an hour or so. She shouldn't stir. If she does, just try to keep her calm. She won't feel like moving much. Don't let her lick the wounds."

With that he headed out the door. Everyone else I had met in the new world wanted to be with other people when they met them. He left just minutes after meeting me. But he would return. No one would put that much effort into saving a dog and not keep caring for it.

I looked around the office and saw that it looked like he lived here also. He had a bed in one room and an area converted into a kitchen stocked with food. I double-checked that the dog was resting soundly, and then I went out to the SUV to get a change of clothes. I was still nervous around the large pack of dogs, but they left me alone.

I walked back in and changed out of the bloody clothes and put them in the trash. I thought of the shower, and I couldn't resist. I took my underwear off and stepped into the shower area. I turned it on and twisted the knob until it reached a deliciously hot temperature.

Now I had hope. John was obviously an experienced vet. He had sewn up the dog like he had done it a thousand times. He was much younger than I expected, not even thirty. The people on the radio had said he was an older man. Someone must have confused him with Sam, apparently the only other resident of Myrtle Beach.

I knew I could convince him. He was still using his skills to help animals when people were gone. How much more rewarding would it be to use his skills to help an actual person?

I hadn't felt clean in days. He had soap and shampoo, and I used those, scrubbing every inch of my body. After a few minutes the water began to turn cold. I felt guilty that I had used all his hot water. I would help him refill it when he got back.

I realized that I didn't have a towel, and I stepped out to look for where he kept them. For a bachelor's pad converted from a vet's office, it was really quite clean, organized and well stocked. But he apparently didn't use towels or had them somewhere I couldn't find. I stood in the middle of the room, wet and completely naked.

And then the door opened, and John walked back in.

I covered my breasts and groin with my arms and yelled, "You said you would be an hour! It's only been twenty-five minutes."

"I'm sorry," John said. "I shopped quickly. I brought some towels back because I knew I'd used them all up cleaning up blood."

He stood there in a new T-shirt and jeans, holding shining new white towels, staring at me.

"Turn around!" I yelled.

"Right. Sorry." He turned around and handed a towel over his shoulder to me.

I took it and wrapped it around me. "Now go out while I change."

He walked back through the door without even glancing back. I finished drying off and changed into fresh clothes. I was angry, but at myself. How could he have known I was in here naked after taking a shower?

"You can come back in," I said, and he came back through the door. "That was my fault. You didn't know. Let's just pretend it didn't happen."

"Okay," he said. He kept his eyes locked on mine. I noticed that he smelled of cigarette smoke, an odor I detested. I'd lived with only one foster parent who smoked, and I couldn't get out of her house fast enough. We stood in silence for a moment until he spoke. "Did you come here for a reason, or did you just wander by?" He was so very direct. He skipped all the normal social processes. He was awkward, and what had just happened didn't help.

"I'm looking to find people," I said. I would wait a little to bring up helping to extract the insulin.

"Did you put out all those flyers?"

"Yep." So he had seen the flyers and ignored them.

"Sorry I didn't go. I keep to myself. Well, to myself and a couple of hundred dogs, cats and occasional farm animals."

"I'd say most people keep to themselves these days, just not by choice."

"Oh, I think it's great," John said. "I'm not really a people person."

I must have given him a funny look, because he immediately corrected himself.

"Wait. That sounded wrong. I'm not glad that everybody's dead. I'm just the type who can deal with it better. I've always liked to keep to myself. That's what I thought I'd be getting when I became a vet."

"And you didn't?"

"It turns out that most of a vet's life is spent dealing with the owners or the vet techs or the front desk people or the groomers or suppliers. But not anymore. Now I just help sick and hurt animals." He smiled. "Dang. I did it again. I really don't mean to seem like I'm happy about the virus."

I wasn't sure that was true. "You must not have lost anyone."

"My parents both died a year before the virus. They were older. I was born late in life."

"That's unusual," I said.

"What?"

"Most people are born pretty early in life."

He seemed puzzled and then laughed. "Well, you found me," he said. "For whatever that's worth. Do you need anything before you go?"

He was trying to get rid of me. I couldn't believe I had found someone who liked to be alone more than I did. Did I seem this way to others? Now the roles were reversed, and I was the one trying to be with people.

"There's hardly anyone else around the area. Maybe I could stay a little bit, and we could get to know each other." No. That sounded like flirting, and that's exactly what I didn't want. I would need his help for a long time. I couldn't have a romantic relationship with him that could end and make him go away. And he was probably too old for me. I thought of numbers and then asked without thinking, "How old are you?"

"Twenty-nine," John said. "How old are you?"

"Twenty-one."

I had learned that the rule for romantic relationship age ranges was half the age of the older person plus seven. It was a mathematical expression of social intuition, and it worked pretty well. Half his age plus seven was twenty-one and a half. I was just below the acceptable age.

Good.

"Maybe I could help with some of your veterinary work. You obviously needed an extra pair of hands today."

He paused at that. "That's true. I lost a cow the other day because I didn't have an assistant."

"A cow?"

"Sure. I help any animal that needs me. Plus I like the milk. I was milking her every day until the accident."

"So what do you think? Do you mind if I hang around?" I couldn't believe I was having to act like this clingy person who needed other people.

"I guess for a little while. But nothing ... ," he made a gesture of pointing back and forth between us, " ... is going to happen."

"Of course. I'm just ... lonely." I hoped that sounded believable. It was normal for most people.

And then I thought I understood what he was trying to say. "Is there a ... reason that nothing will happen?"

"What? Are you asking if I'm gay?"

That would be perfect. No possibility of complications.

"Believe me, I'm not gay."

Dang.

"Our little encounter will haunt my dreams," John said. "It's just that ... I'm happy with my life as it is. That part of life leads to pleasure, but I've never found that it leads to happiness. The opposite really."

"I feel the same way," I said. I didn't realize it until he said it, but I agreed with his perspective completely. Romantic love had caused far more hurt in my life than it had brought happiness.

"I think God intended it for pain as much as for pleasure," John said.

"I don't know what he intended, but it sure works out that way." I was beginning to understand John, and I thought I knew how to handle him. He was like me. He needed space. Lots and lots of space. "Tell you what. I'll go do a little shopping and come back later. I'll make some dinner."

"How about you come back in the morning? I do have something you can help with then. There's an injured dog that I haven't been able to capture to take care of it."

"Okay," I said. He was still reluctant, but it was a start. "Is there a place I can stay for the night around here?"

"You can use my old place. It's just a couple of blocks away."

He gave me directions. I found the little house that he used to call home but had abandoned for the vet office. I looked around for photos or anything that would give me a clue about him, but there was little. He had moved all his personal effects to his new home.

The house didn't smell of smoke, which meant he must have started smoking since he moved into the vet office, or he always smoked outside. That's the kind of thing you only did if someone else was in the house who you didn't want to expose to smoke, but I didn't see any evidence that anyone else had ever lived here.

I slept uneasily that night, excited that I was finally making some real progress on the huge task I had ahead of me. Sometimes I looked at the list of steps, and it seemed impossible. That my death was inevitable. But now that I had someone experienced in medicine and science, it looked less daunting.

I normally didn't give much thought to what I wore, but I dressed carefully that morning. I picked something practical for going out dog trapping, but I made sure it didn't look pretty or flirty in any way. I wore jean shorts and a simple white top with buttons down the front.

I didn't know what time to come over in the morning, but I suspected with all the animals to feed that John got an early start. I arrived at 7:00 am and found him filling bowls.

"I've been having to drive farther and farther to find dog food," he said. "There's not nearly the same amount as the endless supply of human food. I'm hoping to find a dog food plant somewhere, but the search is hard. Man I miss the Internet."

"I don't think dog food grows on plants," I said.

"What? Oh." He smiled. "I meant a dog food factory."

"What about the cats?"

"They pretty much feed themselves by hunting. There's no pest control to keep down the rodent population so the cats are thriving."

I helped him fill the bowls with food and water, and the dogs started wandering in. John greeted each one by name.

"I name every animal I work with," he said. "It's getting hard to come up with new ones, but I don't repeat them. Each one is a unique creature. They have individual personalities, you know."

I had little experience with animals. The pets at the foster homes never liked me, and I was never given one of my own. It's too permanent a gift for a child who only stays for a little while.

I had injected before leaving and needed to get some food. "I'll make breakfast for us," I said. John stayed outside to have a cigarette while I cooked pancakes on a small electric griddle. We ate sitting in chairs in the waiting room.

"I don't have a real eating table," John said. "I just always eat standing up. I keep things clean but with what happens on the tables and counters around here … well the idea of putting your food on them isn't appetizing."

We threw the paper plates away, and I washed our forks in a sink that he said was only used for dishwashing. The office was small. I had now seen every part of it. That made me wonder something. "Where do you keep your cigarettes?" I asked. I figured the first thing a smoker would have done was hoard for his precious addiction.

"Do you want one?" he asked, reaching for the carton in his pocket.

"No," I said, holding my hands up in disgust.

He saw the look on my face. "I allow myself just one pack a day. I get one from the store every day and don't keep any here, so I won't cheat."

At least he was trying to control the vile habit. "Are you ready to go get that dog?" I asked.

His face brightened. "Yeah. Great. This will be good. I had forgotten that other people could be useful."

He got some equipment, some shots, a leash and two long poles with loops on the end. We left and got into a truck with a covered truck bed he had parked around back. He started to slowly drive through the nearby neighborhood.

"So why do you do it?" I asked.

"This? Take care of animals even after the paying customers are gone?"

I nodded. It made no sense to work so hard with no benefit.

"I've always loved animals. I made it my life's mission to heal and take care of them. That didn't change when the people were gone. In fact they need me more. There are a lot of domesticated animals that are having trouble surviving. The first days after the virus I spent most of my time just releasing animals left in homes or backyards."

I thought of the very young children who we now knew must have perished in the days after the virus struck. Why hadn't I thought to go searching house to house?

"You feed those dogs, maybe twenty or so. But there have to be more than you can take care of."

"Sure. Finding food is nothing for us, but it's a big problem for them. They can't open doors or cans. You don't want to know what many cats and dogs ate in the first days."

I wish he had never said that. It didn't take much imagination to realize what they found to eat. I shivered, and he said, "Sorry."

He kept driving. "Look for a large light brown German shepherd. I named him Colby. He has a bad cut on his back left hip. Looks like maybe a bite or cut from a fight. Last I saw, it looked infected."

This seemed like a good, simple life. His career had a purpose. Something bigger than himself. I never got that feeling at the 7-Eleven.

We drove for over an hour, and neither of us said anything. Most other people always felt the need to fill the silence with chatter. John turned a corner and shouted, "There!" and we pulled up to a dog matching the description. I could see the nasty wound, even from the street. The dog sat on the front porch of a house.

"Be careful," he said. "A wounded animal can be dangerous. If you can loop his neck, then do it, but don't get close. I'll handle that. When we have him down, I'll inject a tranquilizer. I wish I had a dart gun, but I haven't been able to find one."

The porch was railed in, and the dog could only get out by coming by us. John approached on the left, and I went on the right. The dog watched us warily. We got within a pole length, and I waited to see what John would do. He started talking in a soothing tone, gradually moving the loop closer and closer.

The loop approached the dog's head, and just when I thought John had him, the dog sprang up, snarling, and ran toward me. The old Sugar would have screamed and run, but something had changed in me. In a swift motion, I put the loop out, got it over his head and pulled it tight. I had done it.

"Wow," John said.

The dog began to salivate like I'd never seen anything do before. The white foam spilled over his cheeks and onto the ground.

"Oh, no," John said as the dog struggled on the end of my pole. He was very powerful, and I could hardly hold my pole.

"What?" I said while John tried to put his loop onto the thrashing animal. He didn't answer.

I lost my grip on the pole, and it clattered to the ground. The dog charged me. I turned and ran, but I was no match for his speed. He bit into my left leg. I fell to the ground, facedown. His teeth ripped into my calf, and I felt fire shoot up through my body. I turned to face him, and my leg twisted in his mouth, tearing more flesh with his teeth.

He let go of my leg and leapt onto my chest, clawing and snapping. I put my arms up to shield my face, and he bit into my right forearm. I pounded on its nose with my left arm, but he wasn't affected at all. He was mad with rage.

Then he jerked back into the air. John held the pole and pulled the dog off me and onto the ground. John tightened the loop and then twisted and twisted it, strangling the dog. For a horrible minute he struggled, fighting in fury, and then went still. John held him another few seconds, making sure he was dead and then dropped the pole and ran over to me.

"I'm sorry. I'm sorry," he kept saying over and over. My left calf and right forearm were ripped open in several gashes. The front of my shirt was shredded, and my chest was streaked with cuts and scratches.

John started to pull me up. "Let me rest for a minute," I said.

"We have to get you back to the office now."

"Why?" I said.

"You've been infected with rabies."

-24-

I didn't know much about rabies, but I knew it was almost always fatal. I had worked so hard to keep from dying from lack of insulin, and now this would take me in a mad, foaming fury. John helped me into the truck and then drove off with screeching tires. I was bleeding, and my arm, leg and chest felt like they were on fire from where the dog had torn my flesh.

"Don't worry," John said, but his voice betrayed his fear. "We need to wash the wounds out thoroughly and then administer an immunoglobulin immediately. Then I think four doses of vaccine for the next fourteen days."

"Do you have all that?"

"Yes. It's one of the first things I got after the virus. I knew I'd need it. I give myself vaccinations and boosters. I'm so sorry."

John drove at a reckless speed back to the office and slammed on the brakes in the parking lot, lurching me forward, nearly into the dash. He hopped out and came around to my side to help me inside.

He took me in the back, to the shower area, and sat me down on a stool. He grabbed the showerhead on the end of the flexible hose and turned the knob to a gentle flow.

"Washing the wounds thoroughly will remove most or maybe all of the virus. I'm sorry. This will hurt."

He ran the water over the wound on my right arm first, and it stung. The water draining into the hole in the floor was tinged red. He used soap, and I gritted my teeth at the burn.

"I'll have to stitch that one," he said, looking at the deepest gash that the dog's teeth had ripped. He ran the water over my left leg, which was worse than my arm. The wound circled my calf since I had twisted around while he was biting. I tried not to look at it. I ached and burned, but I had never felt so tired in my life. The adrenaline surge had left my system empty and drained.

"We need to wash all the wounds," John said. "It spreads through saliva. You'll need to wash and scrub your chest. He didn't bite there, but his saliva dripped all over the scratches and cuts."

He handed me the showerhead.

"I'll step out," he said. "Be thorough. I know it hurts, but get it as clean as possible. The virus doesn't live long when exposed, and this step is important. It could prevent it entirely."

"You do it," I said. "I can't be thorough. I can barely focus with the pain." It hurt even worse now than when the dog was on me. I thought I might faint from the pain and shock.

"The cuts and scratches are all over your … "

The dog had ripped through my shirt. The wounds were on my upper chest and across both breasts. "Go ahead," I said. "It has to be done right." I pulled the remains of the shirt apart and unbuttoned the tattered bra, exposing my breasts. I looked down and saw deep red scratches all over. One cut went from my collarbone all the way down my left breast, crossing the nipple.

John hesitated and then ran the water over my chest. I closed my eyes and gritted my teeth, trying to keep from passing out. He soaped his hands and cautiously scrubbed all the wounds. At first he seemed uncomfortable touching my breasts, but I think the clinical side of him took over, and then he did the task carefully and thoroughly.

"Did he get you anywhere else?" John asked.

I thought for a minute, having trouble concentrating. I didn't see anywhere else and felt no other spots of pain. The ones I had were enough. I wanted to curl up in a ball and sleep. "No, I think that's it."

John went to the fridge and returned with a shot.

"This is the immunoglobulin," he said. He drew it up into the syringe. "Do needles bother you?"

Despite the pain, I almost laughed at that. I shook my head no.

He injected the immunoglobulin, and it burned going in. "Am I going to die?" I asked.

"What? No. Rabies is very treatable. The only people who die are the ones who don't get treated before symptoms, which don't manifest for days. You're going to be fine. You'll need to stay for fourteen days to take the four vaccinations," he said. "But you can stay as long as you like. I'll take care of you. I'm sorry. I shouldn't have endangered you like that."

Fourteen days would take me to the limits of the insulin I had. I had more than enough vials, but it was supposedly only good for twenty-eight days unrefrigerated.

"I need to stitch your arm."

He had gotten over his fear and excitement and was now a professional, calmly caring for a patient.

"Have you ever stitched a person before?"

"No. But it shouldn't be any different. The main difference is that a human doctor would be better at cosmetic stitching to minimize scarring. Most of my patients have fur to cover the scars."

"Do you have any anesthesia?" I couldn't imagine sitting there, feeling him sewing in my flesh.

"A topical, but it won't numb it completely. I have others, but I don't know how to dose it safely on a human."

John applied the topical ointment, and the pain dulled. He started stitching. I had to look away, trying not to think about it. I grew cold and started to shiver, and then we both realized I was sitting there still virtually topless. It seemed pointless at this stage, but I felt I should cover up. I slipped the remains of my shirt off, which didn't cover anything now, and then reached for a towel and put it over my chest.

From that point on we went back to maintaining the illusion of my modesty. I awkwardly held the towel while he stitched. When he finished, he stepped out and got a new shirt from my car and then turned his back while I slipped it on. A bra would be too painful to wear.

He put an antiseptic on the wounds on my arm and leg, which stung again. I turned around, lifted my shirt and rubbed it on my chest. It burned like white-hot fire on my left nipple that had been cut. I pulled my shirt back down and turned around.

John wrapped my arm and leg with bandages. It was still morning, but all I wanted to do was sleep.

"I've got some antibiotics that have been in the fridge since the virus, about a year and a half. They're a little past expiration, but I think they'll be okay. Worst case, they'll just be less effective."

While he got the antibiotics, I shuffled to the other room and lay down on a mattress that must have served as his bed. He came in with the pills and a glass of water. I took the pills and lay back down, pulling the covers up around me.

Then I slept, watched over by a man I had known for less than a day.

-25-

I woke up hours later, starving and feeling awful from low blood sugar. John came in and I said, "I need food. Now. Something sugary."

He brought back a Pop-Tart, which was perfect, and I unwrapped it and wolfed it down. I waited for a few minutes for my system to level out, and my wounds reminded me that they were still fresh.

John squinted his eyes, which I now knew meant that he was thinking. "Why do you have a tattoo of an upside-down clock on your stomach?" he asked.

He must have an eye for details, because the numbers were small, and the two times he had seen my stomach, he'd had a lot more to look at.

"You noticed that?" I said.

"Yeah. I've got a doctor's eyes. I've got to quickly assess a patient and look for even minor details to diagnose the problem."

Since I'd be staying for at least two weeks, there was no point in hiding it. I wouldn't bring up asking for his help yet. I'd find the perfect time later. "Can you guess?" I knew he liked to show how clever he was.

"The numbers are very small. Most people wouldn't notice, so it's not for decoration."

I nodded.

"And it's upside down, so it's meant to be seen from your perspective."

He was getting there. I thought he might be able to figure it out.

"You asked for a sugary treat," he said. "No, 'asked' is the wrong word. You demanded."

"Sorry."

"It's okay," John said. "So I'm guessing you're diabetic, and the clock is a system for keeping track of injections."

"Bingo."

"Is that why you came here?"

"What?"

"Do you need insulin? I've got some in the fridge. It's for dogs, but it should work. It's extracted from pigs. Their insulin is very close to human."

"No. I've got plenty. Although I would like to keep the vials I have with me in your fridge."

"Sure. Let's get some protein in you. But first let's check your blood sugar, and then get insulin if needed," he said and then paused. "Hey, this is cool."

"What?"

"You're my first human patient. Don't worry. I'll take good care of you." He checked my bandages and then, strangely, he touched my nose. "Oh, that's not good."

"What's not good?"

"Your nose is dry. Not a good sign. And I'll need to put a cone around your neck to keep you from licking at your wounds and tearing the stitches out."

I laughed, and it hurt. I had bruises on my ribs from where the dog had pounced on me. He took me to the kitchen area, and I saw that he had bought a small dining room table.

"Where are the vials?" he asked.

"In my purse, in my car."

I sat down at a chair. He went outside and came back with my purse. He set it down on the table, opened it and then carefully took out the gun and set it away from us on the counter.

"That's Clint," I said.

"Eastwood. Makes sense. Good name."

He found a blood sugar meter and the vials of insulin. He handed me the meter. I pricked my finger and put the blood on the test strip. It read 145.

"That's just a little high, and I'm gonna make you some beans, which shouldn't spike it. Does three units sound about right?"

"Perfect."

"Hey," he said. "Can I give the injection? I'm awesome with shots. You think a human doctor gets good at it? Try injecting a cat that can scratch your face off if you hurt it."

"Um. Okay." I couldn't believe I was okay with letting this man I barely knew do this, but I was. He had treated my injuries, stitched my wounds and seen me completely naked.

"Which one are you using now?" he asked, looking at the vials.

I pointed to it. John held the vial up to the light. "This one's a little cloudy. You've got plenty, and I've got some as a backup, so I'm going to throw this one away. All right?"

I nodded. He put the syringe into a new vial and drew out three units. He sat down in the chair beside me. I lifted my shirt up to show my stomach.

"What time is it on the belly clock?" John asked.

"Six," I said. Without a bra on, I had to lift my breasts out of the way. I tried using my left arm, but that blocked the site, so I just tucked the shirt under and cupped one in each hand. John did the injection perfectly and so quickly that I barely noticed it.

"How was that?" he asked. "Are you gonna bite me?"

"Not this time."

He opened a can of beans and heated it on the small stove he had obviously added. I figured a vet's office didn't normally have one. We ate the beans, and then he put the insulin in the fridge.

"I'm going to give you the first vaccine shot now," he said, "and then on days three, seven and fourteen."

"And I'll be okay?"

"Perfectly safe. I did some reading while you slept. In every case where a person was bitten by a rabid animal and got the vaccine well before symptoms, not one reported getting rabies."

Good. Now I only had to worry about one thing killing me.

"Aren't the rabies injections painful shots in the stomach?" I asked.

"No. Not anymore. These are just given in the deltoid. There may be some redness and swelling, but that's about it."

"Where's the deltoid?" I knew gluteus was the butt, and I was glad it wasn't going to go there.

"The upper arm, same as I gave the immunoglobulin."

John did the first injection. My body's immune system began to recognize the weakened intruder and learn how to fight it. All my troubles stemmed from an immune system that thought my own pancreas was a foreign invader. At least it would be doing me some good now.

"I need to check on Avery now," John said.

"Who's Avery?"

"The other patient in the hospital. The dog you helped with yesterday."

That seemed like so long ago.

John wanted me to stay down, but I wanted to see how she was doing. I never cared much for animals, but I had helped save this one. He had her in a small cage with a cone around her neck. She perked up when we entered the room, lifting her head from the concrete floor. I thought she was a mix of lab and beagle, but I don't know dog breeds very well.

He gently examined her, talking the entire time in a calm, soothing tone. He had a wonderful bedside manner with both animals and humans. The question of the bed came up later that night.

"You take the mattress," John said.

"Where will you sleep?" I felt guilty kicking him out of his own bed, but sleeping beside each other on the tiny twin mattress wouldn't work, for a variety of reasons.

"I have a cot. We used to use it when we had to stay overnight to watch an animal. I've had many a night on it."

We were both early risers and woke at about the same time the next day. He wouldn't let me help feed the dogs or do almost anything.

"Just sit still. Doctor's orders."

He gave me my morning injection of insulin, correctly using the seven o'clock spot without even asking. I thought the dose was a little high, but amazingly I just accepted it. He made a breakfast of biscuits and orange juice, which explained the dosage.

After breakfast he carefully unwrapped the bandages on my arm and leg, checked my wounds and stitches and then treated them with an antiseptic. He rewrapped them and said, "Keep a careful watch on the cuts on your chest. The long cut starting on your collarbone and going down is the deepest, and you need to watch for redness or swelling."

I thought a moment. He was a doctor. Well, sort of. Well, he was my doctor now, and it was best if we kept our relationship practical and clinical. "You're my doctor. You can't be squeamish or uncomfortable in treatment. If the wounds on my chest need to be checked, then check them."

"That's a good attitude," he said.

I unbuttoned my shirt, and he looked over the cuts, wiping the antiseptic cloth over them. "Looks great," he said.

"Will there be scars?" I asked.

"The lacerations on your chest should fade almost completely."

I knew he was in clinical mode when his vocabulary switched.

"The deeper laceration on the breast and nipple, I'm not so sure about. That will likely leave scar tissue. I'm sorry. I know very little about cosmetic medicine. Most of my patients don't care."

The next few days we had a strange dance between relationships. Sometimes we were just two people living in same building. I would shower, and he would carefully stay out. I kept myself modestly dressed and covered like I normally would. When I bent over in front of him, I would put my hands over the opening in my shirt.

And then other times we were doctor and patient. John started putting on a lab coat when he treated me. With the lab coat on, he took on a doctor's tone and diction. He would examine my arm and leg, and then he would lift my shirt and examine my left breast. Only one time did he look at my right breast, which had only minor cuts, and that was to compare coloration of the nipples.

And he respected my privacy. He didn't take the privilege any further than he had to. On day six he said, "That's healing fine. There will definitely be a scar, but I don't need to check it anymore."

We had developed a routine, or perhaps I just fit into the routine he already had. In the mornings, he fed the dogs and I made breakfast. Just before lunch, we went to the store to buy a single packet of cigarettes.

"I have to ask," I said.

"What?" he asked and looked at me warily.

"How can someone as smart as you are smoke? You're a doctor. You have to know how bad they are."

"Of course I do."

"Well."

"It's stupid," John said. "You wouldn't understand."

"Most people start as teenagers because their friends pressured them into it."

"That's definitely not my story. I didn't have a lot of friends."

I looked at him expectantly.

"Fine," he said. "I started in college." He didn't say any more.

"And?"

"Now you're making me crave a cigarette," he said. He looked at me and sighed. "It was an excuse to get away from people."

"What?"

"I saw that smokers always had a built-in reason to leave and get away from people, no matter what was going on. I started saying that I smoked. I could leave any social setting at any time. To make it believable, I started puffing on a few. I thought I could control it. Like everybody else, I got addicted.

"I tried to quit, and almost did. Then I survived the virus and well, it seemed like I was ... "

"Invincible?"

"Yeah," he said. "I'll try to quit again. Sorry I stink. I never smoke in the office. It's bad for the animals."

"You didn't smoke in your house either," I said.

"No."

"Because it was bad for ... ?"

"No one else," he said. "I just made it a rule there too. That way I had an excuse to go out if someone was at my house."

And I had thought I didn't like to be around people.

I felt much better the next week, and I helped him with his rounds, as he called them. If he didn't have an animal to care for in the office, he drove around and looked for any creature that might need help. We mended a bird's wings. We got a stuck kitten out of a drain. We patched and treated everything in, on and over creation.

We worked easily together with no need for idle chatter. We could both be by ourselves without feeling any pressure to give the other companionship.

"Now I'm wondering if I should have been a doctor," John said on day fourteen when he gave me the fourth vaccine injection. "It's so much easier."

"Huh?" That didn't seem right.

"You can talk," he said. "I just have to ask you, 'Does this hurt?' I don't have to guess or worry about getting bitten or scratched."

That made sense.

"And there's just one anatomy to learn. I can't imagine having all of my patients having the exact same internal structure."

Now was the time to ask.

"Can you remove a pancreas from a pig?"

"Sure," he said. "I remember when I first cut into a pig in vet school. It sure wasn't like in the anatomy book. Everything looked like one big goopy mess. But the professors showed us, and after a while, I could identify everything. Removing organs on a dead animal is easy. I could do it in my sleep now. What's hard is working on a live animal."

He wiped the injection site with a cleaning pad and then paused. "That's sort of a weird question."

I didn't say anything. I just let him think. I learned that he liked to reach his own conclusions. He walked to the fridge, opened it and picked up a vial of insulin, turning it in his hands to read the tiny print.

"Like everything else, it expires, doesn't it?"

I nodded.

"And no one makes any more of it."

He put the vial back and shut the fridge. He already knew the next part.

"And you'll die without insulin," he said. "How long?"

"Maybe two more years."

He looked straight at me. "And you want me to help you remove the pancreases of pigs to extract the insulin?"

"Yes. I haven't found any doctors anywhere. We've talked to people around the nation. You're the only one who can do it."

"That's probably true."

"So," I said, "will you help me?" I couldn't wait to get started even if the first steps would be gory.

John took off his lab coat and hung it back up on the hook. He turned back and looked at me.

"No," he said.

-26-

I wasn't angry. I was too much in shock for that. "Why?" I asked.

"I've spent my life helping animals," John said. "And you want me to use my skills to kill them."

"But—"

"And we're not talking about one or two. It will take maybe a dozen a month."

"I figured about ten."

"It'll be a slaughterhouse, and you want me to be the head butcher."

"But a vet has to kill animals all the time," I said. In the past, people always brought old or sick animals to be put to sleep.

"And I hated it!" he yelled, the only time I had seen him show any real emotion, except for the day of my attack. He calmed himself. "I despised euthanizing the animals. Sometimes that's best for a suffering animal, but half the time, people just don't want to pay the cost to keep their pet alive. Do you know how much money I lost keeping animals alive when the owners didn't want to pay the medical costs?"

I didn't answer.

"It tore my heart out to put animals down that had more life in them."

"Are you a vegetarian?" I realized that we hadn't eaten any meat, but I had assumed it was because he didn't have any, since it was long expired in the stores.

"I'd be a hypocrite if I wasn't. I can't have anything to do with killing. Never again."

"You killed the rabid dog."

"It would have died soon and infected others before it did. It had to be put down."

"You don't have to do it," I said. "Just get me started. Teach me like your professors taught you."

"You'll need more than a hundred pigs a year. And full-grown ones with large pancreases. You won't be able to manage that yourself."

I couldn't believe he didn't want to help me. "People have managed farms before. It's not that crazy an idea." I figured I could distribute the meat to people. Maybe even start a little trade.

"Sugar," he said. "You don't understand. Yeah, you probably could manage a farm, and if I showed you, you could learn to remove pancreases. But you can't just squeeze the insulin out. It's a hugely complex process to refine it. I don't have any idea how to do it."

Did he think I was stupid? We had spent two weeks together. He had seen my ability with numbers. No. He knew I wasn't stupid. He thought I was naïve. A silly young girl who didn't understand how hard things are in the real world.

But I couldn't get upset. That wouldn't get me what I needed. "I've researched it. I've got all the steps listed out."

I went to my car and got the books and the printout I had made of each step, listed with details and notes. I came back in and dropped them all on the table with a heavy thud. John picked up the pages and read through them.

"This is impressive research," John said.

Exactly.

"But it just convinces me even more. This is impossible."

Impossible if your life didn't depend on it.

He pointed to one of the first steps. "Do you know what it means to 'concentrate the filtrate in vacuo'?"

I didn't answer.

"Do you?"

"No," I said. "The books all assumed the readers knew the basics of chemistry and lab procedure."

"It means to separate a solid from a liquid in a vacuum."

"See, you knew that."

"Do you know where to find Tricresol?" he asked.

"No."

"Neither do I."

"Didn't you take chemistry in college?" I asked.

"Sure, but I don't remember any of it. And it doesn't mean I know where to find these chemicals. There's probably only one place it was made, and that may not even be in the US or in this hemisphere."

His practical concerns didn't bother me. These were legitimate questions. But his complete resignation to failure was upsetting. He didn't even want to try.

"And even if you gather all the chemicals and equipment needed and go through all the steps successfully, you have to prepare it completely sterilely. If not, you're injecting bacteria into your body. And a bad batch, too weak or too strong, could kill you."

"So that's it," I said.

"I'm sorry," John said. "It can't be done. Don't spend your last years trying in vain. Enjoy your time. You'll still get more time than most creatures on this planet."

That was his argument? That I would live longer than most dogs, so I should be happy with it and just relax?

"You could stay here with me," John said. "We can stretch the insulin as long as it will last. When it's gone we can carefully regulate your diet. I'll take care of you until—"

"Until I'm dead? You just want me to give up? No."

Kyle couldn't face my death. John wanted to gently welcome it.

I would have neither. I might die, but I was going to die fighting.

We hardly spoke that night. He saw me preparing to leave and did nothing to stop me. He had a sick cat to tend to and spent the evening watching over it. He did say the antibiotics he had left seemed to be less effective as they passed expiration and that the cat might not make it.

I couldn't work up any emotion over one less cat in the world. Far more cats than people now lived on the Earth. And soon there would be one less person.

I barely slept that night. I kept going over and over ways that I could change his mind. I found the Bible that he read from occasionally and looked for something that would convince him. But most of the Bible was filled with things that made no sense. They killed animals constantly, but I didn't think that would convince him. I wasn't asking him to make a sacrifice to his God.

I tried to think of a logical argument, but the numbers kept defying me. He valued the lives of animals. How could I convince him that I was worth the hundreds and thousands that it would take to keep me alive?

I'm not proud to say this, but at one point in the night I got up with the intention of seducing him. I put on nothing but a bathrobe and stood just outside the door to where he slept. But I had just spent two weeks effectively training him to think of my body as a clinical case. Why would he feel any desire for the scarred body he had now seen so many times?

I felt like a fool and rushed back to bed when I heard him stir.

Since I couldn't sleep, I packed my things to leave first thing in the morning. I didn't feel betrayed by John. He had made no promises. I had been the one to try to work my way into his life. I recognized that in some ways I had manipulated him. He had no obligation to me at all. I wasn't angry with him. He owed me nothing.

But I was deeply disappointed.

I had rested my hopes in him. The tasks ahead seemed insurmountable.

Even someone with his skills was intimidated, and I didn't know a tenth of what he knew.

I tried to wake in the morning before him, to avoid an awkward good-bye, but he was already in the kitchen preparing breakfast. For the first time in two weeks, I gave myself my insulin injection. Something so familiar seemed strange. He had taken it over as part of my care, and I had let him, happily. It had felt so good to be cared for.

John walked over and took my hand. My heart leapt. He had changed his mind.

And then he looked at the wound on my arm and said, "Everything looks good. You should be fine to travel."

He had taken the stitches out a few days before. I would have a scar on my right arm, an ugly one on my left leg, and a thin but noticeable one down the left side of my chest, carved straight down my breast. That one would remain hidden. In the two years I had left, I couldn't imagine having a relationship with a man and letting him see it.

But those were the least of my scars. Others had been cut into my soul, and no one would ever see those.

We ate breakfast, and then I put my things in the SUV. John gave me the vials of insulin he had.

"I'm not likely to find a diabetic dog or cat, anyway," he said. "That's the kind of thing that only gets noticed by an owner. Not a vet driving around the streets."

We didn't say good-bye. John stood outside, smoking a cigarette as I packed. His final words for me were, "Good luck."

I drove off with a stabbing feeling of homesickness. I had lived in a dozen foster homes with good people who had provided for me, but I had never felt taken care of. When I was younger, I had so desperately wanted to prove I could take care of myself that I started independent adult life as soon as I could.

Even with Kyle, I had never let him take care of me. We partnered in the endless chores of living, but I could handle it on my own. I had done it before him, and I did it after.

I hadn't developed feelings for John. I knew what love was, and I had been hurt too badly to let it happen again. I only knew this as I drove away, something tugging and pulling at my mind and my heart:

I would miss him.

-28-

I typed my address into the new GPS, and it plotted the reverse route of how I had come up. But I would gain nothing taking that same way. I had already been down that path and come up with nothing.

Less than nothing.

I had wasted valuable time and injured the body that I needed to keep strong for the fight ahead. My leg still hurt, and I couldn't yet stand to wear a bra on my tender chest. That's a trapping of the old world that I think I was finally done with.

I had to start finding things I needed to make the insulin. I looked at my list. After researching and writing out the steps to extract and purify the insulin, I made a list of supplies:

Sulfuric Acid
Alcohol
Centrifuge
NaOH, Sodium Hydroxide
Filter paper
Beakers
Acid water (not sure if this is just the sulfuric acid mixed in water)
Ammonium sulfate
Alkaline water (with a pH of 9.0)
Something to test pH level
Tricresol
Sodium chloride
Mandler Filter
Glass vials

And after John explained what it meant to concentrate something in vacuo, I added Vacuum Concentrator.

But it was probably called something else. I should have asked him. I thought that a lot of these supplies could be found at a hospital, especially if they had their own lab. I zoomed out the map on the GPS and looked at possible routes home that would take me through a big city that would have a large, sophisticated hospital that did its own lab work. And it was obvious.

Atlanta.

It was almost the same amount of time to get home. The GPS said a couple of hours more, but it assumed I was briskly driving seventy down the interstate. I'd spend a few days there gathering what supplies I could, and then I needed to get back home to the insulin. The insulin vials I had with me had stayed unrefrigerated for two weeks, and then refrigerated again for two weeks at John's. They're supposed to last four weeks unrefrigerated, so I wasn't quite sure how long they would last.

I had the veterinary insulin John gave me, but I wanted to try that safely at home to see how my body reacted to it. It was extracted from pigs, so it would be a good test. I prayed that I wasn't allergic to it. I'd be slaughtering cows if that were the case. Assuming I survived the initial allergic reaction.

Atlanta also offered some small promise because it had a large initial population and a chance of finding a doctor. I'd use the same thinking that Sam had used for finding John. I'd look at hospitals and doctor's offices. A doctor would probably still be working, and it made sense.

To have good odds of having a surviving doctor, a place would need a population of around 3,840,000 (1 in 9,600 survivors times 1 in 400 who are doctors). I bet Atlanta and the surrounding area had a population around that. The odds of me finding the doctor were still low, but it made Atlanta the best choice.

The GPS said five hours and twenty-three minutes, most of it on I-20. I filled up with gas at the station John used, which he had hooked up with a generator like my station at home had. The trip took me a little over ten hours. I stopped once to talk to a fellow traveler, a woman about my age. She had just come from Atlanta, but had nothing useful to tell me. She had the journal that so many survivors kept, and I flipped though it politely. I understand, of course, since I'm doing the same thing, that when you go to the effort to write something down, you want someone to read it someday.

She was, apparently, just a wanderer. Originally from San Francisco, she now traveled the US, never staying in one place for long. She hadn't heard of any doctors either. She mainly asked me if I knew of any men around our age. I didn't give her any useful information either.

The GPS showed over twenty hospitals in the Atlanta area with a cluster of five downtown and another a couple of minutes up I-75. I stopped to fill up for gas and saw an electric-blue Corvette parked on the side of the station.

It had a nearly full tank of gas, and the keys were in the ignition. It was a convertible, like Bella had been, which I loved.

I looked around to make sure it didn't belong to someone else. I wouldn't steal from anyone. I knew what that felt like. I didn't see anyone or any sign that anyone had been around recently. The car wouldn't start. The battery was dead, which actually encouraged me that it was free for the taking.

The SUV had jumper cables, and even though I had never done it before, I followed the instructions on a tag on the cables and got the car started. I moved my supplies and abandoned the unnamed SUV. I left the keys in the ignition and a note on the windshield that said, "Runs great. Take and enjoy."

I stopped at the first hospital I came to downtown. I had prepared myself for the grisly scene, and it was much the same as the hospital in Tallahassee. Bodies, mostly skeletal, lay everywhere. There was destruction at the front of the hospital, but as I walked deeper in it was relatively unscathed.

I followed signs to the lab, which was in the basement. It was completely dark, but I had a flashlight. I got a large bag and began collecting all sorts of glass beakers and tubes.

I found a centrifuge almost immediately. I didn't really know how to recognize one, but it had "centrifuge" written right on front next to the brand name and model number. It was about the size of a large microwave. I tried lifting it, but it weighed at least two hundred pounds, more than I could possibly lift. I could have shoved it onto a cart, but then I still would have had to get it up the stairs. I'd look for another one at a hospital that had a lab on the ground floor. If I couldn't find one, I'd come back and figure out how to get this one out of here.

I started looking through the various chemicals they had in stock and found Tricresol, neatly labeled and in a line of other chemicals in alphabetical order. That was the example John had used of something he didn't know how to find. I felt much better, at least about my chance of gathering the supplies.

They had alcohols, isopropyl and ethyl, and I didn't know which was called for so I took both. I found sulfuric acid amidst a variety of warning labels. The bag was getting full, and I wanted to carry the sulfuric acid separately, so I made a trip back to the car and carefully put the supplies in the trunk.

I made a separate trip for just the acid. I knew it would be safely contained, but it spooked me to carry it. I couldn't find the ammonium sulfate or sodium hydroxide, but then I had the idea to go to a college campus to the chemistry department. They would probably have all these chemicals.

I bagged up a number of other things that I thought might be useful in working with chemicals, including the filter papers, and left feeling pretty good. I drove to the next hospital and found the lab on the third floor. They had a similar centrifuge, and I puzzled at how to carry it out.

I thought I would get a cart to wheel it down the halls and then put it on boards to slide it down the stairs. I left the lab and headed to a nurse's station I had passed, where I thought I had seen a cart.

I turned the corner and a saw a man who looked desperate and scared. And he had a gun.

-29-

I stopped in my tracks and stared at the man. The gun was holstered at his hip.

"Are you a doctor?" he said.

I thought about running, but his question stopped me.

"My child has been bitten by a snake," he said.

I thought it could be a trap. But there was no reason to lay traps now. If he wanted to hurt me, all he had to do was pull the gun out. I had stupidly left Clint in the glove compartment.

"I'm not a doctor, but I'll see what I can do."

"Okay," he said. "Follow me."

He ran down the corridors, down the stairs and out the building to the parking lot. He stopped at a large white van and opened the sliding door. Inside I saw two children, a girl of about twelve and a boy, maybe five. The boy had tears in his eyes and was holding his arm.

"Do you know what to do?" the man asked.

"There's steps to take if it's poisonous, but first we need to know what bit him." I was no expert, but I was terrified of snakes and had watched many YouTube videos on how to identify the poisonous ones. I remembered lecturing Kyle about them before he went hunting. I asked the little boy, "Can you tell me what the snake looked like?"

The boy just stared at me.

The girl said, "He doesn't talk."

"Did either of you see the snake?" I asked.

The man shook his head. The girl said, "Danny showed it to me. He was holding it in his hand. When I saw it, I screamed and then it bit Danny."

"What did it look like?"

"Black."

"How big?"

"About this big." She held her hands about a foot apart.

"How was its head shaped?"

"What?"

"Like a triangle or round?"

"I don't know."

"Was it black all over?"

"No," she said. "It had a bright orange belly."

"A red-bellied snake."

"No," she insisted. "I said orange."

"That's its name, but it can have a yellow, orange or red belly," I said.

"Is it poisonous?" the man asked.

"No," I said, and he and the girl both breathed a sigh of relief. I looked at the little boy's arm and saw two tiny puncture marks. "I've got something for the bite to prevent infection, which is really the only worry." My car was only a few aisles down, so I walked over and got some of the rubbing alcohol. I thought about getting Clint out of the glove compartment, but the man had proven his trustworthiness. He was taking care of two small children. Mathematically they couldn't possibly be his own, so he must simply be doing it out of the kindness of his heart.

I brought the alcohol back and said, "This will sting a little." Surprisingly the boy didn't flinch when I poured it over the bites.

"Thank you," the man said. "My name is Michael. This is Olivia and Danny."

With the drama over, I finally took the time to see the people before me. I hadn't seen a child in two years. Olivia was a pretty girl with light blonde hair. Her eyes had a mix of fear and sadness, but that was understandable considering what she must have been through. Danny had dark brown hair and large blue eyes, with tear streaks running down his face.

Michael was one of the handsomest men I had ever seen in my life, and this was something I normally hardly noticed about men. He had a mustache and a charming smile, now that his worry was gone. He looked to be in his early thirties. He reminded me of the star from *Magnum, P.I.* I had watched all the seasons on Netflix.

"Hi," I said back to them. "My name is Sugar."

Olivia laughed. Michael smiled and Danny just stared.

"It's great that you're taking care of these children," I said.

"Right after the virus, I went house to house searching for children who were trapped. After a few days and a few hundred homes, I found Danny," Michael said.

I hadn't even thought of that in the first days. I thought only of my own survival. When I searched for children it was already too late.

"And you found me there too," Olivia said, emphasizing it loudly. "Because we're brother and sister."

"Right, of course," Michael said. Then he leaned over to me and whispered, "I found Olivia wandering around a few weeks later. I've had them ever since."

"He takes care of us, and we'd be dead now if it weren't for him," Olivia said. "We have to do just what Michael says because he knows best."

"That's right," I said.

"You should come back to our house with us," Olivia said. She was almost pleading. Her eyes locked onto mine. I imagined she was deeply looking for a mother figure, but I was the worst possible choice.

"I'm sure Sugar has someone she loves to get back to," Michael said. "A pretty woman like her wouldn't go too long without a man coming to call."

"Not really," I said. "But I do need to get back home soon. Hey, could you help me carry something down to my car?"

"Sure," Michael said. "It's the least I could do after you helped us."

"Well, I didn't really do anything. The snake bite would have been fine."

"But you saved us all a few hours or days of terror," he said. "That's not nothing. Let's go get that for you." He turned to look at Olivia. "You stay right here with Danny. I'll shut the van door and lock it. Don't open it for anyone. There are dangerous people in this world."

She nodded as he shut the door. Michael and I started walking back up to the lab.

"How did you immediately know that they weren't my children?" Michael asked.

"If both parents aren't immune, the odds of three in a family surviving are astronomical. Ninety-six hundred to the third power, or about one in … "—I calculated for a moment—"eight hundred eighty-four billion seven hundred thirty-six million."

"Wow, pretty and smart too. I guess you only need a man for the muscle."

We walked into the lab, and I showed him the centrifuge. I thought he might question why I wanted it, but he simply unplugged it and heaved it off the counter. He was strong. He wore short sleeves, and his sizable muscles bulged with the strain.

I chitchatted nervously, something I never do, while we walked back, much slower this time with Michael carrying the heavy centrifuge. "Does Danny speak at all?"

"No," Michael said, breathing a little heavily. "He's dealing with it in his own way. They both lost their families."

"Did you lose anyone?" What was I thinking? What an awful topic to bring up.

"I was lucky, I guess. I didn't have anyone close to me. I was raised in the foster system. And I lived alone since the day I turned eighteen."

"How old are you?" I asked, continuing the too-personal questions.

"Thirty-two."

Half his age plus seven was twenty-three. I was only a couple of years under that. And the social rules certainly would have to change with the selection so vastly reduced.

When we reached the ground floor, he had to stop and rest. He was sweating hard.

"Let me help," I said. We still had a long walk back.

"Okay," he said, but he looked skeptical considering my small frame.

He hefted it up, and I put my hands under it, my arms touching his. The hair on his arms tickled mine as we walked. I didn't think that my support helped at all, and it made it a lot more awkward to walk, but Michael didn't complain.

We finally made it to the car, and he put the centrifuge into the trunk. He saw the other strange supplies. "A woman after my own heart," he said, which didn't make sense. "Are you some sort of scientist?" he asked.

"Not yet," I said, "but I'm working on it."

We walked back to the van, and the door slid open.

"Is that a converbable?" Olivia asked, looking at my car.

"Yes. It's a convertible," I answered.

"Could we take a ride in it?" she asked with wonder in her eyes.

"Sure, if it's okay with your … with Michael."

He made a show of considering for a minute and then said, "Let's go."

He picked up Danny, and we walked over to the car.

"Can you drive, Michael?" Olivia asked.

"It's Sugar's car," he said.

"It's only been mine for a few hours. Have fun. You'll have a better sense of what you're comfortable doing with the kids."

Michael smiled and I handed him the keys. I took my purse out of the passenger seat and put it on the floorboard in the rear. Danny climbed into the rear seat behind the driver, but Olivia got in and moved him to the other side and sat there herself.

I made sure they were buckled in securely, and Michael slowly pulled us out of the parking lot. We moved down the street, and I watched the kids' faces. Olivia beamed, but Danny seemed a little uneasy with the light wind blowing in his face.

Olivia asked, "Can we go really fast?"

Michael looked over at me with a sly smile and a wink.

"It's fine with me," I said.

Michael made a few turns, and we merged onto I-75/I-85 that went through downtown Atlanta.

"I've driven this section a lot," Michael said. "It's almost all clear, and I know where all the stopped cars are."

With that he floored the gas and we roared forward. The wind blew in our hair, and I felt alive for the first time since being injured. The children both laughed, the first sound I heard Danny make. We couldn't hear enough over the wind to speak, but we didn't need to.

Michael drove smoothly, with a mastery of the machine and the road. He looked over at me and smiled. I felt more than alive. I felt like I belonged.

I knew the impossibility of the task ahead of me, but for that brief moment, beside a man who seemed unafraid of anything and with the laughter of children in my ears, I forgot all my troubles. My need for insulin. The men who couldn't abide my future.

Michael kept his eyes on the road, but occasionally glanced over at me. I saw him take in the scars on my leg and arm. And then he looked at the scar on my chest that traced a line that led underneath my shirt, now billowing in the wind.

If I had a future, if there could ever be a future with a man in my life, I wondered how he would react to seeing that the first time. Men want their women smooth under their touch.

We slowed, then turned around and sped even faster back up the same road, going against what would have been the flow of traffic. We pulled back into the hospital parking lot, and Michael stopped next to the van. I stepped out, and Olivia put my purse back into the passenger seat. The children reluctantly hopped out and got back into the van.

"What do you say to Ms. Sugar?" Michael said.

"Thank you," Olivia said. Danny nodded his head up and down.

We stood for a moment not saying anything.

"If you're ever in Tallahassee, stop by," I said.

"Maybe," Michael said.

"I'll give you my address."

I reached for my purse to get a pen and paper, but Olivia said, "Here's something to write on." She scrambled through some things in the van and handed me a scrap of paper and a pencil. I wrote the address down and handed it to Michael.

He tucked it into his shirt pocket and winked at me.

"Maybe we'll go to the beach someday and swing through Tallahassee," he said. "But now we have to get home. It's getting late."

Michael got in the van, waved and drove off. I drove down the road a bit and slept at a hotel. That night I missed something I had never thought of having.

A family.

-30-

I drove into Tallahassee the next day with an overwhelming feeling of defeat. I had been successful at gathering some of the supplies, but a collection of supplies was nothing if I didn't know how to use them. I had outlined thirty-four distinct steps in preparing insulin, and I still didn't know how to do the very first one, extracting the pancreas from a pig.

When I pulled in my driveway, I saw with relief that Scotty was still running. Edith had faithfully done what I needed. I opened the door and checked the insulin in Bertha. Everything was as I had left it.

I drove to Edith's house. She looked happy to see me. We hugged, and I thanked her for her tireless work.

"I had gotten worried about you. You were gone for so long. Are you okay?" she said, looking at my new scars.

"Yeah," I said, even though it wasn't true.

"Kyle's been worried sick about you."

"He has?"

"He did most of the work to keep the generator filled."

That was surprising. Strangely, when I thought of Kyle, I also thought of Michael. I had to admit that I was attracted to Michael. Not just because of his good looks. Seeing a man care for children, really loving them, was attractive on an entirely different level. I think there had been a real spark between us.

No. What was I thinking?

I couldn't fall in love. If I was going to die, which looked more and more likely, then it would be cruel to drag a man and his children through that. And I didn't need the distraction.

I went home, glad to sleep in my own bed. In the morning I arduously hauled water from the creek so that I could take a bath. I missed the hot showers from John's and would have to figure that out someday. I stepped out of the lukewarm bath and wrapped a towel around my body and hair. Then I heard, "Sugar! Sugar!"

It was Kyle beating on the door.

I heard him open the door and barge into the house, walking around until he found me in the bedroom.

"You're alive!" he said and ran over and hugged me.

He nearly crushed me in the embrace. I had trouble keeping the towel on when he let go and stood back to look at me.

"What happened to you?" he asked.

His eyes took in the changes to my body that he was once so familiar with.

"I had an accident. But I'm okay now."

"I'm so sorry," Kyle said. "I should have been with you." He put his hands on my bare shoulders. "I won't leave you again." His right hand started to move from my left shoulder, but he took in the scar on my chest and changed hands. His fingers traced my collarbone, and then the back of his left hand glided down the top of my right breast.

I shivered, an automatic reaction, and pushed him away. "You will leave me."

"No, I—"

"You'll leave right now, because I need to put some clothes on."

"Let me prove that I've changed. I'm committed to you. For however long we have."

"You need to leave."

"Have dinner with me tonight, and we can talk. I'll show you."

"I don't know. I'm … "

"Please," he said.

I wanted him gone so I could think, and apparently there was only one way to get rid of him. "Okay."

"My house. Tonight at seven."

"Okay. Go."

He smiled and finally left. When I heard the front door shut, I took the towel off my head and brushed through my hair. I remembered the full-length mirror in the corner of my bedroom. I stood in front of it and took the other towel off, looking at my entire body in a mirror for the first time since the attack.

The scars on my arm and leg were mangled flesh on the canvas of smooth white skin. The scar on my chest and down my breast looked like someone had tried to cut my heart out. I had worried for years about the injections leaving scars on my stomach, and that was now the one piece of me left unflawed.

I dressed, and after injecting and eating, I decided to go to the FSU chemistry department and see what they had. I found bigger centrifuges, and they even had a machine labeled as a vacuum concentrating system which sounded like what I needed "to concentrate the filtrate in vacuo." They had all the chemicals I needed. I decided to store everything there, including the stuff I had gotten from the hospitals in Atlanta. This would be the place to work. It was designed for this.

I would have to bring a generator here and hook up the machines directly to it. I couldn't hope to figure out how to wire the generator to power the enormous building, and even if I could, that would waste a lot of the power. I'd never find every little thing plugged into the power.

I looked around for manuals on how to operate the equipment, and found a couple of them, but they made no sense, using terms I didn't understand. I would first have to start reading and try to gain a basic understanding of chemistry and lab practices.

I left exasperated at all I had to learn and dreading the dinner with Kyle. I didn't know what I felt toward him. That morning I had been seconds away from dropping the towel and pulling him toward me.

I went home and changed my outfit three times and finally settled on a simple dress that covered my chest and shoulders. I resolved that nothing would happen that night. I would listen to what he had to say, but he wasn't going to charm me into bed. It would be so easy to slip back into the habit of him.

I drove to Kyle's house and arrived at exactly seven o'clock. He wore a coat and tie, which I had never seen him in. The ever-present ball cap was gone. His house was rearranged to have the table out of the small kitchen and in the center of the living room. He had the generator off and candles everywhere. The table was set with fine china, and he served a ham that he had actually cooked pretty well. It was delicious.

We chatted about what had happened in Tallahassee while I was gone. Laura's pregnancy was coming along fine, and everyone was excited to have a child in the community. That made me think of Olivia and Danny and the joy on their faces when Michael drove.

Kyle wanted to know about my trip, and I spent most of the time talking about Jacksonville and Savannah. Kyle was furious at Rigby for stealing Bella and putting me in danger. I said almost nothing about Myrtle Beach except to say that the veterinarian wasn't able to help me.

"We'll figure out how to do it, together," he said.

I didn't respond.

After the meal he brought out dessert, a cheesecake, which he knew was my favorite. We ate it in silence. It tasted great, but I could only handle a few bites. I put my fork down, and Kyle seemed to suddenly grow nervous.

When I pushed the half-eaten piece away, he said, "I have something I'd like to ask you."

He had already asked me two dozen questions that evening. He reached in his coat pocket and took out a box. Then he walked over and got down on one knee. My heart leapt in my chest.

"Sugar, my love, would you marry me?"

I sat there speechless. He had thrown away what we had before, what I had thought was a lifelong commitment, because of his fears. Had he really changed? Would a formal marriage make the difference? I didn't know what to say.

And then he opened the box.

It was the largest diamond I had ever seen. The ring was exquisite, a large central diamond with other smaller ones in the gold band. It reflected the light of the candles, and rainbows danced and flitted around the room.

And it was meaningless.

A diamond used to represent a great cost, a tremendous investment. Now it was nothing. He had probably gone down to the mall that morning and picked the best ring they had in the jewelry store. It had cost him nothing. There was no investment. He hadn't changed himself for me.

He was still the same man who had left me when he thought I would die. Now that I had a small hope, he would stick around for a while. But when times got hard, when I failed to extract the insulin and wasted away to nothing on a starvation diet to keep my blood sugar in control, he would leave again.

"No," I said. He fell onto both knees. I stood and left while Kyle stared at the worthless ring.

I drove home in the dark with the top down on the car. The August air was warm in the evenings, and I watched the glorious night sky as the wind blew through my hair. I parked the car in the driveway and walked inside, putting my purse on the kitchen table.

I thought for a moment and remembered that I might have left a vial of insulin in my purse. I opened it up, took Clint out and laid him on the table and started digging through, looking for the insulin. At the bottom of the purse I saw a wadded-up piece of paper. I pulled it out and unfolded it. In large letters it read:

HELP.

-31-

The note was obviously from Olivia, one of the two children I had seen since the virus. I wondered what kind of trouble she and Michael and Danny could be in. Then I started to think. She must have written it when we rode in my car. She had asked Michael to drive and moved Danny so she could sit directly behind Michael. Where he couldn't see her.

I didn't know what to think. Michael was a loving father to them. I had met them when he was trying to save Danny from a snakebite.

Olivia had written an address in smaller letters at the bottom of the note. I went to the GPS, and it estimated four hours and thirty-eight minutes to get to their house. It was ten o'clock at night. If I left then and drove at highway speeds, I could get there by three or four in the morning. I had just driven the roads, and they were fairly clear. It would be a risk going full speed at night, but I wanted to arrive in darkness while they were still sleeping.

I started to pull out of the driveway, but I went back and got Clint off the table and got back in the car. I drove north on I-75 in the dark with my bright headlights on, trying to concentrate on the road, but my mind kept thinking about what the note meant.

Was it just a childish act? Perhaps Michael hadn't allowed her to stay up as late as she wanted. I had done plenty of silly things when I was her age. When I was eleven, I called my social worker saying my foster parents were abusing me. After the police came and investigated, they found that my foster parents had taken my cell phone away as punishment for not doing my homework.

If it was something like that, then we would all have a laugh, and I'd get more time to spend with Michael, which frankly didn't sound so bad. As I drove, I convinced myself that it was probably an exaggeration or a misunderstanding. Maybe they really did need help, but Michael wasn't the problem. Olivia could be worried about Danny not talking or something like that.

I pulled into the neighborhood at 3:35 am. They apparently had taken up residence in a very rich section of Atlanta called Buckhead. All the houses were huge. I suppose if I were raising children, I would pick a big house with a pool and a tree house.

I almost decided to sleep in my car and wait until the morning to talk with Michael, but I felt a little uneasy remembering all the deliberateness Olivia had gone to in order to secretly give me the note. I drove up the street with my lights off and found the house easily. Michael's white van was parked in the driveway, and I heard the sure sign of habitation, a generator humming from somewhere in the backyard.

The house directly across the street had a large, open garage, so I drove the car in and pulled the garage door back down. I went into the house and found a spot upstairs where I could watch through a window without being seen. I set my phone to wake me up at 6:00. I tried to get a couple hours of sleep lying in yet another stranger's bed, but I couldn't even keep my eyes closed for more than a few seconds.

At 5:59 I turned the alarm off and went back to look out the window. I injected and then ate some small snacks I had from the car. At 7:05 the lights came on in what looked like a bathroom window. A few minutes later the front door opened, and Michael stepped outside carrying Danny on his shoulders. A small dog ran out. Danny and Michael watched it until it relieved itself on the front lawn, and then they all went back in.

For hours I watched the house with nothing happening. I began to feel creepy. If Michael found me here, spying, would it ruin any chance of a relationship? If I found a guy stalking me, that would be it. I couldn't believe I was considering our romantic chances when I had so much else to worry about. But he had seemed like such a kindred soul. His childhood had been just like mine.

Around two, Michael, Olivia and Danny came out front wearing swimsuits. I had seen a clubhouse with a large swimming pool at the entrance to the neighborhood. There were also tennis courts and a gym for the rich people to enjoy. Michael wore swimming trunks, and he was even more handsome than I had realized. His arms and torso were well muscled, and his chest was hairy, like a man, not some pretty boy who teenage girls posted on their walls.

They got in Michael's van and drove off. Now was my chance.

I waited a few minutes to make sure they didn't come back for some forgotten item, and then I walked across the street and opened the front door. The house was immaculately clean, especially considering that two young children lived there.

But it was also clear that it was a house centered on children. Michael had painted one entire wall in the living room in chalkboard paint, and the kids had decorated it in drawings up to where they could reach. Above that height, Michael had written in crisp handwriting their daily schedule:

7:00 am – Wake up.
7:05 am – Brush teeth
7:10 am – Take Fluffy outside
7:30 am – Breakfast
8:00 - 11:00 am – School
12:00 pm – Lunch
2:00 pm – Fun time (Pool today!)
5:00 pm – Dinner
6:00 - 6:30 pm – iPads
8:00 pm – Brush teeth and baths
8:30 pm – Pills
8:45 pm – Bedtime
9:00 pm – Lights out

They had a room that was clearly a schoolroom with books, pencils, crayons and every school supply the kids could possibly use. Each kid had a bedroom. Olivia's was an explosion of pink and frills. Right next door, Danny's had been decorated in a jungle theme with wallpaper filled with elephants, zebras and lions.

The huge house had many unused rooms, but Michael apparently slept in the master bedroom. It was decorated simply, but I saw a gun safe within easy reach of the bed. It had an electronic keypad to open it.

I looked through the rest of the house, from the basement to the attic, but found nothing I wouldn't expect to find in any family's home. The dog was in a cage in the corner of the living room and woke up and began barking at me.

This was silly, and I felt like a creep, invading their privacy. I hurried outside and across the street. I got the car out of the garage, closing the door back down, and parked it in front of their house. I waited in the car, trying to look innocent.

They came back around four. Michael pulled in the driveway and stepped out looking cautious. Olivia and Danny came out behind Michael. They were all still in their swimsuits. Olivia made eye contact and seemed to have a question in her eyes. Danny ran to me squealing in excitement.

"I'm not a stalker," I said, lying. "Olivia left me a lovely note inviting me to come visit."

Michael looked at Olivia, and she nodded.

"I've told her we have to be very cautious about telling people where we live," Michael said. "The world isn't safe anymore. Especially for children."

He face was stern for a moment, and then he looked into my eyes and smiled. "But I think we've proven that you're okay."

Danny held his arms out, and I picked him up. We walked inside, and I made a show of admiring the house. The kids wanted to show me their bedrooms, but Michael said they had to get changed out of their swimsuits first. Michael stepped away and came back changed from his swimsuit to jeans and a polo shirt, which made it much easier for me to concentrate.

"Can I help with dinner?" I asked. "The schedule says it's almost time."

"Sure," Michael said. "Kids, you go play in the backyard. Come in, when I call, and wash your hands."

"What are we having?" I asked.

"Spaghetti with meatballs," he said.

Pasta. Heavy carbs. I decided to simply be honest about myself. We had to start off right. Well, except for the fact that I came to spy on him for endangering children that he obviously loved like a father. I'd keep that to myself.

"I'm diabetic so I have to plan ahead for meals."

"I can switch our plans," he said. "Maybe hamburgers, I have the meat thawed already. You could eat yours without the bun."

"No. Spaghetti is fine. I'll inject now. Should I go somewhere else to do it?"

"Doesn't bother me," he said. "One of my foster mothers was diabetic, and I often gave her injections."

I checked my blood sugar and then injected a little bit higher dose to handle the oncoming rush from the pasta. I didn't really help in the preparation at all. Michael was a master in the kitchen and made meatballs like a professional chef, adding ingredients I didn't even recognize.

"How long will you be staying?" Michael asked.

"Oh, just a few hours. I got Olivia's note, and I didn't want to disappoint her. And there's no way to call ahead anymore."

"A few hours. Nonsense. The drive up here was at least five or six hours. I insist you stay the night. I'm not sending a woman into the wilds at night. You can see we have plenty of room."

"Okay," I said.

"Why not stay a few days? Enjoy the new world. There are no obligations or schedules. We so rarely get to see other people, and I have to be so cautious to protect the children."

"I couldn't stay more than the night. My generator at home will run out."

"So some food will spoil in the fridge?" he said. "Are the stores in Tallahassee as cheap as here?"

"No," I said. "It's the insulin in my fridge at home. I have to keep it refrigerated."

"No one can refill the generator for you?"

"Sure, they did on my last trip, but I didn't ask anybody this time." I wanted to stay. To take a break from the worry of the task ahead of me. A few days wouldn't hurt. But I couldn't do anything to risk the insulin. That was my life.

"Is Tallahassee where that preacher broadcasts from?" he asked.

"Yeah. Ralph. Have you heard him?"

"Sure. I listen on some Sundays. I'm not real religious, but it's good for the kids. And I like to hear other people's voices. I can call him on the radio. Could he get someone to fill your generator?"

He turned to look at me and I nodded.

"We'll call after dinner," he said.

Michael finished the cooking, and when he thought the noodles were perfect, he drained them in a colander and asked me to call the kids in. The kids came running in, and he pointed them to the bathroom to wash their hands.

I set the table, and we all sat down to eat. The food was delicious. Olivia chattered the entire time, telling me about their life. Danny didn't say anything, but he wouldn't take his eyes off me.

"So," Michael said, "let's get to know Sugar. What were you before?"

"Nothing much. I was nineteen when the virus hit." I hated saying that because it made me sound so young. "I grew up in foster homes, like you, and got on my own when I was eighteen."

"And you must have managed to gather insulin and keep yourself alive in the new empty world. Impressive. I'll add that to the list."

"List?"

"Beautiful. Smart. And now resourceful."

I blushed and wanted to change the subject. "What were you before?"

"The most unimaginably boring job."

"I'm sure it must have been interesting. You're too smart to have a boring job." I was so bad at flirting.

"Oh, I liked it, but most people fall asleep when I start talking about chemical equations and lab procedures."

"What were you?" I asked.

"A simple professor. I worked at Emory in the chemistry department."

What?

I jumped up and ran to the car and got the list from my purse.

When I came back in Michael said, "Is something wrong?"

"No," I said, out of breath from the run and the excitement. "Does this make sense to you?" I showed him the list.

He looked at it for a moment and said the most beautiful word: "Yes."

"Could you follow these steps? Do you understand it? Do the terms make sense? Does it look possible?"

"This is very advanced chemistry and lab procedure," Michael said. "It would require a lot of knowledge and skill, and of course equipment and chemicals."

"And?" I asked, my head spinning.

"And I have all of those," he said with solid confidence.

I couldn't wait to be subtle. "Can you help me? I'll die if I can't make more insulin. The supply I have will last maybe two more years."

He didn't even hesitate. "Of course. What kind of monster wouldn't help you?"

I almost cried with joy.

"Now, Sugar, I don't want to … sugarcoat it," he said. "This will be difficult. Sterilization is a major concern. You should expect it to take many batches and failed attempts."

"But should we be able to do it in two years?"

"I think so," he said. "Do you know how to remove a pancreas from a pig?"

"No. I tried and couldn't do it."

"Well we can tackle that one first. We may have to read a lot of books and slaughter a few innocent pigs, but we can do it. I should be able to make a chemical test that will identify insulin and confirm that we've found the pancreas."

The other men, Kyle and John, had turned in fear. Kyle afraid of my death, and John afraid of the death he would have to inflict. Michael hadn't even blinked an eye. He was ready for the challenge. Fearless.

We went off the kids' normally strict schedule that night and just talked and got to know each other. At 8:15 Michael sent the kids to bathe and get ready for bed. While they bathed, we got on the radio and managed to make contact with Ralph. He agreed to let Edith know to fill the generator and check the insulin fridge, and said he would do it himself if she couldn't.

The kids came back down in pajamas. Danny's were stuck to him because he forgot to dry off.

"Is it pill time?" Olivia asked.

"Just Danny tonight," Michael said. "The kids got sick a week or so ago. Olivia first and then Danny a few days later. I had been working on making penicillin, and it was ready just in time. It seems to have knocked the infection out. I've kept dosing them a few days after symptoms to be sure."

"I don't get my regular pills?" Olivia said.

"No," he said. "You're fine. Now off to bed. I'll read to Danny first."

Michael took Danny upstairs, and with us alone, I finally asked Olivia why she wrote "HELP."

She thought for a moment and then whispered, "Because I couldn't think of another way to get you here. Things will be different now."

"How will they be different?" I asked.

"You'll be Michael's wife and our mother."

-32-

Michael put Olivia to bed. He could tell I was obviously exhausted and showed me to a spare bedroom. I slept soundly until I heard the dog barking in the morning. I woke to find them about their normal routine.

I set the table again while Michael made breakfast. I showed the kids how I injected the insulin. Olivia was fascinated, but Danny was scared, so I turned away from him and let Olivia watch. We ate breakfast and then started on school.

Michael was teaching Danny his letters, but had to handle it carefully since Danny wouldn't talk. Michael would say a letter and have Danny point to it. He knew up through G, but had trouble after that.

When we got to Olivia's math lesson, they were both amazed at my ability to do problems in my head. They made a game of it, trying to find my limits. I can keep huge numbers in my head. I'm not quite like some autistic savants I had seen on YouTube videos, who can instantly answer difficult math problems, but with just a little time I can solve most anything without writing anything down. We got up to multiplying two seven-digit numbers when Michael told Olivia to let me have a break for the day.

He asked if I could explain it. All I could say was that I felt the numbers in my mind like solid objects. A multi-digit number was like a three-dimensional map. At some level, the entire world was just numbers.

After school, Michael asked, "So when do you want to get started on extracting the insulin? I don't look forward to the first step, but the rest should be fascinating."

"Let's take a little while," I said. "It's all I've thought about for so long. Now that I feel like we can really do it, I want to enjoy just living life."

"Okay," he said. "Well, I'll be thinking about it. Part of me can't wait to get started."

That day's fun time was riding bikes. Michael found one for me in a nearby house. We got our helmets, which Michael insisted on, and rode through the neighborhood. Danny couldn't ride a two-wheeled bike yet, but he had a tricycle that he nearly rode the wheels off of. We went slowly at first so he could keep up. When he got tired, Michael put him in a child's seat on his bike, and we took off, struggling up hills and then delighting in rolling down the other side.

Olivia's energy was amazing, and she nearly exhausted both us adults. We turned around, picked up Danny's tricycle on the way back and got home tired, but feeling great. Not just from the exhilaration of exercise, but from the completeness of it all. For the first time in my life, I felt like I was part of something bigger than myself.

The next week passed much the same. Each day Michael had a different activity to do. We went to a museum. We picked flowers in a field. We did everything together, even the mundane chores like shopping. The kids had strict limits on what they could get, a rule hard to enforce with aisles of well-preserved candies and cereals and everything kids would love to gorge themselves on.

There was no school on Saturday, and Michael let the kids have unstructured playtime. He and I spent the day organizing school lessons for the next week and making meal plans and the other preparations that have to be done to keep a family running.

We talked and learned about each other's past. Like me, he had been in and out of nearly a dozen foster homes. He had even spent some time in a boys' group home, a place he hated. I could still see the anger in his eyes and the way his body tensed when discussing it. But he held nothing back from me. We were an open book to each other.

I told him of Kyle, my journey to find a veterinarian and the attack that left me scarred. He touched me for the first time when looking at the scar on my leg. He held my leg and ran his hand over the mangled flesh. He didn't shy away from it at all.

I sat at the table with a cup of tea and told the story and showed the scar. I was surprised when he took my leg and placed it across his leg and felt the scar. He did everything with such deliberate confidence that it didn't feel like an intrusion, just the natural flow of our conversation.

When I showed him the scar on my arm, he touched that also, seeming to take it into himself with his touch. He hadn't seen the scar on my chest yet, and I quivered at the thought of him running his hand down the scar onto my breast.

On Sunday we listened to Ralph's church service and spent the rest of the day resting. After lunch we napped on a hammock in the backyard while the kids played. Next to him, I fell asleep in the warm sunshine, but I think a part of him stayed alert, always listening for the children.

I checked with Edith on the radio to see how things were going.

"Chekov the generator is runny fine, and Helga the fridge is keeping all your medicine cold," she said.

I asked if she minded if I stayed awhile longer, and she said it was okay. I had a few vials and could keep them in Michael's fridge.

Michael spent a few hours each day at the chemistry lab at Emory making preparations. He never left the neighborhood without his gun holstered at his side. He let me watch the kids, a sign of trust that I recognized. The children were a delight, and I loved my time with them. I wished Danny would talk, but we didn't pressure him at all. Considering the trauma he had been through, he was doing remarkably well.

On the days Michael worked in the afternoon, I fixed dinner and had it ready when he came home at five. I wasn't near as good a cook as he was, but he and the children enjoyed it.

"I've made every meal for myself, or the kids when they came, for the past ten years or more," Michael said one night. "I'd forgotten how wonderful it was to be cared for."

"You didn't have a woman in your life in all that time?" I asked.

"No," he said with sadness in his eyes.

That night, after I had been there three weeks, we put the kids to bed. I read to Danny, and Michael to Olivia. We both liked to get to sleep a little after the kids, but had made a habit of enjoying an hour of time just with each other. We would talk or sit next to each other on the couch and watch a DVD or listen to music.

We lived in a new world from before the virus. Time passed differently. Three weeks might seem like a short time, but when there were no other people, no other adults, you could pour yourself into someone completely. I knew what love was. I had experienced it before. And now, amazingly, when I had given up, it had come again.

And there was no reason to hold back.

Michael, so confident in everything else, had barely made a move physically with me. We would sit close together, but he hadn't even held my hand yet.

Michael sat down on the couch, and I snuggled up beside him, on his left.

"What do you want to listen to?" he asked.

"Something soft," I said. "And romantic."

He pushed a few buttons on the remote and played something with a saxophone that I didn't recognize. He picked up another remote and dimmed the lights. I turned to face him and put my hand up to his face, rubbing the stubble on his cheek with my fingers.

"Sorry," he said. "I didn't shave today."

"That's okay. I like it." I moved my hand down onto his chest and felt his heart beating. I leaned in and kissed him. The kiss was deep and slow and passionate. Michael put his hands on my hips. His fingers just touched the bare skin of my belly. We kissed more. He cautiously moved his hands up. He looked in my eyes, and I let him know that it was okay.

His hands moved to my breasts, just touching the bottom of them with each hand. I had given up wearing a bra after the wound on my chest. I wondered how he would react to seeing it, but I felt confident that he would accept me. I started to unbutton my shirt, but he pulled away when I reached the third button down.

"What's wrong?" I asked.

He didn't say anything.

"Is it the age difference?" Maybe he was uncomfortable being with a twenty-one-year-old when he was thirty-two.

"No," he said. "That doesn't bother me." He paused. "I want this, but … I need to take it slowly."

He stared at the spot between my breasts that I had unbuttoned my shirt to. I was still covered, and he couldn't see the scar. I didn't know what to do. We had time now that I thought had been gone. He would help make the insulin, and a vast future stretched ahead of us.

I took his hand and put it on the center of my chest and let him feel my heart beating.

"We can go slowly," I said.

"I've had … bad experiences as a child."

That explained why a man as handsome and successful as he was hadn't had a woman in his life for so long. So many children in foster care came from abuse or even suffered abuse while in the system. We each had scars that needed time to heal.

I lay down on the couch and put my head in his lap, lying on my back looking up at him. He moved his left arm, not knowing where to put it. I took his hand and put it back on my chest, our skin touching. He felt the rise and fall of my breathing. I gently moved his hand under my shirt, and he cupped my unscarred right breast in his hands.

We stayed there for minutes, enjoying the intimacy without the pressure to go forward. After a few songs, I sat up and kissed his cheek and said, "Good night."

As I walked to the top of the stairs, Olivia peeked around the corner, and when she saw me, she ran back to her bedroom. Her face beamed with a smile.

33

The next day, after school, Michael went to the lab. He said he was almost done making the test to indicate the presence of insulin. We could cut out everything we thought was a pancreas in the pig and use his test to determine for sure. Part of me suspected that someone as educated as Michael would actually be able to use the pictures in the books to find the pancreas, but I remembered that John said it was hard without someone to show you the first time.

I talked with Olivia after laying Danny down for a nap. He didn't nap every day, but some days he still needed it.

"You have to give Michael and me privacy," I said.

"I know. I'm sorry," she said. "You can be his wife now, and everything will be perfect."

I didn't say anything, not wanting to get her hopes up, but it was probably too late for that. For both of us.

I realized how wise Michael's caution had been. I wasn't taking any birth control, and I thought it was the fertile time in my cycle. God or nature had arranged a woman's desire to be strongest when she was primed for making babies, and the night before, I had been very willing.

When Danny woke up, I put the kids in the car and we drove to a nearby CVS. I found the same brand of birth control pills I had used when I was with Kyle. I was glad that Jane, from Savannah, had told me that they wouldn't expire for a long time. Otherwise I would have had to use one of the other methods, which were a lot more trouble. I took a few boxes' worth and let the kids pick out a small toy each.

"What are those?" Olivia asked.

"Just some pills I need to take," I said.

We drove home, and I put all but one box in a drawer in my nightstand. Olivia had followed me upstairs and into my bedroom. I opened one box and took out the package with its ring of pills. I popped out the pill that I thought matched where I was in my cycle and swallowed it.

"Michael said I could stop taking my pills," Olivia said.

"Yep," I said. "You're not sick anymore. Danny is done with his too."

"I took pills like those," she said.

"Pink like these, or white like these?" I asked. The pill package had twenty-one pink pills and seven white pills.

"Not the same color," she said. "The same type of package. Twenty-eight little pills in a ring."

"Why?" I asked.

"I don't know," she said. "Michael just said I had to take them."

That didn't make any sense. "Olivia. When did you start having your cycle?"

"What?"

This was an uncomfortable conversation, but I guessed it came with the territory. "Your period."

She gave me a blank look.

I was going to have to be explicit. "Your monthly bleeding."

She blushed and looked away. "A few months ago."

"Was it bad?"

She didn't answer for a moment, then said, "Yeah. Really bad at first."

"The pills Michael gave you help to make it better." I never thought I would have this conversation with anyone. Did she know the facts of life? Did I need to tell her? I felt for Michael, a man having to handle this himself.

Well, if I wanted to be a part of this family, then I guess this was my job. I remembered the miserable conversation I'd had with my foster mom when I got my first period. I had no idea what it was. I had thought it was a complication of the diabetes and that I was going to die.

"Has Michael ever talked to you about … intimate things?"

"Intimate?" she said, and her face changed completely. Her eyes went wide, and she looked like she had been caught in a crime.

How should I start? "When a man and woman love each other … they want to spend time together like Michael and I do … some of that time they like to spend … " This was miserable. I'd just say it. "They like to spend time together without their clothes on."

Olivia ran from my room, down the hall to her room and slammed the door.

I was messing this up. I walked to her room and opened the door a crack.

"Go away!" she screamed.

"I just want to talk about it," I said.

"No, no, no, no, no!"

"It's okay," I said.

"I don't have to!"

"Okay. If you don't want to."

"I don't have to anymore!" she yelled. "You'll be his wife now. I don't have to do that anymore."

I felt like someone had punched me in the stomach. I pictured Olivia's note with *HELP* printed in large letters.

"Don't have to do what?" I asked.

"I don't have to be intimate." She slapped her hand over her mouth and then said, "Don't tell him I told you. He made me promise."

I wanted to throw up. I sat on the bed beside her. I had to be sure.

"Did he … did he touch you?"

"Don't tell him I said anything. You have to promise."

"I promise," I said. "What happened?"

"He would put … himself … in … "

I stopped her with my hand on her arm. That was enough. I couldn't stand to hear anymore. My head spun and I wanted to run. I wanted to get in the car and drive far away and never come back.

But I had to protect the children. Michael would be home soon. He came every day at almost exactly five o'clock. I looked at a clock on the wall. It said 4:51.

"We have to go, now," I said. I took her hand, and we went downstairs and found Danny playing with the dog. I picked him up and said, "We're going for a ride."

Danny's eyes brightened, but Olivia was afraid. She knew things were different now.

"We can stay," she said. "You can do that now. I saw that you liked him touching you. You smiled the entire time."

"We have to go," I said.

I got my purse and carried Danny and dragged Olivia to the car. She stood on the sidewalk as I buckled Danny in. "We have to go, now," I said. "Please."

She got in the car. I turned the key, and the engine hummed to life. My phone showed 4:55. The neighborhood had only one entrance and exit, and we could easily pass Michael as he came home. I pulled out of the driveway and turned the opposite way of the neighborhood exit.

I drove down the street and turned left and then right. I picked a house with a garage that was already open and drove the car in. I pulled the door down and took the kids inside. We'd wait until dark and then drive away. Michael probably wouldn't be too suspicious at first, thinking we were late getting home from somewhere. When we didn't return by dark he would go out looking for us, probably at the normal spots like the museum or the park or the pool.

We stayed in the living room. Fortunately I went in first, because I had to hold the children back when I saw a skeleton. I shut them behind the door and quickly threw it outside and closed the curtains. We waited for night to fall while I held the children in silence.

I would take them back to Tallahassee. I didn't know how, but I'd take care of them or find someone who could. We'd never have to see Michael again. He'd soon figure out that I knew and wouldn't dare show up. The children would be safe. He couldn't hurt them anymore.

But what about the other children?

If I let him go, he would just find others. He had probably done this before in the years he was alone before the virus. What had happened to those children?

People disagree on what morality is. Some people think that it matters who you sleep with or what paperwork you have before you do, but that means nothing. Protecting children, that's the only morality that matters.

I probably wouldn't live much longer now that I didn't have Michael to help with the complex process of extracting the insulin, but I could accept that. If I'm remembered after I'm gone, I want to be remembered for one thing. I protected children.

I told Olivia to stay there, watch Danny and wait for me. I got in the car and backed out of the driveway.

I took Clint out of my purse and held it in my hands.

34

Michael's van was in the driveway when I pulled up. I parked behind it and walked to the doorway with Clint in my right hand, my arm held stiff at my side. I opened the door, and Michael called out from the kitchen, "Oh, good. You're home. I figured you and the kids were running a little late. I started dinner. I hope you didn't have anything planned."

I took a deep breath and walked into the kitchen. I wanted to lift the gun and fire and be done with it, but I froze when I saw him, standing in front of the sink washing off some carrots he had grown with the kids in the garden.

"Where are the kids?" he asked. "I didn't hear them come in."

"They're not here," I said.

"What?" he said and turned to me. He saw the gun in my hands. "What happened?" he yelled. His gun was still strapped in a holster at his side. He normally took it off and locked it up right when he came in the house, but his routine must have been disrupted when he couldn't find anyone home.

"You happened," I said. I still couldn't lift my arm to do what had to be done.

"Where are Olivia and Danny?" he screamed.

"They're safe," I said. As enraged as I was, I couldn't stand for him to think they were hurt. "And they'll stay safe. I know, Michael."

"You know what?" He stopped and looked back down at my gun. Comprehension spread across his face.

"Why?" It was a stupid question.

"Because I'm a monster," he said. "I thought with you here I could put it behind me. That the beast would stay away. I haven't ... I haven't done anything since we met you."

He put his hand on the holster on his hip. I raised the gun and pointed it right at him. I wanted him to try to draw his gun. It would be simple self-defense then.

"I'm not going to shoot you," he said. Slowly he unsnapped the strap over the gun. With the tips of his fingers, he took the gun out and laid it on the floor. Then he kicked it, and it slid across the tiles, between my legs and out of the kitchen.

"How could you be … you and … that at the same time?" I asked.

"I was put into foster care because of my father," Michael said. "He … did things to me."

"You think that makes this okay?" I put my finger on the trigger. I remembered how easy it had fired when I killed the pig. I had stood there in fear, and it had surprised me. I still couldn't bring myself to squeeze the trigger, but maybe I would slip. It would fire, and this would be over.

We stood there, the gun trembling in my hand, and Michael looking down at the floor.

"Danny would have died without me," Michael said. "He would have died a horrible death. A three-year-old starving in a house full of decaying bodies. All the doors had child protective covers on the knobs. No one else looked for the children in the first days. I was the only one. I had to search hundreds of houses full of putrid death."

"You looked so you could prey on them."

"No!" he yelled. "I never touched Danny that way. That's what my father did with little boys. I just wanted to help children. I saved him."

"Do you think this is some sort of sum that cancels out? You saved Danny so you earned enough points to take Olivia?"

"I didn't look for Olivia. After Danny, I kept looking in houses for trapped children. Did you look for trapped children in Tallahassee?"

"No," I said. I had searched, but it was weeks after. I hadn't thought of the children until it was too late.

"I searched hundreds more, maybe thousands over the weeks. I stopped when I figured it had been too long for any others to have survived. Then we found Olivia, a ten-year-old girl wandering the streets, filthy with infected cuts."

Why was I letting him talk? He'd convince me that he deserved a chance. I believed in forgiveness, but some things were unforgiveable.

"That still doesn't explain anything," I said.

"No," he said. "It doesn't. I'm broken, Sugar. They took me out of foster homes because of what I tried to do. They put me in a boys' home. I wasn't tempted there. I put it behind me. But some of the bigger boys. They—"

"They did to you what you did to Olivia."

"No," he said, then, "Yes. But I never saw it that way."

"I don't care how you saw it."

"It's like there's another part of me. A monster inside me that comes out. You've been with me all these weeks. I wasn't faking. That's who I really am."

I thought of a movie I had seen years ago. The leading man was a werewolf. He hated it and didn't want to hurt people, but when the full moon came, he did. The movie was gory, meant to thrill teenagers with the werewolf feasting on innocent people, but it disgusted me. A woman loved him, and she looked for a cure, but there wasn't one. Finally, in tears, she shot the werewolf with a silver bullet. It thrashed about and then died.

The dead werewolf transformed back into the man. The woman cried over his body, until he sat up with no bullet wound in his chest.

But if I killed the monster, the man would stay dead.

The gun was getting heavy, so I put it back down at my side. Even with my need to make insulin, I hadn't missed the old world in a while. I had gotten used to the new world. But now I deeply longed for the old ways. It would have been so simple.

I would have called the police, and they would have taken him away. He would become somebody else's problem. A judge and jury, who didn't know him, who didn't love him, would decide his fate. And they wouldn't have to kill him. They could put him in prison for a time, or maybe an institution where someone could help him with his problem.

Now all the burden rested on me. When I had walked in the house with white-hot anger, I was ready to put a bullet in the monster. But he wasn't transformed. He was the man, simply making dinner for the family that he loved. A family he had made me part of.

I had to make a decision. I was the judge and jury. I thought about taking him back to Tallahassee and having an actual trial before the people there, but I couldn't transport and control a man of his size and strength. He was cooperating now, but instinct is a powerful thing. He wanted to live, and he had proven that he couldn't control his base desires.

I would decide his fate, standing in the kitchen with a gun in my hand.

"Have you done this before?" I asked.

He didn't answer.

"Answer me!"

"Yes," he said. "Only once in all those years. As a professor you can imagine that I got the attention of some of the female students."

That wasn't hard to believe with how handsome he was. "Having a relationship with a student is unethical," I said, "but it isn't a crime. They were adults."

"I wasn't interested in older girls, and I just thought that would be something I didn't have in my life."

"You aren't attracted to women?" I asked. What had happened between us?

"You were the first grown woman I ever thought about in that way."

What was different about me?

"I politely turned all the female students down, but one woman on campus, a graduate student, but not one of mine, was so persistent that I decided to give it a try. We dated for a while, and I found out that she had gotten pregnant as a teenager and had a daughter."

He looked up at me with shame in his eyes.

"We got very serious. Well, in her mind at least. She was okay that nothing physical happened between us. I think she was just looking for a husband to help take care of her and her daughter. She started having me babysit. I thought it would be okay. I thought the monster was gone after so long."

He didn't finish the story, and he didn't have to. So it had happened before and had happened again with Olivia.

"With Olivia," I said, "you were conscious of it. It was planned. You bought her birth control."

"When I ... failed with her the first time, I knew it would happen again. I tried to resist every time. When her cycles started ... I had to protect her from getting pregnant."

It seemed perverse that he thought of it as protection.

"In all but that, I was a good father to them."

"Why didn't you give them to someone else who could raise them and wouldn't be tempted? There must be women out there who are desperate to love a child."

"It was a year before anything happened. We had become a family. I couldn't send them away. They had both already lost a family."

He stopped for a moment and then said, "Have you ever known anybody who tried to get over an addiction?"

"I had a foster mom who smoked. She kept putting them down and saying she was done, but she would always start again in a few days," I said. "But this isn't smoking cigarettes."

"I know it's so much worse," he said, "but it feels the same. Like your foster mom, I kept telling myself that I'd get control of it. And then you came. I was attracted to you. Last night, when I sat on the couch with you, with your ... holding you, I felt close and excited and ... "

My stomach turned at the thought that he had touched me. He looked at the gun that I held at my side.

"What are you going to do?" he asked.

I had to decide. The fury was gone. I saw a kind and gentle man before me, with a beast inside him. But the beast had to be dealt with. It all came down to one question.

"Would you do it again?" I asked.

"I'll never touch Olivia again," he said. "Just never leave me alone with her. You can keep her safe."

Sadly, he thought there was still a possibility of keeping the life we had.

"You'll never see me or Danny or Olivia again," I said. That blow affected him physically, and he sat down in a kitchen chair. "If I left you here, could you resist? Could you stay away from children for the rest of your life?"

"I always think I can," Michael said, looking down at the floor. "But the beast comes back. I need help."

He did need help. But we lived in a world that could no longer help him. There was only me here. Me and the gun.

I raised it back up, pointing it at him.

"What are you doing?" he asked, looking up.

To find the strength, I had to say out loud what the crime was. To make it plain, not veiled by restrained words, or covered in excuses and reasons. "Michael, you raped a child."

"Just let me go," he begged. "I'll stay by myself. I'll never see another person, especially a child. I can extract the insulin for you. Just bring the pancreases."

As much as I wanted that, I couldn't risk another child being hurt. He had done it before, and he would do it again. I couldn't watch him constantly, and I couldn't live with myself if he got away to hurt another child.

"I'm sorry, Michael."

"Have someone else do it," he said. "I don't want you to live with the guilt. For the rest of your life your hands will be covered in it."

"In what?"

"Blood, Sugar."

I pulled the trigger and, like with the pig, it surprised me when it fired. In the movies people fly backward, but the shot rang out, and a small black spot appeared on Michael's shirt. We both stared at it as it turned red.

It was cruel to let him suffer, so I raised the gun again.

"No," he said. "Just let me fade away. It doesn't hurt like you think it would."

I put the gun down on the kitchen counter. Michael tried to stand, but slipped off the chair onto the floor.

"Promise me you'll take care of them," he said.

"I promise."

"I know what Olivia will think of me, but tell Danny that I was his father. Let him remember me purely. He was the only thing I did right in my life."

I nodded.

Michael looked at me until the life in his eyes slipped away. I had killed the werewolf, but, as the monster died, the man died with him.

-35-

I picked up Clint and stepped out of the kitchen feeling empty. The dog, Fluffy, barked in her cage in the corner of the living room. I couldn't leave her trapped, so I opened it, and then she followed me out to the car. I didn't like dogs, but I decided to take her with me so the kids would have something of their old life.

Twice now, they'd had one world, one life, destroyed and replaced with another. I knew exactly how that felt.

I picked the kids up from the house, and we started the drive back down to Tallahassee. We stayed at the same hotel I had used before on the last trip back from Atlanta. Olivia didn't question what we were doing, and of course, Danny still said nothing.

On the drive home the next morning, I tried to think about what was best for the kids. Once again my own death loomed. I wouldn't give up, but Michael had repeatedly emphasized how much careful skill and knowledge the process took. Why hadn't I learned how to do it from him?

Because the world had seemed secure. The world is never, ever secure. Any feeling of safety is always a temporary illusion.

Should I watch the kids for two years, only to die and have them suffer yet another loss? Maybe someone in Tallahassee would take them in. That would be best.

Bill and Laura. She was pregnant, and they wanted to start a family. Now they'd have an instant family. I had promised Michael that I would take care of Danny and Olivia, and that meant providing for them after my death.

I drove home and found that once again Edith had kept everything safe. The insulin sat securely in Bertha. We hauled some water from the creek, and I had the kids take a bath and get cleaned up. We went shopping at a nice store in the mall. I bought a beautiful dress for Olivia to wear. Danny picked out Spider-Man shorts, a T-shirt and shoes, which was perfect since they made him look even cuter.

We drove over to Bill and Laura's. They were outside in the front yard working in the garden. Laura's belly was just starting to show. They had chosen a large home, and I knew that they had at least three empty bedrooms.

They stood and waved at me, and then looked with curiosity at the children. I made the introductions. Then Bill invited everyone in to have some lemonade. After the drinks, I sent the kids outside to play. Bill had already gotten a swing set, even though their baby wouldn't be able to use it for a while.

I had never been much for small talk or subtlety, so I just explained the circumstances, saying that Michael had died, not giving the details of what he had done or how he died. When I was finished, they stared at me holding their lemonade.

"You show up on our doorstep with two children, and just want us to take them in?" Bill said.

"Two damaged children," Laura said, "who will certainly have issues from the *multiple* traumas they have suffered."

"They don't have anyone else," I said.

"They have you," Laura said. "You're young, but old enough to raise a family. You've already spent a few weeks with them, and they're attached to you."

Laura wanted a perfect family, not the messy, flawed, damaged one I was presenting her. And then I realized what I had done.

Like countless social workers had done to me, I had dressed up two children and tried to sell them to someone. I apologized to Bill and Laura, and took the kids and went back home. I still had to find someone to care for them, but not like I had just done. There was a community meeting at the end of the week, and I'd go to see what people thought.

Olivia and Danny adjusted well to life in my home over the next few days. They seemed fine, but I knew well the hurt that hid behind their smiles. When you first go into a new family, you hide everything. It's not a conscious choice. You have to do it to protect yourself. You don't know how the people will react.

The children were easy to care for. Frankly, the dog was the most work, but I couldn't take her from them. I made sure the kids were fed and bathed. I didn't do school like Michael had, but I did read to them a lot. Danny fell asleep each night on the couch as I read him countless books we bought from the library.

When Friday, the day of the weekly meeting, came, I took the kids and they ate lunch with everyone. The adults were all excited to see children. Ralph bounced Danny on his knee and made him laugh. Edith braided Olivia's hair.

Kyle was there, but it barely fazed me after the horror with Michael. Kyle didn't speak until I sent the kids outside to play while we all sat down to discuss community news and issues.

"I can help you with them," he said. "They seem like great kids."

"I need someone to love and care for them after I'm gone," I said. "You never wanted kids. You've told me that a hundred times. You just want to use them to get to me."

He didn't deny it and walked away to sit in his regular seat at the end of the large table that had been cleared of dishes. Ralph started the meeting with a prayer, and then we discussed various things that people felt were important. When everyone had finished, I brought up the children.

"They need someone to take care of them after I'm gone," I said.

"What do you mean after you're gone?" Edith asked. "Can't you make the … inicillin?"

"I'll try, but I have to plan for it not working. I learned how much skill it takes while I was away. I still haven't even figured out how to find the pancreas in a pig."

Edith patted my hand and said it would be fine, but the look on her face betrayed that politeness.

"I'll take them," Ralph said. "It's the right thing to do."

I hadn't realized it until then, but a sudden fear gripped me. I couldn't stand the idea of a man having Olivia alone. Ralph was a good man, willing to do the right thing. I had no reason to suspect him, but the evil had hidden itself perfectly well inside of Michael. We lived in a world where it was too easy to get away with such things.

"They need a mother," I said.

"I'd do it," Edith said. "They're wonderful children, but I'm too old. I might not last to raise Danny."

Bill and Laura sat there quietly, and no one mentioned them as the obvious choice. I suspected that they had talked to everyone before I got there. No one else volunteered or made any suggestions.

"Well we don't have to decide anything today," Ralph said. He looked relieved that I hadn't accepted his offer.

The meeting ended, and everyone went their separate ways, except for me, Olivia and Danny. I knew that I should get to work on trying to make the insulin, but with Danny and Olivia there, I could easily find excuses not to start.

I was afraid. Starting the work would mean starting the process of failing. Michael, an experienced chemist, had said it would be tricky. What chance did I have?

I thought of Michael constantly. Had I done the right thing? If I did stand before God one day, would he condemn me as a murderer? The dreams came every night. Michael carried Danny on his shoulders or helped Olivia with her schoolwork. And then, in the midst of their simple, normal life, I would barge in and shoot Michael dead.

Somehow I felt like the monster.

I took the kids to spots around Tallahassee. The park. A children's museum. I had what turned out to be a horrible idea of taking them to the zoo. We were driving around, and I turned in when we saw the sign, which had a smiling zebra. I was absentminded, thinking about what to do with the children, not about what would be in the zoo.

We walked into habitats filled with the skeletons of animals that had died of starvation. I quickly ushered the children back out, and we went to the library, which they loved. I hoped the zoo expedition hadn't scarred them. Given their experiences, it was probably nothing.

I hoped by the next get-together that someone would have a change of heart about caring for the children. We were late to the Friday meeting because I wasn't used to getting the children ready on time.

Everyone was gathered around the table, already eating. I made Danny a plate. Since he wouldn't talk, I really didn't have a sense of what he would eat, so I put a little of everything on it. Then I made myself a plate, avoiding the carbs, and sat down.

I had apparently interrupted Ralph, and he waited, watching me intently until I had myself and the children settled.

"I was just introducing everyone to a new member of our community," Ralph said. "He moved here from Savannah."

Savannah? I looked up from wiping Danny's mouth.

"Everyone, I'd like you to meet Rigby," Ralph said.

-36-

No. No. No. No. No.

I couldn't have Rigby, the car-murdering psychopath, here in Tallahassee. I looked across the table at him. He smiled and gave a little wave. He looked completely different from when I'd last seen him. Before he had been dirty, with unwashed, stringy hair. Now he was cleaned up, and his hair looked like it had been professionally cut.

"Rigby says that he can fix cars," Ralph said. "And he's happy to help anybody who needs car repairs."

Fix cars? I almost burst out laughing. He was death to cars. And why would anyone need a car to be repaired? If anything broke on your car, you could pick from any of thousands of cars just waiting in driveways.

"Batteries will be the big problem," Rigby said to the group. "They'll start to die in all the cars that are sitting unused. I recommend that you each drive many different cars. Maybe one for each day of the week. If it's okay with everyone, I'll gather a bunch of cars from around town and put them in some of the big parking garages, to keep them safe from the elements. I'll keep those running. We have to think long term. No one will ever make another car. Well, at least not in our lifetimes. We'll have to keep these running for years."

Rigby finished his speech, and Ralph said, "That sounds like a fine idea. I wouldn't have thought of it."

Everyone else murmured their agreement and seemed impressed with Rigby. I couldn't reconcile the young man I saw before me with the half-crazed boy I had seen destroy Bella. We finished lunch and everyone chatted. Olivia and Danny ate quickly and got restless, so I let them go outside to play. There was a McDonald's with a playground next door, and I could see them through the windows.

When lunch was over, I looked at a chart Ralph had made and saw it was my turn to wash the dishes. Everyone else went outside to talk and watch the children play. As I gathered the dirty plates, Rigby said, "I'll help you."

He began making a stack of plates, and I, never one for subtlety, asked, "What are you doing here?"

"You made it sound like a great place to live," Rigby said. "You have a real community here. It's better than Savannah."

"The problem with the community in Savannah was you," I said.

"Yeah. I guess that's true." He carried the stack of dishes over to the sink. Thomas had been assigned the job of filling it full of water. "But the people in Savannah would always see me as ... what I used to be. I needed a new start."

"If you wanted a new start, why did you come here? I'm here. I know what you used to be. Frankly, I don't know if you've really changed. There's more to it than getting a haircut."

"Jane cut it for me," he said.

"She hates you."

"She was happy to cut it when I told her I would leave after she did it. She's pregnant now and didn't want me anywhere near her baby."

"But why here?" I asked again.

Rigby swallowed hard and looked down at the dishes. "Because you're here."

Oh no. I didn't need this. I had children to care for. I had to find a way to make insulin. I didn't need some boy who had a crush on me getting in the way. He was a few years older than I was, but I still thought of him as a boy.

"I got you something," he said and left the room.

I poured soap in the water and began scrubbing the dishes. I don't know why we couldn't eat with paper plates and plastic utensils. There was a virtually infinite supply. But Ralph insisted on fine dining.

Rigby came back in holding a wooden box. Why do men think they can charm a woman with gifts? He held it out to me, and I wiped my wet, soapy hands on my apron. I took it from him. I should have refused, but curiosity got the better of me.

I opened the box and saw a gleaming metal horse. It seemed strange and familiar at the same time.

"It's the hood ornament from your car," Rigby said. "The Mustang."

I don't know what he expected me to feel. Gratitude? I was overwhelmed with grief at the memory of Bella. I wanted to hold it and keep it forever, and I wanted to throw it back in his face. He was the reason she was gone. The only tangible link I had to my parents, burned into a smoldering, dead heap.

I closed the box and set it on the counter. I didn't know if I would take it with me yet. Rigby stood there in awkward silence until I turned back to the dishes. He cleared the rest of the table, bringing me the utensils and glasses. He had enough sense to realize I didn't want company, and left.

I finished washing all the dishes in the cold, soapy water and left them to dry in the drain board. I put Rigby's box in my purse. It seemed wrong to leave a piece of Bella. Kyle tried to speak to me as I left, but I just held my hand up and he stopped. I didn't need any more men. I wished they would all just leave me alone.

I took the kids home and sat them down in front of a DVD of *The Lion King*, while I sat and thought at my little table. I needed to figure out how to remove a pancreas from a pig. Even Michael thought that positively identifying it would be hard. He had developed some sort of test to show the presence of insulin, but I had no idea what it was.

I slept fitfully that night. I dreamed of killing pigs and Michael, and the kids both came in when I cried out. I held them and fell back to sleep, comforted to have them near me.

When I stepped outside in the morning, seven shiny cars were parked outside, lined up along the curb. They were all convertibles, each a different color. Rigby stepped out of the green one at the end of the row.

"I got you one for each day of the week," he said. "What I said to the group is true. We really do need to keep a lot of different cars running. I asked everybody what kinds they liked. I'll get theirs later."

Once, when I was trying to figure out why I didn't really love the foster families I was in, I read a book about love languages, how different people give and receive love. Apparently Rigby's was "gift giving." I had filled out the questionnaire and added up the totals in each category. Mine was overwhelmingly "acts of service." I felt love when people did things to help me accomplish something or make my life simpler.

Rigby had done the opposite. Now he was burdening me with seven different cars to take care of. I couldn't deal with all the things I had to handle now, let alone a line of needy vehicles.

I had to put an end to this.

"Rigby," I said, and his eyes brightened.

"Yeah."

"This can't happen."

"What can't happen?" he asked, and I thought he was sincere. He really didn't know what I was talking about.

"We can't happen," I said.

His shoulders sagged, and the smile left his face. "Yeah, I figured I didn't have a chance after what I did."

I wished that I could say it wasn't that, but it was. I couldn't get over what he had done. Maybe he had really changed. Maybe he was a great guy who just had a rough time after the devastating loss from the virus. But I couldn't see past it.

"I think you can be good for the community," I said. I hoped that was true. That he wouldn't return to his old ways.

He nodded. "Yeah," he said. "Everybody thought the cars would just keep running forever. There are so many things that won't last."

Like me.

Rigby drove off in a car that I think was a Ferrari. I spent the next week reading animal anatomy books trying to get a clue how to be sure I was extracting the pancreas. I took the kids to a different place every day. The most fun we had was when I took them to Walmart and we got giant rolls of bubble wrap. We rolled them out in long strips on the floor and stomped them, hearing the tiny, snapping explosions. I was surprised at how satisfying it was.

For a moment I just wanted to smash everything. If the kids weren't there, I probably would have. For that brief time, I understood why Rigby let his anger out by destroying things.

On Friday we attended the meeting again. I came in to find Rigby and Kyle talking. They went silent when I looked at them. Everyone loved Rigby's handling of the cars. Many had gotten seven of their dream cars, and he was working on getting cars for the rest. He really did seem to know something, both about cars and pleasing people. I knew nothing about either of those subjects.

I ate the meal, barely noticing it or the conversations around me. The kids went to play, and I listened to Ralph blather on about community goals and our plans for the future. A future I wouldn't be a part of if I couldn't make the insulin.

There was a knock on the door. I figured the kids needed something. Deena got up and then came back and said, "There's a man here to see you, Sugar. He says his name is John."

-37-

I got up from the table, walked to the door and saw John standing there. He flicked a cigarette away as soon as he saw me. I didn't know what to say, so I said, "How did you find me?" Though, apparently, I was pretty easy to find.

"Oh, that was the easiest part of what I had to do," John said. "You never told me your address, but you mentioned meeting at Deena's restaurant every Friday. The GPS brought me straight here."

"Why are you here?" The last thing I needed was another man to deal with.

"I ... I don't know ... ," he stammered. "I'm not good with words. Let me just show you."

He walked to his car and got something out of the back. He turned and came back holding a box. He held it like it contained a precious jewel. Like Kyle, he probably thought I would be impressed with a necklace or some other piece of jewelry he had easily found sitting in a store.

He seemed nervous. Was he proposing? Our relationship hadn't been like that at all. I prepared myself to turn him down.

And then he opened the box.

It was the most beautiful thing I had ever seen. The most perfect gift a man could give a woman in this new world.

"Is that what I think it is?" I asked.

"Yes," John said.

Inside the box lay a wrinkled, bloody red-brown pancreas.

"I thought you wouldn't kill animals," I said.

"It was a matter of math," he said.

"What?"

"You're worth a thousand dead pigs," John said. "I'm sorry it took me so long to realize that."

"Did it take that long to make the calculation?"

"What?" he asked.

"Of how many dead pigs I'm worth. Is it exactly a thousand?"

"Oh, yeah. You don't like rounding. It came to eleven hundred and thirty-seven pigs. At eleven thirty-eight, I'm done."

He had changed himself for me. He had done something he hated so I could have a chance.

But I wasn't naïve about men anymore. There was still no guarantee he would stick around. I was going to learn, now. But I supposed I should be polite first.

"Do you want to come in and meet everyone?" I asked.

"No," he said, with a look of horror on his face.

Same old John. He hadn't changed completely, and I was glad.

"Then show me how to do it," I said.

"Do what?"

"Remove a pancreas from a pig," I said.

"Okay," he replied.

I looked at him expectantly.

"You mean now?"

"Yes."

I went back inside and asked Edith if she would watch the kids for the afternoon, and she was happy to help, as always. Olivia was cautious, but it was easy to trust an old woman. Danny went to her readily. In the back of my mind, that didn't actually seem like a good sign. He needed to be shyer around strangers.

"Um, I need to change clothes," John said. That was true. He was dressed nicely in slacks and a crisply ironed buttoned-down shirt. I had only seen him in jeans and a T-shirt with maybe a lab coat on before.

I needed to change also. "Let's just buy some clothes to work in at Walmart," I said. "We'll get an extra set to change into after the work is done."

We drove to Walmart in my car, bringing the ice-filled cooler John had used to transport the pancreas. John got a couple of pairs of jeans, some T-shirts and even a new pair of tennis shoes. I got the same in the women's department and changed in a dressing room. We bought a box of latex gloves and some goggles. He already had a full set of all the surgical tools we could possibly use.

We drove to the same pig farm I had gone to months ago. The last time I had come in fear, but now I was strangely excited.

"It will be easiest to show you on a small one," he said.

"Don't we want to use full-grown pigs with large pancreases?"

"Yeah," he said. "It will be harder, bloodier work. I thought the first few would be for practice."

"Let's try to use every one," I said. "We at least owe that to the pigs."

I knew this wasn't easy for him. We pulled up to the farmhouse, and John began to look around. He opened the barn up and found a large, solid metal table. It must have been a workbench.

"This will be perfect," he said.

"How are you going to get a three-hundred-pound pig onto that table?"

He set up some boards as a ramp.

"How are you going to get a pig to walk up that ramp?"

"I'm a vet. This is the kind of thing I do all the time."

He paused and closed his eyes for a while.

"What are you doing?"

"Remembering myself as I am now. I'm dreading doing this again, but not as much as the first one. It will get easier with time, and eventually it won't bother me at all. It was the same way with the cigarettes."

He pulled some oranges off a tree and found a medium-sized pig nearby. John coaxed it into the barn and then shut the door.

"We don't want to let the other pigs see what happens," John said. "They're actually fairly intelligent animals."

He worked and coaxed the pig, and amazingly, it climbed onto the table and lay down eating the oranges. I pulled Clint out of my purse.

"No," he said and pulled a needle out of his bag. He filled it with clear fluid that he drew up from a vial. "This stuff will run out eventually, but it's easier this way for now."

He walked over to the pig, talking calmly the entire time in the tone I recognized as his doctor's tone. He said a prayer, but I couldn't make out the words, and then he quickly injected into the pig's thick neck. It startled for a moment and then went back to eating the oranges. In a few moments, it laid its head down, and its breathing stopped.

We rolled it over onto its back. John said, "Are you ready?"

I nodded and he said, "You watch and listen the first time, and then if you're ready, do the next one yourself with me watching over."

He skillfully cut in with the scalpel, explaining every step to me. He told me things I didn't need to know, but I enjoyed listening to his expertise. He pointed out each organ and cut it out, setting it aside on the table. I couldn't believe that I could stand here amidst all the blood and stay calm, even interested.

I learned and helped him pull things out. He showed me landmarks for clearly finding the pancreas. He carefully cut it out and showed me its shape and slight color difference from the rest of the insides. He placed the pancreas in the cooler full of ice.

"Do you think you can do it?" he asked.

"I can try."

"First we need to get the body out of here and clean up. Another pig won't come in with all the blood."

We used the tractor to carry the body off far behind the barn. The farm had a well, and we hauled up water and cleaned off the table.

I lured another pig into the barn, but John had to help get it up the ramp and onto the table. Animals just seemed to trust him. He did the injection, but I handled everything else. I was far slower and got confused a few times, but I was able to find the pancreas on my own. I sliced it away from the body at just the places he showed me.

I did the next one almost completely by myself. The insides of each pig had some uniqueness, but I found my way.

"I think five should be enough to get started with," John said. "The first batch won't be about quantity, but quality. Five should give us enough to experiment with."

The sun was about to go down, so for the sake of time John did the last one. When he wasn't stopping to explain, he moved with dizzying speed, cutting in and finding the pancreas in moments. We disposed of the last body, and we both stood there covered in blood.

The old Sugar would have had a heart attack to be standing there. I remembered running to the creek by my house after I got blood on me when Kyle had slaughtered the deer on my deck.

"We should change," he said. "But we'll have to take turns washing off in the well water. You go first. I'll wait in the farmhouse. I promise I won't peek."

The well water would take forever. It would take quite a few buckets to clean all the blood off me.

"I've got a better idea," I said. "We drove over a bridge to get here. We'll put some towels down in the car seats and drive there and clean up in the river."

We threw the latex gloves away, carefully covered the seats of the car and drove to the river. We parked the car by the bridge and found our way down to the riverbank.

"You go first," John said, turning around. I took off my clothes and waded into the water. It was cold but refreshing. I scrubbed the blood off my skin and dunked my hair under the water. I had tied it up out of the way, but some blood had managed to get in it anyway.

"How's the water?" he asked with his back turned to me.

"It's cool, but it feels good," I said. It felt strange. A few weeks ago, as my doctor, he had looked at me naked, but now our relationship had changed. I'm not sure what it was, but it definitely wasn't doctor and patient anymore.

"Why don't you come on in?" I said. "The water's pretty brown, and the sun's going down. You can't see anything." I wasn't trying to flirt with him. I was enjoying the water, and I hated to make him wait there covered in blood. I looked down. I could hardly see my own body under the water.

"Are you sure?" he asked.

I nodded and waded in a little deeper so the water came to just under my shoulders.

He turned around and looked at me. "You're right," he said. "Turn around so I can take these bloody things off and hop in."

I didn't turn around.

"Um ... ," he said while he took off his shirt. He had a farmer's tan.

"You've seen every inch of me," I said. "I think we should be even. Then no more nudity after that."

I was just playing with him, but he dropped his shorts and leapt into the water, splashing me with river water. I was so shocked that I don't know that I really saw anything.

"Are we even now?" he asked.

"Even," I said. We both got clean and enjoyed the water, standing about ten feet from each other.

"It looks like your scars are healing nicely," he said.

The very tops of my breasts were just out of the water, and he could see the scar. "I had a good doctor," I said. It felt good to have hope again. With Michael it had seemed certain that we could make the insulin, and then those hopes were destroyed. Well, I destroyed them.

"What do you think my chances are?" I asked.

"Of what?"

"Of successfully extracting the insulin."

"Oh. Yeah. We've got time. That's the main thing on our side. The steps were pretty intimidating, but we'll just keep at it. Just keeping slaughtering pigs and removing pancreases and extracting the insulin until it works."

"You said 'we.'"

"Sure," John said. "If I'm going to be a pig killer, it's going to be for a reason. I'm here through the whole process." He looked at me. "If that's okay with you."

It was okay with me.

-38-

John slept on my couch that night. With the kids there, my little house was already cramped. Olivia and Danny slept in the only other bedroom. I thought about moving to a larger house, but I loved Rosy too much to leave. John made sure the children knew nothing about his smoking. He slipped out quietly, and I think he walked at least two or three houses down each time.

John moved into the house next door the next day, but it only took him a couple of hours to get settled. We had five pancreases on ice and needed to get started. The kids stayed with Edith during the day while John and I went to work on extracting the insulin.

"You understand that this will be a lot of trial and error," he said. "Expect to fail many times. We have the time."

I nodded. I was nervous. After so long we were actually starting the process. The first thing we needed, that the chemistry lab at FSU didn't have, was a meat grinder to finely mince up the pancreases. We found a butcher shop, and John detached the grinder. We would do all our work and keep everything at the chemistry lab.

Next we bought a generator from Kyle's Home Depot and set it up in the chemistry lab. The building was large so we couldn't just hook the generator up to it. We would have to connect it to a power strip and run each piece of equipment from that.

With the generator and meat grinder set up, we were finally ready to get started.

"Are you ready?" John asked.

I nodded. My entire life depended on this.

John closed his eyes and said a quick prayer. "Lord, be with us in this. Guide our hands and increase our understanding."

"I've never seen you pray when taking care of the animals, or me for that matter."

"I should have, but I didn't because I knew what I was doing. It was arrogance," he said. "I guess God wanted to put me somewhere where I'd learn a little humility."

"So I guess you believe in God then?"

"Yeah. You don't?"

"I don't know," I said. "If he created it, this world's a pretty horrible place. I've seen that lately." I thought of Michael. "And he just let billions of people die. None of the religious people have been able to explain that to me. It doesn't make any sense. Ralph talks about judgment. Edith talks about his love and mercy."

"Yeah, it's pretty hard to see that right now," John said. "I don't get it."

"What?"

"I don't get it. It doesn't make any sense to me."

I'd never met a religious person who didn't try to explain everything. He wasn't trying to sell God to me.

"He's God," John said. "He doesn't have to explain himself to us. He's done this before."

"What?"

"The flood," John said. "He's done it before. We shouldn't act surprised that he did it again."

I found his honesty refreshing. If there was a God, then maybe he didn't always go around explaining things to people. We just had to deal with the world as it was, and right now that meant extracting insulin so I could keep living in this world he had made.

The second step on the list said to finely mince the pancreases in the meat grinder, so we did just that. I ran them through a few times. "Does that look finely minced?" I asked, holding the pancreases up in a bowl.

"I guess so," he said.

So much of this relied on vague terms. Or maybe they were precise, but we didn't understand the technical definitions of words. We would just have to do it over and over again until it worked.

The next part was a little scary since it involved working with acid. "It says five ccs of concentrated sulfuric acid per pound of glands. How much is a cc?" I asked, feeling stupid. I hadn't thought to look that up.

"It's a milliliter."

I needed to weigh the pancreases. The only scales in the lab were electronic, so I had to start the generator. It was far out in the hall, so it could vent the exhaust safely. I pulled the cord, and it sputtered to life. Then I hooked the scale up to the power strip connected to the generator.

The pancreas pulp weighed 1.23 pounds. "That means we need six point one five milliliters of acid."

I cautiously picked up the bottle of sulfuric acid, took the stopper off the top and was about to pour it into a measuring beaker when John yelled, "Wait!," which scared me and nearly made me spill the acid.

I carefully put the bottle down. "What?"

"The scale you used is measuring in kilograms," he said. "And did you zero it out with the bowl first so it didn't include the weight of the bowl?"

"No." I didn't know what I was doing.

We poured the pancreases into another bowl, changed the scale to pounds and zeroed it out on the glass bowl we would use for pouring in the acid. My simple mistake would have cost us the day and the entire batch of pancreases, which would have taken another day to collect.

"Two point four two pounds," I said. "That's twelve point one milliliters of acid."

"Hold on," John said.

What had I done now?

"We're working with acid. We need to have safety precautions ready."

He was right. I had nearly spilled the acid on myself when he yelled for me to wait. We looked up the first aid for sulfuric acid burns on one of the many posters around the room. It said to use a mild soapy solution and to flush the burn with it. The water didn't run in the lab, but we had brought a lot of bottled waters. I'm glad we read the first aid instructions. Apparently pouring straight water on a sulfuric acid burn can make it worse because the acid reacts with water.

We found liquid soap in a bathroom and made a bucket of soapy water and kept it nearby. I put on rubber gloves and poured the acid into the glass bowl with the pancreases. The instructions said to stir the mixture for three to four hours.

"How do we know which it is?" I asked.

"What do you mean?"

"Is it three or four hours or in between?"

"I know you like to be precise, but everything isn't like that."

"Then how do we know when it's done?"

"When it looks all dissolved."

"What do we stir it with?" I guess we should have figured that out first. We couldn't use just anything because it might dissolve in the acid. I found a drawer conveniently labeled "Stirring Rods" and took out a glass rod about the size of a drinking straw.

"Do we stir it continuously?" I asked.

"I don't think so," John said with less confidence than I wanted him to have. "Just every few minutes so the acid can work through and dissolve the pancreases."

We took turns stirring and reading the next steps and setting up everything we would need. I noticed that I hadn't seen John smoke all day.

"Don't you need a cigarette?" I asked.

"I'm gonna quit. I don't want the kids to see it."

"That's admirable, but I need you to be a hundred percent. Withdrawal can be bad."

"I can handle it."

"Don't handle it now. Do it later. After we figure this out."

He hesitated, but turned and went outside. When he came back, reeking of the smell I had somehow almost grown fond of, I said, "Look at step eight. How do we 'practically neutralize the filtrate with NaOH'?"

I had the NaOH, sodium hydroxide, ready and set out on the counter.

"We need to be able to measure the pH level," John said. "Sodium hydroxide is a base to cancel out the acid."

John found a pH meter, an electronic device with a long probe. "It's neutral when the pH is seven point zero," he said and began to lecture about the pH scale.

I knew it from my research, but I let him talk anyway. I looked through the rest of the steps while he explained. When he was finished, I said, "Step twenty-four is the big one."

John looked at the list. "'Let it sit in an ice chest for a week.' That's the easiest part," he said.

"That's the part that burns time."

"We have time," he said. "More than a hundred weeks before we have to start worrying."

That was easy for him to say. I was already worrying.

"We can use that week for resupplying," John said. "We'll use up chemicals and materials in here. And, of course, we'll need to get more pancreases."

"Should we get multiple batches going at once?" I asked.

"Not at first. There's too many things we don't know. I think we would waste our time pointlessly repeating things before we've figured out if we did the steps right."

While we stirred and waited, we discussed the next step. We had to add alcohol to the mixture until the concentration of alcohol reached 60 to 70 percent. John was a little confused on that, but I explained the simple math of it.

At three hours and fifteen minutes, we guessed that it looked properly dissolved. We measured the volume of the pancreas and acid mixture, and then carefully added the correct volume of alcohol to get about a 65 percent concentration.

Then we got to use the centrifuge. It would separate the solid material by spinning rapidly. We connected it to the power strip and poured the solution into glass tubes and put them in the centrifuge. The instructions just said to "centrifuge the mixture," but the machine had a number of options on it, the most important being the rpms. We didn't know what to set it to, so we picked what looked like a standard setting.

It was these dozens of little decisions that worried me. Each one had the potential to mess things up, and sometimes we wouldn't even know if we had made a mistake.

We ran the centrifuge for a while, again guessing at the amount of time. When we took the tubes out, there was definitely a separation of materials. We removed the solid materials and poured the liquid through filter paper. Then we had to neutralize the solution.

John measured the pH with the meter, and I carefully added sodium hydroxide until it reached a perfect 7.0.

I felt good. We were making progress. It was getting late in the afternoon and would soon get dark, but we had to keep going. We could set up lights connected to the generator. I didn't know if we could just stop and pick up in the morning. The solution may not sit and wait for us. Whatever chemical processes were happening in it would keep going. The insulin molecules might break down. We had to reach step twenty-four, cooling in ice for a week.

We struggled to figure out the vacuum concentrator, but after an hour we got it working. It concentrated the filtrate to a fraction of its original volume.

"Next is says to heat the concentrate to fifty degrees Celsius," I said. "I have no idea how to convert that to Fahrenheit."

"Add thirty-two and then multiply by nine-fifths," John said.

"That would be a hundred forty-seven point six," I said. John was still amazed at my mathematical abilities.

We heated the concentrate to 147 degrees, which the instructions said would result in "separation of lipoid and other materials." We were about to remove those by more filtration when John once again said, "Wait."

"What now?"

"I did the temperature conversion wrong."

"Are you sure?"

"No," he said. "Zero degrees Celsius is thirty-two degrees Fahrenheit, and a hundred Celsius is two hundred twelve Fahrenheit."

"Then it would be multiply by nine-fifths and add thirty-two," I said.

"Then we got it too hot," he said.

"I think it will be okay."

"But we don't know for sure." He thought a moment. "I think we have to start over."

"What? No." That would mean we had just wasted everything, including our time.

"Do you want to continue with a possibly imperfect sample?" he asked.

I took a deep breath. "No," I said.

"We knew we would make mistakes. It's best to catch them before the weeklong wait. We learned a lot today."

"Okay," I said, disappointed with our first failure.
John looked me in the eyes. "We have time," he said.

-39-

I took off the next day, a Sunday, to spend time with the kids. John set up a simple vet practice in his home. His first patient was Fluffy, and since he lived next door, I got John to take over the dog's care. He wanted to start feeding local animals, but I didn't want them all around my house, especially with the kids there. My dog attack had taught me that lesson. The world we lived in was becoming wilder and more dangerous.

I started to wonder about the kids' education. Michael had taught them traditional school lessons. Danny, of course, needed to learn to read and write. That would be needed in any society. I wanted to teach the kids how to think in numbers, not the moronic way math was taught in schools where you follow mindless algorithms without really understanding the numbers themselves.

I had spent so many hours fruitlessly arguing with teachers that it didn't matter *how* I got the answer if I got it right. They had wanted me to show my work. Sometimes I didn't even know how I got the answer to simple arithmetic problems. I just felt it. I couldn't explain the geography of numbers that I saw in my head.

But Olivia was twelve. Did she need to learn the useless skills that they used to teach sixth graders? What would our world need? Farmers first of all. As the population grew, the supplies in stores wouldn't last. And who wanted to eat canned and boxed foods forever? I was certainly getting tired of them.

I didn't see how I could educate the kids and still work on the insulin. The extraction process was obviously going to take nearly our full time. I'd have to make do. I'd read to them and ask Edith to do things that stimulated their minds while she babysat, but I was no good to them dead. And, frankly, a year or so delay in their education wasn't devastating. There were no tests to prepare for or other students to compare with.

The next day John and I extracted (a cold word for the bloody process) five more pancreases. We followed the same routine of bathing in the brown river, but this time I turned my back when he got in. We brought soap and got completely clean. I had grown used to the blood, but that didn't mean I wanted it on me all the time.

We waited until the next day to start the insulin extraction process, so we wouldn't have to work late into the night. We began early in the morning and got to step nine, using the vacuum concentrator, before making a mistake. We didn't know how to use the equipment and spilled the sample.

"We need to start taking notes on everything," John said. "One day we'll do it all right, and we want to be able to repeat the process."

I got a stack of notebooks, and we began taking the notes. We even got a video camera and a hundred memory cards and recorded each step. Not the long ones, like stirring the acid solution for three hours, but each important part of the process.

We began a pattern. One day to extract the pancreases. One day to experiment with the process until we messed something up, and then one day for me to spend with the kids and for John to help whatever animals in the area needed his attention. I realized that John's day with the animals was also his day away from people. He needed the space, and I completely understood how he felt.

We took Sundays off. John attended Ralph's church the first Sunday. Then I decided it would be good for the kids, so I started going with them. Ralph loved having children there, and the tone of his sermons changed completely. It used to be all hellfire and brimstone and God's judgment for our sins. With Olivia and Danny there, he told stories from the Bible. Some I knew. Some I had never heard.

He didn't skip any parts for the sake of the children. If the story included something gory or weird, he told it as it was. There is some pretty strange stuff in the Bible. It made interesting conversation topics for John and me, which we needed with the long hours we spent together.

Ralph would preach on some insane story, like Lot offering his two virgin daughters to the townspeople of Sodom, and then we would have something to discuss on Monday. Monday was pig day. We talked while we worked and then bathed in the river.

I could stand to talk religion with John because he never tried to sell it to me. If something didn't make sense to him, he said so. The Lot story confused him also. He thought it was a vile thing for Lot to do.

"I'm not in to having kids" he said, "but if I were, I certainly wouldn't treat them like that. Your family is above all else."

One Sunday, Ralph told the mythical story of Adam and Eve and their nakedness in the garden. Like them, John and I were beginning to develop a casualness about our bodies. The clarity of the river varied, and some days you could see more than other days. He still turned when I came in and out of the water, but I didn't even bother turning when he did. The nakedness of a man to a woman is completely different than a woman's to a man.

As the weather grew cooler, bathing in the river was no longer an option, and I missed it. I couldn't quite say what I missed. It wasn't a big turn-on. Well, not for me. Sometimes it obviously turned John on, but he never acted on it.

Kyle and I had been lovers. Our relationship was primarily sexual. Michael and I had, in a way, been a mother and father. I had wanted to move it forward, but thank God, it hadn't progressed much.

John and I were partners. It doesn't sound like an intimate word, but it is. We were focused on the same goal. He had given up his life to pursue this with me. I wasn't ready to have a romantic relationship with him, for two reasons.

One, we could easily fail and then I would die. It would be cruel to add romance to our relationship. I knew we were becoming attached, but adding that element would hurt even more when I was gone.

Two, our relationship was stable now. I had learned the hard way that romance is anything but stable. I needed John's help, and I couldn't have anything jeopardize that.

So John and I lived and worked as partners. He had even begun spending some time with Olivia and Danny, and partnering with me in their education. They were fascinated by his veterinary work. I figured they couldn't be getting a more practical education than that.

I decided to tell John about their past, including what had happened with Michael. I brought it up when he came back in from smoking, while I was once again stirring the solution for three hours.

"You did the right thing," he said.

I was scared that he would think I was a murderer. The image of Michael lying on the floor with a bullet wound in his chest still haunted me at night. I would cry out, and the kids would wake up and come in to sleep in the bed with me.

"Did … ," John started to say, but hesitated.

"What? Just ask it." I didn't have any secrets from him.

"Did anything happen to you in the foster system like what happened to Michael?"

"No," I said. "I had good foster parents. I was a bad foster kid. Not bad in a disobedient way, usually. I just didn't connect with any of the families. They never seemed like my real mom and dad."

"Even though you lost them so young?"

"Six isn't young when it comes to losing your parents. I still remember them. Clearly. They formed the core of who I was."

This made me sad for Danny, knowing his core had been formed under such horror.

"How did they die?" he asked.

I didn't answer for a few moments, thinking. "Are you sure you want to know?"

"You don't have to tell me."

"No," I said. "It's okay. They both worked in a lab."

"Like this one?"

"I assume so, but I don't know. It was high security, so I wasn't ever allowed to go there."

"Does the lab have something to do with how they died?" he asked.

"Yes," I said. "They developed it, and they were the first killed by it."

"Developed what?"

I paused a moment and took a breath. "The virus," I said.

The look of surprise and horror on John's face was too much for me, and I burst out laughing.

"That's a little sick," he said, but he was smiling.

"I'm sorry," I said. "I just wanted to see if I could get you to believe it."

I finished laughing, stirring the solution while I did. He rolled his eyes. He stood close to me, watching the solution. I took in the smell of him. Sweat and smoke.

It sounds awful, but somehow I found it comforting. We took turns with the laundry, and one day, when it was my turn, I left one of his shirts out, unwashed, and kept it in my closet. Just smelling it made me feel better sometimes.

"The truth is rather ordinary," I said. "My father died in a car accident. We got a little insurance money, and my mom set up the trust fund. She went to work, but got cancer and died within a year."

"So they didn't have anything to do with the virus that killed billions of people?"

"No," I said. "That was some other people or God."

"Well God's certainly responsible," John said. "Something that big has to be in his plan."

"I get what you see in God now, but I still don't know if I believe. Especially in one so specific like you believe in."

"What doesn't work for you?" he asked.

"All the dumb rules," I said. "Why would the God of the whole universe care so much about how people act? He supposedly has rules about when you can work and what you can say and who you can sleep with."

I set the stirring rod down, carefully, since we were working with acid. "Ralph clearly didn't approve when Kyle and I were together without ever getting married. What was the harm? Why have rules about sexual relationships? It's a cultural thing. Different things are okay for different peoples at different times."

"I'd say what Michael did was never okay," John said.

That stopped me cold. He couldn't convince me that everything from two thousand years ago still applied today, but that one was absolute.

"Do you believe in marriage?" I asked him.

"Yeah. I do."

"Even nowadays with all the trappings of civilization gone? Bill and Laura had Ralph marry them. He just sort of declared it."

"Promises matter," he said. "And they mean more when they're backed up by something. When you invest in something, it makes it harder to walk away from it. That's where the ring tradition came from. A man proves he's committed to a relationship by giving something that cost him a lot. Like a diamond ring."

Or a pancreas.

-40-

Remember when I made fun of people who worried about the winter, and I thought they were stupid for not just coming down to Florida? Well I completely take that back. There are some good reasons not to live in Florida.

Some very, very good reasons.

John and I progressed steadily in working with extracting the insulin. With every step, we had to research and experiment. In February we finally made it to step twenty-four, which involved leaving the mixture in an ice chest for a week, so now every attempt burned at least eight days off the calendar.

My research had shown that the potency of the insulin was measured by testing it on rabbits. A unit of insulin is defined as one-third of the amount of material required to lower the blood sugar of a two-kilogram rabbit, which had fasted twenty-four hours, from its normal level of 0.118 percent to 0.045 percent over a period of five hours.

While we waited for the solution in the ice chest, we trapped rabbits and soon had a few to work with, and if nature took its natural course, we would have more than we could handle. I had speculated that rabbit might taste good, but John and the kids had grown attached.

In April we made it to the final step, still having no idea if the insulin actually worked. I sat nervously holding a precious vial of the clear liquid, and we drove home and put it in Bertha, along with all the other vials. That evening we isolated the rabbit closest to 2.0 kilograms and didn't feed it anything, which the kids seemed to think was cruel. Exactly twenty-four hours later, we measured the blood sugar of the rabbit, and then John injected it. We waited until eleven o'clock, five hours later, and measured the rabbit's blood sugar again.

It had barely lowered at all.

"That amount is probably due to normal body processes," John said.

Disappointment washed over me. "So our insulin did nothing?" I asked.

He nodded. I stood there, and for the first time, John pulled me close and held me tight.

"What did we do wrong?" I asked.

"It could be anything. We could have left it alkaline too long. Insulin is destroyed in an alkaline solution."

"What do we do?"

"We keep trying," he said. "We still have more than a year. Now we know all the steps. We can do more than one batch at a time, and we try different variations on each batch. We still have time."

There were hundreds of variables to control, and we didn't know which ones needed to change. Michael had seemed so confident that he could do it, but this was what he had done for a living. I had probably killed the only chemist left in the country. I didn't know what the numbers were, but I figured there had to be far fewer chemists than doctors, and we hadn't been able to find a doctor.

The year was quickly turning hot, but John and I didn't resume our baths at the river after extractions on the farm. Those had been done in playful, less worrisome times. Now we drove home from the farm, bloody and sweaty, and immediately set to work. We had gone through quite a lot of pigs, and now we didn't bother with coaxing them onto the table in the barn. The pigs ranged far and wide around the farmhouse. We simply found them, shot them once clean in the head and cut them open.

I could remove a pig's pancreas with my eyes closed.

Michael had figuratively said that my hands would be covered in blood, but his prophecy had been literally fulfilled. We always had a few batches in an ice chest and more in preparation. We sat in the lab late at night with blood in our hair, meticulously reviewing notes and watching videos, looking for something we had done wrong or something we could do differently.

On May 1, Bill pounded on my door at 2 am. Laura had gone into labor, and he didn't know who else could help. I went next door and woke John, and we drove over. John masterfully helped with the birth, and his confidence helped calm the frightened parents down. Laura had been given drugs on her previous two deliveries and had never experienced the full pain of childbirth.

It was enough to convince me that it was something I never wanted to go through. I could handle blood now and assisted John, which in an uneventful birth is mainly just playing catcher. The baby, a healthy boy, came into the world screaming and bloody, but I cleaned him up and had him in his mother's arms before the sun came up.

A few weeks later, on a Monday in late May, we once again drove to the farm. Ralph had preached on Cain and Abel the previous day. John and I talked about it as the now-familiar road passed by. I couldn't understand why Cain's offering of fruit wasn't acceptable to God. In a lot of the stories, it seemed like God played favorites. Sort of the whole point of the Old

Testament seemed to be that he just picked Israel as his favorite nation and let them slaughter everybody else.

Was I one of God's favorites, or was I just going to be used as an example to the righteous?

"We're going to have to find a new farm soon," John said, changing the subject. "We need to let this population rebuild."

We parked near the farmhouse under the large tree, like always, and prepared to hike around to find the donors. The pigs tended to congregate near some orange and pear trees, so we walked over to a far one across a pasture that we hadn't been to before. Four pigs lay under the tree. We had to approach cautiously since they were beginning to suspect us.

The pears weren't ripe yet, but the pigs didn't seem to care. I held the pears in my hands so they let us near. I dropped the pears in the middle of the group, and then I pulled Clint out and shot them each in the head, quickly and cleanly. I had become quite a good shot. I had practiced a bit because I hated the idea of not getting a clean kill and causing the pigs to suffer.

John was a lousy shot. He had practiced with me a few times, but was always obviously uncomfortable with it. Once his lethal injections ran out, I did all the killing.

The hardest part was rolling them over. John and I strained and got each on their backs. We each had a medical bag with scalpels and tools, and John also carried the cooler. I picked my two pigs, and then John said, "One, two, three, go." We raced to see who could get the extractions done first. John won, as he usually did, but I was only a few seconds behind him.

As I placed the pancreas in the cooler, a clap of thunder sounded and shook the world. I looked up. The sky had begun to turn dark.

"Let's get home," John said. "Four is enough."

As we walked back across the pasture, the rain came swiftly, and within minutes we were pelted with raindrops. We ran the last hundred yards and slammed the door of the farmhouse behind us, each soaking wet. I had left the convertible top down, so our changes of clothes were soaked also.

"We're not driving home in this weather," John said. "I guess we'll just hang out here until it's over."

Florida has regular quick afternoon showers. So we waited in the kitchen, dripping onto the floor and looking out the window for the storm to abate. The sky grew darker, so I found some candles and matches and lit them around the room. After about half an hour, we realized it was getting worse and that we might be here for a while.

I was shivering and John said, "Let's go find something dry to wear."

I was wearing a soaking wet T-shirt and had given up wearing a bra since the dog attack, so my shirt clung to me and showed everything, almost like I wasn't wearing one. When he looked at me, John kept his eyes on mine, but if he stole a glance when I wasn't looking, I didn't mind.

We found towels and a change of clothes for John. The man who had lived here must have been about John's size, but the woman was apparently a large woman, and nothing of hers was even close to fitting me. I grabbed one of the man's button-down shirts, stepped into the bathroom, toweled off and put the shirt on. It came to just below my hips.

I came out, and John had already changed, wearing jeans and a shirt similar to the one I had on. Wood was stacked by the hearth, and John put it in the fireplace and crumpled some newspaper underneath. He lit it and the wood, which had been drying for two years, quickly caught the flame.

We sat by the fire and warmed ourselves as the storm raged. "I guess we'll open some cans for dinner," John said. "We can heat them over the fire."

"Uh, oh," I said when I thought of dinner.

"What?"

"I'll need insulin, and it's in my purse."

"Okay."

"Which is in the car."

"Oh," John said. The storm was violent with winds blowing hard. We could hear some tree limbs crack occasionally. He stood up and walked to the front door. "I'll run for it."

I should have been the one to go get it. It was my insulin. But I liked him braving the storm for me. That thought warmed me more than the fire.

He opened the door and ran to the car. The rain was so thick and the sky so dark now that I couldn't see him or the car just fifteen feet away. In a few seconds he came back in carrying my purse, his shirt soaked.

"Let's get you out of that wet shirt," I said. Before he could move to go get another shirt, I unbuttoned his shirt and slipped it off him.

I know what I had said before about not letting anything happen with John, but that theory didn't stand up next to the dark and the fire and the storm blowing outside, while I felt safe and secure with John beside me. I took a towel and dried off his chest and back.

I took my purse and got a vial and a syringe. "Why don't you give the injection," I said. "If I remember right, you're great at it."

I handed him the vial and syringe. I could have easily unbuttoned just the two buttons over my belly, but that's not what I did. I looked John in the eyes and unbuttoned the shirt I was wearing from the top to the bottom.

"What ... what time is it?" he asked, pointing at my stomach.

"Three o'clock," I said, but that wasn't true. I was due for an injection at the six o'clock site. He pushed the shirt aside at my belly to try to reveal the three o'clock site, but he couldn't easily hold it out of the way and pinch the skin with one hand and give the injection with another.

"Will you hold the shirt out of the way there?" he asked.

"Sure," I said and pushed the shirt completely away on the right side, revealing my right breast in all its unscarred glory. I'm not sure what he thought was happening at the moment. Maybe he thought I was casual since he had seen me before, and we had grown comfortable with each other when bathing in the river. Then he could only catch fleeting glances through murky water. In a few moments, I'd make sure he didn't have any doubt.

He injected the insulin quickly and smoothly, and then set the syringe and vial down on the coffee table. I didn't cover myself back up and stood there, nervous. He had seen my scarred breast before, but it had been as a doctor.

I didn't want him to see me with a doctor's eyes now.

I let the shirt fall, and he looked at me in the firelight. He put his right hand to my collarbone and traced the scar with his fingertips, down my chest, over my breast and across the nipple. I had little actual feeling in the scar, but just the thought of his hands on me made me shiver. His hands moved to where I did have feeling, and my whole body trembled.

Then we heard the crack of the great tree outside as it fell and crashed onto the house.

-41-

John pushed me back and shielded me with his body as the tree smashed through the house. Glass and wood shattered through the room. Branches of the tree pinned John against me, and me to the wall.

The storm still raged, and a torrent of water poured down on us through what used to be the roof. I struggled to breathe with John crushed up against me. John put his hands on the wall and pushed. I heard branches snap against his back.

He tried to say something, but I couldn't hear over the wind and water and my blood pumping. He pulled my arm hard, and I was tugged through the tree, branches scraping at my bare back, chest and legs.

I heard "house" and "down" as he continued to pull me out. I wanted to stop under the porch, which still had a roof that shielded a little from the rain, but he kept pulling. As we stepped off the porch, the rest of the house collapsed.

I had stood outside before in many storms, but I'd never felt winds like this before. The raindrops stung like needles, and I could hardly stand up. We ran to the barn, falling in the mud and getting back up several times before making it through the opening where the door had once been.

We moved to the back, out of the rain, and a mother pig and several piglets scooted out of our way. John sat down hard on the ground, exhausted. He had a large bleeding gash in his back.

"Wait here," I said, and I ran back out into the storm and to the farmhouse. I went to what I thought had been the kitchen. Under the rubble, the kitchen table amazingly still stood, and after some digging, I found one of our medical bags.

I ran back to the barn where John stood, about to follow me. I sat him down and said, "You've got a bleeding wound on your back. I need to stitch it closed." I had seen John do it several times when treating animals and me, but I had never done it myself.

"Don't worry about me," he said.

"You can't protect me if you die of blood loss or infection," I said. "Lie down and talk me through it."

I cleaned the glass and wood out of the wound and then disinfected the cut with alcohol, which must have burned, but John didn't scream. Then I disinfected the needle and thread with the alcohol. "Okay. I'm ready."

"Get the mirror out of the bag so I can see it."

"There isn't one."

"Are you sure?"

"I can see everything in the bag," I said. "There isn't a mirror, but my phone is in there." Clint was also tucked in safely at the bottom.

"So?"

"So I can take pictures or video and show you."

I took a shot of the wound and held the phone up for John to see.

"You'll need to do a few subcutaneous stitches first."

"What's that mean?"

"Under the skin."

John zoomed in on the picture and showed where to put the stitches. John described the technique. I set my phone up to record a video and pushed the needle into where he indicated, in the deep bleeding center of the wound, and drew the thread back out. He watched the video and told me what I had done wrong. I pulled the thread out and tried again. He watched the second video and said it was good enough. I repeated the process three more times, closing up the inside of the wound.

"For the skin, start at the top," he said, "and put the needle in about two millimeters from the wound edge. Put it in at a ninety-degree angle. Don't worry about making it pretty. Just hold the wound closed without overtightening."

I used a tool that looked like needle-nose pliers to hold the curved needle and thread it through his skin. I showed him the video and he nodded. "Keep going," he said. I worked my way down the wound, stopping every second stitch to show him the progress with a picture.

"Tie it off with a square knot," he said.

"I was never a Boy Scout or a sailor."

He slowly moved his arms up from his side and took some thread, showing me how to tie a square knot. I tied off the wound and disinfected it again with a small amount of alcohol.

John cautiously sat up and said, "Good job," and then, "Man, I could use a cigarette."

For what seemed like the thousandth time, I again washed blood off my hands. We were both shirtless and covered in mud. John had on jeans, and I only had on a pink pair of panties.

"Do you think the barn will withstand the storm?" I asked.

"It's a hurricane," he said. "But I think this will hold up. There are no trees nearby to fall on it."

I silently said an actual prayer that we and the children would be safe. It was the first time I had prayed since begging for my life when the virus struck.

John found an old blanket and wrapped it around me. He cleared out an area in the dirt and found several pieces of wood to build a fire. He found a gasoline can and was able to get the fire started with a little bit of gas and the spark from banging two metal tools together. We sat by the fire with the mother and little pigs huddled in a corner, afraid of both the fire and the weather.

An hour passed with no change in the storm. John looked over at me. "Are you okay?"

"It's just been a tough evening." I had thought it would turn out much better. I had been ready to give myself to John.

"No," he said. "You look bad."

"Thanks," I said. What did he expect?

He opened the blanket and put his hand flat on my chest. What did he want? I was too exhausted to make love now.

"Your skin is pale, and your heart rate is accelerated," John said in his doctor tone. "Your blood sugar is low. You're exhibiting signs of hypoglycemia. I injected the insulin, and you haven't had anything to eat since. On top of that you've experienced high stress."

That was putting it mildly. I should have recognized the signs, but my brain was fuzzy.

"We have to get you some sugar quickly," he said. He looked around the barn and saw nothing to eat. "I'll go check at the farmhouse and see if there's any food in the rubble."

"It's pitch-dark now," I said, "and there's a hurricane blowing outside."

"You have to have something. Now."

And then he looked over at the mother pig and the babies snuggled up to her.

"That's all protein," I said. "I need sugar. Carbohydrates."

"Not the meat," he said. "The milk." He walked over to the pigs. "Let's get the milk flowing." He clapped his hands loudly, and the piglets woke up and started rooting for milk. John grabbed a metal pan and carefully put it under a teat. When he touched the pig, she started and thrashed, kicking hard, nearly knocking him off his feet. He tried again with the same results.

He stepped away and let the pigs calm down again and resume nursing. After a few minutes he said, "Forgive me," and reached for a large knife hanging on a pegboard of tools.

"Will the milk flow if she's dead?" I asked.

John paused. "Good point," he said. "I could get some out, but maybe not enough. She needs to be sedated."

"Do you have sedatives?"

"No, but I've got the next best thing." He put the knife back and found a shovel. He held it up and approached slowly. He seemed to consider the amount of force to use and then in one swift motion, he brought the shovel down on the mother pig's head. She flinched and the piglets squealed, but she didn't move after that.

John grabbed a teat and carefully worked it to release a small amount of milk. He brought it over to me, and I drank the sweet milk. He repeated that on the other teats (I think I counted twelve), sometimes pulling hungry piglets off.

"You're still going to need something to eat. I don't want you going all night without food." He rummaged around the barn but found nothing. The hurricane still battered the world outside, and it was too dangerous to go out. We didn't have a blood sugar meter so we would have to go by feel.

He picked up the knife again and grabbed a squealing piglet and took it over behind the tractor. I heard what sounded like a whispered prayer, and then the squealing stopped. In a few minutes, he came back with strips of raw meat. He put them in the same pan and cooked them over the fire, holding the pan with the shovel.

I ate the meat greedily, feeling profane to do it in front of the piglet's mother and siblings. He cut and cooked more meat. We ate some and saved the rest for in the morning. I began to feel better as my blood sugar reached a normal level.

"I'll stay awake and watch to see if anything happens with the hurricane," John said. "You try to get some sleep. Hopefully it will be done by the morning, and we can get home."

"Do you think Olivia and Danny are okay?" I asked. Tallahassee was south of us, and the storm would be stronger closer to the ocean. We had left them with Edith, like we usually did.

"Edith has a good, sturdy old house," John said. "It's gone through plenty of hurricanes before this one."

"Hold me," I said.

John came over and sat down beside me. I opened the blanket, put my arms around him and wrapped us both up. I fell asleep with my head against his chest.

-42-

I woke with the first light of dawn. The hurricane had passed, and the world was quiet. We ate the rest of the meat and stepped out of the barn to survey the devastation. The farmhouse had nearly completely collapsed. We rummaged through the rubble. John found a shirt for me to wear. I dropped the blanket and put the top on.

I found my purse, which had two vials of insulin in it, but one had been broken. I didn't inject. Low blood sugar was more dangerous than high. I'd wait until we had some carbohydrates.

The hood of my car was smashed in with a large branch and wasn't drivable. I didn't grieve this car for a moment. It meant nothing to me. I could only think about getting back to the children.

"We'll walk down the road until we find a car that's drivable," John said. He carried the medical bag, and I carried my purse. We couldn't find any shoes for me, so I walked barefoot, staying in the grass on the side of the road.

Trees were down everywhere. Some completely blocking the road. We passed several homes in the morning, but they either didn't have cars, or the cars wouldn't start. One of the cars was flipped completely upside down. At one of the homes, we opened some cans and had lunch after I injected. I put on a pair of shoes and socks. I don't think I could have made it much farther without them.

Around noon we finally found a home with a truck that would start. John drove and I rubbed my sore feet. The drive back to Tallahassee was slow, because we had to drive around fallen trees and other debris.

We drove over the bridge spanning the river where we used to bathe. It had swollen far beyond its old banks. The normally gentle water rushed under us. I longed to be able to call and get assurance that the kids were okay. From now on, we would have to get portable radios that would let us keep in touch with the children.

As we approached Tallahassee, I surveyed the damage. Power lines were down all over, and the irrelevance of that fact made me laugh for a brief moment. Many roofs were stripped bare of shingles. Trees and limbs and trash were strewn everywhere. Falling trees had smashed a few houses.

I was saddened to realize it would stay this way for a very long time with no crews of workers to clean up like they had after a dozen past hurricanes. We drove straight to Edith's house, and I was relieved to see it relatively unscathed: shingles missing, shutters torn off and one window broken.

John pulled into the driveway. Olivia and Danny came running out, nearly knocking me down as I stepped out of the truck and opened my arms to hug them both. Edith followed slowly behind them.

"I was so worried about you, Sugar," she said.

"We were worried about you and the kids," I said.

"This old house can take anything Mother Nature has to throw at her. The kids were scared, but we made it. And now you're here and everything is fine."

It did feel fine. Everyone I cared about was okay.

John and I took the kids to the mall, and we all bought new clothes. Even though it was in a huge, sturdy building, I was worried about the chemistry lab at FSU, so we stopped by, since it was on the way to my house.

The campus had seen better days, but the buildings were all standing, minus quite a few windows and doors. The chemistry lab, in the heart of the building, was untouched, and I breathed a sigh of relief.

"Let's head home now," I said. We were all exhausted and needed to sleep. I don't think John had slept all night long. I had held on to him all night, and every time I stirred and looked up, he smiled down at me.

John drove us in the truck back to my side of town, which by the looks of things had taken a harder beating. We stopped at a convenience store, and he bought a pack of cigarettes and then smoked one out back, where the kids couldn't see. I'd probably have to go to Kyle's Home Depot and get shingles and whatever other repair materials were needed. Kyle would be the perfect person to do the repair work, but I had no way to pay him. The only thing he wanted from me, was me.

We got back in the truck, and as we drove around trees and debris, Danny spilled his juice cup and a bag of Cheetos Edith had given him. He began to cry, so I slipped into the backseat and helped pick them up. While I was bending down to the floorboard, the truck came to a complete stop.

"We're home," I said. I sat back up and looked out the window. "Where are we?" I asked John.

He didn't answer for a moment. "It's our neighborhood," he said. He pointed to a street sign that read "Oak Avenue." It was the only thing left standing. Rosy, my beautiful home, would have been three down on the right from the sign. All that was left was a concrete foundation and a pile of rubble like all the other houses that had been on the street.

Nothing remained of the house I loved. Not the walls. Not the roof. Not the chimney.

And not Bertha, the refrigerator that had held all the vials of insulin that would keep me alive.

-43-

John, the kids and I scoured through the rubble of my house and neighborhood looking for any vials. We found a few shattered ones, but nothing with any viable insulin in it. I found Bertha's crumpled frame two blocks away, but the door was missing, and she no longer held a single vial.

When we gave up hours later, John asked, "What do you have left?"

"One vial, already opened." I took it out of my purse and held it carefully.

"How many units left?"

"Five hundred and twenty," I said. The number was like a length of fuse on a bomb.

"You use about thirty units a day, right?" he asked.

I nodded.

"How many days is that?" John asked. He wasn't good with numbers.

"Seventeen and a third," I said, "but I could stretch it with a low-carb diet."

"How much insulin do you produce yourself?"

"None. I've been diabetic since I was eight."

"Then DKA will set in quickly once the insulin is gone."

DKA. Diabetic ketoacidosis. The nasty process of the body destroying itself when the blood sugar is unrestrained.

"Then we just have to get back to work immediately," John said. He tried to sound positive, but I could hear the fear in his voice.

We drove back to Edith's, and she happily let us stay in her home. We needed every minute now and didn't have time to set up a new house.

"You rest today," John said. "Watch your blood sugar carefully and give the minimum dose you can. No carbs at all."

"What are you going to do?"

"I'll go make some more extractions, and we'll start again in the morning."

"You haven't slept at all."

"There'll be time for sleeping ... later."

"I'll go with you—"

"No!" John said. "You have to rest. Keep your system stable and as unstressed as possible."

I had never heard him speak so firmly.

"Where's the gun?" he asked.

I took it out of the medical bag and handed it to him. He'd barely ever fired the gun and had never used it for killing.

John drove off in the truck, and Edith began fixing dinner. She asked about what I could eat, and I helped her prepare my portion with little to no carbs. Kyle stopped by but didn't speak to me. He told Edith that the community was meeting tomorrow afternoon to talk about recovery plans. Ralph's home had been irreparably damaged, but he had simply moved next door.

John came back late that night with ten pancreases in an ice chest. The few hours he was gone must have been a fury of slaughter. He was covered in blood. The kids were watching a DVD with Edith. I grabbed a towel, washcloth and soap, and took John outside to a rain barrel that, unsurprisingly, was full.

I stripped John's ruined clothes off and scrubbed him clean and washed his matted hair. The rain barrel was next to the generator, so we couldn't talk over its unending noise, but we didn't need to.

I slept with Olivia, and John slept with Danny. We both woke early in the morning. I injected just three units and had a light breakfast of eggs provided by the chickens Edith had in her backyard. We drove to the lab and started two separate batches with five pancreases each.

"We'll just have to do as many batches as we can," he said. "We'll take careful notes and videos, and one of the batches will work."

We got to step twenty-four and put both batches in an ice chest. We drove to the community meeting, arriving late. I could tell Edith had filled everyone in. They each had a sad look on their face when they made eye contact, but tried to give a hopeful smile. Kyle's face was emotionless, and he looked from me to John repeatedly.

"We've already discussed the recovery situation," Ralph said, catching us up on what had happened so far. "Kyle will help with any repairs people need. Thomas is going to clear the roads. Rigby will fix cars or find new ones. Fortunately he had several kept safely in a parking garage. Everyone should help with general cleanup to keep our city looking beautiful. You two are exempted, of course," he said, looking at John and me.

That was good, because I wouldn't have done it anyway. Picking up trash seemed less important when death was imminent.

"Which brings me to our next matter," Ralph said. "I've been praying ... "

Oh no. He was going to try to issue some sort of religious rule like no work on Sundays. John and I would be working every minute we had. I'm not quite sure when Ralph became the mayor of our city, but he was definitely acting like he was.

"Sugar needs our help," Ralph said. "While none of us can help with the chemical refinement, we can certainly handle the pigs."

I was taken aback. I didn't know what to say.

"And I think it can be much more," Ralph said. "We'll gather and then raise the pigs. When it's time for slaughter, the pancreases go to Sugar, and the meat and other parts can be used. With the amount of pigs Sugar will need, it will be far more than our small community could possibly use."

"So what do we do with the excess?" Bill asked.

"Trade," Ralph said. "We become expert pig farmers and export the meat and other products to other communities. They become experts at other things and trade with us."

The group discussed it for a few minutes. I thought there would be people who wouldn't want to be in the unglamorous business of pig farming, but they seemed excited. The group would have a purpose beyond each person. We could see a civilization beginning to reform. I prayed that I could witness it.

"Is there anything else we can do to help in this desperate time?" Ralph asked.

"We need a chemist," John said. "Get on the radio and try to find one."

We had asked all over for doctors, and there had to be fewer chemists than doctors. I didn't mention that an expert chemist had lived a few hours away, and I had shot him in cold blood.

"I'll ask around the nation," Ralph said. "We did eventually find a couple of doctors. They're riding circuits now, and one should be in Tallahassee in September."

A doctor wouldn't help now anyway.

"Don't just ask around the nation," John said. "How far will that radio go?"

"Quite a ways," Ralph said. "Before the virus, I talked to people around the world."

"Then do it," John said.

"Getting the farm going will be long term," Ralph said. "We'll handle that. You two focus on the short-term and get the process working."

I loved that he had enough faith to think there would be a long-term. I looked out the window to check on Olivia and Danny and saw them playing with another boy. When I turned to ask, Ralph answered before I could say anything.

"He's the boy I had seen around town," Ralph said. "When the storm started getting bad, I knew I had to find him. He was pretty scared. I think he understands now that he might need other people. And by God's providence, I was out looking for him when my house was destroyed."

"What's his name?"

"He says it's Wolf, but I'm sure that's not his real name."

"It's his real name if that's the name he wants," I said.

John asked Kyle where another farm was, and we said good-bye to everyone. We had to leave the meeting then, to have a chance of finding some pigs for extraction before dark. We entered the address in the GPS and headed straight there. It wasn't a dedicated pig farm. Cows, horses and chickens roamed around, but we found enough pigs for the day.

A group of six lounged in a mud puddle. John loaded Clint and shot all six in a matter of seconds. We waded into the muddy, bloody puddle and cut into the pigs, extracting the pancreases and placing them in a cooler. That would give us enough for one or maybe two small batches tomorrow.

The farm had a long watering trough, full of fresh water from the storm. We walked over to the trough and stripped our muddy clothes off. We poured water over each other, and each scrubbed the other's body clean with our hands.

I desperately wanted to make love to John before I died. I pulled him close and kissed him and put his hands on my body.

"We're not going to have a last time in these days," he said. "We're going to have a first time when the process works and we have a lifetime stretched out in front of us. We'll wait for that. That's how sure I am," he said.

We held each other for a time and then dried off and dressed. Before driving off, we checked my blood sugar, and it was too high, 168, even with the low-carb diet. I injected a few more precious units, and we headed home with the pancreases.

The next days followed that same pattern. I was able to get by with eighteen to twenty units per day with careful control. That would last twenty-six to twenty-nine more days. Each day, we started new batches in the morning and then found pigs in the afternoon.

The rabbits from before had been lost in the hurricane, so we had to spend two days finding more. As we approached one week, ready to work on the first batches to come out of the ice chest, the rest of the community had begun setting up the farm. They were building fenced-in pens in a large park near the middle of town. Some people had even moved into new houses around the farm.

The first two batches failed to affect the rabbit's blood sugar at all. We carefully checked which things we had done differently on those batches. We had to keep trying small changes, varying one thing at a time. We were met with failure after failure, an endless line of pigs giving their lives for nothing.

Two days later, Ralph met us at the lab and said, "We've found a chemist."

We followed Ralph back to the church, where the radio was. Ralph worked the machine, twisting dials and knobs. A man's voice, with a thick accent, came on the line. The accent wasn't Spanish, but it was something close to that.

"This is Mateus," he said.

"Hi, Mateus," Ralph said. "This is Ralph again. I have the girl, Sugar, here. She's the one who was looking for a chemist."

"Yes. Yes," Mateus said. "My son is chemist. Very good. He can help you."

His son? The odds of that were low.

"Where are you?" I asked Mateus.

"In Rio," he said.

"Where's that?" I asked John, holding my hand over the microphone.

John took the microphone and asked, "Are you in Rio de Janeiro?"

"Yes. Yes," Mateus said.

"That's in Brazil!" I said in shock.

"Yes. I know this," Mateus said.

"Can your son get to us, in Florida?" John asked.

"No," Mateus said. "Too far. Too dangerous. You must come here."

"How are we going to get to Brazil?" I asked.

"You fly," Mateus said. "Every airport has many planes. You pick a good one and fly down. My son will come back and help you."

"We'll let you know, Mateus," John said. Ralph spoke with Mateus for a few minutes, and then they hung up, or whatever it's called on a radio.

"We can do it, if we can find a pilot," John said.

"You want to fly to Brazil?" I said.

"We need a chemist," John said. "We're doing something wrong. An experienced chemist will be able to follow the steps and not make whatever mistakes we're making." John turned to Ralph. "You found a vet and a chemist. Can you find a pilot?"

"I'll try," he said.

John and I spent three more days trying and failing in the lab. There was something we didn't know how to do correctly, but we didn't know what it was. The instructions I had found had been a historical reference. Not for an untrained person to actually repeat the steps.

After a long day, we checked back with Ralph, and he said what I had feared.

"I've found a couple of pilots, but no one willing to fly to Brazil. There are too many unknowns. You'll have to stop at least once at an airport along the way to refuel. That's two airports that you'll need to land at without knowing what's there."

"Any pilot willing to do it would be out of his mind," John said. "We can't learn to fly and navigate a plane in the time we have left. I'm sorry, Sugar. We'll just have to keep trying." He looked desperate. Time was getting short.

"I know a pilot who's out of his mind," I said.

-44-

"You want a man with some form of dementia to fly us over four thousand miles, landing at two different airports, and then do the same thing coming back?" John asked.

"Yes," I said. "It's our only hope. We need a chemist. And it won't be *us* flying."

"What?"

"If Sam can even still fly a plane, I can't let you take the risk. I'm going to die anyway, but you have a long life ahead of you."

"We'll decide who's going after we find out if this is even possible," John said. "Every day we spend on this is a day we're not in the lab."

"This is what I want to try. We've got some batches in the ice chest now. They still have a chance. We'll go while they wait."

John didn't argue anymore, and we started driving to Myrtle Beach right after saying good-bye to Olivia and Danny. We stopped at a car lot and took a Jeep, a vehicle that could more easily navigate around or over all the debris from the hurricane.

John drove faster than I thought was safe, and we made good time. When night fell, we stayed in a hotel room in a town call Ridgeland, South Carolina. We slept in the same bed, holding each other through the night.

In the morning we drove to Sam's house. As we pulled up, we saw him staring into his mailbox, wearing a bathrobe and slippers.

"The mail usually comes by this time of day," he said to us as we stepped out of the Jeep.

John gave me a wary look, and then I asked Sam a pointless question. "Do you remember me, Sam?"

Sam looked at me and said, "Have we met?"

Sam appeared healthy. He moved without trouble. I figured he was in his late sixties, and he had kept himself in good shape.

"Can we come inside and talk to you?" I asked.

"Certainly," he said. "I always like company. I've just retired, and I don't get to see people like I used to. When I was flying the charter jets, there were always interesting people to talk to. My wife is out, but she should be home soon."

We went inside and sat down at his kitchen table. I didn't think building up to the topic would do any good, so I just asked him, "Do you think you can still fly a plane?"

"Of course," he said. "I only retired a few months ago. I could have kept going, but it was time for me to finally spend some time with Mary, not bounding all over the world."

Mary was his wife.

"I lost my daughter because of that," he said and then looked at me. "You remind me of her. What did you say your name was?"

Sam was the only person I had told my old name to because the name Sugar made him confuse me with his daughter, who he had often called Sugar.

"I'm John and this is Sugar," John said, extending his hand.

Sam shook John's hand. "I used to call my daughter Sugar."

Now we were about to go down a conversation path we had trod a few times before. I interrupted. "Sam, could you fly a plane for us?"

"I told Mary I would give that up, and I'm true to my word. But, oh, I miss it sometimes. She should be home soon. I'll introduce you."

I had to get him back in the present. What had triggered it before? "Sam, can we step outside for a minute?"

We walked out the front door. "Look at all the other lawns in the neighborhood, Sam." All the other lawns were overgrown, untouched for years.

He looked up and said, "That's unusual. The homeowners association will be furious. It's like they've all moved away."

"Where have they gone, Sam?"

He paused for a minute, and then sadness washed over his face. "It hits me again every time. I have to relive it." He looked over at me. "I remember you, but not him. You're—"

"Call me Sugar now. This is John." He had almost said my old name.

He nodded. "Mary's not coming home, is she?"

"No," I said. I felt awful. His disease could at least take him away from the pain of his loss for a while. But I had to talk to him while he was completely with us. "Sam, I need a pilot. Do you think you can still fly a plane?"

"I can drive a car and do everything else needed to keep myself alive, unfortunately. I've spent more hours flying a plane than driving a car. I think flying will be the last thing to go. It's so deep inside me."

"Could you help me?"

"You want me to fly you somewhere? I could forget where I was going."

"I'll be there to remind you."

"*We'll* be there," John said.

"Where do you want to go?" Sam asked. "I might be fine for a short hop."

"To Brazil. Rio de Janeiro."

"That's forty-five hundred miles from here! That would take nine or ten hours. We'd be flying over water some of the way. We'd have to stop and refuel at an airport that we couldn't see ahead of time. I could easily die doing this."

I wasn't going to lie to him. "Yes. You could."

"Perfect," he said. "I can't think of a better way to go. If you're willing to risk your life, then so am I. You understand the danger?"

"Yes," I said. "I'll die without it."

"Then let's go see if I can still fly a plane," Sam said. "Keep talking to me while we're driving to the airport. Keep me in the present." Sam started to get into his car.

"Would you like to change out of your bathrobe?" John asked.

Sam looked down and then went back in the house. He came out a few minutes later, dressed in a slacks and a buttoned-down shirt, and said, "Who are you, and what are you doing here?"

"Sam, … "

He burst out laughing. "I'm just kidding. I'm good for now. Just keep me focused. I'll drive." He looked at our Jeep and held out his hand for the keys.

"Are you sure?" John said.

"You'd better trust me to drive if you want to trust me to fly."

John handed him the keys, and we drove off as fast as the Jeep would take us. Sam whipped around corners and made both of us nervous, but he had complete control of the car. A few minutes later we pulled into the Myrtle Beach airport.

"Let's find one I'm used to," he said. "I flew charter planes for rich people, and lots of rich people used to come to Myrtle Beach."

Sam drove around the airport, looking at planes until he found one in a hangar that he apparently liked. It looked like the ones I had seen rich people fly in movies. I think it was called a Learjet. Sam looked the plane over inside and out and even under the hood, or whatever it's called on a plan. He finally decided it was ready to fly.

"She has enough fuel for a short flight. First, I'll take her up and down to see if she and I can both still fly. If it works, then we're good to go. If I die, then I'm finally done with this life. Don't be sad for me. I won't be."

Sam was almost giddy with excitement. He backed the plane out and slowly taxied down the runway. We watched him turn it around at the end of a long runway. Then it just sat there.

"He's forgotten," John said.

We waited for minutes with nothing happening. We finally decided to get in the Jeep and go get him, but the engine roared to life, and the plane shot down the runway and lifted into the air.

And the plane flew away, toward the ocean, out of our sight.

-45-

"He's killing himself," John said. "He's going to fly across the ocean until the plane is out of fuel."

I couldn't say that I blamed him. Our idea was absurd. It would be a good way for him to go, rather than waiting for the disease to ravage his mind.

Maybe I should learn from him. We were failing at the insulin batches. John and the children would have to watch me die. At the end, it would be easy for me and hard for them. I'd slip into a coma, and they'd have to sit by while I wasted away.

I stared out, contemplating this path, with the sun starting to sink low in the sky. I had fought. I had tried. But now I had to think about the others and what would be best for them.

And then we heard the roar of the engines and saw Sam's plane heading back toward us. He took a loop around the airport, got aligned with the runway and descended. We both held our breath, but he touched down, in what looked like a flawless landing.

The plane slowed to a stop and then waited on the runway, not moving. We hopped in the Jeep and headed out to the plane. We parked on the side of the plane, and when we got out, Sam lowered the door and walked down.

"Something's gone wrong," he said. "I don't know whether it's my radio, but I couldn't hear anything from the tower. It's like the whole airport is shut down." He looked at us curiously. "Are you my passengers?"

He was confused, but he had done it. We explained the situation to Sam, and at first he didn't believe us, but the memory slowly came back.

"I'm sorry," he said. "I remember you, Sugar. But I don't remember him at all."

"I'm in short-term memory still," John said. "But it doesn't matter. I think this can work. Let's fuel up and fly to Tallahassee. We'll get supplies there and plan the trip to Brazil."

"We can't do a night landing at an airport that's shut down," Sam said. "We'll have to leave in the morning." And then he looked at me and said, "Thank you. I can fly."

We spent the night at Sam's house. He got out old maps and did some basic planning for the flights to Tallahassee and Rio. We often had to remind him what was happening, but sometimes he slipped into old times, and we let him stay there. We became his rich passengers or his extended family. We were whatever his mind could make fit the situation.

In the morning Sam woke before us and was startled to find us in his house. We told him about the flight to Tallahassee, and he grew excited. After I injected a precious few units and ate breakfast, we drove to the airport and spent an hour fueling the plane. Most of that time was spent in finding the fuel truck and getting it running.

We agreed one of us would always stay beside Sam in the cockpit, so I climbed into the other seat beside him. The array of instruments and dials was dizzying, but Sam's fractured mind took it all in like it was second nature. The plane had sophisticated navigation that I assumed was somewhat like my car GPS. Sam punched in the destination and flight plan.

"As soon as the tower clears us, we can be on our way," he said.

"There's no tower, Sam."

He looked at me and said, "Oh, yeah."

He taxied to the runway, and then I was pushed back as we quickly accelerated and lifted off. We got into the air, and after he turned the plane around, the instrument panel showed we were going southwest, which made me feel good.

The flight took barely an hour, and Sam was delighted that he could fly at any altitude he wanted, not having to worry about regulations and collision safety. The Tallahassee airport came into view and I tensed, but Sam landed it with hardly a bump.

We found a car in the Hertz rental lot, because Sam had a Gold club membership that he insisted we use, and drove back to Edith's house. Olivia wanted to hear all about flying. She had never been on a plane before, and Sam regaled her with stories. That day we gathered supplies for the trip. I couldn't depend on finding food quickly, so we packed enough to feed all three of us (me, John and Sam) for a week.

With the range of the plane, Sam decided we would fly from Tallahassee to Caracas in Venezuela and then to Rio. Simon Bolivar International Airport in Caracas was large and should have good runways and refueling trucks. We got on the radio again and called Mateus.

We explained that we would leave the next day, refuel and spend the night in Caracas, and then land in Rio the day after that.

"You will be at Rio airport in two days, yes?" Mateus asked.

"Yes," John said. "And your son will be ready to go?"

"Yes. He is very happy to be chemist again. And to save a life. This is good."

With all the preparations made, we all sat down together for dinner. Edith had made a large meal, but I had to eat very conservatively to keep my blood sugar in check with the low doses. I was a little hungry all the time now. Even if the chemist came back and was successful on his first batch, we would be pushing it. I kissed the kids good night and hugged them like I might never see again, because I likely wouldn't. What we were doing could fail in a hundred different ways.

John had insisted on going, and I gave up arguing with him.

We woke early in the morning, to have as much daylight as we could. We drove to the airport, fueled the plane and loaded it with our supplies. Sam taxied out to the runway, and I said, "My insulin! It's still in the car." I had injected while we drove and ate a small breakfast after loading up. "John, will you run back and get it?"

Sam lowered the stairs, and John set off at a jog. When he was at the car, I took the insulin vial out of my pocket. "It's time to go, Captain," I said.

"Will you be the only passenger today, ma'am?"

"Yes," I said.

Sam raised the stairs, and John started to run back. The plane shot forward on the runway, and I watched John out the window, for what was probably the last time.

Sam and I might die, but I wouldn't let John die with us.

-46-

Sam had us at cruising altitude in minutes. We soared at an even five hundred miles per hour. At that rate, it would take us less than four hours to reach Caracas. Seeing the clouds from above amazed me. This was only the second flight in my life, and the first one had been so short that we didn't get very high. For a moment I forgot and just watched in wonder.

And then the clouds parted, and we were over open ocean.

Any mistakes now meant certain death. I had lived my life the past months on the edge of death. With the insulin in my pocket so low, I sat with my feet dangling over that edge. Sam started giving me what must have been copilot instructions, and I had to remind him, "I'm a passenger, Sam. I'm riding up here because I'm the only one."

"Right," he said. He looked around, disoriented. "Where are we headed?"

"Caracas."

He checked the instruments, seeming to confirm our navigation. The jet had an array of displays, one of which I thought was showing our present position, and the compass showed we were heading southeast. We briefly passed over the coast of Florida, then open ocean again and then barely fifteen minutes over Cuba. A tiny slice of Haiti zipped by at the expected time, and then we would have an hour and a half over the Caribbean.

John had left his pack of cigarettes, and I fiddled with it, passing it from one hand to another. I stepped away from the cockpit for just a second and opened John's bag. I took out a shirt he often wore, and held it to my face. I hoped it would have his scent, but Edith had apparently washed it thoroughly, and it just smelled of the soap she used.

About forty-five minutes over the ocean past Haiti, Sam began clearing our destination from the navigation. "What are you doing?" I asked.

"Don't worry, Mary. I guess I can tell you where we're going now. We'll be in Aruba in a few minutes, and then we start the honeymoon," he said with a wink.

"We're not going to Aruba, Sam. We're going to Caracas."

"Baby, who ever heard of honeymooning in Caracas? Aruba will be fun. We can spend our time on the beach. Or did you just want to stay in bed the entire time?" He reached over and rubbed his hand on my leg and up my thigh.

I didn't know whether to keep him in this memory and convince him that we were going to Caracas or try to jolt him out of it. We turned due south and began to descend.

"Sam. I'm not Mary."

"You can be whoever you want to. It's just you and me. Your parents can't affect us out here."

"Sam, Mary's gone. The virus took her."

"You were sniffling through the whole wedding. But you'll feel better once you get out in the sun and away from the stress of the wedding. It's all over now. Nothing to plan."

"Sam, Mary's dead. Most everyone is dead. You have to come back to the present." Aruba was a tiny island, but I didn't know if we could even find the airport. He hadn't put it into the navigation. He had just turned our current destination off. When he had flown to Aruba as a young man, they probably didn't have GPS guidance.

"She's dead?" Sam asked.

"Do you remember?"

"The virus," he said. "I wanted to die with her but God wouldn't take me. Of all the cruel, damn jokes. He left me with my disease and took her."

He pushed down on the stick, and the plane began to descend sharply. I couldn't see anything but water below us. "Sam!"

"Mary," he said, looking at me. "I'll be with you in a moment."

"Sam! It's me, Sugar."

"Sugar?"

I hated to lie to him, but we were going to crash in a few moments. "Daddy, it's me, Julie. Don't crash the plane."

"Julie?" he said. "I would never hurt you, Sugar." He leveled the plane off.

"Dad, you're taking me to Caracas." I knew there was no memory like that, but I had to make it fit somehow.

"To get away from Ryan?"

"Yes. He won't find me there. We'll just stay a little while. But you have to put it back into the navigational computer."

He hesitated and then punched it back in. I breathed a sigh of relief as we resumed our course. We landed in Caracas, and he came back to the present when I showed him the emptiness of the airport. We fueled up and settled in for the afternoon and night. I kept the insulin doses low and could feel the effects of slightly high blood sugar.

The flight to Rio would be all over land, but it would push the fuel range of the plane. We unloaded everything we could and planned to stop in Brasilia if the fuel didn't last. We took off early the next morning, with Sam's mind temporarily in the present. We had a tailwind much of the way, and fuel wasn't a problem. I kept Sam talking for the entire six-hour flight, which was nearly impossible for me, but it seemed to help. He slipped in and out, thinking he was at various points in his life, but as long as I kept steering his mind back to flying to Rio, he kept the plane going. The disease had ravaged the memories he loved most but left his skills completely intact.

We landed in the afternoon, and I wanted to kiss the ground when I stepped out of the plane. We didn't know where to go and just waited, assuming there weren't many planes coming and going and that Mateus would see us.

In a few minutes a car drove up, and an old man stepped out.

"Mateus?" I asked.

"Yes," he said, and relief flooded over me.

"We'll go get your son, and then we can fly out in the morning," I said.

"I am very sorry," he said. "But I have lied to you."

47

"What?" I asked Mateus. "How did you lie?"

"It is not my son," he said. "It is my … "—he paused, trying to find the word—" … grandniece."

That made more sense mathematically. With a large family, the odds increased of having two survivors in one family. If you extended to distant relations like a grandniece, it covered many possible people.

"Why would you lie about that?" I asked.

"Who would think that a young woman could be a studied chemist? You would not have believed me."

I didn't care about arguing his sexist assumptions. "So she is a chemist?"

"A chemistry student."

Student?

But something else struck me then. Why did he want to have his grandniece taken away by foreigners so much that he thought he had to trick us into coming to get her?

Before I could ask anything, he said, "We must go quickly and get you out of view. You will come to my home, and in the morning you take my niece far away from here."

Mateus ushered us into the car, almost pushing me. Sam sat in the front passenger seat, and I got in the back. "Unfortunately, you are very beautiful. I did not realize this."

That seemed like a strange way to compliment a woman.

"To be safe, it is best, you must hide in the floorboard."

"Why?"

He reached back and pushed my head down. He seemed afraid enough that I decided to cooperate. We drove for at least a half hour, and I grew uncomfortable. The car stopped, and from the light changing, I could tell we were pulling into a garage or some sort of enclosure.

"I do not think you were seen. Very few people in city, of course, but you never can be sure. You can get up now."

I sat up and stretched and saw that we were in a parking garage. Mateus got out, and Sam and I followed him to the stairs.

"You know what protects her the most?" Mateus asked.

"What?" Sam asked, even though the question was rhetorical.

"Twenty flights of stairs. We live up there. I am old and cannot defend her, but up twenty flights of stairs, no man comes to check."

With my blood sugar staying a little high, I was tired all the time now. I couldn't possibly make it up twenty flights. So I asked them to wait. I checked my blood sugar and gave a dose that should level me out. We waited a few minutes and then started the arduous climb.

The two old men made me look weak. I had to stop every few floors to rest. I munched on a pack of beef jerky and drank from a water bottle. Eventually we made it to the top, me covered in sweat, Sam and Mateus helping me to walk.

Mateus opened the door and said, "Sou eu. É seguro sair."

A young woman, maybe in her mid- to late twenties, stepped out from around the corner. She was one of the most beautiful women I had ever seen. She had long, full, curly black hair and golden-brown skin.

"This is Isadora," Mateus said.

Isadora smiled, first at Sam, then at me. I was too exhausted for small talk, so I just asked, "Are you a chemist? Mateus said you were just a student."

"Grandfather doesn't understand what I did. He just wants to protect me," Isadora said in flawless, lightly accented English.

"Are you?" I asked again.

"I was a PhD student in biochemistry. I had just begun work on my dissertation. I was at Stanford, when the world first heard about the virus."

"Then why are you here now?"

"I saw quickly what the virus would do. My professors and I knew better than most. When it started to spread in China, I went home to die with my family, here in Brazil."

"She is not actually from Brazil," Mateus said. "She was raised in Portugal until her family moved here. This is why she talk so funny," he said, laughing, and Isadora smiled at him.

I didn't need to hear her life story. "Can you do this?" I asked and held out the sheet of instructions for extracting the insulin.

She read it over for a few minutes.

"Do you have a lab with equipment?" she asked.

"Yes."

"Then, yes, I can," Isadora said. "I'm sure it will take a few batches to work through the process correctly, but this is standard chemistry. Very hard for a layman, tricky for a professional, but definitely doable."

With that settled, I felt safer. Time would be close. She would have to start from the beginning and each batch took at least nine days. I didn't know if I could live through two more batches, but I'd do everything I could to stretch it out.

"Why are you hidden up here?" I asked. "What is Mateus protecting you from?"

Mateus answered before Isadora could. "Where you live the few people who are still alive are good people?"

"Yes."

"That is mostly true here," he said. "Mostly."

I was still exhausted so I sat down on the couch. The men sat down in chairs across from the couch. Isadora brought me a glass of water, and I thanked her.

"In the first days after the virus, some of the survivors, some men, found guns and began to do as they wished. They took whatever women they wanted. They killed any who opposed them."

"No one fought back?"

"Some did. Some died."

"There are guns and every kind of weapon you can imagine just waiting to be picked up," I said.

"We live in a world of unlimited resources," Mateus said. "Everything is simply a matter of what you are willing to do. These men were willing to do more than others."

"Grandfather kept me hidden, up all these stories," Isadora said. "Any other young women have been rounded up. Every day he walks up and down getting supplies."

"But this life of hiding is over for her now," Mateus said. "She will go to America with you."

"You can come with us," I said to Mateus. "The plane can easily hold more people."

"I am old. I was born here. I will die here," he said. "But maybe I will move to a lower floor, yes?"

"Why haven't you simply left here?" I asked Isadora. "The city is huge, and they can't possibly watch everything all the time."

Mateus answered, "Where would she go? To another town to be captured or killed by evil men? This world is not safe for a woman. Other places in Brazil may have good people. Or they may not. But your home is safe. If your town would do so much to save you, it must be good place."

That was true.

"Young women are a valuable commodity these days," Mateus said. "One of the only rare resources. This is why I had to lie and say the chemist was a man. To know you were not seeking to find women."

"Could we take any other women with us?" I asked.

"Any women who would want to leave have been taken by the men. They are kept in an apartment building a few blocks from here. I'm sure you can imagine what they are used for."

"A few blocks?" I said. "Why would you stay so close? The city is huge."

"If we stay in the area these men claim, we are safe from others that I might not know about," Mateus said. "They keep this part of the city clear. They don't care about me, one old man."

I felt bad for the women, but there was nothing I could do. I was no soldier.

"It is a horror," Isadora said.

We would leave in the morning and put this behind us.

"I feel most bad for the children," Mateus said.

"Children?"

48

"The women have children," Mateus said. "I talked to one of the men, I should say monsters, one day. He talked all about their vile ways like it was the most ordinary thing. I thought men that evil would not be bothered with children, but he said it keeps the women under control. They will not risk their children."

"Why hasn't anyone done anything?" I asked.

"Those who have tried have died," Isadora said. "The men live in an apartment building with only one way in or out, unless you jump, which some women have done. The only ones who go in are the women they capture."

"How many men are in the building?" I asked.

"I think five," he said. "But enough of this sad talk. The world is evil, and we can only do our small part. You will help Isadora get out, and she will help you make the insulin."

Sam had stayed silent this entire time, but then asked to have something to eat and to go to bed. He was handling himself well, or at least he hadn't questioned what was going on. Isadora made a simple meal of rice and beans. I had to skip the rice, of course.

They put Sam in an apartment across the hall. After Sam settled down I stayed up for a while asking Isadora and Mateus all about the men and the building where they kept the women and children. When they were ready to sleep, they started to put me in a separate apartment, but I worried that Sam would wander off, so I decided to sleep on the couch in his. I tried to sleep, but I lay on the couch wide awake. I couldn't get my mind off the trapped women and children.

We were about to abandon them so that I could live. The rational part of my mind said I was doing a good thing. I was freeing Isadora. I couldn't fight five armed men.

But the other part of my mind kept hearing Mateus's words. "Everything is simply a matter of what you are willing to do."

What was I willing to do?

I had spent all the time since the virus trying to save myself. Was my life more valuable than others? I might be worth a thousand pigs, but I wasn't worth more than an innocent person, especially a child. My morality didn't come from a god's commandments or a country's laws. I didn't know what foundation my beliefs of right and wrong were built on, but ever since Michael, I knew this at the core of my being: children should always be protected. That came above everything else, including my own life.

I put Clint in the bottom of a deep bag, buried in random things. I could never hope to simply walk up and start shooting. Isadora had said the only people who could get in were the women who were captured.

In the morning I left a note for the others, telling them to fly back without me if I didn't return by the next day. I explained Sam's condition and that Isadora would need to keep him focused the entire time.

I took a normal injection of insulin, ate breakfast and left the vial in the apartment. If I couldn't do what I planned, then I didn't want to live as a prisoner in the compound. I would go comatose and die soon, and not be left as a plaything for the men.

I didn't know the city, but it didn't take me long to find the things I needed. I looked through stores and soon found a tight bra that pushed my breasts together, and I hid a small switchblade knife in between them. Mateus had described the men as organized and systematic, so I hoped they wouldn't simply attack me when they saw me. He said they sometimes traded women with groups in other cities, so they would want to keep the women as unharmed as possible.

I didn't know if God would bless the murderous plans I had, but I was so afraid that I prayed despite my lack of real belief. I just needed to get one of them alone. I walked down the street toward the building trying not to act intentional. I was almost shaking with fear, but that probably worked in my favor, to keep them from suspecting me.

I stopped in buildings, putting cans of food and other things in a bag, like I was foraging for supplies. After a few blocks a man with an assault rifle stepped around a corner and said, "Pare!"

I turned away from him, as if to run, and he yelled again, this time doing something with the gun that made a clicking sound. I slowly turned back around and held my hands up, still holding the bag.

He walked toward me with the gun pointed at me. I felt like a fool. He could kill me or do anything he wanted right now. He weighed twice as much as I did and was probably five times stronger. But there was no going back now. It was all about what I was willing to do.

When he reached me, he took the bag, then stepped behind me and prodded me forward with the barrel of the gun. We walked up the block and turned the corner. He took both my arms and held them behind my back with one of his strong hands. He pulled me over to a door at the front of a large building.

He knocked five times in a rhythm that was clearly a signal to those inside. Another man with a gun opened the door. He looked at me and smiled. "Americano?" he said to the man holding my hands.

The man holding my hands behind my back must have nodded or something because the man at the door smiled again. The doorman put his gun down and patted me all over, checking for weapons, I assumed. He put his hands between my legs and on my breasts. But he didn't check between my breasts.

"Nome?" he asked, looking at me.

I guessed that meant name and said, "Sugar."

"Você fala português?"

I shook my head no. He rolled his eyes and then stepped back. The man behind me let go of my hands and pushed me forward. The doorman got on a walkie-talkie and spoke to others in rapid Portuguese. I heard "Americano" several times.

In a few minutes, four more men came down the stairs and into the lobby. That meant there was a minimum of six, and they must have left at least one or two guarding the other women.

The men looked at me like a prize horse. Some put their hands on me, and I stood still, enduring it, hoping they wouldn't find the knife. The bra was so tight that they would have had to remove it to find the small switchblade. They started to argue, I assumed over who would get me. For a moment, I thought they might just kill each other, doing the job for me, until another man came down and they all shut up.

He seemed to be the leader. He looked me over and then took the bag I had been carrying and looked through it. He laid everything out on a table and eventually found Clint. I hadn't thought that I could make it up there with my bag and Clint, but it was worth a try.

The man held the gun and seemed to like it, tucking it into his pants in the small of his back. The man pulled out a deck of cards, the apparent method of deciding who would win the prize, and then pointed to the youngest, a teenager, maybe eighteen years old, and gave him some instructions. The young man took me by the arm and directed me upstairs. We skipped the first four floors. I wondered why they would go to such effort, keeping the women on the fifth floor and above, until I realized it was a way of keeping them trapped. Jumping from the fifth floor was almost certain death.

Another man guarded the stairway. The young man walked me past him and out onto the fifth floor. In the hallway, a half dozen women gathered, and four of them held children. Each of the children looked two or under,

216

which made sense because they would have all been born after the virus.

When the men had leered at me and put their hands on me, I had tried to work up hatred, but the fear and revulsion hadn't let it come to the surface. Now I saw these women and the children held here like animals, and I felt rage. I let it burn inside me.

Ten more women came out from apartment doors down the hall. They each looked at me with sorrow in their eyes.

"Ela é uma criança," a woman said.

"Americano?" one of the women near me said.

I nodded.

Another woman, holding an infant, came over and said, "I'm sorry," in a thick accent. She stroked my hair, and tears filled her eyes.

The young man went back down, leaving only the one guard at the end of the hallway. I thought about charging him, but he had an assault rifle and could shoot me down. The commotion would bring all the others.

I started to look around, and the women allowed me into their apartments without hesitation. Everything that could conceivably be used as a weapon had been taken away. No knives or forks or anything heavy that could be used to smash a head.

I counted sixteen women and nine children. Three of the women were currently pregnant.

"Am I the youngest?" I asked the woman who had spoken English. She looked to be in her late thirties, the oldest woman here, but still very attractive.

"Yes," she said. "There was a girl of sixteen, but she jumped. Unlike some others, these men do not like the very young, and they are traded quickly. What is your name?" she asked.

"Sugar."

"Like sweet?"

"Yes," I said.

"I am Gabriela. These first days will be hard for you. You are new and different and will catch their interest."

I heard two shots, and all the women startled, but I recognized the sound of Clint, which I had fired so many times. Each sound was instantly followed by a ping of metal. The man who had Clint must have fired at a couple of metal targets.

"Are they soldiers?" I asked. "Can they fight well?"

Gabriela laughed. "They are just fools with guns. One of them is a dentist. He insists on keeping our teeth well cared for. Another drove a taxi. All they know of fighting is how to scare women and shoot the few men who were fool enough to try to rescue us."

The leader came up the stairs, and said, "Eu ganhei. Você é meu primeiro."

I looked at the woman. "What did he say?"
"He won. He gets you first."

49

Gabriela squeezed my hand. "It will be over soon," she said.

I suspected that the card game hadn't been a fair one. The leader wanted this new treat for himself. He motioned for me to follow him, and he walked toward the stairs. He still had Clint tucked in near the small of his back. This would work. I could get him alone and then get the gun.

He waited until I caught up and then motioned for me to go ahead of him. We started up the stairs until the guard stopped him, pointing at his back. The man took Clint and handed him to the stair guard. The guard systematically pointed to various places, and the leader patted himself down, making sure he had no weapons. It looked like an official check-in procedure. These men had turned kidnapping and rape into an organized process.

We walked to the sixth floor, and no one else was there that I could see. He walked down the hall to a door, opened it and motioned for me to go in. I walked into a standard, small apartment. I became acutely aware of the switchblade still between my breasts.

This was my chance. We were away from the others. I didn't know what to do. I couldn't get the knife out in a quick motion. It was packed in tightly to keep it from being easily discovered.

He said, "Cama," and pointed to the bedroom.

I decided to play along and lull him into a false sense of security. Men were at their weakest when desire took over.

I walked into the bedroom and looked him in the eye with all the confidence I could fake, with my heart pounding and my stomach turning. I said, "Cama," hoping it meant bed or something like it and tried to smile. I motioned for him to lie down.

He paused, and I thought that my chances would all be over if he just grabbed me now. He sat down on the bed, seeming suspicious and ready to jump. I began to unbutton my shirt, and his attention was soon drawn. My hands were shaking. He almost stood up to undo the buttons, but I managed to finish quickly and dropped the shirt to the floor.

I tried to give him what I thought was a sly look and then turned around. I reached behind my back and unhooked the bra. With the tension released, the knife nearly fell to the floor, but I put my right hand up and caught it.

I stood in terror, with my head turned over my shoulder keeping an eye on him. I don't know what horrified me more, showing myself to him or what I was about to try to do with the knife. In one motion I dropped the bra, turned around and put the knife in the small of my back, held in place by my pants.

He looked at my left scarred breast and said, "O que aconteceu?"

With his attention on my chest, I stepped in closer, within my arm's reach. He just kept staring, and I kept thinking, What am I willing to do?

This man had a life. A reason for the way he was. He had suffered pain. I thought of Michael. Had this man had a chance as a child? Was he abused and never given a sense of right and wrong? Was he haunted by demons that took control of him?

But none of that mattered. Whether he was evil in his soul or had just been carried on a wave of cruelty that others inflicted upon him, what he had done and what he was doing was evil, and there was only one way to stop it.

I spoke his crimes out loud. Like with Michael, it helped to steel my will. "You kidnapped innocent women."

He didn't even look up at me as I spoke. He didn't understand a word I was saying.

"You raped them and held their children captive. You murdered those who tried to stop your evil."

And then I thought of the pigs.

I reached behind me, pulled the switchblade out and pushed the button to extend it. The man looked up at the sound, raising his chin. I slashed the blade across his throat, cutting deeply. He put his hands up, unable to scream, blood pouring out over them.

He looked me in the eyes and then fell to the floor. I stepped back and waited, watching the blood spill out onto the carpet, making sure he was dead. I put my shirt back on and left the bedroom, shutting the door behind me.

I had to think about what I should do next. I had seen eight men, which left seven more to deal with. The guard on the stairs below was obviously in an assigned position and wouldn't leave. They had a procedure where men who came up with a woman would check their guns in. If another man came up with a woman, he would be unarmed, and I might be able to kill him with the knife, but I needed a gun if I had a chance of killing them all.

I thought about just trying to sneak out with the women, but the men had covered that avenue thoroughly. There was a door to stairs at the other end of the hall. I went to check it and saw it was secured from the other side. From what I could see out a tiny window in the door, it appeared to have been welded shut. The front entrance was the only way out.

I wondered how long they considered a reasonable amount of time to pass before they would check on us. I couldn't wait for that. With my heart pumping fast, my blood sugar would start to fall soon, and then I'd be useless.

I had to go now while I was able. I went back in the bedroom and put my hands in the pool of blood. I smeared it in my hair and down my face, to look like I was injured.

I walked to the end of the hall, quietly opened the door to the stairwell and peeked out to see the guard still there below, holding his rifle. I held my left hand on my head so the blood appeared to come from a head wound and put the retracted switchblade in my right. I opened the door so it made a slight noise and started to stagger down the stairs, blood dripping down my left arm onto the floor.

"Help," I said.

"Não outra vez!" the guard said. It didn't seem to be a cry of alarm, but one of exasperation.

He watched me walk down the stairs. He lifted his rifle and put his finger over the trigger. When I stepped off the last step, he moved a little closer and looked at my bloody head. The women down the hall had seen me, and the ones with children quickly took them inside.

Gabriela said, "I will help you," and started to walk toward me.

The guard turned, pointed the gun at her and said, "Pare!"

Gabriela stopped, and with the guard's back turned to me, I sprung the blade and stuck it in his neck. He brought his hands up. I pushed the knife deeper, twisting to cut off any scream. He was heavy, and I struggled to keep him from making noise as he slipped to the floor. I lifted the gun to prevent its metal from rattling on the concrete landing.

Gabriela ran forward and began to drag the man backward. "Keep the blood from the floor!" she said in a loud whisper. She lifted his head so that the blood spilled on his chest. We pulled him into the hall and then through the first door. I retrieved the blade from where I had sheathed it in the man. Gabriela handed me his gun, and she picked up Clint from the box in the stairwell.

Then she came back in and shut the door to the first apartment, hiding the body. She wiped a small spot of blood from the floor with the hem of her dress.

"How many men are there?" I asked.

"Eight men," she said. "But now six. They are all downstairs playing cards."

"We need to get the women and children off this floor now," I said.

Gabriela moved down the hall telling each woman to come out quietly,

221

with their child if they had one. When they saw her with the gun, they knew it would end today with their deaths or their captors'.

Some of the babies squalled, but that was ordinary noise. In fact, complete silence from a hall full of women and children would have drawn attention. She had them all take off their shoes, and each mother carried her child.

I checked the stairwell, and after I made sure no one was there, I had the women softly pad up the stairs. If a child was crying, we kept the mother back so the sound would be normal, not the distinct echoing on concrete and steel in the stairwell. Gabriela told them to climb as high as they could.

When the last child calmed and the mothers had all climbed the stairs, Gabriela turned to me. "If we die today, I am glad. It is better."

"We need to get the men between us," I said. "One of us should go down to the floor below. When they come to this floor, they'll be trapped between us."

"Do you know how to fire the gun?"

"Pull the trigger?" I said.

"You have thirty rounds in that magazine. That is it." She lifted my rifle and moved a switch. "Those fools had it on full auto. It is now on three-round burst. Do not just spray bullets. Point at a target and shoot."

I had become quite good with shooting Clint, but I had never touched a rifle in my life.

"Move the switch again to here to fire a single shot," Gabriela said. "Are you experienced with shooting?"

"Not a rifle."

"Then leave it on three-round burst. It will cover your mistakes."

I nodded, but then I said, "No. You take the rifle."

"You are safer with it," she said.

"I know how to shoot Clint."

She looked at me strangely.

"The pistol," I said. "I know how to shoot it. You take the rifle."

She hesitated, and then we switched guns. Clint felt familiar and comfortable in my hand. Six bullets remained. The leader hadn't reloaded.

"You go down one floor," she said. "If the worst happens run away."

I wouldn't, but I didn't say anything. I would see this through to the end.

"I'll draw them up here. When you see all have passed, come up, lie on the stairs and shoot them. Keep low."

I crept down the stairs to the floor below and slowly opened the door so it wouldn't make a sound. The stairwell door to the women's floor stayed propped open so the guard could watch from the stairwell, but all the other doors were closed. I could hear the men talking below. I opened the first apartment door and stood in the doorway, watching through the tiny window in the stairwell door.

I heard Gabriela scream, a terrifying high pitch, and then she fired a single shot. It would sound like one of the men shot a woman. This would hopefully explain the empty hall. The other men would think the guard had shot a woman and the rest had fled into their rooms.

I watched through the door in the window and counted as one, two, three, four and then five men, each armed, ran up the stairs. For agonizing seconds the sixth man didn't come. I didn't know what to do. If I went up, he could come up behind me. But Gabriela couldn't defend against five men by herself.

I stepped to the door and looked out the window and saw nothing. I opened it and didn't see any of the five men above me or the one below. They would be walking down the hall now, prime targets with their backs turned.

I had to go now.

I walked up and lay down across the top of the stairs with Clint pointing out into the hall. The door was still propped open, and five men slowly walked down the hall with their guns drawn.

I looked down behind me, knowing that shooting would likely bring the final man from below. But I could take out a few before he came. I rested my arms on the floor and carefully took aim at the back of the closest man.

I took a deep breath and squeezed the trigger. The gun pushed up and back, a motion I had become accustomed to, and a hole puffed out in the center of his back. He fell to the floor. The mathematical part of my mind kept the numbers of the situation echoing through my brain.

5 bullets. 4 men on this floor. 1 below.

The four remaining men took a few seconds to comprehend what had happened and where the gunfire came from. I put the barrel back down, picked the next target and squeezed the trigger again. I stupidly aimed for his head and missed completely, the bullet punching a hole in the ceiling. I recovered and fired again, hitting him once in the chest.

3 bullets. 3 men on this floor. 1 below.

The three remaining men turned around and fired at me into the stairwell. I slid back down one stair. The bullets bounced off the concrete and metal all around me. I could tell their guns were on full auto, and I was amazed at how quickly their rounds emptied the magazines.

Ninety bullets had sprayed around me.

They started to reload. I knew I had to fire now, but I slipped while trying to crawl and slid down three stairs.

A quick burst from the other end of the hall rang out, and a man screamed and fell. I crawled back up to the top and saw that the two other men were gone. They must have ducked into apartments. The man Gabriela had shot was on the floor clutching his leg and reaching for his gun.

I thought about saving my ammo, but he was looking right at me and Gabriela had ducked back into the doorway. I fired once, and the round went into his groin and he fell back, dropping his gun.

2 bullets. 2 men on this floor. 1 below.

Gabriela stepped out, and we looked at each other. One of the men stuck his gun out from the door, not looking, and fired in her direction. He was on burst shot now. The three shots missed, but she jumped back into the apartment doorway, spraying two more bursts at him.

The other man stepped out and fired a burst in my direction, and I heard the whoosh of air as one passed by my ear. I fired at him but the shots hit on the doorframe beside him.

1 bullet. 2 men on this floor. 1 below.

I remembered the one below and looked back down expecting him to be standing there ready to shoot, but the stairwell was empty. We were in a standoff. They each had multiple clips, and they knew we didn't have any extra ammo. The men only had to get us to waste the shots, and then they could step out and kill us with ease.

But they wouldn't be keeping count of our bullets.

I couldn't help but count everything, even with death flying around me. I relied on the fact that none of the men seemed to know English and yelled to Gabriela, "You have twenty bullets left and I have one, but they aren't keeping track."

Gabriela caught on and fired two bursts, both to keep the men from coming out of the apartments and to make them think we were running out of ammo.

1 bullet in Clint. 14 with Gabriela. 2 men on this floor. 1 below.

Gabriela fired again, dropping her count to eleven. One of the men reached his arm out and blindly fired three bursts at Gabriela. She returned fire with a burst, leaving eight in her clip.

I rotated Clint's chamber around, leaving five empty slots ahead of the one with a bullet in it. I pulled the trigger. It made an empty click. The man on the right side briefly stuck his head out, and Gabriela fired, but he ducked back in.

I heard her gun make the clicking sound, knowing she had five rounds left. The man stuck his head out quickly again, and we each pulled the triggers three times, clicking away.

The same man stepped out slowly, ready to jump back behind cover, and I pulled the trigger again, clicking through the last empty slot. He looked straight at me and smiled. He walked toward me with the gun pointed straight at me. Then the other man stepped out and walked toward where Gabriela was hiding.

When they were both in full view, I aimed carefully at the man's head. It had to be a kill shot. I pulled the trigger, and the bullet tore through his eye, shredding the brain behind it.

Gabriela stepped out and shot the man, but he returned fired and blood sprayed on the wall behind her.

0 bullets. 0 men on this floor. 1 below.

I sat in silence, not knowing what to do for several moments, and then I heard a noise downstairs. I stood up and looked down to see the youngest man, a boy really, coming through the door. He looked up at me, and I saw fear in his eyes. He raised his gun, and I pointed mine at him and yelled.

He dropped his gun, and I kept mine pointed at him. I slowly walked down the stairs. He could have easily gotten out of the narrow line of sight that I had over the stairs, but he stood there paralyzed. I made it to the bottom and aimed my empty gun at his chest.

"Por favor!" he said.

I knew what that meant. *Please.*

I didn't know what this boy had done. Maybe he was as trapped as the women. He could have come up and killed me at any point.

I looked up at a noise and saw Gabriela coming down the stairs, blood running down her right hand from a wound in her upper arm. She carried the rifle in her left hand.

She reached the bottom and stood beside me. The boy said, "Gabriela, por favor! Eu não fiz nada!" to her, and held his hands out as she raised her gun.

"Isso é certo. Você não fez nada," Gabriela said.

Gabriela looked at him, flipped the switch to single shot and pulled the trigger.

-50-

We could hardly convince the women to come down. They couldn't believe the men were actually dead. Eventually one of them cautiously descended the stairs and returned to report to the others. The women held their children as they walked out, shielding their little eyes from the bodies and blood.

Three of the women without children picked up rifles, but I didn't take one. The women followed me to Mateus's apartment building. I dreaded climbing the twenty floors to get him, but he had apparently seen us coming. Mateus, Sam and Isadora came out the front door as we arrived.

They stared in amazement.

Finally Mateus said, "Your name should not be Sugar."

I found a first aid kit and cleaned and sewed up the wound in Gabriela's arm. The bullet had gone through and, though I wasn't a doctor, I thought it would heal without trouble. She would have a scar from my amateur stitching job.

"It will be a scar to wear with pride," she said. "I will always remember you by it."

"You could come back with us," I said. "All of you could." It would be a tight squeeze on the plane, and we might have to stop an extra time for fuel, but I wouldn't abandon these women now.

"I will stay here," Gabriela said. "This is my home. We will build a new Rio. We can defend ourselves now. We will not be naïve anymore."

We decided to fly home the next day. I needed all my wits to keep Sam focused, and I was so exhausted now that I thought I would fall to the ground at any moment. We found first-floor apartments to set up in, and most of the women quickly claimed one for themselves. Like all virus survivors, none of the women had anyone to go home to. They had become each other's family.

I cleaned the blood off me with bottled water from a nearby store and fell asleep within seconds of lying down on a bed. That evening, five women came to speak with me. Only one of them spoke faltering English.

"Gabriela has her guns, but we will not feel safe here," she said. "We are not from the city. We will not live well here. But we cannot go back to the countryside that we were taken from. We will not feel safe there either." She looked to the other four women. "Is it safe in America?"

"Yes," I said. Mostly.

"Can we come with you?"

Before I could answer, she said, "We have simple skills, but we can work hard."

I would let them come even if they had no skills. "You're welcome to come," I said. It's not like we didn't have the room. Maybe they could even help with something. "What skills do you have?"

"Fernanda sews. Alessandra can cook almost anything. We can each do something."

"What is your name?" I asked.

"Mayara."

"What do you do?"

She looked embarrassed and then said, "I worked on a pig farm."

I almost laughed out loud, but knew that she wouldn't understand. I had the useless skills of a convenience store clerk, while these women had the vital skills needed in this new world.

"How many children do all of you have?"

"Four," Mayara said. "I do not have a child. I do not know that I ever will. If I could get pregnant, it would have … "

With that she choked up. These women had been through a hell I couldn't imagine. The few minutes I had spent with one of the men would stay with me forever, and he had never even touched me. I prayed the children would be okay. That was why I had done it.

We radioed Ralph that night and let him know we would start flying back the next day and would likely take two days, again landing in Caracas to refuel.

"How's John?" I asked.

"Sick with worry," Ralph said. "He's been working in the lab and helping to gather pigs. He'll be glad to know you're okay."

I fell asleep that night with the face of the young man begging Gabriela not to kill him running through my mind. I woke early and went outside to watch the sunrise. Gabriela brought me a hot tea. I wondered how she had heated it, but didn't ask. She stood beside me, watching the dawn, sipping on her own glass and holding her rifle.

I remembered what the young man had said even though I didn't understand it. "What did it mean when he said 'Eu não fiz nada'?" I asked Gabriela.

She took a sip of her tea and said, "He said, 'I did nothing.'"

"Did he do anything?"

"Did he rape us?" Gabriela said. "No. He did not even capture anyone."

I wanted to ask her why she killed him, but I would not cast judgment on her. My hands were just as bloody.

"He stood by and let it happen," she said. "Maybe in the old world there would be some lesser punishment."

Alessandra cooked breakfast for everyone, and her skills were impressive. I took a normal dose of insulin so I could stay fully alert to keep Sam focused. He had no idea where we were, but I explained that he had flown us here, and that seemed to put him in the right mindset.

The five women going with us hugged the ones staying behind. Mateus decided to say his good-byes at the apartment.

"If I saw the plane, I would be tempted to go with you," he said. "But I am too old, and I think I will stay with these women. I am the only man these children will see for quite a while. The women will probably shoot any other man that comes near."

Isadora held Mateus for a long moment, and while she did, I realized something. "You don't have to go anymore," I said. "You were leaving because of the danger."

She let go of Mateus, with tears in her eyes, and said, "I will come. You need me. I thought the education I had spent a lifetime acquiring would go to waste."

We found a few cars in the garage and drove to the airport. When Sam saw the plane, he turned back into a focused pilot. He greeted everyone as they came on and talked to Isadora like she was the stewardess, either because she was dressed in a pantsuit or because she was by far the prettiest among us.

I climbed into the copilot's seat, and in a few minutes, we were in the air with the sound of the jet's engines roaring and babies crying at the change in pressure. The trip home went smoothly. Taking a full plane of people seemed to help Sam settle into any of a hundred old memories.

We landed in Tallahassee in the late afternoon the next day. When the plane rolled to a stop, Sam just kept saying over and over again, "I did it. I really did it."

I couldn't wait to see John and the kids, and in my excitement, I nearly left my insulin vial on the plane. I went back on and picked it up from near the copilot's seat. I held it up to the fading light of day and read the amount left.

101 units.

51

John, Olivia and Danny ran out of the house as soon as we pulled into the driveway. John hugged me so tightly that I thought he would break one of my ribs, but I loved it. I breathed in his familiar smell. The cigarette odor was thicker than usual. He smoked more when he was upset.

"I'm sorry I left you behind," I said.

"It's okay," he said. "You were trying to protect me. I guess the trip was pretty uneventful then?"

"Not exactly," I said. I would tell him what happened later. Much later. "I brought home some ... settlers would be the word, I think." The other women were getting out of two other cars that we drove home from the airport.

"Where's the chemist?" John asked, looking over the women and obviously getting worried. He still thought the chemist was a man.

"*She's* right here," I said. Isadora walked up and introduced herself.

"I'm Isadora," she said. "You must be John. Sugar says that you are very intelligent. I can see it for myself in your eyes."

Was she flirting with him? I couldn't tell. Maybe it was just the way of her culture or maybe everything a beautiful woman did seemed like flirting. Even her accent seemed different.

"How much insulin do you have left?" John asked. He didn't seem to be flustered by Isadora.

"101 units."

"Then we have to get started immediately. Are you ready to go to the lab, Isadora?"

"Yes," she said.

I talked to Mayara and introduced her to Edith. Edith said she knew a little Spanish, and I explained that the women spoke Portuguese. I told Mayara to tell the women to pick out houses in the neighborhood. "You can each pick a car too. If it won't start, we can help jump the battery."

"We do not know how to drive," she said.

"Oh." That was a problem for another day. "Edith, can you take them to a grocery store to pick out a few days' worth of food and diapers?"

Edith immediately set to helping the women. She spoke to them loudly in English with a few mispronounced Spanish words thrown in, but they didn't speak either of those languages, so it didn't matter.

"You two girls head to the lab," John said. "Sugar, you can get Isadora oriented while I go get some pancreases I have in a refrigerator by the new pigpen downtown."

I started to get in the driver's seat, but Isadora asked to drive.

"The trips to and from the airport was the first time I have driven in two years," she said. "But I had to go slow with the other women and children in the car."

I handed her the keys and gave her directions as we drove. She raced down the empty streets at speeds far exceeding the old speed limits.

"So, John he is your husband?" Isadora asked.

"No," I said. "He's my … " I didn't finish. I didn't know what he was. We arrived at the chemistry building in minutes, and I walked her up to the lab. She immediately put her long hair into a ponytail and put on glasses that she kept in her purse. She found a lab coat and was transformed from looking like a fashion model to a scientist.

I showed her all the equipment and the thirty-four steps we had written up and posted on the walls. "Are you familiar with all this equipment?" I asked.

"Yes," she said. "I've even worked with some of these specific models." Her accent was now almost completely gone. I showed her the generator and how to plug everything into a power strip connected to the generator. We always left the equipment unplugged when not using it to avoid damage from electrical spikes.

John arrived with an ice chest of fresh pancreases and smiled when he saw Isadora. I had to admit her new look did inspire confidence.

"Show me how you have done the steps," she said to John.

"We have videos," he said. He got a laptop and hooked it up to the generator and took a memory stick with a recent video and plugged it into the computer. Isadora watched our steps in silence, making notes. I felt like I was back in school being graded.

We fast-forwarded through the long, repetitive steps like stirring the mixture for three hours. After watching the video with complete focus, Isadora looked up at John.

"This is very impressive for a layman," she said. "I did not think you would have figured out this much."

"Sugar did all the research to find the steps," John said. "And this is a recent video. We messed up a lot the first times. And even this still didn't work. I tested a batch on the rabbits while you were gone. No effect on their blood sugar."

"This video shows everything you did?"

"Yes," I said, wanting to make sure Isadora remembered I was here. "This captures everything from the moment we come into the lab."

"Is this the pH meter you used?" Isadora asked.

"Yes," John said.

Isadora looked around the room and found two vials of clear liquid, labeled 4.0 and 10.0. "Do you calibrate the pH meter each day?"

John put his head to his hand and said, "No."

She proceeded to clean the probe on the meter and then tested it with each of the solutions. "The meter is reading low, so when you thought the solution was neutral at seven point zero, it was actually still alkaline. Insulin is destroyed in an alkaline solution."

I would have died because of something so stupid. There was probably a manual in a drawer around here somewhere that would have told us that, but the machine had worked so easily that we didn't think that it might need calibration. My head hurt just thinking that my fate depended on such a trivial thing.

"There are other small mistakes in your technique," Isadora said, "but these are easily corrected. I am most worried about maintaining sterility of the product."

"I can take a few germs as long as I can get the insulin," I said.

"When they're injected, the germs skip the body's protections," John said. "It's as dangerous as an open wound. Isadora is right. Sterility is vital."

"With only a hundred units left," Isadora said, "and at least nine days to make a batch, your immune system will be compromised from high blood sugar and lack of food. We'll need to keep you on an extremely low diet."

"Why don't you go home and rest," John said, "and let me and Isadora get a few batches started tonight? I've got thirty pancreases. That'll make six batches. With Isadora's skill at least one of them should work, and then you'll have enough to carry you through while we perfect the process."

I wanted to stay. I wanted to make it or at least watch it being done. I had worked so hard on this for so long. It was my life at stake. And, frankly, I didn't like leaving Isadora and John alone deep into the night.

"What's your blood sugar now?" John asked, getting a meter out.

I tested and it was high, 172. I had last used a tiny dose to conserve the insulin. I felt tired and shaky. I needed some water. John brought a bottled water, and I sucked it down.

"Take a small dose to lower it a little bit, and then go home and rest," John said.

He was right. In my current state, I would slow things down or cause mistakes. I had to trust John. He had proven himself over and over. I injected just two units and drove back to Edith's house.

Olivia was enjoying watching the babies and toddlers while the Brazilian women set up their houses. They had picked two down the street from Edith, three women in one and two in another. They hadn't even considered living alone.

I remembered my days of solitude, and they seemed strange now. I still needed some time to myself, but I had people I loved now, and I wanted to be with them.

I read to Danny until we both fell asleep in his bed.

52

John came back sometime late in the night and got a few hours of sleep. Isadora stayed in the house next to Edith. I thought she would want the company of the other Brazilian women, but she seemed to distance herself from them. She definitely had a different accent, which I assumed was from growing up in Portugal. She controlled the accent, slipping in and out depending on the situation and company. I didn't know if it was a conscious choice, or just a subtle mastery of social situations that I would never have.

The next day John ate the huge breakfast that Edith and Alessandra prepared for everyone, and then left again with Isadora to the lab. I had a single hard-boiled egg. While the community was setting up the pig farm, they had also gotten a few chickens. Having a fresh egg was delicious compared to the canned, preserved foods I was used to, but I was left hungry. Isadora and John decided I should do the minimum insulin to keep my blood sugar below 160.

At this rate I still used twelve units, barely eating. John and Isadora came home that evening.

"We have six batches ready," he said. "Two were put in the ice chest last night and the rest today. They'll have to sit for seven days, then steps twenty-five and twenty-six. Then they sit overnight, and we finish the next day and test on the rabbits."

"How many units are left?" Isadora asked.

"Eighty-seven," I said. "Twelve units per day barely kept me under one sixty. That would last seven more days."

"That should just make it," John said. "It's hard to say how quickly DKA will set in, but I don't think it will in one day. You can try to stretch the insulin."

I had stretched it as far it would go. "What do we do while we wait?" I asked.

"You rest," John said. "Isadora and I can make a few more batches tomorrow."

"We've done all we can," Isadora said. "More batches won't help. I need to know the results from these before I know to do anything differently."

"Will these work?" John asked.

"At least one should have some potency to carry her through another week," she said. "Then we get better each week until we have a pure insulin. This will work. They did it a hundred years ago, and I can do it today."

John and Isadora stayed up planning the next steps. I wanted to stay up with them, but the exhaustion took over, and I fell asleep on the couch. John must have carried me to the bed, because I found myself next to Olivia in the morning.

She was snuggled up next to me, breathing in and out gently. Isadora and John had confidence, but I knew nothing was certain. This could be the last week of my life. Technically I would last a little while in a diabetic coma, but I wouldn't be aware of it. I didn't want to spend the time just sitting around.

After breakfast, all the Brazilian women but Isadora left. Edith was going to introduce them to the others in the community and show them around. Mayara wanted to get started helping with the pigs. A new light came into her eyes when she realized the importance of the pigs and how our community had decided to make it our focus.

"I want to do something," I said. "Something fun with the kids. Something they can remember me—"

John cut me off. "They won't have to remember you. You're going to make it," he said, almost insisting it would happen through the force of his will.

"It is a good idea," Isadora said. "But we should do something relaxing. That won't stress your system."

She had said *we*, automatically putting herself into our group. I tried not to resent it. She had left her life to come save mine. She didn't have anyone else.

"A beach is close to here, no?" Isadora said.

"Less than an hour," I said. That sounded perfect. The kids would love it, and I could still take it easy. "Let's go today."

We told the kids, and they were ecstatic. For a moment I thought Danny might actually say something. He clearly understood everything we said, but I had never heard him speak a word. We went to Ralph's to see if the boy, who still called himself Wolf, wanted to go, but they were flying radio-controlled airplanes together and having a ball. The boy didn't want to leave Ralph's side now.

We all drove to the mall to buy swimsuits. I found SpongeBob ones that Danny liked and a modest one-piece for Olivia that would sparkle in the sun. I decided to go a little more daring for myself. John had seen all of me, but sometimes getting close to seeing everything was more tantalizing. I had never worn a bikini before, but I picked out a red one that I hoped he would like.

We all changed into the swimsuits in the mall, but I wore a T-shirt over mine. I felt too weird to wear a bikini anywhere but the beach. Isadora surprised me and wore what appeared to be a modest swimsuit from what I could see. She also wore a T-shirt. She had a cloth around the bottom of her swimsuit that almost looked like a skirt.

We got everything we could possibly need for a beach trip: sunscreen, sand toys, Frisbees, beach balls, towels, beach umbrellas and food for the day. We piled in the car, excited and feeling like a family. I didn't know what family role Isadora filled, but I decided to think of her as an aunt.

I took a couple of extra units of insulin. I wanted to enjoy this day. John drove us south quickly, and we could barely keep Danny in his seat. He was bouncing with excitement. I rode in the back between the kids, and Isadora sat in the passenger seat.

"I hope it's not crowded," John said, and Isadora laughed out loud and touched his arm.

We found a lovely stretch of beach, and John pulled the car right up to the sand. I rubbed sunscreen on the kids, feeling more like a mother than ever before. I lectured them about not going far in the water and always staying by an adult. I told them to play in the sand first, and then we would go in the water. I put my insulin vial in our cooler full of ice and drinks, to keep it from spoiling in the hot sun.

And then it was time to reveal my swimsuit. I took a deep breath and lifted off the T-shirt. I was somehow a little self-conscious in front of John, but he smiled, looked me up and down and then winked at me in a playful way.

"The red looks very good on you," Isadora said. "It is perfect for your skin tone."

Isadora looked for a moment at the upside-down clock point tattoos on my belly and nodded, seeming to realize what they were for. She crossed her hands at the waist and lifted her T-shirt over her head.

And she was topless.

-53-

She rubbed an oily sunscreen over her body, including her chest, and her golden-brown breasts gleamed in the sun. John and I stared in amazement. Well, my reaction was amazement. I'm sure John's was amazement mixed with something else.

"Will you get my back?" Isadora asked John.

John looked from Isadora to me. I didn't say anything, so he took the bottle of lotion and quickly rubbed her back. She turned back around to face him and said, "Thank you."

Olivia looked up from the sand, and her jaw hung open.

Danny looked up, and a smile crossed his face. "Nursies!"

John visibly shook himself out of the trance and began setting up the towels and a beach umbrella. Isadora helped him, her left breast brushing his arm as they arranged our supplies.

I thought about taking my top off, but putting my scarred breast on display next to Isadora's perfection made my courage falter. I also wanted Olivia to acquire her sense of cultural appropriateness from me. I suppose I couldn't blame Isadora. This must be what women in Portugal did. I started to lay out my towel, when I was suddenly struck with realization.

Danny had spoken.

I walked over to him and said, "Danny?"

"Nursies!" he said again, pointing at Isadora's breasts like they needed more attention brought to them.

Isadora looked at Danny and said, "Did your momma nurse you?" in the lilting tone women use when speaking to young children. She didn't realize that Danny hadn't spoken for years. She turned to John and said, "When I have my babies, they will nurse at my breasts. It is best. And the formula will all be much too old by then."

Danny stopped his play and said, "Momma," and tears filled his eyes. I

236

picked him up and held him for a few moments, until he wiggled free and went back to the sand. If this is what it took to help Danny move forward, then so be it.

I sat beside him and helped him build a sandcastle. I said everything we were doing out loud, and he repeated a few of the words. "Water ... Build ... Sand."

John took Olivia out to play in the waves, but Danny wouldn't go near the ocean. He was content to stay on the beach while Isadora and I sunned ourselves. I couldn't imagine why she did. Her skin couldn't get to a more perfect color.

After a while, Danny kept pointing at the car, and I asked him, "What do you want?"

He wouldn't answer, but I decided to not give him what he wanted until he tried to speak. I didn't know if it was the right way to handle it, but I had to make these kinds of decisions now.

Finally he said, "Glasses."

I realized he wanted the matching SpongeBob sunglasses I had bought him. "You can get them from the car," I said.

He trotted up to the car, opened the door, rummaged around and came back smiling, wearing the goofy glasses that were too big for his head.

"You are good with him," Isadora said. "And the girl." She paused. "It does not seem possible that you are the same woman who ... " She didn't finish the sentence, but I knew what she meant. I didn't feel like the woman who had killed men like slaughtering pigs. I couldn't even believe that I was a woman who killed pigs.

Danny put his hand on my shoulder and said, "Spilled." His sand castle was knocked over, so I helped him rebuild it.

John and Olivia came back. They were thirsty and John asked, "Where's the cooler?"

"It must be still in the car," Isadora said. We had grown used to her breasts now. She seemed so comfortable and at ease, that we all accepted it. Maybe it was a better way.

John went to the car and brought the cooler back. "It was spilled out in the back floor," John said, "but the drinks are still cold."

They enjoyed sodas while I had a water, but the coolness was refreshing, and it tasted good. They ate lunch, peanut butter sandwiches and chips. I had beef jerky. I supposed people would still be eating the well-preserved and ubiquitous beef jerky years from now.

After lunch, Isadora watched the children while John and I swam deep into the ocean. He wanted me to take it easy, but I loved to feel the power of the vast water. I got tired on the way in and held on to John's back as he swam. He was a strong swimmer, having grown up at the beach, and he pulled me along easily.

As the sun set lower in the sky, we regretfully decided to head back before nightfall. It had been a perfect day. We packed the trunk of the car back up, and Isadora put her T-shirt back on. I heard John whisper, "Finally," and the kids climbed into the back of the car.

I stepped in, still barefooted, and there was a pop. Something stabbed into my right foot. I lifted my foot. Blood dripped out of it from a small cut. I held it out, and John quickly cleaned it out with water and wrapped it up with a towel.

"There were shards of glass in it," he said. "Isadora, can you clean that up so Sugar or the kids don't step in the glass?"

While I held the towel on my foot to stop the bleeding, Isadora leaned back and looked in the floorboard. She began sweeping up, and then she gasped.

I looked down and saw the shattered remains of the last vial of insulin.

-54-

I was thankful for a few things. That I was the one who stepped on the vial. Anyone else would be left with the guilt. That John and I never made love. It would make the loss easier. I know he would hurt. We loved each other, but the physical would have drawn us even closer.

That Isadora was here. She could take my place in John's heart. The children would need a woman in their lives, and Isadora was a good woman who loved children.

John put me on a near-starvation diet, only allowing me to eat when my blood sugar dipped low. Despite Isadora's objections, he took a batch out of the ice chests early. They finished the process, but it had no effect on the test rabbit's blood sugar.

We had six more days to go. Isadora thought we could try taking a batch out one day early, but I had to last that long. On the second day without insulin, my blood sugar began to climb even without food. I had read historical articles about people surviving before insulin therapy for months, even up to a year, on restricted diets. They must have been people still in their honeymoon phase of diabetes, when their body still produced some insulin. My body produced none.

The fatigue and weakness kept me virtually bedridden. The only thing I could do was continue to write this journal that you read now. Sometimes even typing on the laptop exhausted me. I had an unquenchable thirst and had to pee all the time. John bought some test kits from the pharmacy, and my urine started showing ketones, toxic acids that would kill me. It was a sign that my body, desperate for energy that it couldn't get from sugar, was breaking down fat for fuel.

Sometimes after I had fallen asleep with the laptop on my chest, I would wake and find John praying by my bed. I kept my eyes closed and listened to the prayers, wondering if I was the only other being hearing them, or whether

God was receiving them in some distant heaven. John begged God to keep me alive. He offered himself in my place.

If I were about to meet God, I hoped he wasn't the sort that made deals with lives, balancing some sort of cosmic equation that required a certain amount of suffering. Sometimes John was angry with God. He told God that it seemed cruel to let me get so close.

This was how I knew that he thought I wouldn't make it. He was positive and encouraging when he saw I was awake, saying I would make it to the first batch of insulin. But when he prayed, he asked for a miracle.

On the third day, I began to vomit, but there was nothing in my stomach, and all the retching produced was bile and blood. My blood sugar was somewhere over 400, but even minutes after taking it, I couldn't remember the exact number. I knew confusion had truly set in. Once my mind let go of numbers that meant it was done.

These last few sentences took over an hour to write, and I'm afraid they may be my last. I hope someone finishes my story, just so it will be complete. I've asked John to, but he still insists that I'll be there to keep writing it myself. With the delirium setting in, I don't know what my last words will be before slipping into a coma, so please count these as my last:

Danny, Olivia and John, you were the only family I have ever truly known since my parents. I love you all.

-55-

John

I'm finishing this journal because Sugar asked me to. It was one of the last things she said before she slipped away from us.

There are so many things that I regret. That I wish I had done differently. I should have studied how to keep a diabetic animal alive without insulin. I could have removed a pancreas from a dog or a pig, sewed it back up and learned how to keep it alive as long as possible. I would have had to torture dozens of animals through a painful death, but I would gladly do that now.

There's not much to tell of what story she has left. Her body lies in a coma, feeding on itself, hungry for the energy it can't get from food without insulin. If she doesn't pass before then, we'll finish the insulin extraction process tomorrow. But I fear she's too far gone, that her body has destroyed itself, and now we're just watching the shell waste away.

I want it recorded here what I never said to her aloud. I love her. She is the strongest woman I know. Tiny and frail to look at, but fearless when facing the worst monsters the world has. Not fearless. That's the wrong word. She was full of fear when she faced Michael and the men in Brazil, but she kept going despite the fear.

Sugar was willing to lay down her life when it didn't benefit her at all. I don't know what I think of God now, but I've seen Him through her, and she is the only thing that kept my faith from shattering.

I've asked the others to put their thoughts here, and then we will leave this as a memorial.

Isadora

I've talked with John, and now I see that Sugar thought I might be trying to tempt John away from her. What kind of fool would I be to try to oppose the woman who walked into a building full of armed men carrying only a tiny knife?

I have had many feelings toward Sugar in the brief time I have known her, but the foremost of them is fear. People see me as beautiful and smart, but she is both of these things and more. She is a force of will. She fought to stay alive, facing almost certain death, both from within and without.

Knowing her strength now, I am amazed that she didn't stop me, by whatever means she could, from doing what looked like trying to steal her man. When I took my top off on the beach, it wasn't to tempt John away (although I admit I know the effect that breasts have on American men). I wasn't thinking about coming between two people who obviously loved each other.

I was thinking about the new world we were going to build and the culture it would have. I love my homeland, beautiful Portugal that I will probably never see again, and I wanted some of it to be here.

I see how selfish it was now. I was worried about something as meaningless as self-expression when she was thinking about spending her last moments with the people she loved. I'm sorry that I distracted from that, and I'm glad she was able to accept my silliness and enjoy that last day.

I'll raise Olivia, beautiful Olivia with scars like Sugar, to be like her. Strong despite what the world has done to her.

Edith

I never know what to say in these kinds of things. I'm not good with words. Haven't we had enough death?

I supposed that's not what I'm supposed to say, but it's what I feel. If God wanted another soul, why did he have to take a young girl and leave an old woman?

Oh, that's not what these notes are meant to be. Let me just say that Sugar was my friend. What more is there?

Rigby

I had a simple schoolboy crush on Sugar, and I got over that quickly when she turned me down. I didn't need a woman. I needed a community. A place to belong.

And because of her kindness to me, when I had hurt her so much, I came here and found a home. If it weren't for Sugar, I would still be an angry young man destroying everything in my sight. She showed me there was still good in the world, and I want to be a part of it.

Ralph

Sugar ruined my theology. Everything I knew and believed said that her lack of belief should condemn her to damnation, but I can't reconcile that with the person I know she was and the God I love.

When Sugar slipped away from us, I did what we always do when good non-believers die. I rationalized that there was probably some conversion experienced we didn't know about. That God had reached her somehow. But I talked to John, and her own words closed that possibility. She left us in unbelief. She was beginning to open to the idea, but that doesn't meet the criteria I had preached about so many times.

I can only pray that there are ways of God that I don't understand.

Sam

I write these words in the few moments of clarity I have. I hate to think of the burden I'll be to this community, but they all insist that I stay. Perhaps one day, when it gets worse, I'll just fly away, straight up to heaven to be with Mary and the children.

I know I'll see Sugar there.

Everyone else saw me as broken, but Sugar, in her broken body, knew I could still do something valuable. That I was valuable. Even when my mind slips, I can still remember that feeling.

Kyle

The Sugar of two years ago just couldn't understand the pain I felt when I lost everyone that I loved in the short, terrible week of the virus. I didn't get to talk to her, but I think she would understand. She knows what real love is now. She knows the fear of losing someone who's become a part of you.

This is the second time I've lost her.

I didn't think that I wanted kids, but seeing Danny and Olivia has changed that. Even if I didn't see the joy they brought to our community, I would have still helped take care of them. For Sugar's sake. It's the only thing I can do for her now.

Olivia

I asked Danny what he wanted to write. I think his words say what I feel better than anything I could put here.

Good-bye, Mommy.

-56-

The light was indistinct and small at first, but as I floated toward it, I saw that it was a place, an island in a void. I saw grass and hills and trees and people, enjoying the warm, golden light that covered it all.

My feet touched down on a sandy shore, and I thought of the last clear memory I had, of our day at the beach. The people along the shore looked up and smiled at me. Animals roamed all about, which answered a theological question I had always had about whether animals had eternal souls. I wondered how many pigs I had sent here.

Actually the exact number shone clear in my mind: 147. Every number of my life stood out, easily accessible. Large ones like the number of days I had lived—7,726, and the number of units of insulin I had taken—148,965, and small ones, like the number of people I had truly loved—5.

Two of the people on the shore began walking toward me, hand in hand. Their faces weren't like I remembered them from my childhood, but I didn't need to recognize their faces to know they were my parents. I ran toward them across the warm sand, and they held out their hands. But it wasn't to embrace me. They were holding up their hands to tell me to stop.

I skidded to a halt a few feet in front of them, and they simply said, "Not yet."

Why did I have to wait?

I hadn't seen them in fifteen years. All I wanted to do was hold them tight. I felt a sharp sting in my belly at the old nine o'clock position. My parents smiled, and I began to feel sick and weak. What was the point of heaven if you could get sick?

They seemed to move away from me, even though we all stood still in the sand. The world went dark, and a buzzing flooded through my body. I fought to get back to my parents, but I couldn't see anything. I realized now that I hadn't passed the qualifications for heaven and God, in his cruelty, had allowed me to see just a glimpse before throwing me into hell.

But this couldn't be hell because the voices of the people I heard around me would never be sent there. I heard John and Olivia talking, and even Danny yelling, "She waking up!"

John said, "Fluids!" and I felt another sting in my arm. I opened my eyes and saw him attaching an IV to the needle in a vein in my arm. The fluids made me shiver, and John and Isadora threw blankets over me. Danny and Olivia crawled into my bed under the covers, and I drew warmth from their bodies.

"It worked," John said.

"The insulin?" I asked.

"Yes," Isadora said. "It's not near standard strength, but we can perfect that in a few batches. Until then we just have to give more milliliters than you're used to."

John tested my blood sugar, and it was still high—360, but it dropped every few minutes as the insulin did the job it was designed to do. They gave another injection, and within an hour, I needed to eat to keep it level. I was amazed at how fast it worked. They kept the IV for the night, flushing fluids through me to purge the toxins and replace electrolytes.

The next morning I injected a larger amount than usual to get eight units and then ate a light meal, an egg and a biscuit, which was a carbohydrate. My blood sugar never got above 100.

That afternoon after a large meal, I was able to walk. I had lost twenty pounds, 18 percent of my body weight, but I could put that back on quickly with the ample supply of ham, bacon and sausage. Mayara ran the pig farm for the city, and people brought in more pigs from the surrounding area every day.

Alessandra and the other Brazilian women helped start crops in various places around the city that we hoped to harvest in the fall. Isadora perfected the insulin-making process with each batch and soon had it near the concentration of insulin produced in the old world.

In a few weeks I was completely recovered and helping the community in various jobs: extracting pancreases, educating the children, tending the crops or helping John. He cared for the animals, including pigs, obviously, and a number of chickens and a few cows. But he had mainly become the community doctor. We stitched wounds that came from the bloody business of slaughtering pigs and began working with Isadora to grow antibiotics.

John finally quit smoking and, strangely, a part of me missed it, but of course I wanted him to be healthy. I still kept the shirt of his I had taken and hoped it would keep the smell for a long time.

John proposed on a warm evening, and we planned the wedding for a week later. Isadora, Edith and Olivia helped me buy a beautiful dress from a bridal shop.

"Oh, you look absolutely radiated," Edith said when I stepped out of the dressing room.

We were married with Ralph officiating, the whole community attending, and Mateus and the women in Brazil listening on the radio. Sam was John's best man, and at one point in the ceremony, he thought he was the groom. Isadora was my only bridesmaid, and Olivia made a beautiful flower girl. Danny had the job of ring bearer, but he heard it as "bear" and made growling noises all down the aisle.

Ralph had asked how religious I wanted the ceremony to be, and I told him not to hold back. I didn't know where I stood with God, but the people I loved believed in him, and that was enough for me, for now.

After the wedding, I had no idea where we were going, but soon recognized the route as we drove down the road to the old farm, which had been destroyed in the hurricane. This seemed like a strange place to go. I couldn't say the bloody memories there were exactly pleasant, but we stopped well before the farm, pulling off at the bridge by the river where we used to bathe.

We walked down to the riverbank and slowly undressed each other and waded into the water. We had soap, and like before, we cleansed our bodies, but this time we put our hands on each other, delighting in every touch.

We made love for the first time on towels on the riverbank with the sun setting in the sky. We spent a few days at a house on the beach, enjoying each other and the solitude, but after that we were both hungry to get back to the people and life that we loved.

Kyle and I were able to talk again. Surprisingly, my marrying John made it so Kyle and I could relate as friends. He believed in marriage and wouldn't do anything to hurt it. He told me that he hadn't married me because of losing his fiancée. He felt like he would be betraying her to marry me so soon after her death. I could finally understand the pain he felt. I didn't blame him anymore.

Unsurprisingly, he began to take an interest in Isadora. I told him to take her to the beach. After that, they were inseparable.

Most people in Tallahassee moved to within a few blocks of each other and the farm. As we thrived and sent meat to other communities, people from other places started moving in to be part of a growing, productive life. They could survive easily enough where they were, but that life couldn't give them purpose. Something larger to live for.

John and I lived in a four-bedroom house with Olivia and Danny. Our days were filled with teaching the children and caring for animals and people. Our nights, after the kids were fast asleep, were spent in love.

I had bought a large supply of birth control pills. Both John and I were happy with the family we had. Olivia and Danny were our children, even though not from our bodies. We loved them as completely as any parent ever loved a child, and I couldn't imagine a life without them.

A few months passed and as summer turned to fall, mild as it was in Florida, we began to harvest the first of our crops. Fresh food tasted incredible compared to the cans we had grown used to.

It took some getting used to though, and my stomach felt bad for days. I was nauseated and had to carefully regulate my insulin since I threw up some of the food, especially in the mornings. It didn't go away like John expected it would, and he gave me an examination. I thought he was playing and it would lead to more lovemaking, but he had a serious look on his face.

"Sugar," he said.

"Yes."

"Let me see those pills you've been taking."

I got up, went to the bathroom and came back with the box. He looked at it and flipped it over to read something on the back. He laughed and pointed to tiny print on the back of the box. It was a date that had passed some time ago.

An expiration date.

Please leave a review on Amazon.com

ACKNOWLEDGMENTS

First, I want to thank my wife, Cheri, for her support while I wrote this novel and through a very dark time in our life. She is always my first reader and always first in my heart.

I am deeply grateful to Orson Scott Card for his patience and guidance. Reading his stories for the past three decades showed me what I wanted to be as a writer. His advice over the past year took my craft to the next level.

My publishing team made this personal work professional quality: my editor, Sheila Haab, who improved both the story and the writing you just read. My proofreader, Tricia Parker, who found the numerous mistakes you didn't read. And Greg Simanson, who made the wonderful cover that caught your attention.

The feedback of my beta readers was invaluable: David Seay, Reubin Felkey, Bill Felkey, Sandy Wilson, Doug Wallace, Lauren House, Samuel Norwood, David Norwood, Diana Norwood, Lisa Norwood, Cherie Wood, Katie Pollock, John Pollock, Baylee Lowery and Sarka-Jonae Miller (find her hilarious books at sarkajonae.com).

Deep appreciation to the others who supported and believed in my writing: Donna Felkey, Todd Abbott, Geneva Bailey, Jayne Love, Amy Helwig, Bill Reed, Carmen Reed, Tom Norwood, Kavitha Mehra, Larry Mathers, Kirk Curnutt, Eric Seales, Christine Tiday, Janet Robinson (find her delightful books at janet-robinson.com), Doris Knight, Dan Jones, Bob Vinti, Tracie Griggs, Velma Bailey, Carl Bailey, Wes Norwood, Bekah Norwood, Bethany Norwood, Elijah Norwood and Robert Inman (find his wonderful books at robert-inman.com).

Much thanks to my writing group: Doug Wallace, Cathy Harmon, Marcus Mann, Jessica Winn, Megan Oliphant, Celesta Hubner, Keith Ward, Steven Novick, Janini Viswanatha and Elise Stephens (find her lovely books at www.elisestephens.com).

And finally, and ultimately, I want to thank my Lord and Savior Jesus Christ. You have carried me through the darkness..

ABOUT THE AUTHOR

Travis Norwood lives in Montgomery, Alabama, with his wife and five children. Like Sugar, he would be perfectly happy living in a world emptied of almost all people. But not you, of course. He sincerely hopes you survive the apocalypse..

Visit TravisNorwood.com to read blog posts and to sign up for notifications on new books.

Twitter: @TravisLNorwood

Facebook: facebook.com/TravisNorwoodAuthor

OTHER BOOKS BY TRAVIS NORWOOD

Suspended Between
Julya's scream shatters through the metal of the starship when a simple number destroys everything she dared hope for in her life—love, a future, happiness. One simple number...

101

4,096 colonists lay in deep suspension. Some of Earth's best, they are chosen to colonize a new world and are on a 200-year journey through space. Julya was one of them, dreaming of the life she'll live when she awakes on the new colony.

But Julya isn't asleep anymore.

When an accident causes two suspension pods to fail—those of Julya and an engineer named Dax—both are forced to face the unthinkable…

What happens when you are in deep space, on a spaceship never designed for the living, with only one other person? Can you survive? Can you find love? Can you face the unexpected?

What happens when you awake early? Not just early, but 101 years early?

Anora's Question
Eight-year old Anora and nineteen-year old Sylene are separated by more than just age and distance. Anora lives in a small world of rooms, halls and advanced machinery, where men and women live together in families. Sylene lives in a primitive world of tents, forests, and simple tools, where men are kept in subjugation to women.

Anora asks a simple question that Sylene must answer. What causes a woman to be given a child?

Each girl's journey starts with this question. But in time Anora realizes that there is a much deeper question at stake. The answer will shake the foundations of both their worlds.

Printed in Great Britain
by Amazon